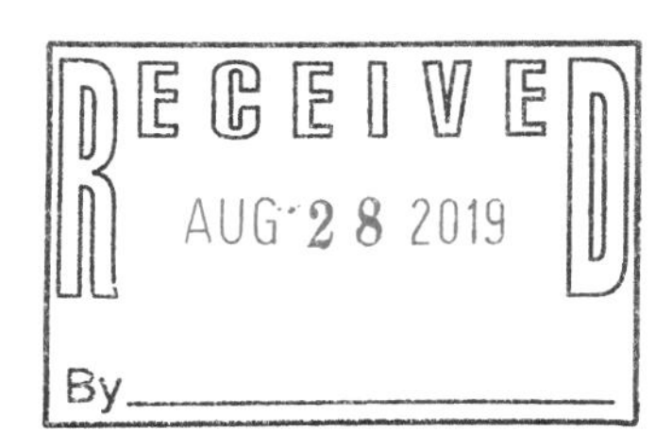

ANTE UP

CHRISTINA C JONES

WARM HUES PUBLISHING

Cover art by Christina Jones,
Images courtesy of DepositPhotos.

AUTHOR'S NOTE

I recently said about this book that it didn't start "in the box", and I was never able to put it in one either. It's a romance, kind of. Suspenseful, kind of. A little dark. A little funny. A little sweet. A lot outside of what you might be used to from me. I'm going to be honest here – I'm terrified. Sick to my stomach, heart racing, *terrified*, but I can't pinpoint exactly why.

Of course I want you, the reader, to enjoy it. I want these characters to resonate, and I want to have represented them properly, and I want to have done them justice. I hope that I've delivered their story in a way that humanizes them for you as much as they were for me.

I hope that nobody curses me out for where/how it ends LMBO!

In many, many ways, this project has been an incredible challenge for me. It has pushed my boundaries of what a romance has to be, challenged my definitions of what an "alpha" man does and doesn't do, and frustrated me to no end with the depths of where these characters pulled me. And it hasn't just been the story – physical challenges, stress, kids, *life*.

This hasn't been an easy project to deliver by any means, but I do so with the knowledge that I put so, *so* much more than just words onto these pages. We're in such uncertain times right now, more than usual, and it's my hope, as always, that the story contained here can offer you a few hours of escape, for whatever reason you might need it.

I dedicate this to… you. Yeah, you. ☺

ONE

ASHA

I shot him.

With a gun purchased on a shadowy corner of an obscure street I had no business being on, from a man that made my skin crawl. His eyes were burnished blacker than his clothes, reflecting the sparse streetlights as he undressed me with his eyes. But he took my money and handed me a loaded gun that I took in trembling, gloved hands.

And he didn't touch me, which was all I could really ask for.

I waited for him at home, while my mama worked the night shift to support his sorry ass, and my basketball prodigy brother was at an away game overnight. I was supposed to be spending the night with a friend.

Her mama was one of those that felt like if your kids partied at home, it was safer than in the streets. She thought nothing of letting us into her liquor cabinet, even into the good stuff, and she drank with us sometimes too. That night, I goaded her. Implied she was old, so she'd drink with us and spill all her secrets about the men she screwed and used for money to prove she wasn't "some old dried up bitch".

While they were wrapped up in their story, I dropped a pill from the stash I'd found in the bathrooms months ago in each of their glasses. I'd thought about this long and hard, done the dosage calculations to make sure I didn't do them any harm, timed how long it would take me to get to my house and back, figured out the quietest route. While they snored away, slumped over on the couch, I traded my shorts, tank top and bare feet for all-black running gear, and headed out.

I knew his patterns, knew his mannerisms. Knew he'd come staggering home drunk a little after eleven. Knew just a little bit of tinkering with the lock would make it stick. Knew his drunk ass would flip, thinking mama was trying to keep him out again. Knew he'd start yelling and beating on the door and making a whole bunch of noise that our useless neighbors were so accustomed to that it would go ignored. Knew he'd kick the door in, since he'd done it before.

"Bitch, you think you gone keep me out of my own house?"

Those words sent a chill up my spine, but I was ready, not stupid. I didn't need him to know it was me, or need him to know why. I didn't need to offer him a soliloquy, pour my heart out about the ways he'd failed my mother, or brother, or me.

I just needed him *gone.*

So I steadied my nerves, steadied my hands, and pulled the trigger, staggering back from the recoil.

He dropped.

I heard his gurgle of pain, heard a woman – *a woman he'd brought with him to my mother's house* – scream, even through the ringing in my ears. I aimed at him and pulled the trigger again, and suddenly, it was like someone had stuffed my head with cotton. His wounded groans, his mistresses' screams as she took off, my footsteps as I went the opposite way, everything was muffled as I sprinted through the kitchen, through the back door I'd left open for this purpose.

I didn't stop running. *Couldn't* stop running until I got to the dumpster two blocks away.

Dump the gun. Swallow ¼ of a pill, so it's your system, just in case.

When I got back to Shani's house, she, her mother, and sister were still drooling. My hands shook as I tipped up the open bottle of vodka and poured some in my mouth, cringing as it burned its way down my throat. I changed back into my shorts and tank top, then eased myself back into my empty spot as the pill took hold, clouding my vision and my mind. Laying my head down on the table, I closed my eyes, suddenly tired, and then… terrified.

What if I'd forgotten something? What if someone had seen something they shouldn't? I hadn't expected him to bring a woman home… even with my ski mask on, in all black, in the darkened room… would she be able to tell someone it was me?

My blurry thoughts drifted to my beautiful, weary mother, to my talented, handsome brother. To the bruises *he* had lain on both. To the constant fear he'd instilled in me. We'd be better off without him, definitely, but if I went to jail for it, would they honestly be better off without *me*?

I'd considered everything… except that. Failure wasn't an option.

The next time I opened my eyes, it was one in the morning, and the phone was ringing.

I smiled.

"Red, were you even listening to me?"

Startled, my eyes cut in Jackson's direction.

No, I wasn't listening. I was *thinking*.

"I heard you, Jax."

I looked around in surprise as the other waitresses and bartenders rose from their seats, either going back out to the floor or gathering in little groups to talk. Jackson chuckled as he stood himself, pushing his chair against the break room table.

"You really expect me to believe that?" he asked, standing over me with his hands in the pockets of his tailored black slacks. Jackson was the manager at *Dream*, the luxury lounge/club located inside of the *Reverie* casino and hotel.

I gave him a sheepish smile, and he rolled his eyes as he turned to walk away.

"Wait," I called, jumping up from my seat, and grabbing my bag to follow him. He had his eyebrow raised when he turned back to me. "Are you going to tell me what the meeting was about? Just like… a little hint? Please?"

Jackson shook his head, but his eyes held amusement. "I'll let you suffer until tomorrow night, when I remind *everybody* about what's going on. Maybe then it'll actually get through your head. What's up with you lately? You've been distracted."

I sucked my teeth, letting my gaze skirt around the room before I returned to Jackson's handsome face. "Ahmad."

For a couple of seconds, Jackson just stared, but then he blew out a sharp breath of disgust. "Of course. So what is it this time? You need me to—"

"No," I said, brushing my deep red locs away from my face.

"You sure? Because—"

"Yeah. I'm sure. He's just stressing me, is all. It's fine."

"It's not fine."

"You know what I mean, Jax," I almost snapped, trying to be mindful of my tone. Ultimately, even though he was cool, he was still my boss, and I needed this job. "I'll be okay."

Jackson nodded. "Aiight. Well… try not to let him stress you too much. Tomorrow is important, and everybody needs to be on point. Go home, get some rest."

"Yes sir."

"I'm serious, Red. You're one of my best girls, I need you on your A-game."

"*One of*?"

"Don't push it."

I smiled. "Okay, Jax. I hear you. Can I go now?"

"Isn't that what I just said? Go. Go *home*. Not to the tables."

"Okay," I said, grinning as I turned away. "See you tomorrow night!"

"I'm serious! And show some more ass tomorrow, this ain't TGIFriday's," he called after me as I left the break room laughing. The fitted black dress I'd worn for tonight's shift hit me at mid-thigh, and had none of the cutouts I usually gravitated to. I guess it *could* be considered conservative for our typical attire.

The dress code for waitresses at *Dream* was simple: Wear black, and look sexy. The "look sexy" part was subjective, and up to Jackson's discretion. Lucky for us, he wasn't too hard to please. He'd teased me tonight about showing a little more skin, but he was mindful of each woman's individual comfort level. I was all about showing legs, back, and midriff area, but too much cleavage made me feel naked, so Jackson didn't push it with me.

I headed out of *Dream* and straight for the elevator, traveling down to the casino floor. I was well-practiced in my heels from the waitressing, and moved quickly out onto the bustling activity of The Strip at night. Navigating carefully through the crush of people, I moved with a purpose until I made it to my desired location – *The Drake* casino and hotel.

Despite what Jax said, I wasn't quite ready yet to call it a night.

I had a thing about not ending up like my father.

I didn't want to be some drunk asshole, abusing the people who loved me because of whatever selfish reasons abusers used. I didn't ever want to walk around belligerent and angry, didn't want to be a user, didn't want the people in my life to hate the fact that they loved me, when they would rather lose themselves in hate.

I didn't drink, not usually. A glass of wine here and there, and that was all, since I allowed myself the indulgence of my father's *other* vice. It was no good to be wrapped up in both at once.

That was one good thing he'd given me, in the rare moments of his humanity that weren't overshadowed by whiskey on his breath and bruises on my mother's skin. He'd planted the seed of interest in poker in me, and that seed had blossomed into skill, and passion. With everything else happening in my life, it was a hobby still, but this was *Vegas*. With the right push… I could make it my life.

For now though, the poker tables were an escape from reality.

Just that morning, another thick white envelope from *Sunrise Hospital and Medical Center* had arrived, and remained unopened with the rest of the bills I would address when I made it home. There was *always* another bill, another expense, another something sucking the life out of me, and my younger brother, Ahmad, only added to that stress.

All I'd ever wanted was for him to find success, whatever that meant for him. He'd been drafted out of college to the Phoenix Suns – the start of what should have been a promising career. A shattered leg in his second year on the team ruined those dreams, which led to a short bout with depression. Some drinking, some partying, some women, some gambling – he blew through most of his NBA savings before me or mama could get a handle on what was happening.

He cleaned himself up, after a verbal ripping to shreds. Used the last of his money to finish his degree, got a job at the high school he graduated from, and a position on the basketball coaching staff. He was in a good place, I thought.

But Ahmad had a little "gift" too.

Like our father, he preferred the riskier games available in the countless casinos on and off The Strip. He'd taught me how to play poker when I was barely six years old but didn't like it himself, not for gambling. It "moved too slow, took too much thinking", he'd said. He liked the immediacy of craps, the thrill of blackjack, the angst of roulette.

The tables where you lost money *fast.*

But, there was always somebody willing to give you money in Vegas, for a price. People willing to float the desperate and delusional a little cash until their "luck" turned around.

At the time of my father's death, he had a nearly thirty-thousand debt on his hands, and a big, ham-fisted loan shark ready to collect. Ahmad didn't quite have debt yet, but he was heading down the same path.

I'd already covered his debts a billion times only for him to keep doing the same shit. Gambling debts, hospital bills, living expenses… I was hemorrhaging money left and right, and I was *exhausted* with it. Physically I was fine, but mentally, emotionally, I'd been bled dry.

I was college educated, graduated summa cum laude, got a great job. But when the bills and responsibilities were stacking higher and faster than my little corporate worker bee salary could handle, the money-making capabilities of the Vegas nightlife looked promising. And turned out, it *was* -- I doubled my previous monthly income by putting on a short dress and serving drinks, but there was a whole list of other shit that came with even *that.*

So I was basically sick of everything.

Poker was my escape.

I tapped the deep green velvet of the poker table twice, signifying that I was "checking" – staying in the game, without raising the bet. The first three cards – the flop – were already turned, and they were in my favor.

This money was mine.

The table was almost full. Four other players, plus me, and an empty spot across the table. Someone slipped into the empty seat as the dealer turned the fourth card over, but I was too busy not reacting to the card flip to pay attention to the new arrival.

Poker face, Asha. Keep it cool.

Check, new player, fold, check.

My turn.

Raise.

$500.

The guy to my left folded, and the betting started around the table again.

The player directly to the left of the dealer shook his head, then folded, leaving it down to me and the player on my right.

Darren.

That was how he'd introduced himself, in a voice he probably thought sounded slick, but grated my nerves. He was handsome, and smelled good, all of which should have made him more appealing, but then he opened his mouth and ruined it.

"Come on, gorgeous," he drawled, smiling. "Are you really about to make me take your money? That's not a good way to start a relationship, is it?"

Revulsion mixed with the anxiety already roiling in my stomach, and I allowed a snarl to creep onto my face. "Place your bet."

"Damn, no love huh?"

I met his eyes, and shook my head. "No love. Just cards. Play."

Looking away from him, I focused on the pile of chips in front of me. Four thousand, eight-hundred, twenty-five dollars. I was up from the *crazy* two-thousand dollar minimum to sit down at this table. It had taken me a long time – too long – to save up that money, but it was probably nothing to the men at this table. Just thinking about losing it all made my palms slick with sweat, but if I was playing, it was useless to do so at the smaller tables. I wanted wins that were actually worth the gamble.

There was this saying, right?

Take risks. If you win, you'll be happy. If you lose, you'll be wiser.

I was really, *really* hoping I didn't leave here any wiser.

Darren made a big show of tossing his five-hundred dollars' worth of chips into the pot. Then, wearing an expression that practically dripped haughtiness, slid in an additional fifteen-hundred.

"You're not having any regrets now, are you beautiful?" he asked, leaning way closer in my ear than he had a right to be as I surveyed my stack of chips. My lip curled – poker face be damned – and I jerked away, rolling my eyes.

The pot was edging very, very close to five thousand dollars, the kind of pot that would make this night beyond worth it.

"What would you like to do, ma'am?"

That question was directed at me from the dealer, and I swallowed hard.

Eyed my stack.

"Call."

I slid $1500 of chips over the line.

The dealer nodded, then turned over the burn card, putting it with the discarded others. My breath stuck in my throat, remaining there until he flipped the last card of the hand, the "river" card.

Jack of clubs.

Yes. Hell yes!

That little celebration happened in my head, but I forced it not to play on my face. The jack of clubs gave my full house a little more value – aces and jacks instead of aces and fours. I hated full houses, but I was confident in my hand, and confident in Darren's lack of one.

I'd already peeped the tiny beads of sweat at his temple, could feel the nervous shuffling of his feet, his impending anxiety over the thought of losing to a "girl" at a table full of men. With a long glance at my chips, Darren smirked. He slid the exact amount I had left out of his stack and over the line, into the betting area. He said nothing to me, but looked around at the other men at the table, chuckling, showboating, and digging himself further into an idiotic hole.

He was pissing me off. He was really, *really* pissing me off.

We'd been at this table long enough for him to know I was a cautious player. I wasn't fast and loose with my betting, didn't take crazy risks. To the other players, it probably looked as if he was being benevolent, giving the poor confused woman at the table a chance to see the error of her ways and tip out now. To save myself.

But I wasn't anybody's damsel in distress.

The dealer's cards weren't good enough to offer a better hand than the one I had. If Darren took time to study poker as something better than dumb luck, he'd know that, but it obviously wasn't a concern of his. I could tell from the way he played that he wasn't serious – he was just another asshole in Vegas with money to throw around and waste.

I felt no sympathy about taking it.

"All in."

A hush fell over the table.

Outwardly, I was calm and collected as I pushed my stack of chips over the line. Beside me, Darren's mouth dropped open, but he quickly shut it, trying to maintain some semblance of a poker face, but the damage was already done. At dealer's instruction, Darren flipped his cards.

A simple flush.

How sweet.

I let a rare smile to my face as I flipped over my cards, revealing my full house – a winning hand over his flush. The table erupted in noise, but I said nothing, mostly because I was trying to process a five-figure win. For me, it was something that just didn't happen.

I flinched at Darren's reaction to my winning cards, sucking in a breath when he suddenly stood up, snatching his remaining chips from the table. "Until next time, sweetheart," he muttered, way too close to my ear again, and then stomped out of the room.

TWO

ASHA

I shook my head as the dealer passed me my winnings. Inside, I was bursting with happiness, because a pot like this would go far. A nice chunk of the bills, and some toward a little future indulgence I'd done a masterful job of keeping to myself.

I hated wearing a watch, but cell phones were discouraged at the casino tables and while we were on duty at *Dream*. I glanced at my wrist to check the time, noting that I had about twenty minutes until the time I'd designated to leave so I could get some of that sleep Jackson was being so pushy about. It was enough for a few more hands, but even with that last win, I was still feeling… *restless.*

I shifted in my seat, getting comfortable again as the dealer started doling out cards for the next hand. After a quick peek at my own cards – pocket tens – I looked around the table, waiting for the betting to start.

That's when my eyes fell on the man seated across from me at the table.

He was beautiful– deep copper skin, sleepy espresso colored eyes, and a nicely sculpted jaw, framed by a nicely groomed goatee. He was in all black – tailored blazer, top buttons of his shirt undone, no tie. I wasn't easily impressed by good looks, but *damn.* Where the hell had he come from?

He ran his tongue over full, sexy lips as he glanced at his cards, and I clenched my thighs together as my under-sexed imagination planted a very different visual in my mind. I pulled my lip between my teeth, trying to get a grip, and a second later, he was looking right at me.

I averted my eyes as the hand started. I wasn't putting in money on tens, but nobody had raised the pot, so I stayed in, to see the flop. I ended up folding the hand, but I watched the man across the table play, and win. He had a confident playing style, a little aggressive, but not over the top. Won more than he lost in the hands he played through to the end.

Again, I glanced at my watch. It was well past one in the morning, and though I didn't feel tired, I knew my body needed the sleep.

One more hand, I told myself, and then nodded at the dealer, signifying I was in. My stack of chips hadn't really moved since that big win against Darren, and I was thrilled with that. I just… I don't know. Wanted one last opportunity to go up against the handsome stranger across the table.

On this round, I got it.

Four cards rested face up in the dealer's section of the table. Queen of spades, queen of hearts, a ten of hearts, and a nine of hearts. The other two queens were in my hand.

Questions about the dealer's shuffling aside, I was happy with my hand. Only two hands could beat my four of a kind – a royal or straight flush – and even with all those hearts in the dealer's hand, him having those wasn't likely.

"Your move, sir," the dealer said, prompting Mr. GQ to make a move. He ran his tongue over his lips again, glanced at his chips, and then up at me, looking me right in the eyes.

Common sense told me to look away, but I didn't. I stared right back at him, letting the tiniest hint of a smirk grace my lips. Subtly, he nodded, then looked back at his chips for less than a second before he picked up and counted out eight and pushed them into the pot.

$2000 dollars.

Whew.

What the hell did he have in his hand?

My fingers were steady, movements confident, almost arrogant as I casually added my eight chips to the pot, and then added two more, for a total of $2500.

It was very, *very* slight, but I caught the hitch in his eyebrow.

He met my raise and raised me back, sliding a total of $3000 into the pot.

Shit.

I didn't want to push my stack that low, but at this point the only other option was to fold. And you didn't *fold* on four queens. I ran my tongue over the inside of my teeth, then made a decision.

I put the $3000 in the pot.

The dealer flipped the last card.

Eight of hearts.

My heart sank to the bottom of my shoes. If he had that fucking jack of hearts…

He pushed in another $2000.

Holy shit, I'm screwed.

I tried to subtly sneak a glance at him, look for tells, but he was stone-faced, looking right at me. *Everybody* was looking right at me, the whole damn room it seemed, and suddenly, it felt like I was in a fucking sauna.

Four Queens, Asha.

"Ma'am, it's your move."

"Yeah. Check."

I slid my money into the pot.

The dealer indicated for us to show our cards.

The handsome stranger gave a full smile, with gorgeous white teeth – and a damned *dimple*, have mercy – as he turned his over, revealing two kings – hearts and clubs. My shoulders damn near drooped off my body in relief. This time, my hands were shaking, as I turned my cards to reveal my pocket queens, and excitement erupted around the table.

My eyes blurred with tears as the dealer collected my pot and distributed it to me. I blinked them back as I loaded up my chip rack, offering thanks-yous to the people who congratulated me. I was calling it a night.

"Not going to give me a chance to win my money back?" Handsome Stranger called across the table, in a warm voice that stuck to me like honey.

I looked up as I loaded the last of my chips, keeping my smile carefully measured. "It's late," I said, firmly planting my feet before I stood. The last thing I needed was to topple over on my heels, ruining what could have been a seductive exit. "Maybe I'll see you around."

He nodded a little, giving my body an unhurried perusal with his eyes as he sat back in his chair. "Yeah. Maybe so."

Security escorted me to the cash-out desk, where I had them add my winnings to my player account, so I wouldn't have to walk around with actual cash. Those winnings were precious, precious cargo, and I wasn't willing to risk getting robbed or losing a check.

I left the desk with a new pep in my step. It was approaching two in the morning, but I was far from tired, and still not feeling settled the way I normally did. Underneath the shallow excitement of my win, my mind was still clouded with stress. Deep down, agitation still soaked my spirit.

As I turned the corner, my eyes fell on the long bar that took up most of one of the casino walls, backed by a huge aquarium full of exotic fish. My gaze hung there for a moment, following a purple-bodied fish with delicate pink fins that ruffled and trailed behind it as it moved gracefully through the water. The fish was beautiful, but following it with my eyes led me to something much nicer to look at.

Him again.

We were separated by maybe twenty feet, but I could tell there was something dark in the glass in his hand. He was draped over one of the seats at the bar, completely casual, relaxed, like he owned the place as he sipped his drink and looked around. Even with him sitting, I could tell he was tall, and the way his shoulders filled out that jacket… *Jesus.*

My feet started moving before my brain caught up.

I weaved my way through the crowd, doing my best to stay out of his direct line of sight. It wasn't until I was a few feet away that he glanced in my direction, and his eyebrows lifted in recognition.

His eyes did another appreciative sweep of my body before they returned to my face, making me wish I *had* chosen something sexier for work that day. I wanted him drooling over me, fantasizing, barely able to keep his hands to himself.

I wanted… *him.*

"Changed your mind?" he asked, then raised his glass to his lips to drink. "You come to give me a chance to redeem myself?"

"Absolutely not," I said in my lower, more seductive "work" voice, slipping onto the barstool beside him. I angled my body toward his, reducing some of the space between us. "I'll buy you a drink though."

His mouth curved into another one of those dimpled smiles, giving a boyish edge to his face. "Buy *me* a drink, huh?"

I shrugged. "Yeah. You're not one of *those* men, are you? So steeped in traditional gender roles that you can't accept a drink from a woman?"

"Not at all," he chuckled, moving closer to me, enough that the warm, spicy-clean scent of his cologne wrapped around me, stimulating my senses. "I actually happen to appreciate an audacious woman… especially one who can see right through my best attempt at a bluff."

I didn't correct him. Why on earth would he need to know that I *hadn't* seen through it, and was just out there playing for my life in that hand? Instead, I offered a sexy smile, and crossed my legs, a motion that his eyes followed.

"Well… here I am."

His gaze flicked back up to mine. "Yes you are. What's your name?"

I shook my head. "I prefer not to say."

"Where are you from? How long you been playing poker?"

"Neither of those things are your business."

"If you don't tell me anything, how am I supposed to get to know you?"

"Right. That's the point."

"Why is that the point?"

"Why isn't it?"

I grinned at the little tinge of frustration that crossed his face before he grabbed his drink from the glossy, tempered glass surface of the bar and took another sip. The feeling that had swept through me as I approached him sitting at the bar hadn't left – if anything, it was stronger. Sitting here with him had me ready to indulge a need that hadn't been met in more than six months, since I'd started my full position at *Dream.*

Hmm…

Maybe *that* would give me the relief that the poker tables hadn't.

"So… I'm going to get right to the point. Okay?" I put my hand on his knee, biting the inside of my lip as I pushed it up his hard, powerful leg to reach his thigh. I kept moving, squeezing my legs together when my fingers brushed another part of his body.

"Damn," he chuckled, covering my hand with his, and keeping it in place. "I can't even get the drink you offered first?"

I grinned. "Well, you *could...*"

He gripped my hand a little tighter, looking me right in the face. Those deep, dark eyes of his were burning with a level of desire that made a shiver run up my spine. "Or?"

I nodded a little, then leaned in close enough to speak into his ear. "I have something else in mind."

THREE

ASHA

I swallowed the urge to tell him I didn't usually "do this".

It didn't matter what I "usually" did, because the reality of the moment was that his hands were up my dress, firmly gripping my ass cheeks as he pressed his hard, heavy body against mine. I gasped, grabbing his arms and struggling to catch my breath as his tongue trailed from my collarbone to my neck, then up behind my ear while I fought the instinct to move away.

This is crazy.

Crazy crazy crazy.

Somewhere between the bar and door to the room, I'd lost some of that sexual aggression to common sense. I didn't even know this man. He was bigger than me, I was in *his* room at the Drake, for which he'd magically produced a key after I suggested we go somewhere. All the things Jackson warned the girls at *Dream* against, for our own safety, and here I was ignoring every precaution given to me when I first integrated myself into the sinful nightlife of this city.

But… there was no denying the sizzle of chemistry I'd felt when our eyes first met across the poker table. No questioning my intense attraction to his warm, cinnamon-toned skin, easy, dimpled smile, and chiseled features. No escaping the absolute bliss of his lips on my throat, the taste of his tongue against mine, flavored with hints of bourbon from the drink he'd downed at the bar.

I *needed* this, badly, and I was already here now. May as well have a little fun.

"Relax," he murmured into my neck, and then pulled back to meet my gaze. Up close, I could see that those warm, espresso colored eyes were flecked with gold, and carried an intensity that made a shiver run up my spine as he moved his hands down to my thighs, gripping and drawing me closer. "You still want to do this, right?"

I ran my tongue over dry lips, then nodded. "Yes."

"Then loosen the fuck up."

His words carried a little bit of a growl, but I wasn't offended. I *was* tense. I *was* nervous. I *was* wondering what the hell I was doing there.

"Sorry," I said, looking away to catch a much needed breath. "I'm just—"

"Uh-uh. Don't make an excuse. You were sexy downstairs. In control. Confident. That's the woman I want tonight. You can bring her back, or you can go."

"Excuse me?" I snapped, putting my hands against his chest to shove him away, though he didn't budge. "I'm the *same* woman who wiped the poker table with your ass, not even an hour ago."

His face came toward me, and I sucked in a breath as his lips came to a stop just barely an inch from mine. "Nah. *That* woman took my money, then approached me after and offered to buy *me* a drink. *That* woman sat beside me at the bar and rubbed my dick, made a proposition. You, on the other hand? *You* look like you're ready to run outta here." He released his grip on me. "And I'm not about to stop you."

My cheeks flooded with heat as he turned away, with a sexy swagger in his stride as he moved toward the kitchen of his suite.

Was this motherfucker *dismissing* me?

Anger fueled my movements as I stomped over to where he was standing, having poured himself a drink of something from his suite's well-stocked bar. He was lifting it to his mouth when I approached, plucking the glass right from his unsuspecting fingers and knocking back the contents. The liquor flooded my taste buds with smooth caramel notes before the heat kicked in, spreading through my whole chest.

"I'm not going anywhere. Not until I get what I came up here for," I said, putting the empty glass back in his hand. I strolled away with an extra sway in my hips. Since the Drake family built this casino/hotel, which rivaled The Reverie in luxury and size, I'd been wanting to see the view from one of the big floor to ceiling windows.

I didn't even make it halfway across the room before he was on me.

A whimper left my throat as he hooked an arm around my waist, dragging me back against his body. He swept my locs to one side, then bit down on my exposed shoulder just enough to sting a little before he soothed it with a kiss. I shivered as he trailed his tongue from my shoulder to my ear and then back down before he closed his mouth over my neck, suckling at my skin. His hand went to the bottom of my dress, tugging it up around my hips before he pushed it underneath the soft fabric of my panties, raking his fingers over my sensitive skin.

"What's your name?" he asked in a subtle growl against my neck, before he kissed me there again. I parted my legs, giving him room between my thighs as he slid his fingers into me, grinding against my clit with the heel of his hand.

I shook my head, closing my eyes as he nipped me with his teeth again. "We said no names, remember? Leave Vegas in Vegas, that's the rule."

"*You* said no names, not me." He removed the arm that was hooked around my waist to reach up, threading his hands through my hair. "But fine," he said, tugging a little to make me tip my head, giving him better access to my neck as he pumped me with his fingers. "I'll just call you Red."

For a full second, I froze over him using that name, but another tug to my hair pulled me out of it. Damn near everybody called me Red, from friends to family to customers, because of my hair – pencil-sized, deep red locs that hung down my back – so there was no need for alarm. I relaxed again as his fingers closed around my zipper.

He was in no particular hurry as he dragged it down, planting soft kisses along my exposed skin as it came into his view. He brought both hands up to push the arms down over my shoulders, letting the dress drop to my feet, leaving me in nothing except the tiny black panties I wore underneath.

Standing behind me, he nudged me toward the couch, and I followed his instruction, opting to leave on my heels. He put his hand to the middle of my back and pushed, but that time I resisted, tossing him a questioning look over my shoulder. His heavy-lidded eyes were even lower.

"Bend over."

He pushed at me again, and I did as he'd said, draping myself over the arm of the couch. Heat gathered between my thighs as I felt him kneel behind me, and then roughly drag my panties down my legs. I sucked in a breath as he grabbed my calves, spreading my legs wide. It was cool in the room, leaving an uncomfortable chill on my bare, sensitive skin.

But then his mouth was on me, very hot, and very wet, and that was very, *very* comfortable. I pushed myself up on my hands as he devoured me like he was starving, sucking and licking and sucking again before he dipped his tongue into me. He groaned into me, a deep sound of complete satisfaction as he closed his mouth over me, slurping and sucking like my skin was covered in sweet syrup, and he wasn't trying to miss a single drop.

My arms gave out and I collapsed face down onto the couch, trying to keep my feet planted in my heels as he licked me. My fingernails dug into the cushions as my legs began to shake, my knees buckling under blissful pressure. He pushed me forward so that the arm of the couch bore my weight, then hooked an arm around one of my thighs as he buried his face between them.

I was loud. I was *so* loud that the whole fucking casino could probably hear me, but I didn't care. This – mind numbing pleasure that didn't even leave room in my conscious for stress – was exactly what I needed.

I grabbed one of the throw pillows, biting down as I used my elbows as leverage to move away. It was good – it was *so* good – but it was also too good. More than I could take.

"Don't run," he growled, dragging me back into place. He tugged my clit between his teeth, closing his mouth over it, licking and sucking until I was screaming into that pillow for release. I groaned a deep, throaty moan as he pushed his fingers into me again, licking around them as he stroked me into bliss. I couldn't help the little whines of pleasure that fought past my lips as he nibbled all over my ass cheeks, then brought his mouth back to my clit, sucking hard as he worked me with his fingers.

That was the moment I came unglued.

I damn near bit a hole in that pillow as my body tensed and then released, leaving me feeling boneless as pleasure crashed into me. I let my mouth hang open, letting out helpless gasps and whimpers as his hot tongue kept rasping over my sensitive skin, prolonging the ripples of orgasm as it soaked through me, sapping my energy.

He plied me with slow, elongated, licks as my heart rate slowed to normal, and I closed my eyes. I could have fallen asleep *just* like that, ass in the air, his mouth on me, but from the rustling behind me, he wasn't preparing to let me rest – he was taking off his clothes.

I pulled what little energy I had into looking over my shoulder as he stood, toeing off his shoes, dropping his already undone pants, then boxers. His body was nice – he was toned, and obviously fit, but not ripped, or overly muscular – and he wasn't one of the little skinny men that always seemed to be in my face. He was dense, and sexy.

As he stepped out of the clothes, my eyes landed on his thick erection. Just slightly darker than the rest of his cinnamon-toned skin, deeply veined, damn near pretty as he was, and I had to blink hard to wipe away visions of my mouth around it.

He grabbed his wallet from the inside pocket of his jacket and pulled out a condom, rolling it onto his hard length. He looked up at me as he finished, meeting my gaze with a hungry gleam in his eyes, and wicked grin that made me tremble.

Positioning himself behind me, he gripped handfuls of my ass, squeezing and kneading as he used his foot to spread mine apart. Reaching around me, he yanked the cushions and pillows off of the couch. He moved one arm around my waist, pulling me up so that I was on my feet again, then directed me to plant my hands on the seat.

As soon as I did, he slammed inside of me.

"Ahh!" I yelped, in pleasure, pain, and surprise. My arms collapsed, but I didn't fall because of his arm anchored around my waist, holding me in place as he plunged into me. Because of his height in proximity to mine, I felt his full weight behind every stroke, snatching my breath away.

The slight edge of pain gave way to intense pleasure as he burrowed into me, making my eyes water. Our moans and groans echoed around the room, punctuated by the wet, steady slap of skin on skin as he drove his hips against mine in deep, hard strokes, offering me no mercy.

It was perfectly, *exactly* what I needed.

In what seemed like no time, I was coming again, and he was right behind me, slamming into me with a growl that echoed in my chest for a few minutes after. He grabbed another condom, dragged me into the bathroom with him to dispose of the first, then picked me up like I weighed nothing, propping me on the counter.

He sheathed himself and then plunged into me again, with no less vigor than before. This time, I closed my legs around his waist as he stroked me, propping my arms up over his shoulders.

He dipped his head, pulling my rigid nipple between his teeth. He teased it with his tongue until it was painfully sensitive, then closed his mouth over it, suckling it until the pain had melted away.

He did the same thing to the other side, going back and forth, never losing the rhythm of his stroke. I let my head fall back and closed my eyes, keening and moaning as I rocked my hips into his, creating another level of friction that increased the pleasure.

He buried himself in me deep and stayed there, making me gasp as he pushed a hand between us to rub my swollen clit between his fingers. His other hand cupped my breast and squeezed, then moved up to my neck, where he ran his thumb over my throat. Just that action made me swallow hard, but then his hand was around my neck, in a grip that was just firm enough to make a tingle of fear rush over my skin.

A second later, he was stroking me too hard for me to care.

My throat was already raw from earlier, and constricted from the pressure of his hand, but I screamed my lungs out in mindless, absolute bliss as he slammed into me again and again. His mouth crashed onto mine and I parted my lips to accept his tongue. He devoured my mouth, licking and kissing, sucking my lips and tongue, exploring and tasting my mouth, savoring me. Making it absolutely impossible to breathe, but in the moment, the only thing that mattered was how incredible I felt.

And then, the release.

Everything stopped. Static filled my ears and eyes as the orgasm paralyzed me, leaving me momentarily helpless. Feeling came rushing back at ten times intensity, and I practically melted against him, past the point of coherent thoughts or sounds. Loosely, I understood that he was still moving, and then came to his own release, but my mind was elsewhere, soaked in ecstasy, bathed in the feeling of *everything*.

And it kept going, and going, and going as he kept moving in me, renewing the wave of orgasm over and over again until I was weak. I slumped against him as he came, eyes closed but aware as he put his arms around me, with a hoarse chuckle in my ear.

He cleaned up both of us, and then carried me to the bedroom, where I was too exhausted to object to being tucked under the covers with him. I woke up hours later to him behind me, his voice in my ear, asking if I felt okay, and if I was ready again.

"Condom," I muttered, safety-conscious even in my half-asleep state. I felt his hand around my wrist, pulling my arm behind me to maneuver between us. His fingers led mine to his dick, letting me feel the latex over it, and the ridge of the condom.

My eyes closed again as I nodded, rolling my face down toward the pillow as I turned onto my stomach. He caught me at the hip though, urging me onto my back before he settled between my legs and sank in.

I was sore from our earlier romps. Still, my body welcomed him inside, welcomed the pleasant feeling of his weight on top of me as he moved in slow, measured strokes that were nothing like before. Surprised, I opened my eyes to find him staring down at me. His gaze locked with mine, and I closed my eyes as he lowered to kiss me, teasing and sucking my bottom lip before he slipped his tongue into my mouth.

We stayed like that. Easy, deep strokes, long kisses and caresses. Slow, sleepy sex that would have my feelings all tangled up if this man wasn't a complete stranger.

He fell asleep on top of me afterward, and I knew I wouldn't be far behind him. I was completely sated and *finally* feeling at peace. I would be sore tomorrow, which would probably affect me at work, but at least I would have a pleasant memory.

I thought about leaving, but didn't even have the energy to get him off me, let alone find clothes and make it to my car. I closed my eyes and settled in, drifting off to sleep, with one last thought.

Best night ever.

FOUR

ASHA

I woke up alone.

Soreness and fatigue clung to my body as I pulled myself into a seated position, but I still felt good. Really, really good.

I looked around for… whatever his name was, but saw nothing, and heard no one.

Strange.

I climbed out of the bed, wrapping myself in the sheet before I moved around the suite looking for him, with no luck. No clothes, no bags, nothing.

He was gone.

A hint of panic crept up my spine, then dissipated when I made another trip through the living room. My dress, bag, and shoes were placed neatly together on the couch, and when I lifted the dress, my panties were underneath, on top of a thick envelope. My eyebrow lifted in curiosity as I picked it up, flipping it open to pull out a neatly handwritten note.

"Red —

Hope you slept well.

I arranged a late checkout for you so you can stay later, and ordered a breakfast platter sent up. I also hooked up a little something else for you... thought you might need a little TLC after last night. I had to leave this morning, but who knows? Maybe one day you'll get around to buying me that drink.

- K.W."

I tried my best to hold back the smile trying to spread across my face, but I couldn't. Inside the envelope was a blank voucher for the hotel's luxury spa, to be used on whatever I wanted, whenever I wanted. Something I never would have done for myself, not on a large scale. Something just for *me.*

Hm.

I like the way "K.W." operates, I mused, smiling as I tucked the note and voucher in my purse. I checked through the contents, making sure everything was there, then picked up my clothes, carrying them with me to the bathroom so I could take advantage of the luxury shower.

The room service arrived at eight on the dot, and I stuffed myself with fruit and pastries before I ventured back into the bathroom to find a toothbrush and toothpaste. Once I was all cleaned up, I got dressed and left, making sure to stop by the front desk to say that I was leaving.

Two women who appeared to be around my age were working the front desk, which, despite the number of people hanging in the lounge areas of the lobby, wasn't busy.

"Hi," I said, getting one of the women's attention. She looked up at me with a smile.

"Yes, can I help you?"

I swallowed a little, suddenly self-conscious. "Um… well, I spent the night with… a friend. He already left, but the room was his. I just wanted to check out."

"We can definitely do that for you. What's the name on the reservation? We'll just have to call him to confirm."

I averted my eyes. "Um… I don't *know* his name."

Her eyes narrowed in confusion for about a half of a second before they widened in understanding. "*Ah*! What's the room number please?"

"It was P11."

She nodded, then typed a few things into the computer in front of her. I watched her face as she waited for something to load, growing tense when her eyebrows suddenly raised, and her lips parted. She schooled her expression back into a pleasant smile before she turned to me again.

"Was everything satisfactory for you ma'am? The breakfast reached you okay, was enjoyable? Did you enjoy the view?"

"Yes."

"Is there anything else we can do for you? Do you need transportation?"

I lifted an eyebrow. "Um… no?"

"Okay. Well, the bill has already been settled, so you're good to go. Thank you so much for staying with us at the Drake."

"Um… you're welcome."

"Have a wonderful day."

Feeling slightly confused about that interaction, I turned to walk away from the desk. I was barely a few steps away when I heard the desk clerk say to two distinct words to the other clerk that further heightened my confusion – and curiosity.

"Lucky bitch."

I smiled about the soreness between my legs as I climbed out of my car in the parking lot of my apartment complex. Not the most standard reaction to pain or discomfort, but it was a sensation I hadn't felt in way too long. Despite the tenderness of my skin, I felt *great*.

The smile remained on my face as I headed toward my door, only dropping long enough to mentally curse out whoever the hell was parked in my spot. I rolled my eyes at the black Charger and kept moving past it, ready to get upstairs and change out of my clothes from the previous night.

"Aye, Red!"

I froze, with my hand on the rail and my foot on the first of the stairs that led up to my apartment. I quickly recovered, pressing the button on my keys that released the blade from an innocent-looking keychain. My other hand went into my purse, closing around my handy little can of pepper spray.

I turned around, and my lip curled in disgust as I watched a man swing the door closed on the Charger that was parked in my spot.

"What the fuck do you want?"

He frowned over my words as he ambled up to me, staying far enough away that I couldn't reach him with the blade from where I stood.

Finally learned.

"You know you're too pretty to be talking like that, right? It's not ladylike."

"Oh, well excuse the fuck outta me, I've been confused all this time. Again, what do you want?"

"Is Camille up there?"

"Not your business."

He sucked his teeth, then shook his head, mumbling something under his breath. "Look, Red. I'm just trying to talk to the damn girl."

"Well, the damn girl isn't trying to talk to you, Jared. And if I recall, you're supposed to be at least three hundred feet away from her. A hundred yards. Does that front door look a football field away to you, nigga?"

"You know," he said, scratching his head. "One day I'm gonna just knock your fucking head in for that slick ass mouth."

I laughed. "We both you know you don't want it with me, Jared. I told you I would slice your ass to ribbons next time and I mean it. Stay the hell away from this apartment, and stay the hell away from Camille."

"Or what, you're gonna call the police?" he asked, with a smirk that made my finger twitch on the trigger button of my pepper spray can.

"Funny. Speaking of the police, shouldn't you be out serving and protecting instead violating restraining orders, Officer Price?"

He was out of uniform, in regular clothes, but still. Maybe a little duty reminder would get him the hell away from me.

"You just tell Camille I came by."

"Fuck you."

"Have a good day, Asha."

He climbed in his car and drove off, and I waited until he was well out of the parking lot before I put away my blade and climbed up the stairs, glancing over my shoulder as I went.

I found Camille in the living room in front of the TV, curled under a blanket with a cup of chai in her hands, as always. She glanced over her shoulder as I walked up, smiling when she saw my face.

"Oh my God," she said, turning the volume down on the TV. "Is this a walk of shame, Asha? Isn't that your same dress from last night?"

I blushed, shaking my head. "Hold that thought. Has he been bothering you?" I asked, gesturing toward the door.

Camille bunched her eyebrows. "Who?"

"Nevermind. Back to me."

"Go on…"

"I had a one night stand with a complete stranger and I don't even regret it a little and oh my God it was amazing and he was so damn fine."

I spit that out so fast that the words blended together in just a mash of sound. I could practically see Camille's thoughts in a little bubble over her head as she tried to decipher what I'd just blurted out. And then her eyes went wide.

"OH MY GOD!"

"Right?!"

"YOU DIDN'T!!"

"I *did.*"

Camille's mouth dropped for a few seconds before she snapped it closed, shaking her head. "Nuh uh. Nope. I'd believe you if you told me you'd kicked a stranger's ass, but slept with one? Girl I don't believe you, stop lying."

I sucked my teeth, then reached into my bag, pulling out the note and spa voucher. Camille took it from me with a look that gave me strong "girl please" vibes, but her expression grew into shock as she read the note, and then looked back at me like she was seeing me for the first time.

"You *did* sleep with someone! Oh. My. God!"

"Wait a minute!" I said, trying – and failing – to give her a stern look as she jumped up from the couch, spilling ice packs from underneath her blanket. "Why are you acting like I *never* have sex?!"

She laughed as she grabbed either side of my face. "Because you *never* have sex. But you're glowing right now! He tore your ass up didn't he?"

I sighed. "Like he never wanted it put back together."

Camille let out a sound that was half scream, half giggle. "Used protection, right?"

"*Duh.*"

"Was his dick pretty?"

"It was *gorgeous.*"

"Did you give him head?"

"Hell no! I don't know him like that!"

She crossed her arms. "But I bet you let him put his mouth all over your little kitty-cat, didn't you?"

"First of all, don't call it a kitty-cat. Second… he didn't really make it seem like an… *option.*"

Camille's eyes went wide. "Ooooh, tell me more! Sounds like *he* knows the proper Vegas one-night-stand etiquette."

"Oh my God, *shut up!*" I laughed. "What's with the ice packs?"

She glanced backward, noticing that they'd fallen. She turned around on long legs to pick them up, and even *that* movement, like all her others, was graceful. Camille was one of the most beautiful people I'd ever seen. Big brown eyes, high cheekbones, mahogany skin, a body people would kill for.

"Girl, I danced my ass off last night. Dawn and Kora Oliver were in the audience."

"Who?"

"Only my professional music theater idols. They came backstage after, and told me they loved the show. Kora actually gave me her card. Asha, she called me amazing."

"That's incredible!"

"Isn't it?!" she squealed, wearing a huge smile. "Sounds like we both had a great night."

I nodded, returning her grin. "Yep. Cause guess who racked up almost *fifteen* thousand dollars at the poker tables last night?"

"You're *kidding*?!"

I bit down on my lip, shaking my head. "Nope. You know what that means, right?"

"You're still gonna try to go for it?"

"I'm too close not to. If I can pull together the other ten thousand in a week…" I stopped, shaking my head. "Girl, I may have to give up serving drinks and start shaking ass."

Camille laughed. "You can't dance, Asha. You'll end up *owing* the customers money. But listen… you're too close *not* to do this. I have some saved up, and—"

"*Hell no*," I said, holding up a hand. "Friends and money don't mix. Absolutely not."

"Asha, come on! You've been talking about this since we met. You're so close."

"I know. I *know*." I let out a sigh, then smiled at my friend. "If we get to that deadline, and I don't have it yet… then we'll talk, okay?"

Her face spread into a huge grin. "Okay!"

"And it would be a loan. I would pay you back, all of it. With interest."

"I wouldn't expect anything else. What are you doing today?"

"Gotta go see mama. Probably try to catch up with Ahmad, make sure he's staying out of trouble. Work later tonight. You?"

"Sleep, and mindless TV. It is my off day, not even rehearsals, and I'm taking full advantage of it. I plan on sitting my ass right here, all day."

"Mmmm."

I tried to keep my face neutral, but I badly wanted to scowl as I thought about how Jared had been waiting outside. What if she'd come down to her car to go grab breakfast, or he'd decided to actually knock on the door? Or kick it in?

"Why are you looking constipated?" she asked, pulling me from my thoughts.

I shook my head. "No reason. Um, hey… make sure you keep that door locked if you're here by yourself. And look through peephole before you open it for anybody."

She lifted an eyebrow as she dropped back down onto the couch, repositioning her ice packs. "Um, thanks mom, but I'm almost thirty. I already know not to talk to strangers, and all of that."

"Not the strangers I'm worried about."

"What? Wait… Asha, are you talking about Jared? Did you see him? Has he been by here again?"

Before I could respond, she was already off of the couch, practically leaping across the room to pull open the curtains and peer out of the blinds. She produced her cell phone from somewhere, and was already dialing as I came to stand beside her.

"He was waiting outside, in a new car. A black Charger."

She glanced back at me. "He drives a blue Mustang."

I shrugged. "Not anymore."

Camille moved away from the window, pacing as she waited for whoever he was calling to answer. "I'm trying to remember if I've seen a black car following me around. I kinda felt like maybe last week, but then—"

"This is why I wasn't going to say anything," I sighed, finally stepping out of my heels. "I don't want you around here worried about this fool, always looking over your shoulder."

"Cree," Camille said into the phone, holding up a finger for me to hold on. "He was over here again." She was quiet for a moment, still pacing as she listened to whatever her brother was saying on the other end of the line. Then, she nodded, glancing at me. "Yeah, Asha just got home, and she says he was waiting outside, in a black Charger… Okay. *Okay*, I will. Love you."

She hung up, then peered out of the window again. "Cree says he's gonna send somebody by. And have *another* talk with Jared about leaving me the hell alone. You'd think he'd get it by now."

It bugged the shit of me to see her paranoid, fear in her eyes as she peeked out the window. It reminded me too much of a long time ago, a time when my mother had dropped this stupid ass glass my father loved, with a roulette wheel etched into the side. She'd been terrified, waiting for him to get home, knowing how his anger would bubble over and spill, mostly on her but touching all of us.

Camille looked exactly like that right now, and I felt sixteen all over again. Weak, and vulnerable, and helpless to get rid of the monster that terrorized someone I loved.

But... you really weren't, were you?

... no.

I wasn't. It had taken time to discover that, to move in and get comfortable in that knowledge, but I wasn't the harmless little girl I looked like then.

And I wasn't now either.

"I told him I was going to slice him into fettuccine noodles if he came near you, Cam. And I mean that."

Her head swung toward me. "Don't get your ass arrested again Asha," she scolded, even though a smiled tugged at the corners of her mouth. "You *barely* got out of trouble last time. Only because he didn't press charges."

"Only because he knew I'd do worse than I already had if he didn't."

The smile went ahead and stretched across her lips, and she shook her head. "You're such a wannabe bodyguard. You sure you're not some super spy?"

I laughed. "Girl I wish. I would've disappeared Jared's dumb ass a long time ago. Get away from that window, and go back to the TV. Forget him. Enjoy your day."

I turned to walk away as Camille closed the curtains. In my room, I dropped onto the edge of the bed, my head in my hands. Already, I was feeling exhausted again from the weight of the situation between Jared and Camille, but I didn't have much time to dwell. I needed to get to my mother's by ten-thirty to hold any sort of order over my day. So I got up, pulled off my dress, then stepped into the closet to find something to wear.

FIVE

ASHA

I thought my life was going to change, but it didn't.

Really? That was the most disappointing thing.

You watch every episode of real crime TV you can get your hands on, stop paying attention in class so you can think through your plan, forsake teenaged social life, put your damned *soul* on the line, to do something that you thought was going to change everything.

But it didn't.

After my father died, it took my mother too long to decide we should leave that house. She mourned him heartily, *wholly.* She cried, screamed, wanted to know why, couldn't wrap her head around why he'd been taken from her.

She loved him.

She *missed* him.

Watching her lay in bed day after day, wrapped in her grief, too broken to tend to me or my brother, I realized the extent of my naivety.

She wasn't scared to leave… she just didn't want to.

I hadn't saved her from anything – I was the one who'd broken her heart, not the man who'd constantly raised his fists to break her body. So many nights I laid in bed unable to sleep, unable to drown out the simultaneous guilt and rage that dueled within me.

How could she not be relieved that this man – barely worth that title, let alone to be called "father" – was no longer a threat to her or her children? Did she really think the bruises on Ahmad were from basketball practice? Did she *really* think my avoidance of being in the same room with him was just some teenage hormone thing? Did she believe the lies she told people about the bruises and cuts and broken bones, that they were all just because she was clumsy?

Whatever.

At least with him gone, Ahmad and I were safe… until she started dating again, not too long after. She chose men who were essentially photocopies of my father, using her for the sudden riches she'd gained, in the form of a life insurance policy payout. That I could ignore, but then I started seeing the telltale signs of abuse, and there was no way I was waiting around for it to escalate, bleeding over to me and my brother. As soon as I turned eighteen, I moved out, and I took Ahmad with me.

It was only because of dumb luck that my mother ended up with her current husband. He was a security guard at the medical center she frequented after her diagnosis a few years ago. The other men were long gone by the time she met Tim – only a man who really wants you will stick around while you're broke and sick.

He sat with her through the infusions that helped manage her lupus, talked to her, fell in love. He was the one who encouraged her to pick herself up, rekindle the relationship with her kids. Not that Ahmad and I had ever closed the door – I was the one who'd found the treatment center, and paid the bills since she couldn't work – but Tim encouraged her to step through.

I loved my mother – loved her *dearly*.

If I ever let it, the resentment was enough to eat me alive.

But mentally, I wasn't going there. I had entirely too much to do to allow today to be one where I ended up lost, wallowing in memories and nightmares.

After I showered *K.W.* off my skin, I'd dressed in simple jeans and a fitted tee to go see my mother. She and Tim lived in a decent suburb of Vegas. Clean, quiet, and removed from the bright, busy vibe of the Vegas everyone thought of when they heard the name, and the often dangerous, worn-down element I'd grown up in.

I smiled as I pulled up to the house, not just because of the big black Titan truck in the driveway – Ahmad's – but because my mother was outside, fussing with the flower beds. That meant today was a good day.

"Hey baby," she said as I approached. She stood, wiping sweat from her brow as she squinted against the beaming sun. "What brings you by?"

I grinned as she pulled me into a hug. "Nothing in particular. Just wanted to see you since it's been a few days."

"Has it?" My mother stepped back, looking confused as she pulled soil-covered gloves back onto her hands to crouch in the flower bed again. "Weren't you here just the other day? You brought me those cookies, from the little bakery up the street."

My breath caught in my throat. "Mama, that was last week… you don't remember?"

"Oh, was it?!" she laughed and shook her head, not looking up from her flowers. "You know your mama is getting old, baby. Just got a little mixed up."

"You mentioned it to your doctor?" I asked, trying to sound casual even though I felt something else.

"Asha, that woman would laugh me out of her office if I made a fuss about a little mix up like this. No point in worrying them about it."

"It's not worrying them about it mama, it's taking care of yourself. It could be related to your lupus."

"I'm *fine.*"

"Mama, please."

She propped her hands on her hips from her kneeling position, pursing her lips at me. "Fine, girl. I will mention it at my next appointment."

I grinned. "Thank you. Where's Tim?"

"In there asleep in front of ESPN. He's got the window open so I can holler if I need him. Your brother is in there too – if you need somebody to be worried about."

My hands twitched, wanting to form fists. I had been glad to see Ahmad's truck here, but if he was in trouble again… "What is he up to?"

"I don't know. Don't know if it's anything for sure, but I've just got a feeling. Ever since your daddy died… I just wonder sometimes how much different Ahmad would be if he still had his father."

I cringed as I literally bit down on my tongue, keeping myself from speculating that Ahmad would probably be a womanizing, gambling, abusive drunk too, if that man were still here. Especially since it seemed like a couple of those were just genetic, and he and I both struggled with our father's vices.

Instead of talking about any of that, I changed the subject, asking my mother about her flowers. I had little to no interest in the happenings of her garden bed, or her feud with the retired neighbor next door, but I endured it for the sake of the joy on her face as she talked and pruned and fertilized and watered. Before I knew it, almost two hours and several bottles of water from the cooler had gone by.

I excused myself from my mother and went inside, searching for Ahmad. I passed Tim snoring on the couch, and headed toward the back of the house, looking room by room until I made my way to the kitchen.

Still no Ahmad.

While I stood there, wondering where he could be, I heard the shuffle of footsteps and the low rumble of a male voice speaking in hushed tones. It only took me a few seconds to deduce that it was coming from the back porch, but instead of stepping outside, I eased toward the wall that the porch shared with the kitchen, quietly listening.

"… said I had it…why you tripping about this shit………but I'm telling you I'm good for it! Haven't I always been? Just be easy… … gonna get the money. Be easy."

I pushed away from the wall, trying to get to him. I made it to the door at the same time he did – he'd apparently ended his phone call – but the smile that had started to slip onto his face at the sight of me quickly dropped as he took in my scowl.

"What the hell was that about?!" I hissed as I pushed him backward onto the porch, closing the door behind me. "What money are you going to get?! What the fuck is going on with you?!"

Ahmad rolled his eyes as he stepped backward to lean on the porch railing. "Hi to you too, Asha. How was your day? You doing alright?"

"Oh, cut the bullshit Ahmad. Just be real with me. Is this about the same damn thing I overheard before? Do I need to be worried about you?"

"I'm a grown man. Why you always acting like I can't handle myself?"

Because you can't.

Again, I bit my tongue. I stepped to my baby brother, cupping his chin in my hands. We shared the same honey-toned skin, thick eyelashes, dark brown eyes, and inexplicable dark reddish hair. He was handsome – damn near pretty. Too pretty to end up with his face knocked in over some gambling debts – especially when he'd promised me…

"Ahmad, *please*."

Why did it always feel like I was doing all the begging around here, and never for myself? Always for *them* to do some of the work of keeping themselves safe, and keeping it all together.

"Asha, I already told you I'm good. You're always trying to run to the rescue, instead of letting me handle my own shit. I got it."

“Got *what*? What do you need rescuing from? Is somebody—”

“See?” he asked, moving away from my touch. “That’s exactly the shit I’m talking about. You’ve gotta learn to chill. It was nice to see you too.”

He shook his head as he walked off, and I let him. What would have been the point of further pushing the issue, when it was clear he wasn’t about to discuss it with me?

It wasn’t that I had zero faith in my brother, but I didn’t hold any illusions about him either. He’d been in some form of trouble over and over, and ten times out of nine, I ended up bailing him out. If he was insisting that whatever he was into was something he could handle on his own…all I could do was hope for the best.

I had enough other things to worry about.

Smoke filled the air at *Dream.*

It curled in the dim light of the lounge, thick and sweetly perfumed as I made my way to the private room at the back, balancing a heavy tray of drinks in one hand. A weighty baseline thumped in my ears and pounded in my chest, making it hard to hear myself think, let alone keep myself upright in the required sky-high heels.

The husky bodyguard at the door ogled me as I approached, pulling a thick lip between his teeth. "How you doin' tonight Asha?" he asked, in no apparent hurry to step aside and let me through. This wasn't a new occurrence, by any means – he'd been trying to get my attention since I started, but my attention wasn't up for grabs.

"I'm doing fine, thank you. Excuse me."

He sucked his teeth. "Come on, sexy. Why you gotta be rude?"

I fought the urge to roll my eyes. "I'm not being rude. I'm at work, and I'm not trying to lose my job over watered-down drinks because the ice melted while I was out here socializing. Can you let me past, please? You know Jackson is uptight tonight about the owner coming."

His gaze skipped over my face, scanning my body again, lingering at my breasts. "You know I have to give you a pat down if you want to get through here, right?"

"Lewis, I swear to God," I hissed, my lip curling into a sneer. "If you touch me, I will—"

"Relax, sexy."

Lewis's voice was falsely calm as he lifted a hand to quiet me, nervously looking around. No matter what else could be said about *Dream*, Jackson didn't play about the safety of the women who worked there. Harassment was handled harshly, and quickly.

"All I want to do is do my job, so I can get paid, and get the hell out of here tonight. Please move."

He sucked his teeth as he stepped out of the way, mumbling something under his breath about how I "*wasn't that fine anyway*". Instead of checking him about why he was so pressed if I "wasn't that fine", I eased through the door when he opened it and didn't look back, still carefully balancing my tray.

I took a deep breath as I started down the long hall. The door closed, effectively shutting out the loud music from the main area of the lounge, replacing it with the faint sounds of male laughter. The volume grew as I moved closer to my destination, louder and louder until I stepped into the private room.

This room was filled with smoke too, a mixture of marijuana and expensive cigars. The laughter that rumbled in my chest came from the middle, where a poker table was set up, surrounded by six men. Jackson assigned me to the room because he claimed I was the best server on this shift, but I had a feeling it was my punishment for not listening in the meeting yesterday. All he would tell me was that *"the owner"* was in the building, and that there wouldn't be any mistakes allowed.

The men seated at the table *looked* like they all had money. It was damn near a prerequisite to walk into this casino at all, but especially these rooms at the back. This was where the high rollers came to entertain their friends. It was full of dancers, some dressed in sexy cocktail dresses like me, some in… much less. I focused on the task at hand.

Deliver the drinks and get the hell out of there.

I wasn't supposed to, but I steadied the tray with both hands as I carefully made my way to the head of the table. It was part of the rules – part of my training – that I stopped there first, and addressed the host by name according to the labeled chart in the middle of my tray. The last thing I wanted to do was spill all of those drinks.

I read the name that corresponded to the head of the table, then lifted my eyes to the man himself, and a chill ran up my spine.

Shit. Shit!

"I don't even know why you niggas *try* with me, come on," he said, tossing his cards down on the table. A chorus of groans erupted as he raked the pile of money in the middle of the table toward him and started neatly arranging it, adding it to the already obscene stack beside him. "Love to act like y'all don't know who wears the crown around here. Motherfucking champ, baby. Ask somebody."

He and his friends laughed as he kept up his over the top bragging, and they continued their playful ribbing. None of them had seemed to notice me come in, but as I approached him, willing my hands not to shake, Kingston Whitfield looked up, and his eyes zeroed in on me.

I'd heard his name mentioned before in the few months I'd been working there, but he'd never been around. The Reverie Hotel & Casino was one of the most lucrative in the United States – a little fact I only knew because I'd interviewed for the job.

The Whitfield family managed to keep a mostly low profile, at least in the media. Around here, they were basically royalty, and in a city like Vegas, it probably meant they were into some shit I didn't want much to do with. I talked to my coworkers enough to not seem like a bitch, and then at the end of the night, I went home. I didn't *want* to be plugged in.

But still… whispers happened.

Kingston was the type of man fantasies were made of – or nightmares, according to the rumors, if you were unlucky enough to be on the wrong side of him. With the smirk that crossed his face as he stared at me… I wasn't quite sure which side I was on.

His eyes were like magnets, and the vibe he was putting off was like a siren's song beckoning me closer, and it wasn't like I had a choice. I took what I hoped was a subtle breath and took the last steps toward him.

Over his shoulder, I noticed a woman standing back from the table, in the shadows. Her skin was light golden brown –a shade or two lighter than mine – and she was dressed in all black, with her hair in two thick French braids that disappeared down her back. She lifted an eyebrow at me, and I quickly averted my gaze, sensing more than a hint of danger.

"Mr. Whitfield… your Mauve," I said, placing the glass in front of him. He didn't even look at it – his eyes were stuck to me, brimming with curiosity and… lust.

I had to get away from him.

I nodded, even though he still hadn't acknowledged the drink, and started to move away. I'd barely put one foot in front of the other when I felt his hand on my arm, tugging me back toward him. His eyes bored into mine as I tried to balance the tray, staring at me for a long moment before he ran his tongue across his lips.

"How much for a private dance?"

My mouth went dry. "I… what?"

"A private show. One on one. Me and you. How much?"

I blinked.

Does he think…

I swallowed hard, pushing down my anger as I reminded myself of where I was. "I'm a server, Mr. Whitfield. Not a dancer."

His only response was to release his hold on my arm. I moved away from him, and the game went on, as apparently no one had even been paying attention to our exchange. The other men were occupied with their cards or the other women, and I went about my business of passing out the rest of the drinks, unbothered.

"Come here, Red," I heard from across the table, and looked up to see that his eyes were on me again. He motioned for me to come to him, and even though I still had two drinks left on my tray, I went to him as a couple of the players at the table folded.

"Yes?"

Kingston scraped his teeth over his bottom lip, a move that made heat blossom between my thighs, remembering the way he'd used those beautiful, perfect teeth on me the night before. The dress I'd worn tonight was a bandage style, with cutouts down both sides. I saw the flash of one-hundred dollar bills in his hand, and a second later, he'd stuck several into the side of my dress, underneath one of the bands that were keeping my dress together. And then, he plucked out two more, adding them to the ones he'd already given me.

"You deserve a little extra something, for last night."

I ground my teeth together as heat flushed my body, and forced my mouth into a smile. Losing my job for smacking the piss out of my boss's boss wasn't exactly an option when I had responsibilities. I offered a stiff nod, then headed to pass out the rest of the drinks, but I could feel Kingston's eyes on me, still.

"Aye, you gonna look at ass, or look at these cards, man? Let's go, let's play," one of the men who was still in the poker hand said. The dealer had already passed out the "flop" – the first three universal cards for the hand – and was moving on to the "turn" – the fourth card. I was right behind the man who'd spoken, delivering his drink, and I peeked at his cards as he lifted them to recalculate his hand.

He had pocket kings, and there was another king, and two tens, on the table. At the very least, he had a nice full house.

But that didn't stop me from meeting Kingston's eyes with a smirk and subtly shaking my head, making him believe that the other man was bluffing.

"All in."

Holy shit.

I had no idea what King had in his hand, but it wasn't incredibly likely that he had the cards to beat a king-led full house. And there was *no* way I was sticking around to find out. I delivered the last drink as the men began talking, then tucked the tray under my arm to hurry out, moving as fast as I could on my heels.

I was almost at the door to get back into the main part of the club when I heard "*Goddamit*!" bellowed out, loud enough that it seemed to bounce off the walls and reverberate in my chest.

I flung the door open, and walked right into Lewis's beefy frame, with his back to the door.

"Shit," I mumbled. "Excuse me, I need to get through."

"What's the magic word?"

Ughhh.

"I don't have time for this," I hissed, glancing over my shoulder. "Can you let me through?"

Lewis smirked as he turned to face me, but didn't make any effort to let me past. "Tell me the magic word, sexy."

I sucked in a deep breath. "I don't know the fucking magic word! Is it… I don't know! Please?"

"RED!"

I froze, heart racing, further worried by the look on Lewis's face as he stared past me. Before I could formulate a thought – or a defense – a familiar hand was around my arm, easily yanking me backward. The door to the hall slammed shut, and suddenly it was just me and Kingston.

His hand was still on my arm, and he had my back pressed against the wall. He was standing so close that my heaving chest brushed the front of his shirt with every rise and fall.

"You're hurting my arm," I mumbled, not breaking eye contact with him. He was glaring at me – clearly angry. But the heat – and hardness – of his body as he moved even closer, lowering his head to be in line with mine, told an additional story.

He released his grip just enough to take away the sting, but didn't let me go.

"Do you have any idea how much money you just cost me?"

"I don't know what you're talking about," I lied, right to his face.

"*Forty thousand dollars,*" he growled. "Did you think that shit was cute?"

I swallowed hard. "As cute as you thought it was to treat me like a prostitute."

His eyes narrowed, and I averted my gaze, squirming against his grasp. I was trying my best *not* to be turned on by his aggression, but the feel of his body, and the warm spice of his cologne was making that damn near impossible.

I flinched as he released his hold from my arm, then snatched the drink tray away from me.

"Get your ass out of my casino," he said, stepping back.

Immediately, my belly twisted into a knot. "But… but my shift isn't over," I said weakly.

He scoffed, then opened the door that led back out into the club. "It is now." He turned to Lewis, who had obviously been eavesdropping at the door.

"Make sure she finds her way out."

SIX

ASHA

I needed ten thousand more dollars to enter the tournament.

Pulling together the fifty-thousand I needed to enter had always been a long shot. Something inevitably came up – a new bill, car trouble, *Ahmad* trouble, every time I even got close. I'd had my eyes on that tournament for years, but *this* year, with my tips from the club, and bigger winnings at the poker table – especially after the night before last – I was hopeful.

Had been hopeful.

I looked at the money spread over my bed – carefully counted and sorted into stacks. Forty-one thousand, two-hundred and thirty-two dollars. So, *so* close.

Yet, so far.

If I – literally – played my cards right, I could head out to the Drake and win the money I needed. I would have to play more aggressively than I liked to, play at the higher stakes tables, but… I could do it.

But was I really going to blow fifty-thousand dollars entering a tournament that I could easily lose in the first round, when I no longer had a job?

Yeah, the poker money was nice. It was fun, it sent adrenaline pumping through my veins. But it was unpredictable, and I was a woman with grown-up responsibilities. The money staring at me from on top of my comforter could sustain me for at least a year. Maybe a year and a half, or two, if I tightened my belt enough.

Tears pricked my eyes as I turned away, covering my face with my hands.

Fired.

Even though I hadn't slept, almost twelve hours had passed since Kingston Whitfield demanded I leave his casino. Jackson had rushed over, pulling Kingston to the side to ask what was going on. There was a moment of hope, while the two men spoke, where I shook off Lewis's grip. But then, a terse head shake from "K.W.", and Jackson's disappointed gaze was on me.

"*You have to go,*" he'd said. I knew he didn't want to, but he had his own responsibilities. I couldn't expect him to sacrifice his job for me. He gave me the courtesy of at least looking me in the eyes, and I gave him the courtesy of not making a scene.

But now that some time had passed… maybe cooler heads could prevail.

With that on my mind, I packed the money back into the bank deposit bag, then hid the bag deep in my closet. I washed the lack of sleep from my face, and dressed in nice jeans, a sexy top, and heels, getting ready as if I were going to work.

Because hopefully… I was.

Dream didn't get much traffic during the day.

A decent enough amount that the people who worked those shifts made tips they could live on, but nothing compared to the crowd at night. I was glad for that today, because if I walked in here and embarrassed myself… at least there were fewer people there to see it.

I found Jackson back in his office, with lunch spread across his desk. He was *always* here, or at least it seemed that way, so it was unsurprising to find him eating while he worked.

"Red," he greeted warmly, even though he looked a bit surprised. "What's up?" He motioned to the seat across from him at the desk, and I sat down.

"I was hoping you could tell me exactly how bad last night was. What is he like?" I asked, referring to Kingston. "Can I just apologize, or…"

Jackson shook his head, washing down a mouthful of food with a swig of water. "I already tried to talk to him, Red. He's pissed, and pissing off the person that runs the casino where you work wasn't a great idea. Why the hell would you do something like that?"

"He insulted me," I insisted, sitting forward in my chair. "Treated me like I was for sale!"

"Look around you. Not in this office, but look at where you are. It's Vegas. *Sin City*. He's a rich man. *Most* women working in the clubs here are… for sale. Whether or not you agree, that's the reality of where we are."

I sucked my teeth. "That doesn't magically make his assumption okay."

"I didn't say it did. But it happened. What was one of the first things I told you in here when I hired you, huh?"

"You told me a lot of things, Jax."

"True. But you know what I'm talking about. I told you you were going to have to be prepared to hear some horrible shit. Men were going to ask, offer, *demand* shit from you that they had no business thinking, let alone speaking out loud. I also told you that if anybody ever went too far, you could talk to security, or better yet, *me*, and we would handle the shit for you. Have I not taken care of you and every other girl that works here?"

I swallowed, and averted my gaze away from Jackson's questioning glare. "You have."

"Have you ever heard a whisper or rumor of anybody fucking with any of the *Dream* girls, and getting away with it?"

"No."

Jackson lifted his hands, and shrugged. "Then *what the fuck*, Red? I know King, and he can be just as savage as any other man, but he usually conducts himself with… a certain level of decorum with women. What the hell did he say to make you mess with the poker game?"

I pushed out a heavy sigh, and shook my head. "It wasn't what he said, not really. It was… how it made me *feel*."

"Which was…?"

I sighed again. I didn't know how to answer that. I'd had men at the club do things that were far more lewd, far more disrespectful than what Kingston had done, and brushed them off like they were nothing. The rage I'd felt over that "tip" was rooted in the fact that, contrary to reality with those other men, Kingston had been inside me. His fingers, tongue, and dick had been in places that would make a good girl blush, and he'd looked me in the face and tried to pay me for it. I didn't look down on sex workers – it was *Vegas* – but what Kingston had done felt like a judgment.

I didn't like that very much.

"Does it even matter?" I asked, defiantly crossing my arms as I sat back.

Jackson scoffed. "To me? Hell yes, it does. He may be the boss, but I run this club. If he said something to you that I need to address, it'll get addressed." He met my gaze, waiting for me to respond, and when I didn't he hiked his eyebrow at me. "Well? Did he say something I need to address?"

"No."

"Then why the hell did you pull that little stunt?"

"Why the hell are you acting like you're pissed at *me*?"

"Because I *am*!" He shoved away the rest of his sandwich, scowling across the paper wrappings at me. "You're one of my best girls, Red! You're smart, sexy, the customers enjoy you. They *ask* about you. And you come in here after that shit you pulled acting like a victim, but then you can't tell me anything? You're goddamn right I'm pissed at you."

I dropped my gaze to my bright pink nails. "Then maybe I should just leave."

"Maybe you should," Jackson agreed, calling my bluff. "You've got a check coming. I'll make sure it gets to you."

Silenced waged between us for several moments before I finally looked up, meeting Jackson's eyes. He was already watching me. "Jackson… I need this job."

"I know. Another reason for me to be pissed at you." I didn't say anything. *Couldn't* say anything. "I'll try to talk to him again, but I can't make any promises. You fucked up his poker game. Would you be very forgiving if somebody did it to you?" I respond. He already knew the answer. "Exactly. If that doesn't work, I know somebody at the Drake. But, so does King. So again… no promises."

I nodded. "Anything you can do, I'm grateful."

"I know. Damn hothead," he muttered under his breath, then turned back to his computer – my sign to leave. I stood up, and turned for the door, but looked back when I remembered something.

"Hey, you're still coming to that show with me next month," I said, waiting until Jackson looked up to let the grin spread across my face. "A bet is a bet, and I won."

Jackson sighed, then scrubbed his hands over his head. "I thought you said you were grateful. A grateful woman wouldn't hold me to it."

"It won't be that bad."

"It's fucking musical theater. It's bad."

I shook my head. "No, it's not. Not the way my roommate does it."

"That's your friend, you're supposed to say that."

"I'm serious though," I laughed. "You'll enjoy yourself, promise."

"Whatever, Red. Get out of my office before I change my mind."

"About the theater?"

"About your damn job."

Oh.

I got out of his office.

But once I closed the door behind me, something drew my eyes to the left, instead of the direction I need to get me out of the club. There was a door at the end of the hall that I'd never been in, but remembered Jackson pointing it out to me when he first gave me the grand tour.

"That's the main office," he'd said, gesturing toward the door. There was no adornment, no nameplate, just a door. *"Mr. Whitfield's*

office. He doesn't hang around the club much anymore, so there's a good chance you'll never see him."

He'd given me that in passing. It wasn't important. I was essentially a burger flipper. Kingston family were the owners. My presence didn't concern him, and he didn't concern me. Or… wasn't supposed to. My heart raced as I stared down the hall at that door. Started pounding as I took a step toward it. By the time my hand closed around the handle, it was galloping in my chest.

But I turned the handle anyway.

I was so surprised to find it unlocked that I gasped, then quickly slipped inside, closing the door behind me. I didn't have time to gather a first impression of the office before pain exploded at the side of my head.

Before I could react, I was on the floor, with my arms painfully bent and pinned at the wrists behind me. I cringed as a knee ground into the base of my spine. Closed my eyes tight as cold metal – a gun – pressed firmly to my temple.

"Well, well, well," I heard, and closed my eyes. Above me, Kingston chuckled. "You just can't seem to keep your ass out of trouble, can you?"

A second later, the knee left my back, and I was roughly yanked up to my feet. I rubbed my wrists as soon as they were freed, and cast a hesitant glance over my shoulder at the woman I'd seen hovering near Kingston last night. She had a gun aimed at my head, and she didn't look happy.

She looked like death, so I looked at something else.

Kingston was as delicious today as he had been that night at the poker table, and in the club. He wasn't wearing a jacket, just the button-up and slacks. He was missing his tie, several buttons were undone, and his sleeves were rolled up to his elbows, showcasing powerful forearms. A smirk softened the sculpted contours of his handsome face as he looked me over.

"Are you okay?" he asked, clearly amused by my current predicament. He stepped backward, propping his hip against the edge of the desk. When I didn't answer fast enough, I was rewarded with the sharp coldness of metal against my skin. The gun was pressed to the base of my neck now.

"Answer the question," I was told, in a voice that perfectly matched a woman with a gun to my head.

"Relax, Ace." Kingston motioned with his hand for her to lower to the gun, and then turned his attention back to me. "Well?"

"I-I... uh... I'm as okay as someone in my position can be, I guess. A bit of a headache."

One thick eyebrow hiked. "I don't imagine taking the butt of a gun to the side of your head feels particularly good. But... when you decide to walk into someone's office unannounced, you get what you get."

"Won't make that mistake again."

He gave me a broad smile, showcasing those perfect teeth of his. "No. I bet you won't. But since you're here, you have the floor. What can I do for you?"

I glanced nervously back at "Ace", who'd lowered the gun at Kingston's command, but still looked perturbed. I considered easing away from her, then thought better of it. My head was already throbbing.

"My job," I said, turning back to him, shoulders squared. "You can give it back to me."

He stared blankly at me for several seconds, then let out a dry chuckle. "Oh, you're serious. I was waiting for a punch line."

"Yes, I'm serious." I bit the inside of my lip, checking myself for my tone. "Mr. Whitfield—"

"King."

I lifted my chin. "Excuse me?"

"King," he said again, pushing away from the desk to take a few steps closer to me. "Call me King."

Just the thought of it made my stomach twist in knots. "You're my boss. It would be prudent to refer to you formally, Mr. Whitfield."

"I'm not your boss, Red. You got fired, remember? But if I was still your boss, I'd advise you to call me what I requested. I mean… it's not out of line to ask to be called by your first name, is it?"

He followed up that question with a smirk. He knew exactly what he was doing, knew exactly why I was loathe to let "King" cross my lips, in reference to him. I dropped my gaze as he moved in close enough for me to be enthralled by his scent, and the heat from his body. Just like the other night, he pulled at me, without lifting a finger. My nipples strained against the inside of my bra, aching for the feeling of his hands.

"Sir," I started, but my words were met with him shaking his head. I swallowed my frustration, and fought the urge to roll my eyes. "*King…* I'm sorry for what I did the other night. It was wrong, and I shouldn't have done it."

He nodded. "It *was* wrong. You *should* be sorry. But you're not."

"I am."

"Don't lie to me," he said in a low growl. He stepped a little closer as he spoke, violating my personal space without a care. "I don't like being lied to. You stand here and do it in my face, I'll turn you over to Alicia. Understand?"

"Fine." I punctuated the word with a curt nod of my own. "I'm not sorry that I did it. I'm sorry that I lost a job that I need because of it."

"Getting ogled by horny motherfuckers while you pass out drinks is a job you need?" He laughed. "I find that hard to believe, considering what you walked away from that poker table with the other night."

"By chance," I countered. "I could just as easily have walked away with nothing. I've been working here long enough that my tips are consistent. I have responsibilities that require consistency."

His wide, powerful shoulders lifted in a shrug as he walked away from me. "Should have thought about that before you sabotaged my poker game. Hopefully you don't make the same mistake at your next job."

His words knocked the air from my lungs. "So… that's just it? You aren't even going to consider it?"

He smiled. "No. I'm not. I was having a good time last night. Friends, women, liquor, poker… bliss. You fucked it up. So fuck your job. It's that simple."

"So because you were gullible enough to trust someone you barely know, and went all in on an obviously sorry ass hand, you're punishing me for it?"

It was like my words vacuumed the air from the room. Complete silence, all eyes on me. I could feel it. But I kept my chin defiantly lifted, refusing to let myself deflate under his hot gaze. He stared at me, not speaking, for what felt like forever before the edges of his mouth slowly ascended into a grin. He looked past me, to Ace.

"Did she just…?"

"Mmmhmm," she responded, still behind me. "She sure did. And she has a point, too."

The grin dropped from his face and a scowl replaced it. "Fuck her point."

"And fuck your wack ass poker game," I said, crossing my arms.

His eyes came back to me, simultaneously annoyed and amused by my attitude. "My poker game is *not* wack."

"The times I've seen you play tell a different story."

"And what story is that?"

"That your game is wack."

He flashed that smile again, cutting right through my irritation as he leisurely ambled up to me, apparently deciding against being perturbed. "I'm not sure it's conceivable," he started, brushing a handful of my locs behind my shoulder to expose my bare collarbone, "that my game is "wack" when I had you melting all over my dick the other night, Red." I didn't move, didn't breath as he ran a thick finger along my neck, then down between my breasts. "When you close your eyes and remember… I bet you can still feel it. Right *here*," he said, pressing the palm of his hand flat against my pelvis.

I immediately batted his hand away. Not because I felt violated, but because I *could* still feel him, and it pissed me off. What had been a pleasant memory that would take me through the next six months of avoiding men was now a source of annoyance.

"Oh please," I snapped. "You were the one with the note, and the breakfast, and spa vouchers." Behind me, Ace laughed, and I turned in her direction. "What's funny?" I asked, with more sass than I probably should with someone who definitely could – and almost had – kicked my ass.

Ace grinned, one hand still holding her gun, ready to aim if necessary, the other playing with one of the thick French braids. "You are, doll, if you thought the morning after package made you special. Somebody was going to get it. This time, it just happened to be you."

Every drop of moisture in my mouth dried up. Every shred of indignation dissipated, replaced with mortification that heated me from my fingertips to my toes.

Why?

It wasn't as if I felt any emotional connection to him. Not after our night together, and especially not *now*. But I'd thought… I'd thought…

What had I thought?

Had I thought I was special?

I gave a slight shake of my head, then turned for the door without responding. I didn't have anything to say, I just wanted to get the hell out of there, with what little – if any – dignity I had left. I'd only made it a few steps when a hand closed around my wrist, sending a rod of tension up my spine. One glance down told me that it was Kingston, not Ace, who'd stopped me. I was less afraid of him, so I snatched away.

"Wait a minute," he said, getting between me and the door, and holding up his hands in a gesture of peace. "You came in here to dispute your termination, correct?"

I swallowed, then nodded. "Another miscalculation to add to my long list of mistakes over the last two days."

"Maybe not," he shrugged, pushing his hands deep into the pockets of his slacks. He looked so comfortable, so relaxed, so completely opposite of how I was feeling that it made my jaw clench. "You feel like you shouldn't have been fired… play me for your job."

I frowned. "Excuse me?"

"You heard what I said. You think you're such a beast on the felt, prove it."

"How?" I countered. "One round, all in? Are you about to pull out some chips, what?"

He grinned. "No. No chips." He pulled his lip between his teeth as he gave me another once-over, but this time, I was unaffected. Couldn't be, knowing I was just another piece of ass to him. Which is why I was completely unsurprised by what came out of his mouth next. "Clothes."

"Fine."

His eyes widened. "Winner *keeps* the clothes."

"Fine." He ran his hand over his chin as he tipped his head to the side, like he was really seeing me for the first time. I propped my hands on my hips, impatiently drumming my fingers over the stitching on my jeans. "Five Card Draw? Follow the Queen? Omaha?" I asked naming off poker variants his ass had probably never even heard of.

He shook his head, dismissing my suggestions. "Keep it simple. Texas Hold 'Em. Unless you want to back off now, so you don't have to walk out of here naked."

I smirked, then pulled my hands in front of me, stretching and cracking my knuckles to put on a show. "Get a dealer in here, and let's play cards *Mr. Whitfield.* Ante up."

KING

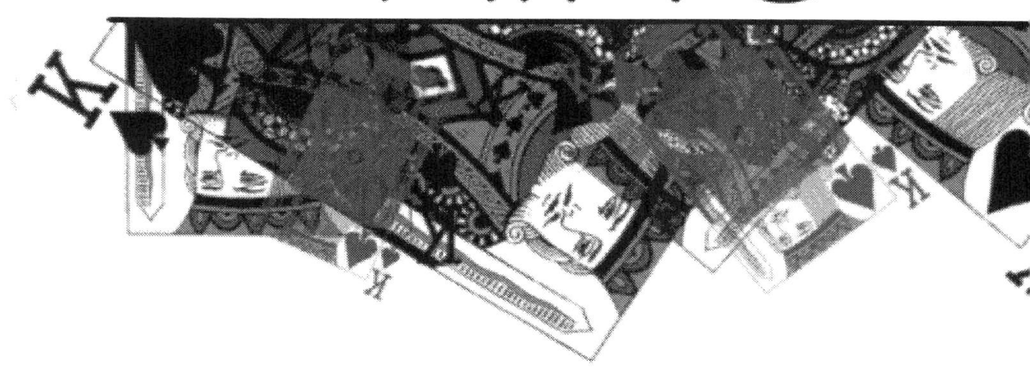

I had every intention of indulging myself in the visual feast of Red's nude body.

I wouldn't feel a single shred of remorse as I, piece by piece, stripped her of every item on her body. I wanted to see her like I did the other night… every inch of honey-toned skin completely vulnerable and bare.

If only she wasn't whipping my ass.

It wasn't that I'd underestimated her – I knew she was good. It was obvious. Her actions at the table – my desk – were bold and decisive. Shrewd. Her body language was relaxed, her expression impassive, giving nothing away. Not even when she won a hand, and she'd done that a *lot* today.

I had her earrings and shoes.

She had my watch, belt, shoes, socks, and I was, quite literally, about to lose my shirt too. But I wasn't bothered. If I was going to get beaten at a game, I certainly didn't mind it from a woman that looked like *her.*

"Where'd you learn how to play?" I asked, intrigued by the woman who'd beat a whole table of players two nights ago, and was replicating that magic right in front of me now. "Internet? Watching the tables? Tournaments on TV?"

Red snorted. "Nope. I had a drunk, mean gambler for a father. He taught me to play so he could use me as practice."

"Seriously?"

She didn't answer. Instead, she picked up the two cards our dealer – Ace – had placed on the desk in front of her.

My shirt was already on the table, folded neatly, as the required opening bet. I picked up my own cards, the ace and queen of diamonds, then glanced up to see Red with her arms above her, pulling her shirt off. My eyes fell to the mounds of her breasts, covered in a sheer blue lace bra that did nothing to hide the deep chocolate of her areolas and nipples. I shifted in my seat as my dick swelled, and she gave me a knowing smirk.

"Are you creeping, or are you playing, Mr. Whitfield?" she asked as she sat back, with an abruptness that made her breasts jiggle. I grinned as I lifted my gaze to her face.

That face.

Thick eyelashes framed dark brown eyes that held an air of wickedness. Full, pillow-soft lips gave an impression of sweetness that didn't match the things that came out of her mouth. Her delicate, softly rounded nose turned upward as she glared across the desk at me, waiting to hear my answer.

Red knew *exactly* how fine she was. She tipped her head, feigning impatience as she swept her locs over one shoulder, giving me a better view of her bare skin. The urge to reach over the desk and tear that sweet little bra off of her made my hands twitch.

"Playing, so I can see that pretty pussy of yours again," I said in a tone that made it clear I wasn't joking. She blinked hard, and I was pleased to see the subtle twitches that let me know she was trying not to blush, or react.

Standing beside the desk, Ace discarded the top card on the deck, then turned over the flop – the three community cards either of us could use to make our hand.

A king of clubs, a jack of diamonds, and a five of diamonds.

Not bad. With the ace and queen I already had, I was well on my way to, if I was lucky, a flush. In a normal game, I wouldn't have bet more, but this wasn't normal. I had a specific mission – and other shit to do. I stood up, undid my pants, and let them drop, leaving me in just my black boxer briefs.

Red's eyes dropped to, and stayed on, my dick.

"Are you creeping, or are you playing?" I asked, throwing the question she'd asked before back into her face. Her gaze flickered up to mine, then back down to the cards. As usual, her calculation was quick. She stood and unbuttoned her jeans, slowly dragging them down her hips to reveal tiny panties that matched her barely there bra. She turned sideways to bend over, pulling them over her feet, and off.

I didn't even give care that I was losing. This was very, very entertaining.

She folded her jeans into a neat bundle, then tossed them onto the pile on the desk. "Call."

Ace turned over the next card, putting it down beside the others.

Nine of diamonds.

I had my flush.

"Check," I said, since it was my turn to decide on the betting. I looked to Red, and she turned around, reaching behind her to unsnap her bra. Her movements were slow, deliberate as she pulled it down from her shoulders, covering herself with one arm before she faced me again. She held her bra with two fingers, holding it over the desk to sway in front of me before she dropped it into my pants.

"I raise you one thing. And it looks like all you have is your boxer-briefs. You putting them on the table?"

"Please don't," Ace groaned. "I don't want to see your dick."

"You can go," I told her, not taking my eyes off Red. "We've got it from here."

Ace didn't waste any time finding her way out, leaving Red and me alone. Red cast a glance back at the door as it closed, then turned back to me, impatiently, with her arm still covering her breasts. "Are you in, or not? I need to go home and get some sleep before my shift tonight."

Was this her "tell"? When I'd watched her at the table, and even throughout our game tonight, she'd been cool and controlled. She didn't talk shit. She played cards. Now, all of a sudden she was impatient, yet speaking confidently about a win that wasn't hers yet. I treated her to a lazy grin that made her roll her eyes and look away.

The fact that winning or losing was of no consequence to me fueled my next statement.

"I'm in."

Her gaze shot back to mine, and I saw the split second of alarm in her eyes before she tempered her expression. "You can keep your boxers on until we're done. Are you pulling the next card, or am I?" she asked, her tone carefully measured.

"Be my guest."

Her eyes rested on the deck of cards a beat too long, like she didn't want to touch them. But then, her graceful fingers reached for the card on top, discarding it before she reached for the next. She didn't turn it immediately. She kept it pinched between her forefinger and thumb while stood there, staring at it.

It wasn't until I cleared my throat that she flipped it over and laid it down, face up.

King of diamonds.

I was *one* card off from an unbeatable hand.

But, as it stood, I still had my flush – five cards of the same suit. The odds were in my favor, and Red still hadn't reacted. I picked up my cards and flipped them over, lining then up with the community cards to show her my hand.

"Show your cards," I told her, looking forward to seeing if what I suspected was true – that she'd tried to bluff her way out. Across the desk, she let out a sigh, then reached for her cards to turn them over. One, and then the other.

The king of spades, and jack of hearts.

"Full house." The words left her lips in a whisper, almost as if she barely believed it herself. She *had* been bluffing – the last card, the river, had won the hand for her.

"I'll take those boxers now."

I looked up from the cards to find her looking at me, that wicked energy in her eyes livelier than ever. Just like the other night, even though I was the one who'd lost, I didn't feel the slightest disappointment. I didn't bother to hide my grin as I moved around the desk in relaxed strides, not stopping until my chest was barely an inch from the arm she was using to cover herself.

From here, I could smell her. Whatever it was that she used on her skin and hair, a scent I'd buried my nose in her to inhale. Vanilla and jasmine and pears and cocoa butter and… arousal. She smelled like sex, and looked like it too, standing in front of me in nothing but those itty-bitty panties, locs framing her face and resting on her shoulders.

I'd wrapped my hands in those locs, used them to pull her head back while I buried myself in her from behind. She'd found the rhythm and fell into it, instead of just taking it while she looked pretty.

Even *that* added to her intrigue.

"A lot of things could happen after I take these boxers off, Red."

She raised her chin, tipping her head back a little to meet my eyes. "They could. But only one thing *will.*"

"And what's that?"

"I'm going to take my winnings and leave."

"You're turned on."

"I've survived worst occurrences."

I chuckled, and to my surprise, she smiled back. Those soft, sexy lips parted and curved, and goddamn, she was… otherworldy.

"We could celebrate your win."

"Oh, I plan to. Alone. Maybe with my roommate."

"Roommate, huh? Is that code for a boyfriend?"

That question made the pleasantry drop from her face, and she gave me a cold look. "The other night wouldn't have happened if I had a boyfriend, Mr. Whitfield."

"I told you to call me King."

"And I respectfully refuse."

"I want you in my bed again."

She blinked, but didn't look overly surprised by the request. In fact, it was almost like she'd expected it. She looked me right in the eyes as she shook her head. "Why would you want that anyway? I wasn't special."

She tried hard not to give any inflection to her words, but her eyes told the truth. Ace's comment earlier had stung… but it was the truth.

"Did you want to be special?"

She scoffed. "I didn't *care.*"

"But you do now."

"I didn't say that."

"I wasn't asking. Your embarrassment when Ace said it, your defensiveness now…"

"Neither of which matters. It won't happen again."

I grunted. "Why the hell not?"

"Because I work in your hotel. Because I think you're an asshole. Because while I may have indulged in a one-night-stand, because I thought I'd never see you again, a *second* night requires…"

"Requires what?"

She shook her head. "Something you can't give me."

"You'd be surprised by what I could give you."

Red let out a little breath of laughter. "The only thing I want from you… is the boxers."

She was serious. She raised her free hand, gesturing for me to give them to her. If nothing else, I was a man of my word.

I took the boxers off, and put them in her hand. "Congratulations."

"Thank you."

She carefully avoided looking at me as she stacked my clothes in a pile. She faced away from me to dress – I shamelessly watched – then planted my shoes on top of the rest of my clothes before she gathered it all under her arm. As she headed for the door, I kept expecting her to stop, and drop them, but she didn't. Well, she *did* stop, but not to leave my clothes. She gave me a slow once-over, her eyes resting on my dick before they came back to my face.

"So… you have a name for it, huh?"

I raised an eyebrow. "A name for what?"

"The morning after package."

I lifted a hand to my face, using my thumb to swipe the hair that covered my jaw. "Don't mistake what comes out of somebody else's mouth for what came out of mine."

She frowned at that. It wasn't the answer she wanted, and I could tell from her narrowed eyes that she wanted to ask questions. But she didn't. She didn't nod, or smile, she just turned and left the office, closing the door firmly behind her.

I chuckled to myself as I went to the wardrobe at the back of the office and began pulling out what I needed to dress. I was buttoning a fresh shirt when Ace slipped in, completely amused by what had unfolded.

"So she *actually* took your clothes, huh?" she asked, taking a seat on the edge of the desk.

I pulled open a drawer. "And one of my favorite watches too," I said, grinning as I picked out a different one from the velvet lining.

"And you let her out of here? Wow. You like her, don't you?"

"I'm fascinated by her. There's a difference. I don't know her well enough to like her."

Ace nodded. "Understood. So… what do you want to do?"

"Well," I said, picking a tie from the limited options in the wardrobe. "I have a meeting to be at in forty-five minutes."

"Whitfiled Inc?"

I nodded. "Yes."

"Understood. Do you need anything from me in the meantime?" Ace asked, even though she already knew the answer to that.

I finished with my tie, and turned to her, looking her right in the eyes."Yes. I want to know everything there is to know about Asha Davis."

SEVEN

KING

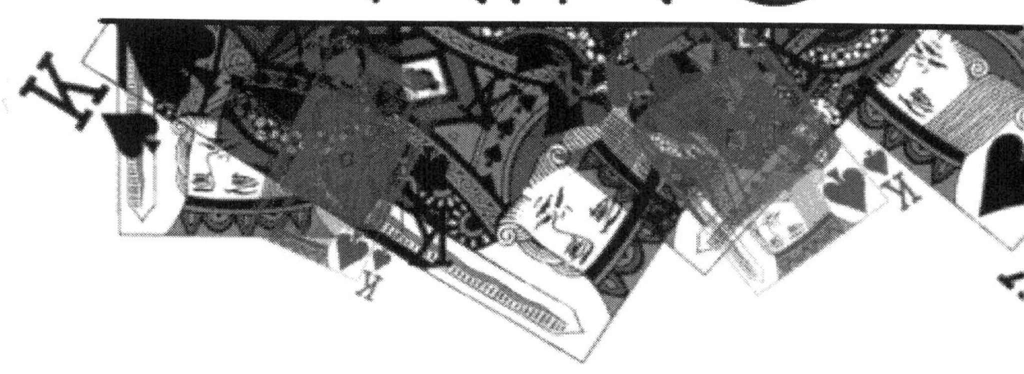

"Ah, his majesty decides to grace us with his appearance."

My sister grinned at me as I slipped into the conference room. I'd been trying not to disrupt the meeting that was already in progress, but her announcement of my arrival turned all eyes on me.

I offered a curt nod around the room, acknowledging the familiar faces, then turned my eyes to my father at the head of the table, who nodded. "Glad you could join us, son. Have a seat."

I took the empty one next to my mother, Angela, who slid a plastic-bound presentation in front of me. Leaning in, I let her kiss me on the cheek – and non-verbally dared any motherfucker around the table to have a slick comment about it.

They didn't, cause they knew better.

I subtly flipped Zora off – she grinned about it – then listened in silence as my father talked about *Reverie's* numbers for the quarter.

They weren't phenomenal, but they were good – good enough to support the next order of business.

"Kingston," my father said. "Talk to us about expansion."

Of course.

That's where I'd been for the last year, traveling the world to scout potential locations for another casino/hotel. Macau, Monte Carlo, Aruba, Sun City. There were plenty of established and up-and-coming gambling destinations around the globe. Our family had turned shit into sugar, created a name with *Reverie* over the years.

Now it was time to spread it.

For the next several minutes, I reported back on what I'd seen in my travels, not bothering with the plastic binder for the facts. I knew them well, and I wanted everybody in the room to know it. I'd been a few minutes late because of traffic, but the depth involved in my short presentation of pros and cons for moving into each of the countries I scouted was enough to prove my competence.

After the meeting, several of our shareholders stayed behind to speak with my father. While they did, Zoraya approached me with a slow, sarcastic clap. "So his royal highness actually did his homework, huh? I thought you would have gotten lost in all that foreign pussy, or started yourself a fight club. Anything except what you were *supposed* to be doing."

"Can you cut the shit Zora?" I asked, pulling her into a hug.

She grinned as she pulled back. "But messing with the big, *bad* Kingston Whitfield is so much fun. I can't help it, baby brother."

"Baby?" I grunted. "I'm thirty-three."

"And *I* am thirty-five. So…" she reached up, lightly tapping the tip of my nose with her finger. "Baby."

Shaking my head, I turned to walk away from my sister, but she caught me, threading her arm through mine as I headed to the buffet in the back.

"What is it?" I asked her, grabbing a *Whitfield Inc.* branded bottle of water. "Why are you tagging behind your "baby" brother?"

She moved in front of me, batting her eyelashes as she gave me an innocent look. "Why would you think I need a reason to tag behind you? You were gone. I can't just… miss you?"

I threw my head back and laughed, making her drop her hand from me. She crossed her arms as her expression descended into a scowl. "Fine. I need a favor."

"Let's hear it."

"I need *Dream* for a night."

I pulled my head back, bunching my eyebrows. "For what? *Waterfalls* is barely two blocks from *Reverie*, and has more than enough space for whatever debauchery that twisted little brain of yours can think of, Zora."

"Debauchery?" she said, dropping her hands to her hips. "We engage in no such thing."

"A bunch of niggas shaking their dicks for screaming women isn't debauchery?"

She smiled. "No more than a bunch of bitches shaking their tits for salivating men."

My eyebrow lifted. "Point taken. Why do you need the club?"

"I want to host an event. Something smaller, more lowkey than what we do at *Waterfalls*. We could pick up some of the *Reverie* traffic, make *Dream* a bunch of money for the night…"

"And put yourself in front of a shitload of potential new customers at *Waterfalls*."

She smirked. "Well… I *guess* that's a small perk."

"Oh bullshit, Zora," I laughed, finally unscrewing the top from my bottle of water. "That's your whole point. You're not born to sharks without becoming one yourself. I know you, and I know you've thought of this from every angle, weighed every pro, every con, crunched the numbers. Don't insult my intelligence by pretending that advertising *Waterfalls* is a byproduct."

"You're right," she conceded, lifting her hands. "I was just trying to make it look good for you. You know… being tactful."

"And you know I'll take candor over delicacy any damned day of the week."

"Fine. Can I have the fucking club or not?"

"Run me the potential dates, and I'll let you know."

Zora's eyes narrowed, shrewdly searching my face. "Is that your way of brushing me off?"

"What do you think?" I asked, keeping my face neutral, which, by the way her expression further deepened in annoyance, got under her skin.

"Whatever, Kingston." She turned to walk off, and I shook my head.

"I don't even know why you're *asking*," I called after her, and she stopped. "Does anybody in this family say no to your spoiled ass?"

Her lips bloomed into a smile as she strode back to me on steep heels that put her closer to my height. "So… the answer is yes?"

"Isn't it always?" was my dry response, but I couldn't help grinning back as she threw her arms around my neck, then kissed the same cheek my mother had.

"Thank you. I knew all that stuff they said about you wasn't true."

I frowned. "Who is "they"?"

Zora's only response to that question was a wink before she turned and pranced away, heading in my mother's direction.

"Hey," I said. "Try to be a little more obvious about eye-fucking my sister, would you. I don't think my father noticed yet."

I directed those words to the person a little to my left, standing at the window trying – and failing – to look like he wasn't staring a hole into Zora. Trei scrubbed a hand over his face, then shook his head before turning to me with confused – but apologetic - eyes.

"How did you even know I was looking at her? You weren't looking at me."

I snickered. "Your ass is *always* looking at Zora," I explained, reaching to shake his hand. "Like a lovesick puppy."

Trei scoffed, but didn't otherwise deny it, because it would have been pointless. He'd had a one-sided crush on Zora since high school – since *he* was in high school. Zora was seven years his senior, and was, as far as I could tell, painfully unaware of the fact he even existed.

His father, Thomas Nichols, was the reason behind Trei's presence at this meeting. He owned a good number of *Reverie* shares, and had been bringing Trei along to these meetings since the boy was fourteen years old. Like me – and Zora – he'd grown up in the "business" of Vegas. Nichols' Fine Wine and Spirits was the primary liquor vendor for many establishments in this city – *Reverie* included.

Our family was part of the reason their liquor business existed.

My father – and his father before him, and his before him – was a savvy businessman. Some would use different adjectives – ruthless, cutthroat, callous – but I preferred savvy. The Whitfield name had been built upon keen, assertive investments. Taking dying businesses that had abundant potential but substandard management, injecting them with resources, and transforming them into companies that made money.

Reverie itself had been a disaster twenty years ago. Even by Vegas standards it was gaudy and archaic, a coral, pastel yellow and seafoam green monstrosity called *The Reef.* The only things my father hadn't ripped out were the huge, multi-story fish tanks that traveled the lengths of the casino, hotel, and club. He renovated around them.

Before I could catch up with Trei, my father caught my attention, beckoning me over to where he stood, alone now. I shook Thomas' hand as I passed him, then joined my father at the front of the room.

"Good job today, son," he said, clapping me on the shoulder. "Glad to see you were on your shit."

"Was that in question?"

My father chuckled, and the water I was sipping turned to lead as it poured into my stomach. "We both know the answer to that," he said, fixing his gaze on me. "But I'm glad to see you're back to business again. We have a problem."

My jaw tightened. “What kind of problem?”

“Beauchamp’s.” Internally, I groaned. He hadn’t said it, but what he really meant was, Beauchamp’s *again.* When I didn’t say anything, my father went on. “Pulled out a gun on the painters. Threatened the new manager I hired.”

“I get the gist. I’ll swing by with Ace. Have a little talk with him.”

My father extended a hand to me and I accepted it with mine. I wasn’t surprised when he pulled me in. “You make sure Alicia does most of the talking. Can’t have you getting in trouble again.”

“Won’t be a problem.”

He made a disbelieving sound, low in his throat, that made my jaw twitch again. “You say that, and yet you have a reputation that precedes you, son.”

“A reputation that has served this family and our business well.” I met my father’s piercing gaze with a steady one of my own. “Which is why you’re sending me to “talk” to Beauchamp, no?”

He held my eyes for a few seconds longer, irritation brewing with every second that I didn’t back down. “I’m sending *you* to remind Beauchamp of the arrangement we made, and to encourage him to honor his end of that deal, because you are a bright young man who I expect to use his intelligence and charm, instead of brute force. I’m sending you because you are my progeny, and next in line to run this business, since your sister has made her disinterest clear.”

“And because you hope Leonard Beauchamp is going to piss his pants when he sees me walk in, and not give you any more trouble because he’s afraid of getting his ass kicked. There’s no need to talk around it. It is what it is.”

“Not anymore,” my father said, tightening his grip on my hand. “When you – when *we* – were younger, and the business was in a different place, we had different needs. Not anymore. Not after that shit you got yourself into.”

I scoffed. "The shit *I got myse—*" I stopped myself, and inhaled a breath through my nose.

"Son," he said, putting a hand on my shoulder. "Your scouting trip around the world was as much about business as it was about giving you a chance to start from scratch. Charting a new course. You have the talent to take these reigns when I hand them to you, and make something valuable to pass down. I won't have you jeopardizing it. You understand?"

My deadlock of feelings about this conversation must have shown on my face, because my father chuckled, releasing his hold on me. "I know, you're a grown ass man. I can't make you do anything, Kingston. But know that if you defy me, and end up on the wrong side of the law, I'm leaving you there."

I smirked. "You know damned well Angela wouldn't let you leave her baby sitting in a jail. I don't know why you're playing."

He didn't smile, but his amusement showed in his eyes as he shook his head. "Discretion, Kingston. Remember that."

"Yes sir," I said, completely serious. "Now if you'll excuse me, I need to go collect Ace. We have a half-finished restaurant to pay a visit."

I viewed my father with an intense level of respect, reserved solely for him. I had no delusions that he came from a background that was anything less than privileged, but truthfully speaking, that privilege gave him a higher regard in my eyes.

See, Daniel Whitfield *could* have done what I observed from many others in his position – rested on that privilege, using it as a cushion to absorb mediocrity. He could have settled into the wealth my grandfather and great-grandfather managed to build, despite the looming tyrants of racism and prejudice. The legacy they'd built could have been the excuse to tread water – simply *maintaining* the business.

But he hadn't.

He loathed contentment and content people, and he'd used the legacy as a springboard, gone after success like a lion stalking a gazelle. The Whitfield name had been built locally before he ever took the reins. In the twenty years that he'd held them, he'd taken us national, and was right on the verge of *global*. That was the empire he wanted to hand down to me and my sister, whether or not she liked it.

He was putting his trust in me.

Did he know how much pressure that was?

"And I got the information you wanted on Asha Davis."

I turned my attention to Ace, listening to her for the first time since she'd climbed into the back of the car. She was my assistant as much as she was my "harmony advocate" – the sight of her was usually a pretty good diffuser of conflict – and she'd been running off a list of things I needed to be updated on. Everything else, she would have to tell me again. About Red though… I was all ears.

"Oh, so *now* you want to pay attention?" she teased, her emerald-toned eyes laughing even though her mouth wasn't. "I knew you liked her."

I shook my head, turning my gaze back toward the window. "I already told you, I don't like her, I'm—"

"Interested," she finished for me, disbelief apparent in her tone. "Which is understandable, because Asha Davis is… *interesting.*"

"How so? Like she has a slew of strange hobbies or something?"

Ace cleared her throat as she used a stylus pen to navigate the tablet in her hands. "Like she has mug shots and a fucked up childhood."

"Show me."

I took the device when Ace handed it to me, staring at the screen as she explained what I was seeing. "Arrested for assault and battery, stalking, harassment, all against a police officer, so I don't know how the hell she got out of *that* shit. She's banned from the Venetian, Bellagio, Aria, and Encore for suspicion of card counting at their poker tables. Before all of that, she graduated college with high honors, with a degree in finance paid for with scholarships.

Her mother has lupus, the stepfather is a security guard at a hospital. Brother, Ahmad Davis used to be an NBA golden boy, but now spends his time at the blackjack tables. She's friends and roommates with a Camille Jeffers, who used to dance at the Crazy Horse, but has moved on to work the high-production burlesque shows. Asha quit her job in corporate finance to work at *Dream*. Based on tax returns… she makes almost twice as much at the club as she did in her cubicle, but most of her money pays her mother's medical bills.

No children, but…"

My eyes shot over to Ace. "But?"

"She was in a lengthy relationship, from college to about three years ago. And well… keep scrolling. You should see a familiar face."

Those words were barely out when I reached the picture she must have been referring to. I narrowed my eyes at the screen.

Dorian Haywood.

Familiar face indeed.

"As we know, Dorian is… volatile. It's not clear if there was physical abuse or not, but it wouldn't be new for Asha, considering the multitude of domestic disturbance calls she grew up with. Her father was kicking her mother's ass on a regular basis. And… more likely than not, Asha and her brother too. Father was shot dead in the family home when Asha was sixteen. Unsolved, but her father had a lot of enemies."

"I see now why you called her interesting."

Ace nodded. "Yeah. The face may be angelic, but the girl herself is not."

As I scrolled back through the pictures on the tablet – copies of police reports, Asha hugged up with Dorian on a college campus, Asha's *mug shots* – I let the information I'd just heard sink in. I hadn't thought there was anything innocent about her, but… *damn.*

"You're in love now, aren't you?" Ace snickered from the other side of the car, and I flipped her off with one hand, gave the tablet back with the other. "Oooh, sensitive about it too!"

I ignored Ace's teasing as the driver pulled up to Beauchamp's. I buttoned my jacket as we walked up to the back entrance and went inside, walking through the obvious signs of renovation – dust in the air, paint cans lining the floor, and most notably, the neon lights that lined the entrance were switched off.

We didn't linger there. Our destination was the back office, where I was sure we'd find Leonard Beauchamp doing what he'd been doing since the contracts that gave Whitfield Inc 60% of his business were signed – trying to find a way to get out of it.

My hunch was spot-on.

Old Leo was a troll of a man, deeply wrinkled and hunched in his age. His advanced years had taken a physical toll, but not a mental one, and the man was cunning, always looking for the upper hand – even when advantages had already been handed to him.

Whitfield money bought this place from the brink of foreclosure and out of outstanding debt. Currently, it was bringing the Cajun restaurant up to the standards of the other restaurants on the strip – full remodel, new staff, fresh menu, award-winning chefs. One of the few things going untouched was the name, which was within our purview as owners. But we hadn't done that. We always wanted to leave the original owner feeling like the place was still, at heart, *theirs.* Like we added value, instead of stripping it away.

Leo didn't see it like that.

"What the fuck do you want?" was the greeting I received, not from Leo, but from his youngest son, Randall. Randall was in his early forties, and if it were possible, hated the Whitfields even more than the old man seated beside him.

I smirked at Randall, then Leo, as I stepped fully into the office, with Ace close by my side. "Now, is that any way to address the man who saved your family's livelihood?" I asked, pushing my hands into the pockets of my slacks. "Impolite, don't you think?"

"Politeness isn't a contracted stipulation." Randall stood, crossing his arms, and I knew how this meeting was about to go.

I nodded. "You're one hundred percent correct. But, our governance over the new design of this restaurant is. Do we need to have our attorneys meet, and review that paperwork again? I'd hope not, since from the outset this was supposed to be a friendly arrangement. We do the work, everybody makes money."

"Your crooked family stole my daddy's business," Randall growled, coming from around the desk. I gave Alicia a subtle nod, urging her not to act.

"I can understand why you might feel that way." Randall and Leonard both looked shocked by my words, but I continued on. "Your father scrapped and saved to build this business into what it was. Legendary on the strip. A black man, owning something like *this*… who would have thought?"

"You're goddamned right," Leo said, shoulders back, un-hunched, chest proud as he looked at me. "I hung that sign over the front door myself."

I smiled. "Oh, I know that. Saw the newspaper clipping and everything."

"So then you and your daddy ought to be giving respect where it's due." Randall crossed his arms over his chest, staring me down.

"We always do."

He scoffed. "That's funny to me, because I haven't seen it for the last… hell, since you came in here, acting like *you* built it. There hasn't been any respect around here!"

"So what should that tell you, Randall?" An expression of bewilderment mingled with the anger already etched into his features, and I fought the urge to smile. "Let me give you a hint – you really think that the piss-poor management that ran this place into the ground deserves respect? The health-code violations, expired permits, employees complaining about a hostile work environment… you think you and your father deserve praise for that shit? You're kidding me, right?"

"See this is why the black man can't get ahead," Randall started, using his hands to emphasize his words, and I rolled my eyes. "You come in here believing these lies, spreading them, trying to tear another black man down!"

"Get out of here with that bullshit. " I shook my head, disgusted. "Black people are out here doing big shit, with nothing but determination on their side. Don't stand in my face and put yourself in the same group as people with *real* barriers to their success. You aren't one of them. You're lazy, and stupid, and you – both of you – dropped the ball with your business, and that's no ones fault but your own."

Randall's face dropped into an ugly, aggressive scowl. "What the fuck did you just say to me?"

"Nothing wrong with your ears, man. You heard me. I know you've got a chip on your shoulder because somebody better at this than you came in to put your business back in order, but I suggest you brush it off. You were made an offer for a certain percentage of your business and you accepted it. The money has been disbursed, and it's been spent too, if that brand new Benz that was parked outside is any indication."

"What's your point here young man?" Leonard spoke up, and I glanced in his direction.

I cleared my throat. "My point… is stay out of the way so we can turn this piece of shit into something, make some money, and everybody goes home happy."

"Watch your tone," Randall growled, and I chuckled.

"Or what?"

"Or you'll be at the cleaner's paying to get blood stains out of that nice ass suit."

I laughed as he stepped forward, fists clenched like he was ready to make good on that threat. He'd barely taken two steps in my direction before Ace was in front of him, perfectly poised, with her gun aimed right at his chest.

Confusion, and then anger set into his expression as it dawned on him that Alicia's pretty ass, in her black platform heels, slim-fitting black slacks, and gauzy black blouse, was *not* eye-candy.

"Oh," he snarled. "I see what this is. You're nothing but a pussy in a suit. Fucking punk. What kind of grown ass man keeps a bitch around to do his dirty work for him?"

I frowned a bit as I nodded, more to myself than him. "You know, that's a good question." I stepped forward, putting a hand on Ace's shoulder. "Why don't you step aside? I've got this."

Ace didn't lower the gun, but her gaze drifted to me with a slight turn of her head. There was an unspoken question in her eyes, "*What about what your father just said*?" but I wasn't too concerned about that. I squeezed her shoulder, signaling that I expected her to follow my direction, despite the message relayed to her from my father. She dropped the gun and stepped aside without a word – but I knew I'd pay a price for that silence later.

I unbuttoned my jacket and handed it to her, then turned back to Randall, who was posted up like we were about to go a few rounds. "Do you really want to do this?" I asked, glancing over at Leo. "The professional way to handle this would be to simply honor the terms of the contract you both agreed to, and signed."

"Hell yeah, I want to do this. You and your bitch-ass daddy tricked us into selling our company. You stole that shit!"

"Nobody stole anything from you," I said calmly. "You're upset because you didn't understand that you wouldn't be in charge anymore, but the terms were clear. That's *your* bad."

"Yeah, well… let's see what you have to say about a contract after I kick your ass," Randall shot back, then quickly threw a jab at me, trying to catch me off guard. I easily dodged the blow, then sent one of my own, relishing the sickening crunch that occurred as my fist connected with his jaw.

The howl he let out sounded inhuman, more wounded dog than man. Leo moved faster than I thought he could to get to his son as Randall crumpled to the ground, holding his face. Beside me, Ace laughed, and I shot her a censoring look that she shrugged off.

"Let's get him to a hospital," I told Leo, but Randall shook his head as he shakily made his way back to his feet.

"Fuck you," he mumbled, then spit out a mouth full of blood as he raised his hands again.

I shrugged. "Fine. But after this… one way or another, we aren't going to have any more problems."

Instead of a simple ass yes or no, Randall responded physically, letting out some kind of half-yell as he rushed me. Once again, I saw him coming, and quickly moved aside to land a blow right under his ribs, knocking the wind out him.

I stood over him as he clutched his side, rocking back and forth.

"So," I said, looking between him and his father. "Like I said. Stay the fuck out of the way so we can make this money."

I was grateful for moments of solace.

No smartphone, no computer, just me, alone in the dark silence of my office. Those were my moments of self-inventory and assessment, sometimes prayer, always an examination of my life, and choices.

What the fuck was I doing?

I planted my fingertips in the condensation coating my half-melted glass of Mauve and coke as I pondered that question. It was an undeniable fact that I'd always been something of a shit-starter. A bright kid by all accounts, but boredom drove me to the role of constant antagonist – for my sister, my teachers, my peers. Over time, I'd mellowed – or at least, matured – into a straightforward man with a low tolerance for incompetence or bullshit, and very little desire to compromise. So easily confused with being an asshole that I wasn't even offended by the accusation anymore.

To those who didn't know me, I was surely some type of spoiled, violent, wealthy playboy-esque legend. And that wasn't entirely untrue. But I was more than that – or had been, at least.

Eight-hundred-thirty-nine days ago, I'd come unhinged.

That's what had my father so concerned, why he wanted me to "keep my hands clean". I chuckled a bit as I pressed my sore knuckles to the cold glass. I'd have to hear an earful about the Beauchamp situation later, but when it came down to it… it had been handled.

I didn't leave things unhandled.

Doing so was what allowed fools like Randall and Leonard Beauchamp to believe that they held any measure of power, when the exact opposite was true. They were allowed what we gave them, and only that. That little meeting had been the reminder.

Not handling things was the first domino in a chain of events that led to a rage that was all consuming and uncontrollable. An experience I had no aspirations to repeat.

So… I handled things.

But, that brought me back to my initial question – *What the fuck was I doing?*

I'd been quiet, which put my parents at ease. Because the same *what the fuck* question that was on my mind was on theirs too. I could feel it in lingering handshakes and hugs, long silences at the dinner table, scrutinizing gazes when they thought I was unaware. Exactly how long could I travel and take meetings and screw beautiful women, all without meaning, before that shit… imploded?

We all wondered, but they were the only ones who worried.

For one, I intended to remind the people who mattered that my family's firm stance of only conducting legal business did *not* mean we would be jerked around. Furthermore, I would never *–never-* again put myself in the position of vulnerability that had led to that… eruption.

Never.

A knock at the door pulled me out of my thoughts. I cleared my throat before delivering the "come in" command that brought Ace through the door. Her eyes went to my unfinished drink, then up to my face.

"Are you coming out to the floor?"

I gave her a nod, then knocked back the rest of my drink before I stood. "Yes. Let's go."

Trying to get myself into a lighter frame of mind, I pushed out a deep breath as I followed Ace down the hall toward the club floor. *Dream* hit us in sensory waves. First, the double-whammy of sound and feeling from the throbbing music. Then, the lingering smell of smoke, filtered in from the designated area on the screened patio. Finally, the blue-and-purple tinted visual of the packed club, with certain sections – VIP – cordoned off with translucent glass dividers.

I bobbed my head, giving in to a subtle sway in time to the music coming from the DJ booth up front, and streamed through the surround-sound speakers. Now that I was out here… it was time to leave my thoughts from earlier alone.

"I was wondering if you were going to come out. I heard you got that ass tapped in poker earlier, thought you might be afraid to show your face."

I grinned as I turned to face Jackson, and shake his hand. "I bet I know where you got that information from."

"I bet you do," he chuckled. "And she was very excited to have her job back. Not that she should have lost it in the first place…"

I shrugged, moving aside as one of the cocktail waitresses came rushing past with a tray of drinks. "You know I don't play about my games, man."

"If I didn't before, I do now."

"And make sure you remember it." I leaned in, so I could speak without yelling over the music as loud. "Zora wants to use the club one night. I told her she could."

Jackson smirked. "Of course. What night? And for what?"

"She's getting the dates back to me. But she wants to do… I don't really know, niggas in g-strings or something. Some shit I don't want to be around for."

"But I have to?" Jackson asked, frowning.

"You're the club manager, aren't you?"

"That's cold, man."

I clapped him on the shoulder. "It'll be a club full of horny ass women, Jax. Trust me, you'll be just fine."

His expression changed as he considered my words, and I chuckled to myself as I turned away. My eyes scanned the crowd, and just as I was about to say something else to Jackson, a flash of red caught my eye.

She was in one of the VIP booths taking drink orders. A tinge of… *something*… ran up my spine as I watched one of the patrons stand up, getting in her personal space, dipping his head to say something in her ear. Something that made her turn up her lips in the same sort of seductive smirk she'd given me the first night I saw her, at the poker tables. Despite her smile, she shook her head and started to walk away, but he was persistent. Unbidden, my hands strained into fists as he grabbed her arm.

In the dedicated light for the booth, I saw her clearly form the word *"stop"* but her smile never wavered. He released her wrist, saying something that earned a laugh before she gracefully exited through the rope barrier, into the main part of the club.

"Don't do it," I heard, and glanced to my side to see Jackson still there, watching the same scene I had. "She's a good girl, King."

I pulled my brows together. "I have it on good authority that she is *not.*"

"You know what I mean," Jax grunted. "She's not caught up in this nightlife shit like most of these other women. She just wants to take care of her family and play poker. That's it."

"I have no intention to interfere with that."

"And she's one of our best servers. You see how the customers respond to her?"

Yeah, I did. And inexplicably, it was getting under my skin.

I watched as she strutted through the crowd in obscenely high heels, wearing a dress she was practically spilling out of, in the best possible way. She was completely covered in front – the dress went all the way to the base of her neck – but the back was virtually nonexistent, dipping all the way down to expose the dimples at the small of her back. And the length… she would have a serious problem if she needed to bend down.

Shit.

The last thing I needed in my mind was a reminder of what she looked like bent over.

In any case, she was an attention-grabber, even if she didn't seem to notice. She strutted towards the bar – where Jackson and I were standing – as if she were completely oblivious to the trail of lustful gazes she'd left in her wake.

She offered Ace a slight nod of acknowledgment, and then her eyes skipped completely over me to shoot Jackson a smile before she made it to the bar to order the drinks she needed. Jackson and Ace both laughed at her blatant disregard, and I couldn't help laughing a little myself.

"Let's sit," I said to Ace, then turned to Jackson. "Put me in a VIP in her section."

Jackson shook his head, but sent us to a section, where Ace left me to go talk to a friend she spotted in the crowd. Less than five minutes later, Asha sauntered up to the entrance.

"What can I get for you, Mr. Whitfield?" she asked.

I sat back on the curved couch and patted my lap, motioning for her to come and sit down. The plastic smile melted from her face, and I grinned. "What's wrong? I'm trying to be a gentleman, and offer a place to rest. Those shoes *have* to make your feet tired."

"I'm fine."

"You sure as hell are," I countered, satisfied by the way she bit down on her lip, trying not to smile.

"What can I get you to drink?"

"Mauve and coke."

"Should I make it a double?"

I smirked. "Are you trying to get me drunk?"

"We're trying to get everyone drunk, sir. It's a casino."

"Fair enough," I nodded. "But no."

"Okay. I'll be right back with that for you."

True to her word, she was. I watched through the glass as she made her way to the bar and back, then drank her in as she came to deliver the cocktail to me.

"Here you go," she said, extending the drink to me. I looked at it, then looked at her, making no move to accept it.

"Have a seat," I said instead, motioning at the other end of the couch.

Asha shook her head. "I have customers."

"They can wait. Take a seat." I took the glass from her as she narrowed her eyes, and for a few seconds, I thought she was about to walk away. But then, she let out a heavy sigh, tossing her locs over one shoulder as she sat down.

She crossed her legs, then tried in vain to tug her dress down to cover her thighs. "What do you want?"

Great question.

I really didn't know, but after the information I'd gotten from Ace earlier in the afternoon, I was even more intrigued than I'd been before.

"What are you planning to do with the suit you won from me this morning?"

She smirked. "It's a nice suit. A *really* nice suit. Probably sell it."

"And my watch?"

"It's a nice watch. A really, *really* nice watch. Definitely selling it."

I nodded, then ran my tongue over my lips. "I'll buy it from you. How much?"

"Make me an offer."

"Five."

She raised an eyebrow. "Five…?"

"Thousand."

Her eyes widened in shock, but she quickly cleared the emotion from her face, fixing me with a steely gaze. "Twenty," she said, without blinking.

I chuckled. "Damn. You drive a pretty hard bargain."

"And you're a crook. Five thousand, for a diamond embellished Rolex? Do you think I'm stupid?"

"That is just about the *last* thing I think you are."

She scoffed. "Could have fooled me." She uncrossed her legs and stood, giving me a perfect view of her ass in that dress as she moved to leave.

"Fine," I called out, and she stopped, but didn't turn around. "Fifteen. More than you'd get selling it on your own."

Over her shoulder, she looked at me, some inscrutable emotion in her eyes. "No."

My eyebrows shot up. "No? Fifteen thousand dollars isn't pocket change."

"It is to you."

"But not to you," I said, and she turned a little more, her face pulled into a scowl.

"According to who? To you? You don't know me."

"But I know everything there is to know *about* you."

Her lips parted, and another… *something* … I couldn't articulate crossed her face. Subtly, she shook her head, then gave me the same look she might have given something stuck to her shoe. "Fuck you, Mr. Whitfield," she said, then turned, closing the short distance between herself and the exit. She stopped there, and glanced back. "And just for the record… I *highly* doubt it."

EIGHT

ASHA

"All in."

Anxiety bloomed in my chest as my father pushed the last of his money into the pot in the middle of the table. I'd been watching and absorbing every move, storing them away in my head. At that poker table with my father and his friends – a setting I had no business being in – I'd learned to recognize "tells", learned the hierarchy of card suits, learned which hands were ideal. That dark, smoky room full of drunk men was... school.

And I was educated enough to know my father was bluffing.

Outwardly, I didn't react. If there was even a chance I'd done anything to cause his loss, I didn't even want to let my mind drift to his retaliation. So I remained stone-faced, even as the drunken, sweaty men around me whooped and hollered over what was happening on the table.

"Show your cards."

The man sitting across from my father smirked. He was a big guy – the biggest in the room, with biceps cultivated during the idle hours of his time in prison. I knew that information from hushed whispers and fearful glances, even from the other men. He was trouble, and my father was a sore loser.

I silently prayed the man had a shitty hand.

He turned over a King and a ten…which meant he had a flush. My father's eyes filled with panic.

"Double or nothing," my father demanded with false bravado, and the other man chuckled.

"Everybody knows you ain't got shit Jimmy. This is probably your ol' lady's light bill money on the table now."

The room roared with laughter, but I swallowed hard.

It ***was.***

"What about my watch?"My father's voice held a tinge of desperation, and the other man caught it, and scoffed.

"Nobody wants that shitty watch nigga. What else you got?"

Nothing.

That's what he had. Nothing, because every time we got something, he drank and gambled it away. My father's eyes darted around, over himself, down at his hands. His gaze landed on his wedding band, staring long and hard, and then… he looked up at me.

I was fifteen, wearing all-white air force one's I'd bought with the money I earned from babysitting, and kept hidden from my father. I wore them with a hot pink velour track suit, with the jacket zipped damn near up to my neck. Tiny silver studs in my ears. Cherry chapstick. Donut bun, and a pink and white headband.

I ***looked*** *fifteen, which had been a source of distress when I wanted the attention of a particular boy who happened to be in the* *twelfth grade. In this room, with these men, I'd hoped it would protect me. I was a child.*

But that other man followed my father's gaze with thoughtful eyes. I didn't understand what was happening, but his scrutiny made me feel dirty. When he turned back to my father and nodded... my stomach turned inside out.

Tears welled in my eyes as they dealt the cards out. A scream settled at the base of my throat but didn't break free as I watched them go through the motions of another round as if... as if... I balled my hands into fists in the pockets of my jacket to try to stop myself from shaking.

Everything was... blurry. The voices were distorted, and the smoke was suddenly even thicker, even more cloying. No one else was horrified. Just me.

There was no raising the pot. The cards were what they were, so it went fast.

The other man had two pairs. Aces and fours.

A dry heave wracked my chest, but I didn't care anymore about being a distraction – nobody noticed anyway. All eyes were on my father, who was staring down at the cards like a man on his last bit of hope. His shoulders were sunken in defeat, nose snarled in defiance... and then he put down his cards.

I couldn't look at them, but he said two words that pardoned me, but didn't lessen my heartbreak in the least.

"Full house."

I hated winning with a full house. Even now. I would play my way through it, but it always set off a twist of nausea that I had a hard time shaking. I never, *ever* went to watch my father play poker again after that night, and if his friends came to the house, I found somewhere else to go.

We didn't talk about it. If I brought it up, I would bet money that he'd tell me I misunderstood, or that I'd imagined it. Hell… I hoped I had. Wished I had.

But the more it played in my head, the surer I was. The fear I lived with after that… it wasn't of my own doing. It wasn't *my* fault. That prickle of terror I'd felt, the greedy look in that man's eyes, the quiet voice screaming *run* in the back of my head… I hadn't imagined that. I didn't make it up.

I reminded myself of that whenever I started feeling guilty about pulling that trigger.

When I pulled myself up out of bed, it was ten in the morning. My eyes landed on the Rolex on my nightstand, completely out of place among my seven-dollar alarm clock, cracked cell phone, and the random assortment of earrings that had accumulated from me taking them off before I tumbled into bed.

I picked it up, running my fingers over the cool, smooth glass surface of the face.

Is it really glass? Or something fancier? Seems like they'd use something fancier on a luxury watch.

It was heavy in my hands – appropriately so. It had been three days since the night Kingston Whitfield offered to buy it back from me, which I didn't understand. He had an obscene amount of money – why not just buy another one?

So I'd taken it to a friend of mine, who owned a jewelry store. The twelve-thousand dollar appraisal value had made my mouth dry up, and I'd had to put a hand on my chest to calm my racing heart. That was the money I needed for the tournament, handed to me on a silver platter. He offered me a check on the spot.

But…

Here I was.

No check. With a watch that belonged to a man I wanted really desperately to hate. But there were already men I hated, and it felt almost obscene to place Kingston in the same category with them. Nothing he'd done to me remotely compared.

Getting on my nerves really didn't qualify.

I couldn't say why I was so enthralled by the watch. It was an exquisite piece of jewelry, sure, but I'd never been into glitzy things like that. I chewed at the inside of my lip as I stared at it, then closed both hands around it as a different, painfully accurate reason came to mind.

It's a reminder of the attention you got from the man.

Quietly, I laughed at myself. Male attention? Now *that* was something I definitely didn't hold in the highest regard. Maybe because I got it in such abundance at the club, it didn't faze me anymore. I appreciated compliments just like the next person, but it had been forever since any one man's attention made me feel like my heart was going to stop.

Which was even more reason to stay away.

A man like that couldn't possibly do my life any good.

I opened the bedside drawer and placed the watch at the back, underneath a mess of important papers. Once it was closed, I went ahead and got up, going to the bathroom for my morning routine.

Today was one of my days off, and if I wasn't selling that watch, I needed to get my behind to the poker tables. Between tips and winnings, I'd managed to pull together another four thousand dollars toward my tournament entry goal. If I played a little more aggressively, I could manage the other five thousand I needed to make the deadline in two days.

Just the thought made me a little woozy.

In two days, I'd be handing over *fifty-thousand dollars* to enter a tournament. There were prizes other than the grand prize, sure. But there was no guarantee I'd leave with *anything.*

But still… win or lose, one way or another, I'd be fulfilling a long-held dream. I smiled to myself as I padded into the kitchen.

Gonna have to come up with a new dream.

Camille kept our fridge stocked with the things she needed to keep her sleek dancer's body – I just gave her grocery money and let her loose – so it was easy for me to grab something light for breakfast. I peeked into her room as I took a bite from the apple I'd chosen. A frown twitched at the corners of my mouth when I saw her empty bed, until I remembered her text from last night. She had early rehearsals, so she was taking advantage of the block of rooms the dance troupe reserved.

I closed her door, then returned to the kitchen with my apple.

I was heading back to my room to get dressed when several loud thumps against the front door stopped me in my tracks. It wasn't that early, but I wasn't expecting anyone.

I was a few steps from the door when whoever it was pounded again, harder this time. A scowl settled on my face.

"*If this is Jared's dumb ass,*" I muttered, pressing a hand to the door to balance myself as I pushed up on my toes to see through the peephole. My eyes went wide when I saw who was on the other side of the door.

"Why the hell are you beating on my door like you're the police?" I started asking, before I'd even turned the lock. I flung the door open, still scowling, but my expression softened as soon as I saw the state of Ahmad's face. His golden-brown skin was marred by cuts and purple bruises, and he had the distinctly swollen beginnings of a black eye.

My mouth was opening to ask what happened when he was shoved into me, and several men I hadn't seen appeared from either side of my door.

"What the hell is going on?" I shrieked, looking from Ahmad's battered face to the casually-well-dressed men who'd pushed their way into my apartment. I was backed up against the table that stood beside the door, and my hands were already in my purse, searching for my weapon.

"You won't need that."

The voice that spoke those words made a chill run up my spine, and my fingers froze just as they wrapped around my keys. My lungs constricted, keeping me from taking a deep breath as another man stepped through my doorway, stopping in front of me.

I didn't move – couldn't move – as he reached around me, plucking the purse from my hands. My hands fell uselessly to my sides as he tossed the bag onto the couch, then closed my door.

Nobody else was in the room.

Or at least, that was how it felt as he touched me, cupping my face lovingly in his hands. Only… lovingly wasn't the right word, though it was easily confused with him. The smile that spread over his mouth was devastating – in appeal and inability to stomach. The heat from his fingertips was scalding, but I didn't move. I didn't dare.

"Hello, Asha."

I ran my tongue over dry lips, knowing he expected a response. "Hello Dorian."

"It's been a while."

"It has. What brings you by?" I asked, breaking his gaze to look at Ahmad, hoping like hell that it wasn't what I already knew it was.

Dorian chuckled, but he didn't move away. "You don't have to play polite with me, Asha. I know how lethal this pretty mouth of yours is," he said, brushing his thumb over my bottom lip. I swallowed a whimper as he leaned in. "And how deeply you can cut with that gifted tongue."

I didn't feel like I was breathing properly again until he pulled back, looking me up and down as he lowered his hands. His gaze rested on my breasts, only covered by the flimsy fabric of my tank top, and that was when I finally moved, crossing my arms to cover myself.

His gaze came back to my face. "Don't you *really* mean… What the hell am I doing here, after you told me to leave you the fuck alone? After you said you never wanted to see my goddamn face again?" His jaw clenched, eyes narrowed when I didn't answer. "Don't you?" he demanded, so forcefully that I flinched, and my hands clenched.

"Yes."

He smiled again, and I swallowed hard, forcing myself not to drop my gaze, even though I wanted to so bad. Dorian was handsome. Disgustingly so. Perfect white teeth, perfect mahogany skin, perfectly athletic body. I'd loved him since I was in the ninth grade, with all my teenaged heart, but he wouldn't even look at me back then.

On my 17th birthday, at one of Ahmad's games, I bumped into him on the way from the concession stands with my friends. He'd graduated high school three years before, and was one of the ones our mothers told us to stay away from. On the streets, he'd graduated from the one pressing tiny packages of illegal substances into addict's hands in exchange for crumpled bills, to the one protecting, to the one hiring. But I didn't care about that. I'd wanted him and that smile since watching him clown with his friends in the cafeteria at lunch.

And then I bumped into him, spilling bright orange soda down his perfectly creased jeans onto his spotless sneakers.

"Yo, what the fuck?" he'd bellowed, scowling as he stepped back. I was scared and embarrassed when I stammered back, *"I'm so, so sorry! I can get some napkins!"* and then he finally looked at me. *Really* looked. And my heart went still in my chest, just before it exploded in tandem with the smile that spread across his face. *"Nah,"* he'd said, looking me over with approving eyes before he pulled his lip between his teeth. *"Napkins ain't gonna cut it. Come sit over here and tell me what you gone do to make it up to me."*

That was a lifetime ago.

Or at least, it felt like it. And now, that face I'd loved so much – too much – was hard to look at. Impossible to abide.

My stomach lurched as I squared my shoulders, refusing to back down. The affection in his eyes was clear, and potent. He wanted me, still.

But I didn't feel good about that.

It felt really, really ugly.

"We have a problem," he said, any trace of humor dropping from his voice.

"We?"

He nodded, then glanced at the other people in the room, reminding me that they were even there. Ahmad's eye had swollen more, distorting his face. He'd slumped down to a seat at one of the barstools, looking like he wanted to bolt away – which was probably why Dorian's guys were standing on either side of him.

"Your brother and I," Dorian explained, then ambled over to where Ahmad sat. "See… I had every intention of leaving you alone, just as you asked. But then Ahmad came to me, asking for a favor. And you know I've always been fond of him… like a kid brother to me. So I said yes. Trying to help a young man out."

A bitter taste erupted in the back of my throat as I turned to Ahmad. Of all the devils lurking in Vegas, ready and willing to pay for souls…he'd sold his to *this* one?

"What was the favor?" I asked, just above a whisper. Ahmad closed his eyes, but my gaze didn't leave him. I moved without thinking until I was right in front of him, shoving his shoulders back to get him to look at me. "*What was the favor?*"

When Ahmad opened his eyes, they were covered in a glossy sheen. Deep brown pools, begging and pleading with me for help. I hadn't seen that look since we were kids. It tore me in half back then, and … it did the same now.

"Money," Dorian said, when my brother didn't answer. This time, I was the one to close my eyes. "Lil' bruh needed me to front him some cash to keep that pretty ass truck in his possession, so I did. I paid it off for him."

My eyes popped open, and flew to Ahmad, who simply hung his head.

"I mean… I figured why keep letting him pay the dealership, when he could just… pay me? I even gave him the option to deliver a few packages for me. Work his debt off."

"You didn't..." I whispered.

Dorian chuckled. "Oh, he *did.* Lil' nigga actually had a bit of swag to him and everything. Paid me back for the truck easily."

"So then what is this about?" I asked, propping my hands on my hips as I turned to face Dorian. "If he paid you back for the truck, why the black eye, and the bruises? Why are you *here*?"

"Because it ain't about the truck," he sneered, stepping into my face. "Come to find out, this little motherfucker likes to live on the edge. Went to some jack-leg casino off the strip after doing some business for me. Got drunk, got his ass jacked for *my* money and *my* property. And I'm ready to collect on his debt."

Nausea overwhelmed my senses, and I swallowed a big mouthful of air, trying to keep my light breakfast in my stomach. "How much?" I asked, my tongue feeling like sandpaper against the roof of my mouth.

"Seventy."

My hands flew up. One to my mouth, the other to my chest. "Dorian," I said, in a shaky breath. "You... you *can't* be serious."

"Oh I'm serious as a gun to the head, sweetheart. Your brother has been dodging me, and had the nerve to get slick at the mouth about it. And well... only *one* Davis gets a pass on that."

"He doesn't *have* that kind of money!"

"No shit," Dorian chuckled. "That's why I'm here. You know what this is, Asha. Know what happens to people with debts they can't pay. Remember?"

A stray tear finally broke free, dripping down my cheek as I looked at Ahmad. Of course I remembered. I couldn't *unsee* the things I'd watched Dorian do to people. And I didn't want to live it again.

"Let's see," Dorian continued, with a sadistic little smirk. "You, your mother, your stepfather. That's three fingers. Maybe I'll send one to his boss... oh, and his homeboys who still play for the Suns. And I can't forget his girlfriend, and the chick he knocked up."

"Knocked up?" My eyes went wide.

Dorian's smile spread. "Oh, my bad. You hadn't told her she was going to be an aunt yet, and I ruined the surprise. Seriously, my bad. But you've got too many people who give a shit about you, man," he said to Ahmad, bending to eye level. "You're not even going to be able to hold your dick, let alone your kid by the time I'm through with you."

"You don't have to do this." I did something I hadn't done on purpose in years – touched Dorian's shoulder. He looked up, surprised, and I yanked my hand back.

Dorian straightened to full height, looked me right in the face, and told me, "Oh, I definitely do. This ain't no after school special shit. I can't give this nigga a pass just because of you. The streets talk. And then everybody is looking for a favor, or just one chance, whatever. Or worse, motherfuckers start looking at me like I'm on some pussy shit. And that ain't happening."

"What if he paid you back? What if *I* paid you back?"

He shook his head. "You know… this is one of the things I loved about you. Loyalty. And I'm sure you make out nice with your tips and shit at *Dream*, but nah… I'm not rent-a-center. No fucking payment plans."

I swallowed my question of how he knew where I worked, and stepped closer to him. "I have money, Dorian. A lump sum for now, and I'll get you the rest. Just *please*. Don't hurt him anymore."

Dorian sighed. As vicious as I knew he could be, I could tell it was troubling him to not give me a break. "Nah, Asha. A couple hundred dollars or whatever, isn't going to cut it."

"I have forty-five thousand."

Those words tumbled out of my mouth and got everybody's attention. I could feel four pairs of eyes on me – Dorian's narrowed. "You have forty-five thousand dollars?"

I nodded. "Yes."

"How?" That question came from Ahmad. The first word he'd spoken the whole time. I didn't look at him though – couldn't. I looked at Dorian instead as I answered the question.

"I saved it. From my tips, and playing the poker tables."

"Show me."

I swallowed the bitter taste in my throat, and nodded again. "Okay. It's in my room. I'll be right back."

"I'll come with you."

He motioned to his cronies to watch Ahmad, and then turned to look at me. I stayed where I was until he raised an eyebrow at me, then cocked his head. "Well?"

"Oh! Uh… yeah. It's this way."

I turned around and headed down the hall. As I passed Camille's door, I was grateful as hell that she wasn't home.

Or was I?

At least then I wouldn't be alone.

I didn't want Dorian in my bedroom. That kept playing in my head as I took my time getting there, then stepped through the open door. I went straight to the closet, but Dorian's hand around my wrist stopped me.

"Where's your phone?" I pointed to where it still lay on my nightstand, and he moved in front of me to pick it up. My chest tightened as he unbuttoned his suit jacket, revealing the gun holstered at his side before he sat down on the edge of my bed. "Get the money."

He wouldn't shoot me. We both knew that. But because I knew he *would* blow Ahmad's head off his shoulders while I watched, to prove a point, I went into my closet for the bank pouch. In anticipation of paying my entry fee, I'd taken the money to a bank in increments, getting them to change it out to stacks for me.

There were four of them. Four impossibly tiny stacks of a hundred one-hundred dollar bills that comprised the bulk of everything I had in the world. The rest of the money was still in the random increments I'd gotten it in – singles, fives, tens, twenties – but they were neatly bundled and labeled.

"It's all there," I said, fresh tears welling in my eyes as I handed him the pouch. "Forty-four thousand, eight hundred and sixty-two."

"You told me it would be forty-five."

"Dorian, I—"

"Relax," he said, raising a hand to silence me. "I'm fucking with you."

His voice was kinder than it had been in the room with Ahmad. He put the pouch down on the bed without opening it, and motioned for me to come closer.

My stomach churned as I stepped between his open legs, but he didn't touch me. He stared up at me like he'd never seen me before. "I came to the club one day," he said, not taking his eyes off me. "You were wearing this dress, and these heels that made your legs… you looked good as fuck."

I closed my eyes as his fingertips skimmed my legs. From my knees, up my thighs, until he cupped my ass and pulled me closer. He put his nose in the apex of my thighs and inhaled, letting out a suggestive groan. My fingers trembled with the urge to dig my nails into his eye sockets.

How far could I get before one of his guys shoots me in the back?

"Twenty-five thousand," he said, and I opened my eyes. He took his hands off me, but the sensation of his touch lingered. "That's how much you're short."

"I'll get it to you," I insisted, taking a step back. "Just give me a little time."

Dorian shook his head and stood up, eliminating any space between us. "That's the one thing I don't have in abundance, Asha." His gaze dropped to my breasts, then came back up to my face, his dark eyes boring into mine. "What are you going to do to make it worth it?"

I flinched as he grabbed the bottom hem of my tank top. He pulled me into him, hooking an arm around my waist, but I shook my head. "Not that."

There was a long, uncomfortable stretch of deathly quiet while he stared into me. "You used to love when I touched you," he said, breaking the silence. "Now you're looking at me like I make your skin crawl."

I dropped my gaze from his, and winced at the harsh breath he pushed out through his nose. I could feel him still staring, and I willed myself not to squirm, not to react at all as he dipped his head, pressing a kiss to my cheek.

"Five weeks. Five thousand a week. Don't be late."

He abruptly let me go, and didn't look back as he grabbed the pouch full of money, dropped my phone back on the dresser, then left the room. A few moments later, I heard my front door slam closed.

Gravity didn't hit me until then.

I dropped onto the bed with my head in my hands, mind racing through the last – I glanced at the clock – fifteen minutes of my life. I'd come face to my face with someone I'd never wanted to see again, because he'd had to kick my idiotic, incompetent, drug dealing brother's ass because he was somewhere he shouldn't be with no protection. That irresponsible, foolish decision – possibly the stupidest in the long list of stupid – had landed him tens of thousands of dollars in debt that even my life savings, the money for my dream, the one damn thing I wanted for myself, couldn't cover.

Oh, and his dimwitted ass was about to be a father.

"This isn't happening," I said to myself out loud. If I closed my eyes, when I opened them again, I'd be waking up from what had to be the worst kind of dream.

Only… I could still feel Dorian's lips against my cheek.

A sob broke from my throat as I pressed my hand to the spot where he'd kissed me. So, *so* much time, and so, *so* much mental energy had gone into convincing myself that Dorian and I weren't meant to be. For years we'd loved hard, then fought hard, then fucked harder, until it finally occurred to me that our "love" wasn't healthy.

It was *toxic.*

By the time I left, I hated *us.* I hated the turbulence we created, hated the havoc he unleashed in me.

I hated that he reminded me of my father.

Devilishly handsome and just… devilish.

Period.

Dorian wasn't a good person, but he was mostly good to me. When he *wasn't* good to me, he was horrible. But I was beyond "mostly". I loved him with everything I had, for years and years of my life. Then came a point where I had to do what my mother never had.

Love *me* a little more.

"A-Asha?"

Coolness swept over me at the sound of Ahmad at my bedroom door. "What?" I snapped, in a voice I barely recognized as my own. When I looked up at his pitiful, battered face, I waited for the familiar feelings of sympathy to overwhelm my anger. Like always. I waited for the love, for the overwhelming need to protect him to cancel out the rage swirling in my chest. Just. Like. Always.

But this time it didn't.

"I… I don't know what to say," he managed to get out, and my lip curled as I stood up.

"I don't want to hear it anyway. What I want," I said, walking to meet him at the door, "Is to put my hands around your throat and wring your *fucking neck*!" He recoiled in surprise at my outburst, taking a step back, but I was right there, getting in his face. "Do you know how long it took me to save that money? I have bailed you out over, and over, and *over.* I'm sick of saving you! When the hell is somebody going to save *me*?"

"Asha, I—"

"*Shut up!*" I screamed, jabbing a finger in his face. "A baby, Ahmad?! By somebody who isn't even your girlfriend? What is wrong with you?"

"I'm sorry!" His voice cracked over the words, and hearing that sound – hearing my brother cry, I…

"No." I shook my head. "No. I don't care about you being sorry. I don't care about you wanting to make it right. You brought *Dorian* back into my life, like you didn't have a front row seat to what the relationship did to me. I gave up my *dream*, Ahmad. I…" I turned away from him, swiping away the tears streaming down my face. "You being sorry doesn't mean anything."

He grabbed my hand, but I snatched it away. "Tell me what to do. I promise, I'll—"

"Don't promise me anything," I snapped, holding up my hands. "What you can do, is figure out a way – a *legal* way – to get him his five thousand dollars next week."

Ahmad nodded. "I'll get it. I swear. And I'll repay you too. I know I didn't deserve it, but thank you for doing that for me."

"I didn't do shit for you." I crossed my arms, and glared at him. "I don't want a dead brother, our mother doesn't want a dead son, and your child needs a father. Work on doing better than the piece of shit that created us, how about that, Ahmad? You want to do something for me? Do *that*. Okay?"

A tear escaped from the corner of his eye, and I looked away. I didn't want to break. Didn't want to falter. Didn't want to give in, just like every other time.

"I'm sorry, Asha."

"Get out, Ahmad. And don't say shit to me until you have Dorian's money."

For the second time, I listened to the heavy sound of male footsteps leading away from my room, then listened for my front door to open and closed. When it did, I rushed out, turning the lock and deadbolt to keep any more surprises from coming through.

And then I sat down on the floor, and cried for the death of a dream I should have known better than to have in the first place.

NINE

ASHA

"You sure you're okay?"

No.

I was glad this was a phone conversation, instead of face to face. I blinked back tears as I shook my head, preparing to tell Jackson a pointless lie. The words stuck to my tongue, refusing to be spoken.

"Uh… I will be," I said instead, and slipped my feet into the flat sandals I'd put down at the end of the bed. "If me taking the day is a problem, I can just—"

"No," Jax cut in. "It's fine. I'm not worried about that. I'm worried about *you.*"

"Don't." A quick glance around my room told me I had everything I needed, so I stepped out, closing the door behind me. "I just need a little break. I'll be on time for my shift tomorrow, okay?"

There was a long pause on the other end of the line before Jackson pushed out a sigh. "I know there's something you aren't telling me Red, but I'm going to let it slide. For now. You know you can talk to me if you're in trouble, right?"

"Of course."

"Or if somebody is fucking with you."

"I know, Jax."

And honestly… I really did. In fact, I was confident that if I told Jackson about this, he'd probably loan me the money in a heartbeat. But I didn't *want* to tell him. He'd done me enough favors, pulled enough strings, let enough things slide while I was running behind my little brother trying to clean up his messes.

This time – this *last* time – I wasn't involving anyone else. Not unless I absolutely had to.

As ridiculous as yesterday's events were, I'd already parsed them in my head. It was cut and dry. There was no way Ahmad was going to be able to come up with five thousand dollars in a week, so that responsibility was going to fall to me – just like usual.

Between tips and poker winnings, I could probably make it. If not… the watch that was still hidden in the back of my nightstand drawer was a desperate route I could take, even though for whatever reason, the thought made me sick to my stomach. With the level of pressure I was under, taking the day off probably wasn't the wisest decision I could have made – I needed those tips.

But I also needed, as I'd told Jackson, a break.

I managed to get him off the phone before I left the apartment, locking the door behind me. Camille still hadn't been home, which I was grateful for, because she wouldn't have left me alone as easily as Jackson had. She would have weaseled the truth out of me, and then called Cree, which meant getting the police involved, which was the absolute *last* thing I wanted to do.

With people like Jared allowed to proudly wear a badge and carry a weapon, I didn't trust them, even a little bit. Cree was the only exception.

I looked around, checking my surroundings before I walked to my car. I kept my hand in my purse, on my pepper spray, and my other had gripped my keys, with the blade extended.

I was tired of men catching me off guard. The next one was going to the hospital.

Twenty minutes later, I pulled up to the front of the Drake Casino Resort, and gave the valet the keys. Normally, I would spend ten or fifteen minutes on an adventure in the parking lot, looking for a space, but the spa voucher in my purse said that my parking would be validated. I wasn't passing up *any* perks today.

Inside the resort, I headed straight for the spa desk, which was just a few steps over from the hotel check in. As I approached, the woman at the counter looked up, absorbing my cheap sandals, cut off shorts, tee shirt and ponytail with a thinly veiled sneer.

"Can I help you?" she asked, clasping her hands in front of her as she spoke.

"Yeah. I saw a video online of this guy giving a woman a massage, but it wasn't like… a regular massage. I think there was like… slow jams in the background while he was rubbing on her thighs, and her feet, and all of that… and he definitely touched her pussy. I think it was called a "vassage". Do you guys offer those? Cause that's what I need. Really bad."

When I finished speaking, the woman's mouth was open in surprise, but she clamped her lips closed and cleared her throat. She glanced around her, then angled her head toward me, and motioned for me to lean in.

"So… we don't offer those here. But there's a place called *Waterfalls*, about two blocks away from here, and…mmmhmmm."

I grinned, for what had to be the first time in the last two days. "Seriously? I've been there before for a show, but I didn't know they were doing… that."

The woman nodded. "It's a new service. You've gotta talk to the owner, Queen Z, yourself. Tell her Kiely sent you."

"I sure as hell will," I said, filing the information away in my head. "Good looking out. I was honestly joking when I mentioned it, cause you were giving me that crazy look when I walked up."

Kiely cut her eyes toward the ceiling. "Oh girl, I didn't mean anything by that." She leaned in a little more. "We *have* to turn up the bougie when we're at the desk. Adds to the ambiance or something. What services are you looking for today?"

"Whatever I can afford with this," I said, digging the envelope with the spa voucher from my purse. I handed it to her, and she turned to her computer, keying in the number printed on the side. I chewed at my bottom lip as I waited for a response. When Kiely's eyes went wide at something on her screen, it felt almost like deja-vu. "What is it?"

She looked up, and I could tell she was scrutinizing me again, for different reasons than at first. She shook her head. "Oh, uh, nothing. Not really. It's just… uh…"

"It's not valid or something?" I asked, as my face heated with embarrassment. Had I pissed Kingston off so much that my "morning after" privileges had been revoked?

"No, not at all," she said, holding up her hands. "Quite the opposite, actually. It's an ongoing pass… covering anything you want, in perpetuity."

My eyes went wide. "I… what?"

"It means—"

"No, I know what perpetuity means. I just… he does that for every woman he sleeps with?" I mumbled, more to myself than anything. How bottomless was this man's money, that he blew forty grand on a single hand of poker, basically gave away fifteen thousand dollar watches, and covered luxury spa services for what was probably a whole harem of women?

"Not at all," Kiely said, and my gaze shot back to her face.

"Excuse me?"

Kiely gave me a little smile. "You asked if he does this for every woman he sleeps with. I know you probably weren't really asking me, but… no, he doesn't." She glanced around again, making sure no one was close. "You didn't hear it from me, but it's usually just a one service voucher."

I swallowed. "Maybe… it was an accident?" I said uncertainly, but Kiely shook her head.

"It requires putting a card on file, and you have to sign in three different places. It wasn't an accident .You must have put it on him *real* good, cause I haven't checked in one of his guests in… a while." She smirked, then handed me an iPad with the spa logo. "Spa menu is on there. Sign in, and check off the services you want. Wine, cocktails, snacks, and lunch are provided if you'd like, just let any member of our staff know what you need. We'll get you back shortly."

I gave her a weak smile, then took the iPad from her hands, going to a nearby couch to sit down.

I haven't checked in one of his guests in… a while.

I shook my head, refusing to let those words mean anything to me. If it were anyone except Kingston Whitfield, they *wouldn't* mean anything. The night we'd spent together was supposed to be between passing strangers – for all he knew at the time, I could have only had a couple of days in Las Vegas. His little "in perpetuity" voucher meant nothing special, not really.

"Ace" had made that clear to me.

Instead of dwelling on that, I tapped the screen of the tablet to plug my information in. Once I was through with that, the spa menu came up, and my eyes went wide at the prices.

"Holy shit," I muttered to myself. These types of luxury services were *well* out of my range. I kept myself well-groomed – manicured

nails, pedicured toes, tamed eyebrows, body hair removal, all of that. But three-hundred dollar massages? Two-hundred-dollar body scrubs? Not in my budget.

That wasn't the case today though.

With all the stress *he'd* caused me, and his obviously deep pockets, certainly Kingston wouldn't mind if I splurged a little. At least, that's what I convinced myself of as I hit the check mark beside something called the *Empress Treatment – Feeling Stressed? Treat yourself to the works! Euphoric Mud Bath, Vanilla Brown Sugar Body Scrub, Full Body Massage, Spa Manicure, Ultimate Pedicure, and Ultra Hydration Facial.* I ignored the numbers beside it indicating the price, and moved on to make myself a lunch reservation immediately following my treatments.

I didn't panic about until I hit submit.

What if that was too much?

These people are going to think I'm crazy, I mused, contemplating putting the iPad on the seat beside me and bolting out the door.

Before I could do that, a gorgeous Asian man dressed in impossibly white slacks and a button-up approached me. "Ms. Davis?"

"Uh… um… yes?"

"We're ready for you. Follow me, please."

He took the tablet from my hands, then waited expectantly for me to get up. His smile seemed genuine, and when I finally stood and glanced at Kiely, hers was too.

"Enjoy," she called, with a little wave before she turned back to the customer at the desk. I took a deep breath, then followed my guide – Daniel, according to his nametag – to an area beyond the front desk.

"I'll be your liaison between treatments, Ms. Davis," he said, showing me to a small room with stone walls. Lush plants rested on shelves, and there was a cabinet at the back, near a plush white chaise. "This is where you can change into a robe, and leave your personal items… including your cell phone. We don't allow anything beyond this point that might disturb the other guests, or take away from your experience."

"That won't be a problem."

I didn't want to talk to anybody about anything. The point of this was to get away… from *everything*. Even if it was only for a few hours.

After everything that happened the day before, I'd been… paralyzed, in a way. I don't know how long I sat in front of that door, crying, but the next thing I knew the sun had gone down, and I was still in the same spot. I went from there to my bed, where I stayed until the next morning, only moving enough to send a few texts back and forth with Camille. In the morning, I got up and forced myself to eat, then called Jackson to let him know I wasn't coming in.

I needed this time to disengage.

And that was exactly what I did.

Following Daniel's instructions, I undressed after he stepped out, and then I followed him to the mud baths. Once I got over the mental block of purposely getting myself covered in mud, I relaxed into it, and discovered that it was just as amazing as rich folks made it sound.

After a quick shower, I moved on to my body scrub and massage. I left those with my skin glowing and my limbs loose and tension free as Daniel led me to the salon for the rest of my services.

My real life troubles were impossible to forget, but by the time I made my way to the spa's restaurant, they felt like problems that belonged to someone else. I practically melted into the small booth I was directed to, sighing to myself as I admired the view of the Drake resort's gorgeous fountains.

"Good afternoon ma'am." I looked up to a smiling server, and returned her greeting. "What can I get you to drink today? Would you like the wine list, or a cocktail menu?"

I shook my head. "Just water for now." I'd already had at least four cocktails through the course of my services, something I rarely did because liquor prices were exorbitant in casinos. Today… it wasn't my problem.

The server nodded and walked away, returning with a tray. She placed an elegant glass carafe of ice water on the table, and poured some into a goblet I suspected was crystal. Confusion swept over me as she poured a second one, putting it in the place across from me on the table. My bewilderment deepened when the bottle of wine I assumed was for another table was uncorked, put on the table, then joined by two elegantly engraved long-stem wine glasses.

"Uh… excuse me," I said, but the server only smiled, then walked off.

A few seconds later, my confusion dissipated as I watched Kingston approach the server, bending to speak a few words into her ear before he looked up, smiling in my direction.

I rolled my eyes as he sauntered up to the table, then slipped into the seat across from me. "You look refreshed," he said, those animated espresso eyes of his gleaming with amusement. "Are you enjoying yourself?"

"Well… I *was*."

He smirked, then picked up the bottle of wine, pouring two glasses. "Until?"

"Until you sat down."

"Damn," he said, sitting back against the plush leather of the booth. "It's like that? I sponsored your pampering today, and I can't even sit down?"

I raised an eyebrow at him, then picked up my glass, taking a long sip of the deep purple liquid. "Am I in trouble?"

"Do you want to be?"

The way he spoke those words – in a low, suggestive voice, while he looked me right in the eyes – sent the best kind of chill up my spine. I shifted in my seat, dropping my gaze from his.

"Mr. Whitfield… what do you want?"

"I want you to stop calling me Mr. Whitfield. The name is King. It's just a name, not a big deal. *I'm* a big deal, but the name isn't."

I shook my head. "You really enjoy trying to get under my skin, don't you?"

He raised his hands in a defensive pose. "I'm not trying to get under your skin, Ms. Davis. I'm trying to get under your *robe*," he said, his eyes lingering over the thick terry-cloth robe I – and most other patrons throughout the restaurant – was still in.

I crossed my arms over my chest, even though there was no way my hardened nipples were showing through. I still felt exposed. "This could be considered harassment."

"It could," he nodded.

"I could sue you."

He shrugged. "You could."

We stared at each other for several seconds before he leaned over the table a bit. "Am I bothering you, Red? Like, *really* bothering you? Because that's not my intention, so if that's what's happening… you can let me know. I'll get up, and leave you to enjoy the rest of your day."

He sat back then, waiting for an answer.

I wanted to badly to say, "*Yes, you're bothering me, leave me alone,*" but his eyes on my lips kept them closed. What was going through his mind? Was he thinking about kissing me? Remembering what I felt like? What I tasted like?

Instead of answering, I took another sip from my wine, savoring the burst of flavor on my tongue – anything to distract me from this moment.

"Asha." Somehow, the way he spoke my name struck a balance of gentle and demanding. I looked up, reluctantly meeting his eyes. "Do you want me to leave?"

I ran my tongue over my lips. "No."

"Good. Let's order."

He was barely finished with the statement before the server was back at our table, notepad poised to write down our selections. They both looked at me, expecting me to start, but I looked at Kingston.

"You mean to tell me you're having me order for myself? I'd have thought you would do it for me. Since you know me so well, of course."

Kingston smirked, running a hand over the perfectly groomed lines of his facial hair. "I was actually trying to back off a little. Give you some room to do your own thing."

"No, no," I said, returning his little devious grin. There was no *possible* way this man knew what kind of food I liked, no matter what his googling or whatever had brought up. "I insist."

He looked from me to the server and said, "We'll both have the scallops and polenta, with asparagus and mushrooms. And bring us a bottle of white wine with the meal. Whatever the chef recommends."

I bit my lip to keep them together as the server walked away to deliver our order to the kitchen. Kingston's eyes were burning a hole in the side of my head, but I kept my gaze pointed out the window at the beautiful view.

Did he have something to do with me getting such prime seating?

"So how did I do?" he asked.

"You did okay… I guess." I hazarded a glance in his direction, and ended up stuck. "How did you know I loved scallops?"

"I didn't. *I* love scallops. I ordered you the same thing so you wouldn't ask for any of mine."

Before I could help it, a giggle burst free, and I clamped a hand over my mouth.

"Nah, now." Kingston reached across the table, pulling my hand down. "I earned that smile, don't cover it up."

"Whatever," I said, then pressed my lips together, hoping he would stop watching me so keenly. Instead, his gaze seemed to intensify, making me squirm a little in my seat. "What?"

"You're beautiful."

I rolled my eyes, latching on to false annoyance in an attempt to quell the butterflies in my chest. "You see beautiful women all the time."

"What does that have to do with you?"

"The same thing *you* have to do with me. Nothing."

He drew his head back and chuckled. "Damn. Shut me down, huh?"

"I'm trying."

"And yet, you didn't ask me to leave. Interesting."

Heat raced to my face, and I shook my head. "Don't read too much into it, Mr. Whitfield. I've spent a lot of your money today, and you're right. The least I could do is share a meal with you."

"So you consider your company a gift?"

I shrugged. "You certainly seem to. Since you continue to seek it out."

He picked up his wine glass, taking a deep sip before he nodded. "You might be right."

"I think I *am* right," I shot back, propping an elbow on the table to rest my chin on my hand. "But the question is… why?"

"Why not?"

"Because of all those *other* beautiful women you see on a daily basis. Women who actually *want* you."

He grinned, and I silently cursed my body for responding to him with moisture between my thighs and hard nipples. "Those women aren't nearly as interesting. That's what separates you from them – not their desire for me. Because unless I just dreamt you wrapping those agile fingers around my dick at the bar that night… you want me too, Red."

"I'm not interesting," I said, ignoring the intimation that I wanted him, because I had no substantial case against it. "I am wholly unremarkable. Just another girl trying not to get swallowed up by this city. Does that convince you to leave me alone?"

"The fact that you think you're ordinary only deepens my curiosity."

I narrowed my eyes, searching his face for some hint that he was just being conversational, not really that fascinated by me. Merely passing time. But the only thing I found was rapt attraction lighting his pupils. I blew out a breath, forcing myself not to squirm.

"Okay. What is it that you think you know about me?" I asked, trying not to let my frustration creep into my voice. He was so… *composed.* There was no way I was about to let him know he had an effect on me—not without a fight.

One thick eyebrow hiked up. "What, you want me to run down a list or something?"

"Works for me."

He shook his head, chuckling at the suggestion. "And give you a chance to correct my misconceptions all at once? What fun would that be?"

"You know what…"

"I don't, but I'm almost certain you're about to introduce me."

Again, an unwelcome giggle slipped from my mouth, and I shook my head. "You really are a piece of work."

"So I've been told."

After that, our food arrived, and there was quiet between us while the plates were arranged on the table. I occupied myself with my food, letting out an embarrassing moan over the deliciousness of the combination of the creamy polenta and tender, buttery scallops. I kept my head bent as I cautiously raised my eyes to Kingston. He wasn't looking at me for a change, but from the smirk on his face, I knew he'd heard my appreciation of the dish he selected for me.

I looked back down at my plate, feeling confused.

Twenty-four hours ago, I'd been crying my eyes out on my living room floor. Now… I was sharing a quiet meal with a man I wished I wasn't attracted to, like the events of the day before hadn't happened.

It was… strange.

But I welcomed it.

"Jackson said you called off work today. But you don't look sick to me."

"I never said that I was," I replied, stabbing a spear of asparagus with my fork.

"Then why'd you call out? You could have had your spa day yesterday, on your day off."

"I didn't realize I needed it until this morning."

"What happened?"

"Not your business, Mr. Investigator."

"You work in my club, so maybe it is."

I rolled my eyes, twirling the vegetable on my fork through a cheesy trail of polenta. "So you're gathering information to rat me out to Jackson? I didn't realize this conversation was between employer and employee."

"It's not. It's between… friends."

I scoffed. "Oh please. Look, I woke up this morning needing to relax, so I called in. Jackson was fine with it. What's the big deal?"

"The big deal is that you're supposed to relax when you're not at work, not get so stressed you need to spend a grand of somebody else's money at the spa."

"Is that why you're interrogating me like this?" I shot back. "Because of the money? Fine, I'll pay *you* back too." I raised the fork to my mouth, snapping the asparagus with my teeth more viciously than necessary. I chewed slowly, trying to prolong the time before I had to say something in response to the fresh stare down Kingston was giving me.

"Too?"

My teeth stopped moving. I swallowed the partially-chewed lump of asparagus, and shook my head. "Just let it go."

Kingston snickered, in a mirth-free way that sent a shiver up my spine, and brought my eyes to his. "That ain't happening. Tell me who you owe money to."

"I'm not telling you shit," I mumbled, looking down at my plate again.

"Is it Dorian Haywood?"

My neck snapped up so fast it hurt. "How the hell do you know that?!"

Just one of his shoulders lifted, in a casual half-shrug that lit another hot fire of rage in me. He reached for his wine glass, took a sip, then said, "Lucky guess. When people are stressed about owing somebody money in this town, they damn sure aren't scared of the bank."

"So his name just *happened* to be the first one you rattled off?" I asked, trying to hold my composure as he gave me another gesture filled with nonchalance. This time it was a subtle shake of his head.

"Oh no, I know quite a bit about your college sweetheart."

My nostrils flared. "We didn't meet in college."

"Ah. I stand corrected. My apologies for the error, but… when you involve yourself with criminals, that association tends to stretch across a lifetime. Criminals are sticky that way. The logical conclusion is that your troubles center around him."

"You don't know a damn thing about my troubles."

"Enlighten me."

"Kiss my ass."

Kingston grinned, then nodded. "Hm. That's okay. I'll just ask him."

I sat up a little straighter at that. "You wouldn't dare."

His grin stretched wider, until he let out an extended laugh that made me clench my fists. "Now… do you *really* believe that?"

No.

I didn't.

In fact, there was very little doubt in my mind that Kingston Whitfield would *absolutely* stick his nose exactly where it didn't belong – between Dorian and me.

"Now," he said, then took another frustratingly casual sip of his wine. "Why don't you go ahead and explain the situation to me, instead of me giving our mutual acquaintance a call?"

I dropped my fork beside my plate and sat back, crossing my arms. Any trace of relaxation I'd found before was gone now.

"My brother is an idiot," I started, then cleared my throat, hating the flood of emotion making my voice tremble. "He got involved with Dorian, and got into debt. I used some money that I had set aside to pay Dorian back so that Ahmad could keep his fingers. Or… hell, his life. Whatever Dorian had decided he was going to take. That's it. You happy now?"

Kingston frowned. "Not at all. You're upset. Why would I be happy about that?" I avoided his eyes as I picked up my wine glass and drained it down my throat, then poured myself another glass… and drained that one too. "What was the money for?" he asked, as I poured a third glass, not caring that I'd emptied the bottle.

"What?"

"You said the money was set aside for something else… what was it?"

I shook my head. "It's stupid."

"I doubt it. What is it? A long vacation somewhere tropical? New place? What?"

I chuckled. "Something much less practical. Poker tournament. If by some… *miracle*, I'd won, I was definitely getting a new place. Somewhere tropical. Far away from Vegas. As far as I could get."

Kingston smiled at me. "A poker tournament, huh? Which one?"

"This one," I said, twirling a finger in the air to indicate my surroundings. "Ace of Spades, here at the Drake."

His eyes went wide. "No shit? Ace of Spades has a fifty-thousand dollar buy-in."

I blinked back a fresh round of tears, and nodded. "Yeah. I know."

"You had it? All of it?"

"Just about."

He let out a low whistle, and sat back. "Damn. And you used it all to pay this debt?"

"Every penny."

Kingston shook his head, then leaned forward again. "You want me to kick his ass?"

"Which one? Dorian or Ahmad?"

"Either. Both."

I couldn't help the smile that freely blossomed, but I quickly brought my wine glass to my lips to suppress it. The buzz of tipsiness was already spreading over me as I sipped again from the cool liquid. "No. It's not necessary. It was a silly dream anyway."

"No such thing. For what it's worth, I think you would have excelled."

I tipped my head. "Yeah, well… we'll never know, will we?"

Instead of answering, Kingston motioned to my plate. "Eat, before your food gets cold."

"I'm not hungry anymore."

He studied me for a few seconds, then nodded. Barely two seconds after he lifted his finger for the server's attention, our lunch plates and the empty wine bottle were whisked away, replaced with a thick slice of decadent chocolate cake with caramel frosting, and a bottle of Port.

"Maybe dessert will change your mind," Kingston said, pouring glasses for both of us from the fresh bottle. As much as talking about my stressors had turned my stomach inside out, the smell of that cake put me back in line, and I picked up the fork, taking a substantial bite.

It was amazing.

The texture was perfect, melting in my mouth almost as soon as my lips closed around the fork. A deep, oaky flavor meshed with the chocolate – maybe bourbon?- and I let out another moan like the one the scallops had earned.

"Glad you like it," he said, the corners of his mouth twitching with amusement before he took a bite himself. "So how'd you meet Dorian?"

I narrowed my eyes, then took another forkful of cake, taking my sweet time to finish before I answered. "Why?"

"Because I'm curious. Obviously."

"Some might call it nosy."

He grinned. "Yes, they might. Call it whatever you want… but answer the question."

"High school," I answered, not bothering to hide my annoyance. "We went to high school together."

Kingston's eyebrows lifted. "Wow… so the two of you go way back, huh?"

"Yep."

"Why'd you break up?"

"I didn't say we dated."

"I called him your college sweetheart, and you only corrected me on the time frame – not the fact that the two of you used to kick it. So… what went wrong? How'd he lose you?"

I shook my head. "That is *so* far from being any of your business."

"That's fine. Just thought I'd ask."

"You shouldn't have."

He nodded. "So… I guess I probably *really* shouldn't ask why you didn't just fuck him and keep your money. A man like Dorian… I'm sure he offered you the option."

For just a second, I was stunned that an inquiry like that had crossed his lips. But I shouldn't have been surprised – getting under my skin with inappropriate things seemed to be a particular source of entertainment for him. I clamped my lips together, saying nothing as I dropped my fork and slid out of the booth to stand up.

Much to my chagrin, the sudden change in body elevation and too many glasses of wine made a bad combination. I was only on my feet a few seconds before extreme dizziness struck me, and I had to grab the edge of the table to stay upright.

Before I could argue about it, Kingston was up from his seat. His arms went around me, and he turned caring eyes down to my face.

"Are you okay?" he asked, and his concern only heightened my annoyance with him.

"I'm fine," I snapped, then further embarrassed myself by almost toppling over when I snatched away from his touch.

His hold around my waist was firmer this time, making me very, *very* aware of the fact that I was naked underneath my robe. "You're drunk. Let me help you."

"I'm not drunk," I argued, as he led me to the back of the restaurant – not toward the entrance. "Where are you taking me?"

"Where you'll be safe until your liquor wears off. This is Vegas. You can't wander around drunk by yourself."

"I'm *not* drunk," I insisted again, and this time I was able to pull myself out of his hold. I wobbled at first, but managed to keep myself upright as I glanced around, realizing he'd taken me to what must be a private entrance – it was quiet, despite the elevator bank in front of us. "Tipsy, maybe. But I've handled myself for twenty-seven years, and I've done alright. I don't need you to protect me."

"I believe you." He shrugged, and pushed his hands into the pockets of his perfectly tailored slacks. "You're a tough girl, Red. I can see that."

For some reason, even though I knew he meant those words as a compliment, they stung. Tough girl. So unaffected, so… *strong*. A term I hated so much it put a bitter taste in my mouth. *Strong*. That's what was expected of me, strength. Take care of your brother while your mother busts her ass at a job to take care of a lazy, trifling man who heaps abuse on his family. Get rid of your abusive father, then play parent to your brother while your mother mourns. Pay your mother's bills when she gets sick, pay your own bills, keep your brother from getting his stupid ass killed. Protect your friend from her abusive ex and weasel your way from underneath a toxic sort of love. Bust your ass for a degree to get a shitty job that barely gets you by. Leave that job for one that isn't shitty, but… has its own laundry list of problems.

Do it all with a smile.

"What if I don't want to be tough?" I asked, my voice thick with more emotion than I wanted him to see. But I didn't have the energy to swallow it. "What if I'm sick of being tough?"

"Then don't be."

TEN

ASHA

He made it sound so simple.

So *easy.*

Like it wasn't a burden I'd been carrying since before I used my first tampon.

I shook my head and turned away, covering my mouth. I was trying not to let out the sob that had been building in my throat, but it broke free anyway. The warmth of Kingston's arms around me made me close my eyes, settling into their comfort. A few seconds later, my eyes popped open as I realized what I was doing.

I laughed as I pulled away from him, crossing my arms around myself. "Maybe I am drunk," I mumbled to myself as I glanced up the hall. "How the hell do I get out of here?" I asked, running my tongue over my dry lips. "I need to get my clothes, and get home."

"You drove?" Absently, I nodded, not looking at him until I felt the touch of his hand on my wrist. "You know you probably *shouldn't*, right? We went through a bottle and a half – more you than me. And that last glass probably hasn't even hit you yet, but will soon."

Sucking my teeth, I pulled away from him again, only to stumble so badly he had to catch me to keep me from hitting the floor. "Di… did you put something in my drink?"

Kingston pulled his head back, but didn't move away from me. "What the fuck? Are you crazy? No, you did this to yourself, knocking back *real* wine like you were drinking damned Lime-a-rita's. Come on."

"Where are you taking me?"

"Upstairs. So you can lay your drunk ass down. And it's not negotiable, so don't bother."

"You can't tell me what to do!" I said, trying to snatch away. But my attempt only made him grip me tighter, and I sucked in a breath as he got in my face.

"Asha," he started, so dangerously calm that it sent a chill through me. "You are woefully mistaken if you think you're about to leave my presence in the state you're in. We're going upstairs and you're going to lay the fuck down until it's out of your system."

Another wave of dizziness almost stripped away my desire to get the last word, but I still managed to retort, "What about my belongings?"

"I'll have them brought up to the room." Before I could come up with anything else, he'd steered me to the elevator, which opened as soon as he jabbed the "up" button. He maneuvered me inside, then pressed the button for the right floor before he deposited me in one corner of the elevator.

He retreated to the other.

"What's wrong?" I jeered, driven to get as far under his skin as he'd gotten under mine. "Scared to get too close without your bodyguard around?"

Kingston chuckled, then swiped the bottom of his chin with his thumb as he shook his head. "Scared of *what*? Of you?"

"Yes."

He laughed louder, folding his arms across his chest. "Why the hell would I be scared of you? You're harmless."

"Ha!" I retorted, so loud that his eyebrow ever-so-slightly twitched upward. "That's how I know you don't *really* know shit about me."

"Are you referring to the little cat fights you've been in? Must not have been too bad, cause you're walking around as a free woman right now." The smile that played on his lips made me narrow my eyes.

"I've done worse."

He scoffed. "Such as?"

The elevator stopped on our floor, and chimed before it opened to set us free. Neither of us moved.

"I watched Dorian beat – almost kill – a man with his bare hands over fifty dollars' worth of coke. Right in front of his family. *Purposely* in front of kids who couldn't have been older than twelve or thirteen. He listened to me. If I'd told him to stop, he would've. But I didn't."

"Why?"

"Because he was killing them. That man… he was bleeding them dry to pay for his habit, and it reminded me of… I decided they were better off. As if it were up to me. With him, I was a person who thought it was up to me."

Kingston studied me for several long moments – for what felt like forever – before he nodded. "That's why you split? Why you didn't want to be involved?"

I opened my mouth to speak, but then the elevator chimed again, and I shook my head. I latched onto the interruption, forcing out a laugh as I pulled myself out of the corner. "What am I even talking about? I'm all over the damn place. Liquor has me…imagining things."

He took me by the arm, leading me off the elevator. "Imagining things. Of course."

I didn't – couldn't – meet his eyes. I'd offered up enough revelations already. The last thing I needed was him looking right through me – something he seemed particularly adept at – and seeing the fresh pain those resurfaced memories had brought about.

Why did you even open your mouth to tell him that shit?

I wished I had an answer for that. Those things that left behind a painful imprint on my psyche were normally kept locked away. My private horrors that I kept to myself, only brought out in my mind for moments of soothing self-injury. Because that's all it was, if I was honest with myself. The memories weren't cathartic, or gratifying. They were the equivalent of cutting my wrists, just with no evidence left behind on my skin, and no knife.

It was sobering.

I was quiet as he led me down the hall to the room – the same room from the night we'd spent together that felt like a lifetime ago, but had barely been a week. He let us into the room, then closed the door, not bothering to flip on the lights. It was early evening, and the sun was still up. The huge, uncovered windows bathed the room in natural light.

Just like the first time, the view caught my attention, but before I could approach the window, Kingston slid the room key into my hand. "In case you need it," he said, then proceeded to point around. "Bedroom is through there, the bathroom is connected. There's ice, water, juice, snacks, anything you need, so you really shouldn't have a need to leave." He reached into the inside pocket of his jacket, pulling out a business card that he glanced at before putting it on top of the room key in my open hand. "If you need to call… call."

I looked down at the thick, elegantly printed black card, quickly realizing the phone number printed on it was his. "Wait… you're leaving?" I asked.

The corner of his mouth turned up. "Yes. Is that a problem?"

"No," I said quickly. "I just… didn't realize." I turned away from him and walked toward the window, hoping my inexplicable disappointment wouldn't show on my face. When he didn't say anything, I turned back, panicking when I saw him heading for the door. Without thinking about it, my hands went to the belt holding my robe closed. "King!" I called, and he stopped, turning to me obvious surprise at the use of his "preferred" name.

I tugged at the belt, loosening the tie, then pulled the robe open. His eyebrows went up as I pushed it off my shoulders, then let it fall at my feet.

"Stay."

My heart rate sped up under his gaze as he raked his eyes over my body. He didn't say anything, just visually drank his fill before met my eyes. I took a deep breath, trying not to squirm. Like with many of my actions tonight, I didn't know why I'd bared myself to him, basically inviting him to…

"Put your robe back on, Red."

I swallowed hard as embarrassed heat rushed to my face. My legs bent immediately, getting me down to the floor to snatch the robe up, covering myself as quickly as I could while avoiding his gaze.

As I turned my back on him, I wrapped my arms around myself tight. From here in the window, it seemed like I could see all of Vegas, and like all of Vegas could see me. Like the whole city had just watched me embarrass myself, and was laughing at my rejection.

"You're intoxicated," Kingston said, from closer behind me than I expected. I closed my eyes as he wrapped his arms around me, pulling me against him so I could feel his erection against the base of my spine. My locs were tightly secured in a bun, and he used that as his opportunity to place a kiss in the bare curve of my neck. I suppressed a moan at the feeling of his soft lips against my skin. "Sleep it off," he said into my ear, "and we can discuss this at a later time."

"I'm *not* drunk." My words came out so forcefully that I surprised myself, but quickly recovered as I turned to him.

"You could barely keep yourself upright ten minutes ago."

"And now I can," I said as I pressed into him. He wanted me…the evidence was poking me in the belly, but for some reason I didn't understand, he was pushing me away. "Downstairs, you were trying to get under this robe."

"And you acted as if you were repulsed by the thought, yet … here we are. Drunk or not, your over-indulgence has you feeling lost, and you think you're gonna find yourself on my dick. And then once we're done… it'll be a regret. I'm trying to protect you from yourself."

"Don't."

I let out a gasp of air as he eased me backward, into the cool wall of glass that was the window. His hand went to my neck, gentle but firm as he glided his thumb up my throat, using it to tilt up my chin.

I met his gaze and didn't back down. I wanted him to see the clarity in my eyes, to know that even if it was pathetic, and the opposite of the front I'd put on before, I knew what I was doing, and exactly what I wanted.

Him.

His mouth suddenly collided with mine. But maybe… collided wasn't the right word – he'd just caught me off guard. There was nothing forceful about the fleeting caresses of his soft lips against mine. His tongue flicked out, traveling the seam of my mouth like he was tasting me, and then he closed both lips over just my bottom one. Then the top. And then his tongue was in my mouth, tasting me there too, in unhurried swipes that made me light-headed.

He pressed his body against mine, sandwiching me between him and the window and he continued a kiss I could only think of as… *indulgent.* The sweetness of wine and chocolate cake lingered in his mouth, and I savored it, keeping my eyes shut tight as I let myself get wrapped in the moment.

In no particular hurry, his hands drifted down, pulling open my hastily-tied robe and pushing it off my shoulders. His lips never left mine as he gripped my ass, using his hold to lift my feet off the ground. He pressed a powerful thigh between mine, using it to keep me up, and free his hands. He kissed a trail from the corner of my mouth down to my neck – a sudden absence of his lips that I hated until I felt the sensation of his tongue on my neck and his thumb on my clit at the same time.

Then, I was lost again, brazenly rocking against his hand, fully aware and fully indifferent to the mess my wetness was creating on his thigh. His teeth grazed my neck at the same time his fingers plunged into me, crafting another dual sensation that sent my synapses into a frenzy. I clamped my hands on either side of his face as he brought his mouth back to me, not wanting him to leave again. I lapped my tongue into his mouth like I was starving, because I *was* starving, and his mouth, and fingers, and whatever else he was willing to give me… they were the oasis where I was getting my fill.

Sweet, blissful pressure coiled and twisted in my pelvis as his teeth grazed my bottom lip just before he pulled away from the kiss. My eyes were still closed, but his weren't. I could feel them on me – deep pools of molten chocolate hungrily watching as pleasure played out on my face. My lips fell open, thighs shaking as he circled his thumb on my clit harder, pushed his fingers deeper. I was… *shit*, he had me so hot I felt like I was on fire, on the verge of melting right through the thick glass pane behind me. If he made one more circle, plunged those thick fingers just one more time, I was going to explode, and it was going to be *exquisite.*

But he didn't.

The sudden removal of his hand was a jolt to my system, and my eyes popped open as he let down his thigh, lowering my feet back to the ground. My fingers pressed to the window, steadying me as confusion took over. He caught my gaze, holding it for a moment before he simply turned around, casually ambling toward the bedroom, leaving me wondering what the hell had just happened.

I followed him.

He was facing away from the door, and had draped the jacket to his suit over the chair that stood in the corner. His hands were at his neck, unknotting his tie, and for a moment I was spellbound by the sight in front of me.

When Kingston turned to me, tie undone and draped around his neck, he wasn't smiling. He was… smoldering.

I went to him quickly, without really thinking about it. Standing in front of him – him mostly dressed, me… not – I felt exposed, but unafraid. My fingers shook as I raised them to his neck, carefully undoing the buttons of his shirt until I couldn't reach the ones that were tucked in. I ran my tongue over my lips as I unbuckled his simple, but undoubtedly expensive belt, then undid the hook of his pants.

His dick was right there behind his boxers, hard, thick, and straining to touch me, but I finished the task at hand – the shirt. I undid his cufflinks, placing the heavy cobalt accessories on the bedside table. I pushed it off his shoulders and let it fall, admiring the smooth copper skin that had been hiding underneath. Even without being "ripped", his body was beautiful to me. No tattoos, just unblemished red-brown skin, poured over a tall, toned frame.

Just like I remembered.

I reached for his pants, but he caught me at the wrists, stopping me. He moved to that chair in the corner and sat down, motioning for me to come to him, and I did. I stood between his open legs, then blinked in surprise when he bent to untie the sturdy-bottomed spa booties I'd forgotten I was wearing. I'd barely stepped out of them when he grabbed me around the waist, pulling me until my shins bumped the front of the chair, and then hiked one of my legs up over his shoulder.

I gasped as his mouth covered me, his tongue immediately going to work. I pitched forward as pleasure shot through me, grabbing his free shoulder to keep myself up. My nails dug in, damn near breaking the skin as he sucked my clit into his mouth, lapping it with his tongue until my thighs began to shake. My inner walls clenched in frenzied response to the sudden onslaught of pleasure. I planted my other hand on his head, trying in vain to push him away. It was too, too much at once, but he wouldn't stop. My mouth opened for a moan, but nothing came out – his fingers burrowed into me, snatching away my breath as he hooked them forward.

"*Ohh my.... Oh my God!*" I cried, as the steady waves of an orgasm began to build. My fingers dug into his scalp and shoulders as that pressure peaked, and peaked, and then… dissipated, as he pulled back, taking away his fingers, leaving me empty again. "What the *fuck*?" I hissed, as he let my leg down from his shoulder.

The only answer I got was a smirk as he eased me backward, and stood, moving around me to take off his shoes.

Tears of frustration pricked my eyes as he, completely casual, put his shoes in the corner near the chair, then picked up his shirt from the floor. Pissed, and tired of the games, I reached for his pants, again. And again, he caught my wrist.

With one hand, he tossed his shirt into the chair, but somehow kept the tie. He draped it over his bare shoulder and then released my wrist, using both hands to reach behind me, undoing my bun.

Then he lifted the tie to my eyes.

My apprehension was only brief, killed by the softness of his lips on mine as he tied the silk around my head. I kissed him back greedily, only growing further aroused by the taste of myself on his tongue.

This time, when my hands went to his pants, he let me do it. I pushed them down, then dropped to my knees in front of him. I was blinded, but my fingers were sure as I reached up, feeling until I found the waistband of his boxers and pulled them down.

His smell made my mouth water.

The scent of his cologne blended beautifully with the naturally earthy-clean smell of *him.* I took him in my mouth, moaning over the velvety-smooth feel of him against my tongue. I didn't waste time teasing – I was going to do to him what he'd done to me twice now. I sucked him hard and fast, sloppily taking him to heaven's door, where I planned to leave him. Only… his grunts and groans of pleasure were so gratifying. His hands gripping my locs was so pleasingly erotic, the salty taste of his precum such a reward that I kept telling myself that the *next* suck was going to be the last.

I reached up, gently gripping, massaging his balls in my hands.

"*Fuck*," he grunted, and I hummed with pleasure at the effect I was having on him. The blindfold had slipped, and I looked up, past the plane of his stomach to find him watching me, and I held his gaze. He blinked away, shaking his head as he muttered something I couldn't hear.

I knew he was right on the verge when he gripped me hard enough to keep me still, pumping into my mouth.

Stop him, Red, I told myself, but my body didn't respond to the command. Instead, I massaged him harder, closed my mouth tighter, lathed him with my tongue.

Suddenly, he tore away from me, bending to rip me up from the floor. He practically tossed me onto the bed, climbing on top of me with the swift agility of a panther, moving my legs apart before he sank into me with a firm, hard stroke.

He didn't move back. He pinned my arms above my head on the bed and stayed there, staring at me with an intensity that made me clench around him.

He sucked in a breath, looking away from me as he closed his eyes for several seconds then turned back to me, shaking his head. "You are so…*fuck*," he cursed, blowing out another harsh breath as he looked away from me again.

"So… *what*?" I breathed, grabbing his face in my hands, turning it down to make him look at me. "What?"

He stared at me a little longer, then shook his head again before he slid out of me. "I have to get a condom," he said, then moved to make good on those words, while I laid there thunderstruck by the fact that I hadn't even considered – or cared – about protection.

When he hadn't returned to the bed after several moments, I sat up on my elbows and looked around, finding him a few feet away, with his wallet open in his hands. He wasn't looking at it though – he was looking up at the ceiling as he took deep breaths, like he was trying to settle himself.

A few seconds later, his gaze drifted down, landing right on me. He pulled a condom from his open wallet without looking, then tossed it aside, keeping the condom in his hand. His eyes stayed on me as he stalked back over to the bed, discarding the wrapper on the bedside table beside his cufflinks.

He situated the condom on his dick, then used one hand to roll it on. His other hand wrapped around my ankle, dragging me toward him. My heart was racing when he pulled me upright, pressing a soft kiss to my lips before he pulled the luxurious silk of his tie back down over my eyes, and tightened it.

"Scoot back," he said, in a tone that let me know it wasn't a request. I did as he asked, using my hands to move backward, back into the place where he'd left me. "Open your legs." Was his next demand, and I followed that too.

And then… nothing.

It was a little disconcerting, knowing that he was seeing all of me right now, in the broad daylight streaming through the windows, and I was seeing none of him. He hadn't left – I could feel him in the room still, could feel him watching, and drinking me in, even though he wasn't saying anything. He *had* to know it was messing with my head.

"Say something," I whispered.

His response of "Something." came from somewhere near my feet, and then his hands were on me again. He lifted my foot, and I let out a surprised peep when my toes entered the warm, wet heat of his mouth. My back arched up from the bed as his tongue hit erogenous zones I didn't even know I had.

Logically, I knew his mouth was on my feet, but I felt it between my legs. He sucked my toes one by one, licked between them, kissed me from the ball of my foot to my heel, then to my ankles, and up my legs.

With the blindfold on, everything was heightened. His cologne and my arousal filled my nose, and very, very faintly, maybe from the hall, there was music. I could still taste him in my mouth, salty and manly and perfect, and the *feelings*... my God.

My nerve endings were on fire. Hyper-sensitivity soaked my skin, and every part of my body seemed to be on high alert. Every place his lips touched was blissfully scorched, every brush of his fingertips branded me with pleasure. He kissed his way up my thighs, taking the time to engulf my pussy with long, slow swipes of his tongue. By the time his lips pressed my belly button, I was panting.

If I didn't come soon, I was going to burst.

He nibbled at the undersides of my breasts, with little nips that were painfully, torturously good. His whole hand covered one breast, gripping and squeezing while he sucked my nipple into his hot mouth. Tears built behind my eyelids as he suckled me like he was hungry, in the perfect blend of pleasure and pain. He switched sides, doing the same thing for the other before he came up, lining his mouth up with mine.

His dick was between my legs. *Right there*, pressed against my opening, but he didn't push inside. Blindly, I reached up, feeling for the soft layer of hair that decorated his jaw, cupping his face in my hands again.

"Earlier... you started to say something. You said I was so... so what, King?"

He smiled – I could feel it under my fingertips. My mouth fell open in a gasp as he sank into me, burying himself as deep as he could go. "So..." he started, pausing as he pulled out of me, then sank back in. "Beautifully," he continued, on another stroke, speaking right against my lips. "Refreshingly..." That time, he mumbled into my neck, then sucked so hard it would surely leave a mark. He moved his mouth up to my ear, nipping my earlobe as he plunged into me again. "Fucked up," he whispered.

And then his mouth was on mine, kissing me so deeply it snatched my breath away. I locked my legs around his waist as he stroked me. Long, hard strokes that filled the room with the steady "*smack, smack, smack*" of skin on skin as he massaged my mouth with his tongue. Finally, he pulled back from the kiss, coming to my ear again as our hips rocked together.

"That wasn't an insult, by the way."

I managed to nod, then breathe, "I didn't take it as one."

"Why not?"

"Because I know exactly why it turns you on."

He stopped stroking, and I could feel his eyes on my face, even though I couldn't see him. "And why is that?"

I flexed my inner muscles, purposely clenching around him to elicit a groan. "Like attracts like. You're fucked up too."

He didn't respond – verbally, at least. His mouth crashed onto mine as he pumped himself into me, unlocking my legs from his waist and pushing my feet up above my head.

"*Shit!*" I cried, squeezing my eyes shut behind my blindfold as he took full advantage of the complete access to my body, burying himself so deep that his hips were flush against me. For what felt like the hundredth time, pressure coiled in me, but this time it seemed to come from a different, deeper place. Almost as soon as I recognized it, it combusted, and the orgasm hit me with a roar that made me scream.

My whole body tensed, and my senses flooded with color. For a long moment, it was like I couldn't even breath, and then everything hit me in euphoric swells that made me gulp as they washed over me.

King drove into me one last time, with a heavy growl that sent an aftershock of bliss through me. My nails dug into the tension of his shoulders, and he relaxed right underneath my fingertips as he released, collapsing on top of me after he let my legs down.

I didn't try to take off the blindfold.

Didn't even try to open my heavy eyelids.

King's head was resting on my breasts, arms tight around my waist. I felt… light. Boneless, and unburdened, and exquisitely gratified.

And exhausted.

I was perfectly happy to let sleep take me. On the way, my fingers absently stroked the smooth skin along King's back, until I reached a long, raised scar on his shoulder. Vaguely, I thought to ask him about it, but his soft snores kept my lips closed, until I drifted off too.

When I woke up, I was alone.

ELEVEN

KING

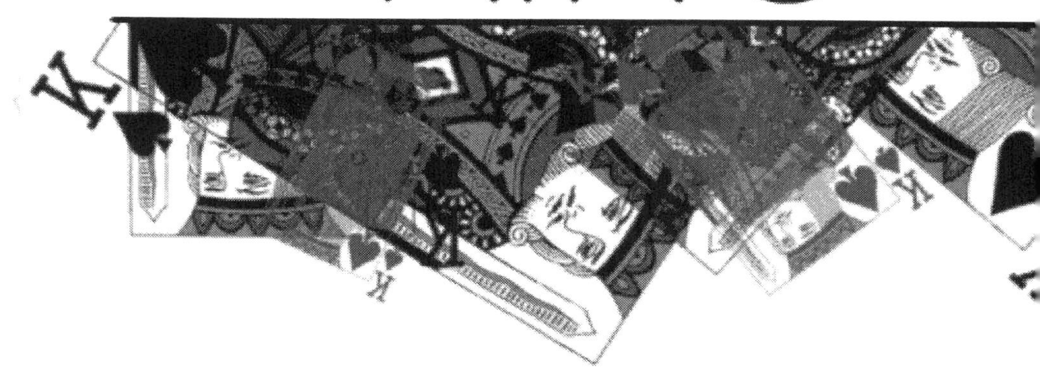

This wasn't supposed to happen again.

Again.

I was supposed to have learned my lesson the first time, about a woman I couldn't seem to keep myself away from, with her fucked up past, tough girl façade, and unintentionally blatant sex appeal.

Turn around and get far away – that's what I knew from experience that I should do this time. I shouldn't get any further involved than I already was, and yet…I couldn't help it. It was as if the knowledge that I *should* leave Asha Davis alone made it that nearly impossible to do.

But… I thrived on challenge.

Two days had passed since our second rendezvous at the Drake, and I'd successfully avoided seeking her out. I cringed over the fact that such a weak thing was an accomplishment, but I had to take my victories where I could find them. I hadn't looked for her at the club, hadn't asked Jackson to send her to my section, none of that.

Too bad that didn't keep her from invading my thoughts.

"Are you going to pull your head out of the clouds long enough to play or what?" I glanced to my right, at my friend Braxton Drake, who'd been the one to speak up. Around the table, all eyes were on me, and I wondered how long they'd been waiting.

This game wasn't unlike the one Asha had conned me into losing. Same room and all, just with different players. Braxton and Lincoln Drake, Steph Foster, Tariq Evans, Brandon Jensen, Avery Anderson. All long-time friends, gathered for our yearly game.

"Check," I said, allowing play to move forward, but after they played their cards, every set of eyes at the table came back to me. "What?"

Across from me, Steph chuckled. "You *know* what. We recognize this from last time."

I frowned. "Recognize what?"

"The same distant ass look you used to get on your face when you were thinking about Robyn," Braxton drawled, and the whole table went quiet, until I let out a dry chuckle.

"Talk about something else," I told Braxton, rubbing my jaw as it twitched with annoyance.

"Damn," Lincoln, his twin, chimed in. "Still a sore subject?"

"Always fucking will be. Why wouldn't it be?" I looked him right in his eyes, then glared at everyone around the table. "Y'all are my boys, but don't *ever* bring that shit up. Talk about something else."

There were a few more beats of silence over the table, and then Lincoln told a joke and everybody relaxed again, continuing to play the round.

"So," Braxton said, as he folded his hand, tossing his cards away. "Let's talk about the last minute tournament entry that happened two days ago then."

Shit.

That was before I resolved to keep my distance.

"Nah." I rubbed my jaw again. "Not that either."

Half the table laughed, and Braxton shook his head. "Fuck you, King," he chuckled. "You can't call everything off limits nigga. Who is this Ashley David chick?"

"Asha Davis," I corrected, and I could feel the collective smirk around the table. He'd baited me, and I went for it. "She's… a talented poker player."

"I've never heard of her," Tariq chimed in, after he'd folded as well. "Not too many black women on the professional poker circuit."

"She's not professional yet. Wants to be."

Braxton scoffed. "Man, ask something important. Like, what does this woman look like? How do you *really* know her? Because the only reason I even paid attention to the shit is because Reverie is *sponsoring* this woman. So… yeah. Spill the beans mothafucker. You're knee deep in it, aren't you?"

"There aren't any beans to spill," I maintained, and as far as I was concerned, there weren't. "She works here, and I've seen her play. She's good."

A grin spread across Steph's face as he pushed more money into the pot. "Works *here*? As in, the casino, the hotel…?"

"As in... *Dream*. Here in the club."

A collective whistle went around the table, and several men shook their heads. Avery chuckled a bit as he pushed in enough chips to match Steph's bet. "So, what you're saying is, this woman is fine as hell. Because otherwise…"

"She wouldn't be working *here*," Lincoln finished, with the words that were on everyone's minds. "So… she one of the dancers?"

"No."

I kept my answer short and simple, hoping they would let the shit go – even though I knew better. To my dismay, the subject of our conversation brought herself around the corner into the room barely thirty seconds later.

"Bartender?" Brandon asked, and I shook my head.

"Just stop talking and play the damn game."

I spoke those words to the whole table, but my eyes were on Asha. She wore a simple, sleeveless black dress made of fabric that flowed loosely around her body, clinging to her curves as she moved toward us with a tray of drinks. She kept her gaze on her tray – purposely avoiding looking at me – and started handing out the glasses backward, instead of starting with me as she should have.

She was flustered – I could see it in her eyes – but she held herself together. Her smile was flirtatious, her demeanor warm as she charmed my friends while handing out drinks.

It pissed me off.

I wasn't at all amused by the long glances at her thighs, the double-takes at her ass as it swayed under that deceivingly sexy dress, just… the attention she was getting from these married-or-almost-married men in general.

"Come on," Lincoln said, after he'd taken a sip from whatever he ordered. His eyes were still on Asha as she bent between Avery and Brandon to put down a coaster, then place a glass on the table. "It won't take us anything to find out. You may as well go ahead and tell us. You can't let us know that Reverie's first sponsored poker player works here at the club, and then *not* tell us which one she is."

"What?"

Asha had handed out all the drinks except one. Mine was the only glass left on her tray as she froze where she stood, her eyes rooted on me, waiting for an explanation.

"Get out," I said, and her eyes went wide as I stood up. I raised a hand, halting the move she was already starting to make. "Not you. *Them*."

"Us?!" Steph asked, then laughed as he looked around. His eyes landed on Asha, and then understanding must have dawned on him. "Oh, shit is this her?!"

"Get the fuck out!" I growled.

"Nigga, relax, we're leaving," Tariq chuckled as he stood, gathering his chips. "We see you need to handle things with uh… are you Ms. Davis?" he asked, and Asha nodded.

"You're Tariq Evans… Kora Oliver's husband, right?"

He shook his head as the group laughed. "Damn, it's like that? That's all I'm known for now, huh?"

"I'm sorry," Asha blushed. "It's just, my roommate is obsessed with your wife. Not like, in a creepy way. She's a really big theater fan."

I cleared my throat, which got another laugh as the rest of the group started toward the door.

"Ms. *Davis*," Braxton said, licking his lips as he raked Asha with his eyes. "I will certainly be looking forward to watching you… compete."

"I will fucking choke you, Brax." I was dead ass serious, but leave it up to them to brush me off, taking their time to actually leave, dropping slick comments along the way. A moment later, it was just me, Ace, and Asha in the room. I turned to Ace, who was giving me a look I couldn't decipher. "Give us a minute," I said, in a low voice.

She raised an eyebrow. "You sure about that?"

"She's harmless."

Ace scoffed. "You think so?"

Incredulity twisted my mouth into a scowl. "What, do you think you're going to step out of here and she's going to kick my ass or something?"

She rolled her eyes. "Of course not." She glanced at Asha, who was still standing across the room, looking stunned, then moved in front of me, lowering her voice even more. "It's not your *ass* I'm concerned about getting kicked."

“I do *not* need protection from this woman,” I snapped, annoyed by the insinuation.

Ace scoffed. “The fact that you think I’m talking about *physical* protection tells a different story.”

I frowned. “What the hell are you… just say what the fuck you have to say Alicia. I have business to handle.”

“We’re family, right? Not just employer and employee?”

“You know that shit already.”

She nodded. “Then as your family, I’m telling you… don’t be foolish.”

With that, she walked off, leaving me just as confused as Asha looked. I quickly recovered though, and approached Asha, who was still holding her tray tightly in both hands. I casually took my drink, then walked back to the poker table, perching against the edge.

“What can I do for you, Ms. Davis?”

My direct address seemed to pull her out of whatever was happening in her head. She ran her tongue over her deep red lips as she finally lowered the tray, tucking it against her side. “Um… *Reverie’s first sponsored poker player*?” she said carefully, but still stumbled over the words, almost like she was scared to say them out loud. “What is… who is it?”

I raised my glass, taking a long draw before I spoke. “Who do you think it is?”

She shifted on her feet, lips parted for a moment before she clamped them shut again and shook her head. “I… I don’t even know what it means.”

I nodded. “It means that, as a casino, Reverie is sending a player to the Ace of Spades tournament at the Drake. We cover the entry fee, endorse the player under our name. It’s good publicity for Reverie, and it helps legitimize the AOS tournament. Good business all around.”

“Yeah,” she said, her voice still shaky as she moved closer to me. “I could see that.”

I finished my drink, then ran a hand over my chin. "So was there anything else?"

"Who is Reverie's player?"

I suppressed a smile over the way she asked that question, scared and hopeful at the same time, eyes glossy with tears. I took a deep breath, trying to calm the clamor of whatever the fuck was happening in my chest from seeing her like that.

"You are," I said. "If you want to be, that is."

The tray hit the ground with a loud clatter, and Asha swiftly covered the distance left between us on impossibly tall heels. "Of course I want to," she gushed, wringing her hands as she stood less than a foot from me. "What would… what do I have to do?"

I frowned. "Play poker…"

"No, I mean… to be able to play. Is it like a loan, or…?"

"What?" I shook my head. "No, it's not a loan. And you don't have to do anything, it's already done. Your name is on the roster."

"So… I'm going to play in Ace of Spades?" she asked, like she still barely believed it.

That time, I couldn't help the smile that curved the edges of my lips before I nodded. "Yes."

She staggered backward a little on her heels as she put a hand to her mouth to choke back a happy sob. Reflexively, I reached for her to help her steady herself, but instead of accepting the assistance, she threw her arms around my neck for a hug.

"Oh my God. *Oh my* God!" she mumbled into my chest several times before she finally looked up, meeting my eyes. I didn't realize how close we were – that I'd opened my legs to let her step between them – until she cupped my face in those soft hands of hers. "Nobody ever… nobody does things like this for me," she whispered.

I gripped the edge of the table to keep myself from touching her. It had been hard enough to stay away when I could keep her at a distance, but having her *right here…* was torture. I bit back a groan as she leaned in, pressing her mouth to mine. She pushed herself right against my groin as she grazed her tongue over my bottom lip, tracing it before she slid her tongue between my lips.

Shit.

The alluring warmth of her pussy was pressed right against my dick, separated by nothing but the thin layers of our clothes. I clenched the table even harder, fighting the need to grab handfuls of her ass, and somehow haul her even closer as her tongue danced in my mouth.

"Thank you for this," she said when she finally pulled back, with a stream of tears running down her cheeks. "You have no idea what this means to—"

"It's not personal," I interrupted, clearing my throat. I moved my hands to her waist to ease her backward, then stood from my perch at the edge of the table, turning my back to hide the obvious bulge of my dick. "It's a good investment for the casino. That's it."

Heavy silence blanketed the room as soon as those words crossed my lips. A few seconds that felt like hours passed, and I turned to see Asha standing exactly where I left her, her expression a mixture of hurt and confusion that made me feel like shit.

Which I deserved.

"Oh. Yes, right," she nodded, then quickly swiped the tears from her face. She avoided my eyes as she went to pick up her tray, not looking at me until she was near the hall that led to the door. "Well… thank you for the opportunity, still."

"You're welcome." I picked up my drink glass, empty except for the large, round ice cube that took up the center. Asha had it out of my hands before I could even say anything about it, and was already turning to leave when I caught her arm.

One look at her face told me she was right on the edge of something I didn't want to unleash, so I let her go. "Would you like a refill, Mr. Whitfield?" she asked, her voice edgy.

"No, thank you. We'll be in touch about the tournament though."

"Great."

I didn't stop her when she took off down the hall, faster than I thought was possible on those heels. As soon as she was out of sight, I scrubbed my hands over my face, trying to shake off whatever had my chest feeling tight.

Fuck.

"So I see you *didn't* take my advice," I heard from behind me. I looked up, and shook my head as Ace came strolling back into the room, hands on her hips. "What the fuck happened? Why did she seem so upset?"

I shrugged. "Exactly what *needed* to happen – a pulled plug."

"Oh, is *that* what needed to happen?"

"Goddamnit, Ace!" I roared, throwing my hands up. "Stop with this sarcastic bullshit and say whatever the hell it is you've got to say."

"You're an asshole," she shrugged, crossing her arms. "*That's* what I've got to say. If all you were going to do was play with her emotions, you should've left her alone after the first time."

"I'm not playing with anybody's emotions."

"*Bullshit*," Ace hissed, jabbing a finger in my direction. "You know, I thought she was just another piece of ass to you, which I never say anything about, because I know you. You're not warm and cuddly, but none of these women can say they weren't treated well. So she worked here... *fine*. You could have acted like the shit never happened – not like it would have been the first awkward situation your dick led you into. But no. You had to poke, and prod, and... play strip poker. And had me dig up her past, and you bothered her at the spa, and you slept with her again, Kingston! All the time you've spent either around her, or finding out *about* her, and I'm supposed to believe nobody started getting in their feelings?"

"I've known this woman existed for less than two fucking weeks!"

"And what exactly is your point?" Ace asked, tipping her head to the side. "You're *obviously* drawn to this woman, and it's about more than sex. She's damaged, and you just can't help yourself."

I grunted. "You know what, Ace… I give you a lot of room, cause we're homies—"

"Let me stop you right there, before you get wherever you're going," Ace snapped, catching me off guard with the emotion in her voice. "We're not like *homies*, you're like a damn brother to me, so don't you *dare* tell me I'm out of line with this. *You're* out of line. A one-night stand is one thing. Everybody knows what's up. But you don't chase a woman you don't want, especially one… like *her.* You hurt her fucking feelings, King, and the shit is foul. To think… I was worried about it happening the other way around."

She didn't give me a chance to respond before she stormed off, leaving me on the bad side of yet another woman tonight.

Ace had been through her share of shit with men, and I'd messed around and reminded her of one. She was projecting, and I fully understood that. But… it didn't change the fact that she was right.

It *was* foul. But that didn't make it any less necessary.

The sooner Asha and I had a boundary in place… the better.

"Are you sleeping with this woman?"

My father had never been a man to waste words talking around an issue when he could address it head on. When he'd called to arrange this meeting, he hadn't said what it was about, but I had a hunch.

A correct one.

I was surprised it took this long for him to address it. I'd submitted Asha's name three days ago, and it had gone under the radar until last night. Early this morning, I'd gotten the call to meet my father at Whitfield Inc. and now here I was… a grown ass man, sitting in the principal's office.

"Currently… no."

Across the desk, my father leaned back in his chair, shaking his head. "I should've known there was something convenient about this sudden sponsorship of a poker player, when we've never done such a thing before."

"My sleeping with her has nothing to do with it."

My father raised an eyebrow. "Now see *that* is interesting. I understand doing a favor for a beautiful woman. You take care of her, she… takes care of you. That's just how it works. But if you're *not* sleeping with her… why the favor?"

"It wasn't a favor. She didn't even know I was going to do it."

"So… it was a gift, then. What makes a man give a gift to a woman he isn't sleeping with?"

"It's not like *that* either."

He smirked. "Okay. Explain it to me then. I'm all ears."

Immediately, I opened my mouth to clarify to my father exactly how there was nothing personal about me creating a sponsorship around Asha. Only… there was nothing I could say that would make it make any type of sense.

At the time that I'd submitted her name, it seemed like the only thing that made sense to do. I was on the balcony of my suite at the Drake, enjoying the glass of Mauve I'd poured after leaving Asha sex-drunk and passed out in the bedroom. I could practically still feel her wrapped around my dick, and maybe *that* had influenced me. Maybe her sweet scent lingering in my nose had fueled my fingers as I moved through the registration process from my phone. Perhaps the memory of her tears made me call it a sponsorship instead of paying for it outright, which I had no problem doing. I just didn't want there to be an implication that this would mean there was anything she owed me.

I wanted her to feel taken care of.

And she had, obviously. Before I pushed her away, that kiss had said it all.

"Look," I said, trying to deflect. "It'll be a positive thing for the casino. We're endorsing a female poker player – women will love it. More importantly, *black* women will love it. We're supporting one of our own, and in turn, they'll support us. And you know, anywhere that women are in Vegas, *men* are in Vegas, buying drinks, stuffing money down the slots, showing off at the blackjack tables. It's good for business."

My father nodded. "Oh, I've already explored all of that, son. And if those numbers hadn't added up, I would already have shot this plan in the head. Luckily for you, it does. But back to this … Asha Davis… have you checked her out yet?"

"I have."

"Before or after you slept with her?"

I sighed. "After."

"Of course."

A low, annoyed groan slipped from my throat before I could help it. "Dad…"

"Son." He chuckled. "I know you didn't think I was just going to let this slip by, did you?"

"I'm holding out hope, actually."

"Well you can put that away. Your mother is worried about you, and she's not alone."

I frowned. "Worried about me why?"

"She's concerned that your wife has left you irreparably altered. She was never a fan of Robyn, and after everything that happened… her disdain was somewhat prophetic, don't you think?"

"I'd rather not…"

"We have to do and face things we'd rather not all the time. It's all in how you handle it, son. But in any case… we know how things with Robyn turned out, and what the aftermath of that was – self-destruction."

I scoffed. "I'm pretty sure *your* head would have been fucked up to if *your* wife had—"

He raised a hand, and out of respect I stopped speaking, swallowing my words with a clenched jaw. "You're right, son. I may have been ready to lose it too, had I found myself in your shoes. You don't have to defend that. That's not what this conversation is about."

"Then what *is* it about?"

"You, right here, right now. The wildness of your scouting trip around the world was widely reported. You broke one of Randall Beauchamp's ribs, and who do you think had to clean *that* mess up? And now, you publically affiliate our casino with this woman whose past is checkered, to say the least."

I narrowed my eyes. "The two of you *encouraged* me to live it up on that trip to get my mind off the shit with Robyn. I didn't want to touch Randall Beauchamp – the motherfucker squared up, so I knocked him on his ass. And I'm not sure what Asha's past has to do with anything."

"If you looked her up, you should know the answer to that."

"Enlighten me."

He smirked. "Okay, so you want to be petulant. How about instead of that, you tell me if her involvement with Dorian Haywood is fueling your interest in her."

"Absolutely not. I didn't even know about it until later."

"But it certainly didn't stop you from pursuing her further."

"I'm *not* pursuing her," I snapped, standing up. It was time for this meeting to end. "She wanted to be in the tournament, and caught a bad break. I had an opportunity to help her out, so I took it. Why is it such a big goddamned deal?"

"Because of Robyn."

I blew out a harsh sigh. "Why does everybody suddenly want to talk about Robyn? Why can't I go without hearing that fucking name?"

"Because your sudden interest in this new woman is… familiar. We've seen this, remember?"

"Asha is not Robyn."

My father nodded. "Yes, Alicia was very clear about that as well," – my jaw tightened – "and before you get upset, she didn't betray your confidence in any way. I have my own sources – even at the Drake. But she assured me that Asha is a very different woman than Robyn was. Despite their similarities in background."

I shook my head. "I'm not sure why the hell you think it matters anyway."

"Well that should be obvious. If you're going to be involved with this woman—"

"I won't be," I interrupted. "So can we call this conversation closed? My only dealings with Asha Davis will be as an employee of Reverie Casino and Hotel. Nothing more."

He studied me for a long moment. "You're sure about that?"

"Positive."

After a few more seconds of thoughtful scrutiny, he nodded, but I knew better than to think he was done with the subject. It was just going on hold.

"Okay. In any case, we'll need to meet her. Your mother has already been making calls. We'll need to get her in for a trial, to see where her skills are, and possibly put her with a coach. There will be interviews, she needs head shots, all of that, if we're going to turn this young woman into a poker star."

I nodded, then reached across the desk to shake my father's hand.

"I'll let her know."

TWELVE

"He says he expects to see *you* next time."

I froze where I stood, earring post pushed halfway through my ear as my brain processed Ahmad's words through the speaker phone. Absently, I shook my head, then finished putting the earring on as I switched back to auto-pilot to finish getting ready.

"Did you hear me?"

"Yes!" I snapped, taking a second to close my eyes. "Dorian wants me there at the next payment. I hear you. I got it."

Shit.

It wasn't enough that we were being blackmailed. Of *course* that wasn't enough. I knew Dorian on a level that I should have expected him to want to inflict the most distress he possibly could. He knew I didn't want to be around him, knew I wanted to keep my distance. In his mind, the only sensible thing to do was to force my hand.

"I'm sorry about all of this, Ash," Ahmad said quietly. The obvious distress in his voice made me put down the mascara wand I'd picked up. As pissed as I still was…a large part of me hurt for my baby brother. "I'm trying my best to make it right."

I swallowed the bitter words I wanted to cut him with. "I know you are. Playing taxi cab through an app? Never thought I'd see the day."

Ahmad laughed, but it was weak. "Yeah… quick, easy money that I can supplement my job with. And I've got something else in the works too. Might fix all of this."

My nostrils flared as those words set off alarm bells in my head. "Ahmad, what the hell do you mean, *something else in the works*? The last thing—"

"It's nothing like that," he interrupted, then pushed out a frustrated breath. "I'm just… I'm *trying*, Asha. I wouldn't do anything like that, after the mess we're in now. It's legal."

I huffed. "There's plenty of shit to get into in Vegas that's legal, but will still leave your ass in trouble."

"It's not trouble Asha, damn!"

"Then what is it?!" I snapped back. "And I suggest you take some of the goddamned bass out of your voice, or *I'm* gonna break your fucking fingers myself. I paid enough for them, hell. Those are my fingers."

On the other end of the line, Ahmad smacked his teeth. "Will you chill? I'm keeping it on the low in case it doesn't pan out, but I promise you, it's legit."

"Like you *promised* you could handle yourself? Like you *promised* you wouldn't get in any more trouble?"

"You don't *have* to keep drilling me, you know? Yeah, I've fucked up, but I get it Ash, I swear I do. I'm not *trying* to let you down. You think I don't recognize how much you've done for me?"

I let out a bark of laughter. "It damn sure doesn't seem like it."

"Well, I do. I just… *fuck*, man." I closed my eyes as Ahmad's voice broke. "I'm going to make this right. I don't know how, but… I swear I will."

Shaking my head, I snatched several squares of tissue from the roll, using them to carefully dab the tears from my eyes so I wouldn't ruin my makeup. "Don't sweat it, Ahmad. Just… *please…*"

"I know. I *know.*"

On the counter, my phone chimed, and I picked it up to see that I'd received a new text. I rolled my eyes at the message, then started packing away the contents of my makeup bag.

"Ahmad, I have to go. I love you, okay?"

"I know. I love you too."

A few seconds passed, and then I said, "Stay safe."

"I will."

"Okay. Bye."

I ended the call, then took my time in the mirror, mentally checking off a list to make sure everything was perfect. My locs were pulled into a neat bun, and my makeup was natural. Minimal jewelry, conservative three-inch heels. The silk tank I wore underneath my sleeveless sheer blouse kept it from being revealing, and I'd chosen the wide-legged black pants specifically because they fit well, without calling too much attention to my ass.

I looked like I was heading to an interview, and… I kinda *was.*

An insistent knock at the door pulled my attention away from the mirror, and I grabbed my cell phone and clutch from my dresser before I headed out. Camille was in the kitchen, earbuds in, probably blasting the music from her next show in her ears as she fixed herself breakfast.

I ignored the knocking to get her attention, letting her know I was heading out. She pulled out her earbuds and grinned at me.

"Where are *you* going looking like you're about to teach a first-grade class?" she teased, stepping out of the kitchen to look me over. "You must have found this *way* in the back of your closet."

"Whatever," I laughed. "For your information… I found it in the middle, thank you very much."

"Sure you did." She went back to the stove, picking up a spoon to stir her oatmeal. "You look cute though. You hungry? I can share…"

I shook my head. "Nah, too nervous to eat right now."

"Nervous about what?" she asked, eyes wide.

I still hadn't told her about Dorian, or Ahmad, *or* about Reverie sponsoring my way into the poker tournament. She'd been so busy rehearsing that she hadn't even realized the entry deadline had passed, and I wasn't about to burden her with any of that, not while she had a premiere on her mind.

"I'll tell you later," I said, glancing at the door as the knocking started again. "Right now, I have to go."

"But you'll be at the show, right?"

I frowned. "Uh, *duh*. I wouldn't miss it for the world."

The knocking got louder, and we both frowned at the door.

"I've got it," I told Cam, shaking my head. "It's for me. I'll see you later, alright?"

I pulled the front door open without checking the peephole first, and closed it behind me as Camille called out her goodbye. I glared at Ace, who glared right back, but I wasn't flinching today.

"Could you act like you have some sense next time you come to knock on my door?" I asked, locking it before I started for the stairs.

"Yeah," she said, from right behind me. "As long as you answer in a timely manner."

Without turning around, I rolled my eyes, silently wondering if I could get away with tripping her. At the bottom of the stairs, she got in front of me, leading me to a sleek black escalade. As we approached, the driver stepped out, coming around the side to open the door for us.

First, my eyes went wide over the fact that the seating in the back had been converted to limo style. Then, I saw who was in the back seat.

"Do I need to sit back here and mediate?" Ace asked, smirking as she leaned against the side of the vehicle.

"I would assume you can sit wherever the hell you want to," I snapped, then accepted the driver's hand to help me inside. I took the seat that wasn't right across from Kingston, so I wouldn't have to look at him, then strapped myself into a seatbelt. I angled my body toward the window as Ace climbed in, taking the seat beside me. The door was closed, and a few moments later the driver was back in his seat, and we started moving.

Desperately, I hoped that neither of them could look at me and know that my heart was racing. I'd known that I was being picked up for this meeting, known that I would be meeting Kingston's family – because they ran the business of the casino, known that it was likely that I would be seeing him.

I *hadn't* known that he'd be personally picking me up.

Don't you fucking dare, Asha, I silently cursed myself as a lump built in my throat. If I'd known he would be in the car, I could have mentally prepared myself for the surge of hurt and anger coursing through my chest. As it stood… I felt just as sucker-punched now as when he'd looked me in my face and told me that the most meaningful thing anyone had ever done for me "wasn't personal".

He couldn't have known how intensely that would wound me.

That's what I told myself all that night, and all the next morning, and that's what I told myself now. Sure, he'd eased his way behind my carefully erected wall with no intention of following through. Sure, he'd sexed me in a way that people who weren't in love had no business doing. Sure, he'd – apparently – decided that it ended there, and decided to give me a parting gift, and *sure* his declaration that the gift "wasn't personal" was delivered in an unnecessarily callous manner. After I made myself vulnerable.

It was shitty of him.

There was *no* denying that.

As pissed as I was, as much as I wanted to mush him in his smug, gorgeous face, I *had* to believe that he was simply… pushing me back into my lane.

He couldn't have known it would cut me so deep.

There was no way he realized the implication – no, the ugly reality – that I was so underserved by the people who were supposed to love me that a gift could mean nothing to him, and at the same time, mean everything to me. He wasn't *really* saying that my vulnerability, my company, my offering of my body, was worthless to him. It was impossible – *had to be* - that the butterflies in my stomach, the electricity when we touched, the passion when we kissed, and the intensity of the connection I felt when he was inside of me, was all one-sided.

Unless…

"Are you hungry?"

The sound of his voice pulled me out of my thoughts, and though I'd intended to ignore him, I was caught off guard enough to look his way, meeting his gaze. I was used to warmth, and energy in his eyes. Today, they were flat.

I looked away without answering.

"Asha," he said, his voice stern. "I asked you a question."

Frowning, I angled my body even further away, turning to the window as much as I could. Beside me, Ace sighed, then tapped my arm.

"What?" I asked, not taking my gaze away from the cars we were passing outside.

"Have you eaten anything?"

"Yes," I lied, hoping it would quell any further questions. "I'm fine."

I was relieved when my fib actually worked, and they left me alone. I settled back into my seat, and stared absently out of the window, letting my mind drift as we moved. It wasn't until we stopped that I realized we weren't anywhere near the downtown building I'd expected, and were instead in front of what appeared to be a private home.

A *huge* private home.

I tried not to let my confusion show on my face. Maybe we were picking someone else up. But that notion was quickly squashed when the door was opened, and King, followed by Ace, climbed out. Ace stopped at the door, turning back to me with an expectant look in her emerald-toned eyes.

"You coming or not?" she asked, eyebrow raised.

I unclipped my seatbelt, and eased out. "Where are we? I thought we were going to the Whitfield building?"

She shrugged. "We are, kind of. This is Whitfield Manor. Daniel moved the meeting here, because Angela woke up with a migraine, but insisted on attending anyway. He's trying to keep her at home."

My confusion must have shown on my face, because Ace grinned. "Daniel and Angela Whitfield – King's parents. This is their home."

She said it like it was no big deal and then walked off, motioning for me to follow her. Kingston had disappeared somewhere.

Inside, the grandeur of the entrance briefly snatched my breath away. Elegant twin staircases flanked a huge foyer, rising up from the sparkling white marble floor. An intricately detailed chandelier hung from the arched ceiling, situated perfectly over the "W" crest engraved in the middle of the floor.

I shook my head. I knew the people had money, but this was… *damn.*

"This way, Asha."

I looked up from the floor detail to see that Ace was across the room, motioning for me to come on. I quickly caught up, following her into what I soon realized was a conference room. Ace stepped out as soon as I was inside, and closed the door behind her. I pulled my shoulders back, holding my head high as all eyes in the room fell on me.

Here we go.

I forced myself not to roll my eyes as Kingston approached me, taking me under the elbow to steer me to the front of the room where everyone was gathered.

"Asha, this is my father, Daniel Whitfield," he said, taking me first to a man who looked so much like him it was startling. Same illustrative eyes, sculpted jaw, nose, and cinnamon-toned skin. I took the hand Daniel offered, and he greeted me warmly, with a smile.

"It's a pleasure to meet you, young lady. I trust Alicia and King took good care of you in getting you here this morning," he said, covering our clasped hands with his other one as he looked me right in the eyes.

I brought a smile to my face, hoping it didn't look like a grimace. "Yes, of course. I have no complaints sir. And it's very nice to meet you too. Thank you so much for this opportunity."

Something flashed in his eyes, and a bit of a smirk played at the corners of his mouth. "It wasn't my doing. You should thank my son here."

"She already has," Kingston cut in, before I could respond. If I wasn't mistaken, there was a distinct note of censure in his tone, which only deepened his father's smirk before Kingston pulled me away, introducing me to the other men in the room – the Reverie shareholders.

They were all a blur to me – older men of varying ethnicities who all proclaimed interest at meeting the first sponsored player for the hotel. That whole "*first*" thing was honestly baffling to me. I never played at the Reverie, since I worked there and didn't want any problems. If this year was going to be their debut at the tournament, why not pick one of the regulars at *their* poker table?

Why me?

Obviously, I had an inkling, but when I reminded myself that it "wasn't personal"… that's where the confusion started to creep in.

"Asha, meet Thomas and Trei Nichols," King said, gesturing to a duo with strikingly similar golden-brown skin, thick curly hair, and dark gray eyes. The only prominent difference between the two men was the fact that Thomas had a sexy, distinguished, salt-and-pepper effect happening with his hair and facial hair, while Trei was obviously younger.

"Pleasure to meet you Ms. Davis," Thomas said, giving me a vigorous handshake. "I wasn't sure what to expect when I was informed a *woman* would be representing the hotel, but I'm hoping to be won over."

I frowned. "What an… interesting thing to say, Mr. Nichols. Do you think that women can't play poker?"

"Again," he grinned. "I'm hoping to be won over." He gave me a nod before he walked away, and I turned my attention to who I assumed was his son.

Trei's gaze was focused on something over my shoulder, but as I started to turn to see what it was, he spoke. "I'm sorry, beautiful. Excuse my bad manners. Trei Nichols," he said, extending his hand in my direction. I accepted it, thinking he wanted to shake, but instead he clasped my hand, lifting it to his mouth to kiss the back of it. "Pleasure to meet you."

I couldn't help it – I blushed.

Trei – and his sexist daddy, for that matter – were handsome men, and those gray eyes set off the tiniest bit of a flutter in my chest. Plus… Kingston was standing there staring a hole in the side of the man's head.

I stepped in a little closer, and let a flirtatious smile linger on my lips. "The feeling is mutual, Trei."

He grinned back, and a deep, intense surge of satisfaction rushed through me as King's murderous gaze shifted to me. I acted as if he wasn't even there, clasping my hands in front of me and angling myself away when Trei released my hand.

"Well, well… who do we have here?"

An unfamiliar female voice made me turn around, and I came face to face with another favoring duo – women this time.

Behind me, Kingston cleared his throat before he stepped up. "Asha, this is my sister Zoraya," – he motioned to the younger of the duo, a woman with the same red-brown skin tone as him, but with softer, almost delicate features, and a mass of dark brown curls that rested around her shoulders. Trei had moved to the side, and was practically panting over her – "And my mother, Angela." – high cheekbones accented a face that was similar to Zoraya's, except set in smooth mahogany skin. Her face was framed by a sleek, chin-length bob with a thick streak of gray running through the front. "Ma, Zora, this is Asha Davis. Our player for the Ace of Spades tournament."

Both women's eyes went wide.

"Oh *my*," Angela said, smiling as she grasped my hand and squeezed, then circled around me, looking me over like I was up on the auction block. "What a *wonderful* canvas to work with. Right, Zora?"

"Mmmhmm." Zora's smile wasn't quite as warm as her mother's, but she repeated the action of circling me to scope me out. "Very pretty. She's sexy, even though she's dressed like she's going to interview for an office job."

"We'll work on that." Angela stopped in front of me, smiling. "You know how to get a man's attention, don't you? You work in the club."

I started to nod, but Zora spoke before I had a chance to. "Of course she does. His majesty over there has his nose wide open over her. And… I get it. She's fine." She moved into place beside her mother, and crossed her arms. "Tell me something, Asha… can you actually play poker, or do you just have my brother pussy-whipped?"

"Zoraya!" Daniel growled from a few feet away. "Keep your voice down!"

She shrugged. "What, Daddy? Don't act like everyone in this room isn't thinking the same damned thing. Everybody in here is grown, so let's put it out there. Mama wants to be hands on with this, because she's excited about sending a message to women, or something, and she asked me to help. We need to know what we're working with."

I shook off the nervousness that had plagued me since I walked into the house, and looked Zora right in her eyes. "You want to know if I can play? Get a dealer, a deck of cards, and your wallet in here and I'll show you."

"Ooooh!" Zora squealed, shimmying her shoulders. This time, her smile was full and bright as she leaned in. "Don't get too sassy with me girl, I bite. And that means *exactly* what it sounds like," she said, giving me a wink before Kingston stepped between us.

"Stop it, Z," he said, sounding more exasperated than stern.

She laughed. "What's wrong baby brother? Scared I'm gonna steal your new pussy and treat it better than you?"

"You're not gay…"

Zora sucked her teeth. "What's your point?"

"That's enough, Zoraya," Angela said, putting a hand on her shoulder. "Asha, I apologize for my daughter's mouth, but… she's right. I love to see young women succeed, so when I heard about this, I insisted that Daniel let me take the reigns as far as the optics of your participation in the tournament. Keeping that in mind… I *do* need to know how you play."

"That's not a problem at all, Mrs. Whitfield."

She waved a hand at me. "Please, it's Angela. Now, let's get this meeting going. I have no intention of taking up your day."

At Angela's word, the meeting was called to order, and I quickly realized that being the "first lady" of this family did *not* mean that she simply sat back and reaped the benefits. It was clear that she was respected around the table, and when she said she was in charge of something, she meant it.

Through the course of the meeting, I learned several important things – first of which was that they wanted me to stop working at the club. It wasn't that I was losing my job, they just wanted my primary focus to be poker, which led to the second thing – they wanted me playing at the Reverie tables.

According to them, I needed to work on some name recognition as quickly as I could. They didn't want the players who *did* play at the Reverie rumbling about my appointment being undeserved. In the two weeks between now and the tournament, I needed to be taking their money.

Which led to the third, and perhaps most important thing.

If by some miracle, I won the overall title… the money was mine.

I didn't even have to pay the entry fee back.

Of course, there were contractual obligations and such. I would go into the tournament and play my best, I wouldn't get drunk and pee on the table if I lost, or anything stupid like that. They would use my name and image for advertisements, so on and so forth.

But if. I. Won.

I was ready to sign on the spot.

But, if my years playing poker had taught me nothing else, I knew how to play it cool. No official announcement had been made to the public yet, so I asked if I could have some time to think about it and they agreed to three days, under the condition that I would move forward with some playing time at the Reverie poker tables.

That agreement was sealed with a handshake.

I walked out of Whitfield Manor feeling like I could fly, and climbed into the same Escalade from before, only it was empty this time. The driver closed the door behind me and I buckled my seatbelt, settling in for the drive back.

Then the door opened again.

Ugh.

I should have known that getting to ride back alone was a little too much frosting on what was almost a perfect cupcake.

I wasn't surprised to see Kingston climb in, but I *was* surprised when he closed the door. I continued what I'd started this morning – ignoring him – expecting that the door would swing open again, revealing Ace on the other side.

That's not what happened.

The driver got into the front and started the engine, and then a partition rolled up, separating him from where Kingston and I sat in the back.

"Are you happy?"

I rolled my eyes, keeping my head turned toward the window. "Sure, I guess. Why do you care?"

"Because you're going to be representing my family's company. Why wouldn't I care?"

A bitter laugh broke from my throat before I could stop it, and I shook my head. "We don't have to talk, you know? I'm perfectly content to just sit here in silence."

"You don't want to talk to me?"

"No," I snapped, as the car finally started moving. "I want you to leave me alone unless it's directly related to my employment."

He scoffed. "You can cut the attitude. I'm just trying to be polite."

"Yeah, don't bother." I finally turned to him, only to find him already intensely focused on me. "Don't be nice to me, don't give me any more gifts, don't present yourself as a shoulder to cry on. Don't do me any more favors. I wouldn't want to get confused, start thinking anything is personal, you know?"

"Asha—"

"*Leave me alone.* Please."

Déjà vu smacked into me as those words left my mouth. I closed my eyes, not even caring about, or hearing what Kingston said in response. I tuned it out, wrapping my arms around myself as I turned back to the window, trying not to let myself get lost in ugly memories.

When the Escalade pulled up in the parking lot of my building, I couldn't wait to get out. I quickly unhooked my seatbelt and tried to open the door on my side without waiting for the driver, so I wouldn't have to maneuver past King's legs.

It wouldn't budge.

“Child lock,” King said, grinning when I turned to glare at him.

Shaking my head, I slid to the side, stopping at his legs. “Excuse me.”

“I’ll talk to Jackson for you. Until you’ve had a chance to think about the terms.”

“I can talk to Jackson myself. I don’t need you to do that for me. I was perfectly fine before you showed up, and I’ll be perfectly fine now that you’ve moved on. Don’t bother lingering. Excuse me,” I said again, more firmly this time. He stared at me for a short moment, then shook his head before he moved, letting me out.

I didn’t respond to the goodbye he called out, or look back.

“See, that wasn’t so bad, was it?”

I looped my arms through Jackson’s, staying close to him as we headed out into the lobby of the crowded theater. When he didn’t answer, I looked up to find him still wearing the same stupefied expression he’d worn through most of the show. I grinned, turning to face him as we stopped near the entrance that led backstage.

"Jax!" I called again, waving a hand in his face. That time, I got his attention.

"What's up?"

I sucked my teeth. "I was trying to ask you what you thought about the show…"

I'd won a bet about who was going to win the NBA final last year, which was the only reason I'd gotten Jackson into this theater. The tickets had been free, and I wanted to prove to him that not all of the year-round shows in Vegas were corny.

Especially not the stuff Camille did.

"Your friend," he said, in a tone that was damn near dreamy, shaking his head. A fresh smile came to my face. As much as he'd protested about coming, from the time Camille hit the stage, Jackson was completely enthralled – him and everybody else in the audience.

Before she made it to the strip, Camille had danced in several different high-end clubs, much to her brother's dismay. But that experience had paid off – on the big-budget, high production quality stage, Cam shined. The songs and burlesque dance routines told a story, and her voice and movements added the sound and imagery to bring it all to life.

She was the lead, so everything revolved around her. Her all white costumes were the most intricate, she showed the most skin, she was always center stage. She *commanded* attention.

And she certainly had Jackson's.

"I have backstage passes," I told him, hooking arms with him again. "The two of you should meet."

A few moments later, I was showing my pass to the security guards, and we were walking into the meet and greet the theater company had put on after the show. When I spotted her, Camille was talking to someone else, but she excused herself once I caught her eye.

"You made it!" she exclaimed, rushing to pull me into a hug. "How was it? Did I do okay?"

I rolled my eyes. “Did you do okay? Girl, *please*. You were amazing! Tell her, Jackson.” I turned to him, and Camille did too, seeming to notice him for the first time. If there was a facial expression for wet panties… Camille was wearing it.

“Red is absolutely right. You were… *incredible*,” he told her, in a low voice I’d never heard him use with *anybody*. “I’m Jackson.” He reached for her hand, and she gave it to him, but he didn’t shake it. He held it in his. “Your friend and I work together at *Dream*.”

Camille nodded. “Yes,” she practically purred. “So I’ve heard. Are you joining us for the cast party later?”

“I actually have to get back to the club tonight,” Jackson said, releasing her hand – something that left Cam looking a little disappointed, and *me* confused. I didn’t know that. “It’s my job to keep it all going smoothly. I left it with my assistant manager to come see the show, but I can’t be gone too much longer.”

She nodded. “I understand that, a man about his business.” Her eyes came back to me, and I could tell she felt the same thing that I’d picked up – Jackson had brushed her off, though I didn’t understand why. “I need to mingle. Asha, we’ll talk at home?”

I gave her another hug before she moved on, then grabbed a glass of champagne from a server who was passing by, and took a sip as I looked around to give her time to get away before I started grilling Jackson. Before I could, a familiar face caught my eye.

I immediately downed the rest of my champagne, then started looking for an exit. I didn’t want to see, or talk to Kingston again after this morning, so *of course* he was here.

And he wasn’t alone.

Inexplicably, my eyes went back to him when I noticed there was a woman on his arm – a gorgeous, golden-skinned woman that had her hand on his chest, laughing at something he’d said. I narrowed my eyes, glaring at him.

Bastard.

It was annoying as hell, seeing him so… happy.

"Hey," I heard from behind me, and turned around. "You ready?"

"Jax!" Just that quickly, I'd forgotten he was there. "Hey, what was up with you blowing off Cam like that?"

"I wasn't blowing her off. I just… have to go."

I nodded. "Uh-huh. I'm not really buying that, but we can go."

I grabbed his arm, remembering that King was there, but then he said "I just spotted somebody. Hold on."

Shit.

Next thing I knew, I was right in front of Kingston Whitfield, getting an up-close view of the beauty I'd seen with him before. I stood there trying not to stare at her, at him, or at anybody else as Jackson and Kingston greeted each other.

"I love your hair," she said to me, smiling. "That deep red is gorgeous."

Caught off guard by the compliment, I choked at first, but quickly recovered. "Thank you. I love yours too. The short cut is beautiful on you."

"I got lucky then, I guess. I cut it all off to spite my asshole of a husband, and decided I liked it."

"What are you over here saying, Nash?" Kingston asked, in a playful tone that sent my irritation through the roof.

She grinned at him. "Nothing but the truth."

He shook his head. "Nashira, this is Jackson, my head manager at Dream, and that's Asha… the poker player Reverie is sponsoring for AOS."

The woman – Nashira, apparently – let a little gasp, and her mouth turned into a little "o" for a moment before she clamped it shut. "So *this* is the woman I've heard so much about."

My nostrils flared. "Whether or not it's true depends on who you've been listening to," I said, with a pointed look at Kingston, who smirked.

“Jackson, Asha… this is Nashira Haley, president of Warm Hues theater. They’re the ones who produced this show.”

Beside him, Nashira sucked her teeth. “Stop trying to be funny, asshole,” she scolded Kingston, swatting him on the shoulder. “My divorce is final, and I don’t care about any of that “keeping my name for professional reasons” bullshit. My name is Nashira *Drake*.”

“As in… *The* Drake… casino resort?”

She smiled, and nodded. “Yep, that’s me! Well… my *family*. Good luck in the tournament, okay? You’re one of very few women… and the *only* black one. I’m rooting for you.”

“Thank you so much. Are you ready now?” I asked Jackson, feeling more and more uncomfortable about how nice this woman was being to me. It was easier to plan on hating her when I could imagine her as a bitch. Jackson confirmed that he was ready, and I turned back to Nashira. “It was nice meeting you. You guys enjoy your date.”

Nashira reeled back like I’d thrown something in her face. “Date?! No! King is here with his mama, I’m just talking to him until she gets back from the restroom.”

“Oh!” I said, feeling my face grow hot. “Well, still… good night.”

I didn’t dare look at Kingston. I already knew he’d be wearing that smug ass smirk, and I just wanted to get away before I couldn’t avoid it.

“Good night,” he called after us, and I rolled my eyes. Jackson and I parted ways in the parking lot – him heading to the club, me heading back home.

Closed and locked inside my quiet apartment, I took a long shower and climbed into bed, spreading the documentation of my contract with Reverie on top of my covers. The loss of my money still stung, but I would be lying if I said that having this opportunity at my fingertips didn’t make it a little better.

If only it didn’t mean a continued connection to *him.*

My face got hot again as I thought about the "date" comment I'd made. Was it obvious that I was… *ugh* ... jealous? There was no point in denying to myself that it was jealousy that made me mad at a woman I didn't know, just for being around him. The thing I couldn't pinpoint was *why*.

It wasn't like I wanted him.

He was handsome, and witty, and rich. All appealing qualities. But he was also an asshole, and an asshole. And, an asshole. And then there was the little fact that he was an asshole.

Factoring that in, I had no *reason* to want him.

My mind drifted to the watch in my nightstand drawer, and I got annoyed with myself all over again. Here I was holding on to something I could be using to pay off this stupid debt to Dorian, all because I felt some connection that obviously wasn't reciprocated.

Hmph.

I was calling that jeweler bright and early in the morning.

I gathered up my documents and put them back in the folder. Of course I was going to sign, but I'd think about it a little longer first.

I put the folder on top of my nightstand, then turned off the lamp and closed my eyes.

A few seconds later, I flipped the lamp back on, and opened the drawer.

The watch was, as I remembered, heavy in my hands, and the diamonds sparkled brilliantly, even in the low light. Despite my anger, a part of me still felt bad for even considering selling it to someone else, when I knew he wanted it back.

Why this watch? Why is it important to him?

I rolled my eyes at myself. Why should I ever care to know anything further about him? I couldn't get it out of my mind though, and on a whim, I picked up my phone and brought up my web browser, navigating it to google.

Why is this important to him?

I thought about it for a few moments, sifting through the reasons that people gave sentimental value to things. After turning it over in my head, I typed out "Kingston Whitfield diamond Rolex gift" as my search term.

The first search were results were ads, and links to sites that sold watches. After the first page though, I ran into something interesting – a message board that seemed to be for local pawn shops, which were a huge part of the Vegas scene.

There, I found out that Kingston's people had apparently put out the word that anybody who accepted a particular watch – the one I had in my possession - was to contact them immediately. I had no doubt that all the jewelry stores in Vegas had gotten the same message.

He wanted the watch back, and I was going to make his ass pay for it.

I was giddy just thinking about how much I might get for the watch as I scrolled down to read a few more posts, which led me to something even more interesting –

"Look at the watch, then look at his wedding pictures from about 7-8 years ago. His father gave him that watch as a gift for taking an official position with the Whitfield corporation, right before he got married. He mentioned it in an interview. He's probably going to pay big bucks to get it back... I wonder how he lost it?"

While the knowledge of who had given him the watch was notable, and explained why he wanted it back, that wasn't what stuck out most to me.

"Married?" I mumbled to myself as I read the message back, then opened another tab in the browser. This time, my search term was *"Kingston Whitfield wife"*.

I swallowed hard as I waited the two or three seconds for the web page to load the results, and when it did, I almost dropped the watch, and the phone.

The first search result, from almost three years ago according to the tiny date stamp under the link, took my breath away.

"Robyn Whitfield, wife of playboy billionaire Kingston Whitfield, death ruled a suicide."

THIRTEEN

KING

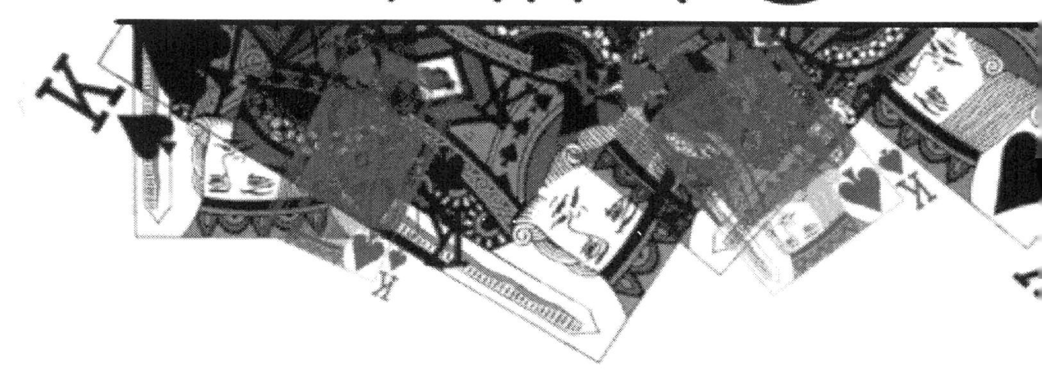

Leave me alone. Please.

Those words were fucking with me to the point that I couldn't get them out of my head. As hard as she'd tried to appear all tough and unaffected, the truth was in her eyes – I'd fractured something.

And it was fucking with me.

Sweat dripped into my eyes as I jabbed at the heavy bag. On the other side of it, Ace was in workout gear too, looking noticeably alarmed as she held it still. I was on edge, and she knew it, but this was the better alternative.

Something was going to get fucked up, either the bag, or… somebody's face.

I actually had a few candidates in mind, and I was rotating their images in my head as I worked myself toward the point of exhaustion. It wasn't just *other* people either – I was pissed at myself, for this thing with Asha.

She was right. She was perfectly fine before I came along, messing with her head. I *knew* that, even before she said it. Knew I should do exactly as she asked – leave her alone – but for whatever reason… I couldn't seem to help it.

I didn't *have* to be in the car when she was picked up for that meeting with the Reverie shareholders, or when they took her back. Yet there I was, insinuating myself into her life, even though I knew better.

I threw another blow at the bag, so hard that it went careening backward, and Ace cursed under her breath as she fell.

"Planting your fucking feet," I barked, and she glared at me as she pulled herself up from the mat.

"Or, you could just go see a goddamned therapist, because *clearly* you have some unresolved issues you need to work out."

"What do you think I'm doing now?"

She cut her eyes up at the ceiling as she grabbed the bag again, nodding when she was ready for me to hit it. "I think you're in here trying to kill yourself cause I wouldn't let you kill ol' boy."

"And I'm still pissed at you about that," I told her, relishing the way my fist popped back every time I landed a punch on the bag. "He deserved that shit. You should have let me do it."

Behind the bag, Ace laughed. "I know you think so, but I promise… killing people changes you. Good guy, bad guy, whoever. You just don't recover from it."

"You'd know, huh?"

I stepped back a bit, and Ace's face peeked out from around the bag before she nodded. "Yeah, I do. You're a brawler, King. And an asshole. That combination is bothersome enough. Don't become a killer unless you have to – and if you ever *have* to… you'll understand why I saved you from it."

"Guess I'll have to take your word for it for now."

She sucked her teeth. "Okay, kill that "for now" shit. Just take my word for it, and come on over here and keep pretending this bag is Bas's face, okay?"

"Gladly."

I didn't waste any time hitting the bag again, and again, doing exactly like she said – imagining it to be Sebastian Gray's face. Ace had never trusted the man – rightfully so, as I later found out – but she'd somehow found it in herself to pry my hands from around his neck.

Well… she *tried* to pry my hands from around his neck. When that didn't work, she'd resorted to other methods. But in any case… she hated him enough that if she said her actions had been saving *me*, not *him*, I believed her. And, I thanked her for it, after some convincing that she hadn't been trying to kill me herself.

Not to mention, the whole *not* being in jail for murder part worked out pretty well. Still though… it bothered me to no end that Sebastian's soul was still on this earth, instead of hell, which I considered more appropriate.

One day.

One day, I was going to make good on what I'd started, but for now, the punching bag would have to do. I poured all of frustration into my fists, and by the time I finally stepped away, my shoulders were on fire and my clothes were soaked in sweat, but… I felt a little lighter.

A little.

I left Ace in the gym to get her own workout in, while I went to take a shower. She preferred solitude, so she could get into whatever killer headspace helped her develop the dangerous vibe she put off to other people, and I… needed to be alone as well.

In the shower, I turned it up as hot as I could stand, letting the damn-near scalding water dig into my aching arms.

Leave me alone. Please.

That shit came to mind again, and I shook my head, but this time I couldn't get it to go away, couldn't keep the memory from materializing. Asha had been the one to speak those words to me, but the memory that took over my brain and wouldn't let go wasn't of her.

It was of Robyn.

"What's up with you lately?" I asked from the doorway, my eyes lingering over my wife's bare breasts and stomach, then drifting lower before I brought them back to her face. "You've been...distant."

She shook her head as she wrapped herself in her towel.

Why is she showering in the middle of the day like this?

"Nothing, my love. Just a little stressed."

The crisp edge of her slight accent made the lie even more discordant, even more exaggerated to my ears. The art gallery had a manager now, and I'd taken her books from red to black. She had a driver, a bottomless bank account, and anything else she might possibly need.

And she had me.

What the hell did she have to be stressed about?

I approached her from behind as she stood at the bathroom mirror. Wrapping my arms around her, I pulled her into me, pressing my nose to the back of her neck.

"We should go out," I murmured, then kissed a patch of deep brown skin that was still damp from her shower. "Dinner, a show, whatever you want to do." I kissed her ear, then met her eyes in the mirror, waiting for her response.

She looked frazzled.

"Uh... can I have a rain check, my love?" she stammered. "I'm really tired, and I feel a headache coming on. I want to be fully present, and energized with you if we go out. I don't see that happening tonight."

I narrowed my eyes. "Of course, beautiful." I smiled at her reflection, but that fearful look didn't leave her eyes. "I want you to be... energized as well. So..." I turned her around to face me, planting my hands on either side of her against the counter. "Next time you meet with Sebastian Gray... you tell him I said... leave you a little energy, okay?"

Robyn's expression broke into complete panic. "Kingston, it's not—"

"No." I delivered that word with a firmness that made her clamp her mouth closed. "You just deliver that message... okay?"

I walked away, intending to leave her in the bathroom to live with whatever guilt my words inspired.

"Kingston! Whatever you think is happening—"

"Whatever I think is happening?!" I bellowed, turning back to face my beautiful, terrified wife. Who the fuck was she so damned scared of? Me? For fucking what? "Do you really *want to have that conversation now? With your stress, and your headache, and your lack of energy? Do you?"*

"No," she whispered with glossy eyes as she shook her head.

I shook my head too, approaching her again. "Nah, let's talk about it. Let's talk about your lying, and sneaking around, and—"

"No," she said, louder this time.

I raised my shoulders, feigning confusion. "Oh, no? You sure, baby?"

She looked away from me, looking at her reflection in the mirror. "Just leave me alone. Please." She turned back, meeting my eyes for barely a second before she closed the bathroom door.

"Fuck!" I smacked the side of my fist against the tiled shower wall, and the resulting pain had the desired effect of clearing my mind. I hated moments like these, where my thoughts drifted to her, because they were never the fond moments. It was always, invariably, the ugly stuff.

I loved the hell out of Robyn, and I chose to believe it was reciprocated. Only through love could we have created the poignant memories I had to dredge up from the recesses of my mind, since they never snuck up on their own.

This was one of those places where I contradicted myself, because a smart man would have recognized my subconscious burying of positive interactions with Robyn as course-correction. My brain was trying to tell me something, despite my refusal to listen.

My wife was a liar. She took advantage of her proximity, using it to manipulate me. One way or another – I was still working on coming to terms with the fact that I'd never get that answer – she had betrayed me.

These were all truths I didn't know until after the fact. I didn't learn her motives until after I learned the truths, and… her reasons didn't change their veracity. It haunted me that she never had to answer for any of it, didn't have to live with the consequences.

But I did.

I shut the water off and climbed out of the shower, drying off before I pulled on a pair of boxers. A freshly pressed suit was already waiting for me at the dressing table in the closet, and I was tucking my shirt in when Ace appeared at the entrance, already dressed for the day.

"You have a visitor," she said, with a note of tension in her voice that made me raise an eyebrow.

"Did I have an appointment?" I asked, sliding my belt through the loops in my slacks.

She shook her head. "No… police usually don't make those."

My hands stilled over the belt buckle. "The police? Regarding…?"

"I don't know. He wouldn't tell me," she said, crossing her arms as she leaned back against the doorframe. "Bastard."

I chuckled a little, then picked up my tie, looping it over my shoulders as I moved in her direction. "Let me guess… Cree Bradley?"

Instead of answering, she rolled her eyes and walked off, leaving me to trail her through the house, into the large front entrance where my visitor was waiting. He had his back to us, admiring the large canvas that hung in the area. From a distance, it appeared blank, but close up, you could see the white, scented wax it'd been embellished with, creating an image spoke to me.

"Detective Bradley," I called out, as I finished with my tie. "What can I do for the LVPD today?"

He turned around, pushing his hands into his pockets. "Not much, actually. We don't have any beef with you. *Police Nationale*, on the other hand…"

I frowned, but before I could speak, Ace stepped forward. "The French police? What the fuck do *they* want?"

His mouth twitched as he studied Ace for a moment longer than necessary, like he was trying to discern something from her question. "I asked myself the same question before my boss called me to sit in on a phone conference with some somber motherfucker speaking that *voulez-vous* bullshit. Apparently, somebody has been harassing Sebastian Gray," he said, then gave me a pointed look.

I exchanged glances with Alicia, who smirked, and then I raised an eyebrow when he didn't say anything after a few moments had passed. "I'm waiting on you to explain why I should give a fuck about that. Somebody is harassing that piece of shit, good for them."

Detective Bradley sighed. "Come on, man. You know why I'm here."

"No, I don't. Make it plain."

"Are you behind it?"

I lifted a hand to stroke my chin, pretending to think about it. "Hm… can you tell me what happened?"

"Pig guts on his front door, threatening voice mails, being followed by suspicious cars, hacked emails. The usual."

I nodded. "That doesn't sound like fun for him at all. Which… makes me pretty happy. Thank you, Detective. I needed this news."

"Cut the bullshit, Whitfield," he said, taking a step closer to where I stood. I didn't get the impression that it was meant in a threatening manner, but I'd barely blinked before Ace was between us, staring him down like she dared him to take another step.

Down girl, I thought, but didn't say. She hadn't pulled a weapon yet, which meant she was cool. This was just her way of letting him know there wasn't going to be any bullshit.

Detective Bradley sighed as he looked her up and down, then propped his hands at his waist as he turned to me. "Just answer the question. Are you behind the harassment, or not?"

"If you had *anything* beyond an accusation, you wouldn't be here interrupting our morning," Ace said, her voice deceptively pleasant.

He scoffed. "I'm here as a courtesy, ma'am. Not trying to create a problem."

"Then don't," she shot back, stepping dangerously close to the man's personal space. "Unless you have a warrant of some sort, you can leave."

"Sweetheart," he said, leaning a little closer to her. "I'll leave when he answers my question. Not until then. So if you don't mind, the grown-ups are trying to have a conversation."

Oh, shit.

I grabbed Ace's hand as she moved it to reach for something that definitely would have turned this into a problem. Pulling her back, I stepped in front of her, keeping my hand on her wrist. "I don't harass, Detective," I said, giving him what he was looking for. "I don't play those type of games. If I wanted to get at Sebastian Gray… I'd get at him."

"But… you *did* get at Sebastian Gray. When he was living here in Vegas."

"There's a police report that says that?" I asked, and the detective's jaw tightened. "Right," I nodded. "I didn't think so."

He grunted. "But the fact remains that you beat the shit out of the man, and left him for dead. But you didn't finish the job. Is that what this is? You warning him that the time is near?"

"Not in the slightest. Tell old Bas' he's going to have to go to the next name on the list of people he's fucked over to figure out who's after him. Pig guts on the front door? Sounds like… I don't know… police corruption or something to me."

Detective Bradley chuckled. "I'll keep that in mind. But, according to that phone conference, Sebastian seemed pretty adamant it was you. And from the story that was relayed to me… you may not want to hear it, but I'm inclined to believe it. A man can do some pretty serious things when he finds out another man is fucking his wife."

I tightened my grip on Ace's wrist as she fidgeted behind me. We both knew me holding her wasn't physically keeping her from doing anything, but in deference, she played along, even though it had to be killing her. Hell… I wouldn't have minded rocking the detective's jaw about that statement myself.

Instead, I chose patience. Cree Bradley wasn't the enemy here. "You can believe whatever you choose to believe. That doesn't have shit to do with me."

"And he's answered your bullshit question now, so you can go," Ace chimed in, stepping out from behind me. "I've just about reached my limit of looking at your face."

Detective Bradley smiled. "Well that's not true at all, is it Alicia? We both know why my simple presence pisses you off so much… be honest with yourself sweetheart."

I hadn't even blinked before Ace was out of my grip and in his face. To his credit, the man didn't flinch, but that little smile he'd given her was gone, and his expression was stern like he understood the gravity of the situation.

Ace's hand was gripping his tie.

If she intended to harm him… there wasn't shit either of us could do.

"Alicia… I'm going to need you to back up," he said carefully, not taking his eyes off of where she held him.

A smile that was half-sinister, half-seductive crept onto her face before she grazed her bottom lip with her teeth. "Or… *what*, Detective Bradley?" she asked, raising her gaze to his face. "What are you going to do? Handcuff me?"

"Perhaps."

She giggled. "Mmmm, you'd like that, wouldn't you? But see…" she tightened her grip on his tie, tugging his head down as she leaned in to say, "If I wanted to fuck you, Cree… you'd already be on your back."

She let him go and walked away, not looking at either of us as she disappeared from the room. My eyebrows were high as I turned back to Detective Bradley, who was staring in the direction Ace had gone, looking stupid.

"Well… I read that all wrong, huh?" he asked, and I shook my head.

"Nah. You didn't." I went to the door and opened it, the universal sign for *"get the fuck outta my house"*. "You have a good day, Detective."

After one last glance after Ace, he turned, coming toward the open door, but stopped in front of me. "Mr. Whitfield… I know this is probably a hard time for you. Sebastian Gray is a dirty sonofabitch, and I can't say that I'm too bothered, personally, by somebody fucking with him. You *know* that," he said, in a low voice, and I nodded. I *did* know. "But… he's back over there in France now. Saint Tropez is *his* playground, just like Vegas is yours. His money runs deep, touches a lot. *Police Nationale* isn't going to just let this shit go."

"I haven't done shit for them to let go," I told him, lifting my shoulders. "I'm not the only motherfucka with a vendetta against him, and I highly doubt I'm the one with the most money or power. Threats are not my style, and I only give warnings to people who might have value to me. He doesn't fit that criteria."

Detective Bradley studied me for a moment, then nodded. "I'll let my captain know that you've denied any involvement, and he'll pass it on. You have a good one."

"Same to you, Detective."

I closed the door behind him when he left, then headed towards the back, where I almost walked right into Ace. She was coming out of what she used as an office/bedroom, and she looked a way I didn't see from her very often – frazzled.

I smirked as I passed her to finish getting dressed. "Had to go change your panties, huh?"

"Fuck you," she muttered, heading in the opposite direction.

"Hey, that was hot though," I called after her, and she stopped, a smile playing on her lips as she turned to look at me.

"Really? It wasn't overkill?"

I laughed. "Nah, he was into it. Probably the only reason he didn't *really* arrest your ass. Why don't you stop playing with that man?"

She raised an eyebrow. "And do what? Ask him on a date or something?"

I shrugged. "Why the fuck not? You're bold about everything else."

For a moment, she tipped her chin up like she was considering it, then shook her head. "I think I'm good. With what he knows, that situation is a problem just waiting to happen."

"You're making excuses."

"Oh, you've got so much nerve," Ace laughed. "If I'm making excuses with him, what do you call what you're doing with Asha?"

I scoffed. "Self-preservation."

"Preserving yourself from *what*?"

"Another situation like the shit I'm still dealing with now," I said, gesturing toward the front of the house. "I didn't know what I was getting into last time. This time I do, and I'm not about to make that mistake again."

She crossed her arms. "Why would you automatically assume it's a mistake?"

"Because life doesn't have to drag my ass through the mud twice for me to get the fucking picture."

"So that's it?" she asked. "You just… give up?"

I chuckled, then turned around to head back to my closet. "Okay, I'm not interested in whatever pseudo-motivational love-conquers-all direction you're trying to take this conversation, so you can pump those brakes."

"I just don't want to see you get used to being a stereotype," she called out as I stepped into my bedroom. "I don't know how long I could stomach it. I was contemplating killing you myself until Asha came onto you at the bar that night."

I grinned, and stopped where I was, listening to what she had to say.

"The broken-hearted bachelor is played out, King. Don't be that guy. Be an inspiration, asshole. Surely, if someone could love *you*… then maybe *I*..."

The wistfulness in her tone as she trailed off made me move back to the doorway and look out. She was still there in the hall, arms crossed, looking to the doorway like she knew I'd be back.

"Nice sentiment, Ace, but… I'm good."

She nodded, briefly closing her eyes before she shuttered whatever emotion was spilling into their emerald depths. "I know. Can't blame a girl for trying though, right? I'll be in the kitchen whenever you're ready to go."

Ace turned and left, and I went to the closet to finish up. I wasn't sure where her newfound sappiness was coming from, but I was leaving that shit to her.

She'd been trained – not by my family, but in the life she'd had before – not to form emotional attachments. Her eventual connection to us was a convoluted story, but in the end, it resulted in a relationship where she was, on the surface, an employee. But below that, Ace was family. If she was finally feeling the need to build more personal relationships outside of that, I was all for it.

I just wasn't in a place to lead by example.

"Anything else I can do for you today Mr. Whitfield?"

I looked up from my phone to meet the pretty, pecan-skinned floor hostess's eyes, knowing she wasn't asking if wanted a drink. I smiled at her, dropping my gaze to the nametag pinned near her ample cleavage.

"Not right now, Sierra. But if something changes, I'll let you know."

She returned my smile with a seductive one of her own as she touched my arm. "Please do," she said, then moved along, leaving me a few feet away from a specific poker table.

It was the middle of the day, but the casino floor was loud and crowded as always. Back here, nothing indicated what time it was – no clocks, no windows – and the drinks were flowing.

There was a certain effortlessness to getting lost in the dimly lit atmosphere of the casino, by design. The residual smoke from a variety of substances filtered together, creating a haze that dulled the senses. The slot machines and roulette wheels droned together in a cacophony that drowned most everything out. For a lot of people, that was the goal. A mindless escape from reality, filling their need for risk-and-reward, feeding their addiction. Others tuned all of that shit out in favor of a singular focus – gambling for a living.

The person I was looking for fell into the second category.

It wasn't the designated time for our meeting yet, so I left her alone for the moment, and simply watched. She was so focused on the hand that she hadn't even taken notice of Ace and I standing there. As she played, I watched her in a way I hadn't before. The first time, I'd been a man scrutinizing a potential lover. The second time, a man enthralled by the beguiling presence of a woman I'd been inside of, and wanted to be inside of again.

This time, I was watching as a businessman observing an asset.

Or at least, trying.

Outside of the poker table, I'd discovered the key to reading her. Asha gave away much more than she realized, especially when she was upset. I'd seen quickly shuttered confusion, hurt, reverence, anger, sadness, a full gamut of emotions in those deep, dark eyes. But here, when her primary focus was on the game, she was impenetrable. She was *cold* – something that, having been on the receiving end of it, I knew she was very good at.

It was captivating.

There she was, this gorgeous woman looking positively bored as she beat a table full of men out of their money. She responded to slick, insulting comments like a housecat plotting to kill you in your sleep might – with a long, impassive stare until the offender got uncomfortable enough to look away. Compliments on how she looked went ignored, but compliments on how she played earned the shadow of a smile. As far as I could see, she had no tells.

Perfection.

As soon as that descriptor crossed my mind, she looked up, and her eyes found mine. She held my gaze for a few seconds before she looked back down at the table, taking a heavy breath that made her chest do a noticeable rise and fall.

I'd just watched her play her way through a hand that added ten thousand dollars in chips to her pot, while barely batting an eyelash. One glance at me, and she was… flustered?

Interesting.

When the hand she was playing was over, Asha cashed out. We had a meeting in ten minutes, so that was to be expected. What I *didn't* expect was for her to approach me, bringing us face to face for the first time in three days.

"You were watching me play," she said, not asked. "Did you need something?"

Unlike the hostess earlier, Asha's question was matter of fact – something that was as disappointing as it was impressive. I'd unambiguously pushed her away, and she wasn't, apparently, a woman who couldn't take a hint. She wasn't leaving a door open, wasn't giving me room to ease my way in next to her, or any indication that I could.

I shook my head. "No, I got what I needed. Are you heading upstairs?"

"To give my answer? Yes… is that why you're here?"

Her tone made me raise an eyebrow. "Is that a problem?"

"Not at all," she said immediately. "Just asking a question. I'll… see you up there then, I guess."

With that, she walked away, and mine weren't the only eyes on her as she moved. She was dressed more casually than she had for the meeting at the house, but even in slacks and a simple blouse, she was an attention grabber. I forced myself to look away, glancing at Ace for confirmation that we were leaving.

We had a meeting to get to.

When we made it to the private room upstairs, the main contributors to this endeavor were already gathered. My parents and sister were with Asha, talking, and further back, the poker coach, photographer, stylist and hair stylist were waiting.

I didn't have to be here.

I really had no reason to be a part of this meeting, but when I said I was coming, no one questioned it. Eventually, we moved to the table, where my mother slid a manila folder in front of Asha, and said, "So… what is your decision, Ms. Davis?"

"I accept the offer," Asha said, without hesitation. "I just wanted a bit of time to be sure, but I complete appreciate the opportunity, and I have every intention of making it far in the tournament. I won't let you down."

Beside my mother, Zora smirked. "That's that corporate charm coming out, which will be good for interviews – and you're going to have a lot of them. The further you get, the more people are going to want to talk to you. The more scrutiny your life, and your past will get. Is that something you'll be able to handle?"

Asha pressed her lips together, taking a moment to consider. "Well… I think the question that needs to be answered first is if *you* found anything you felt was insurmountable," she said, directing her words at my mother and father. "I'm not naïve enough to think that your family hasn't already sifted through my past. As a matter of fact," – she glanced at me, then back to my parents – "I know for a fact that I've been looked into. So, you tell me."

My mother looked to my father, who'd sat back in his chair, and had his eyes narrowed, chin propped in his hand as he studied Asha. After a few moments, he shook his head. "No. We didn't find anything that was too much cause for alarm. This *is* Vegas, after all. I'm certain there will be players with much more checkered pasts than yours."

"I agree," my mother nodded. "If we thought any different, this meeting wouldn't be happening. And as your sponsor, you'll have our support to handle any potentially negative press or anything."

"Which means, we'll have your back." Zora cocked her head to the side. "But… you don't look relieved by that."

Asha shook her head. "No, I am. It's just… I really hadn't considered it too much before now."

"Do you need another day to think about it?" My mother asked, a question that immediately earned another headshake as Asha took a deep breath.

"No," she said, picking up the pen that lay beside the folder. "I don't need any extra time. I'm… I'm sure. I can handle it."

In the back of my mind, a memory popped up, pushing its way to the front. I remember that day at the spa, Asha telling me how badly she wanted to be in the tournament, so she could have a chance at that money. So she could have a chance at… freedom.

I doubted that she was actually confident in her ability to handle a media shit storm that may or may not happen. What I didn't doubt was that she'd fight through it anyway, if it was the only path to her dream.

Without further discussion, Asha positioned the pen in her hand, her eyes skimming the top page of the contract before she signed with a flourish. She did that three more times, on the appropriate pages, then closed the folder and handed the signed contract to my father. He glanced at it, and then put it down, standing up to extend a hand across the table.

"Congratulations, Ms. Davis. You're officially our sponsored player for the Ace of Spades Tournament at the Drake. Welcome again to the Reverie family."

The smile that spread over Asha's face as she accepted that handshake did something to me. In my admittedly short experience with her, this kind of full on happiness was rare, but exquisite on her. After that handshake, she passed around hugs – for my mother, sister, and even Ace, but none for me. It was a slight that I had to eat, because I was the one who'd created that rift in whatever connection we'd started forging. I couldn't be salty about something that was my own doing.

Once the pleasantries had passed, my mother was ready to get down to business.

"Okay Asha, we're going to get the photographer over here to get a few shots of you at the poker table. I don't think we really need the makeup and hair, but as far as your style, we'll jazz you up a little."

"She means *sex* you up," Zora chimed in. "And that's going to go for when you're playing too. None of that "my eyes are up here" bullshit. You have titties, so we're going to use those puppies. Have these boys so distracted they can't even tell the difference between a spade and a club."

Zora and my mother carted Asha off to the other side of the room, and Ace went to go talk with the other members of the security team, leaving me with my father. "You alright son?" he asked, his expression concerned as he came around the side of the table. "You look a little preoccupied."

"Just a lot on my mind." I sighed. "Got a visit from Detective Bradley this morning."

His eyebrows lifted in alarm. "Regarding...?"

"Yes. Apparently someone is harassing Sebastian over in Saint Tropez, and he thinks I'm behind it."

"Are you?"

I looked my father directly in his eyes when I answered. "No. I'm not."

"Good," he nodded. "I was hoping you were… past that. It's been years, son. And you did enough. At some point, you have to—"

"Do *not* tell me I have to let that shit go," I growled under my breath, father or not. "If it was my mother… would *you* let it go?"

He scoffed. "I don't mean to be insensitive, but it wouldn't have *been* your mother. She wouldn't have gotten herself into such a situation, and if she did, she would have been sensible enough to use the resources she had available to get herself out of it. Stop romanticizing who your wife was. Admit to yourself that you made a mistake, Kingston. It will make it much easier to move on."

"I'm perfectly clear on the shortcomings of my dead wife," I said dryly, shaking my head. "her mistakes aside, Sebastian knew what the fuck he was doing, and he smiled in my fucking face like an ally *while* he was doing it. I'll let it go when he takes his last breath."

Blowing out a hard sigh, my father put a hand on my shoulder and squeezed. "Very well. It isn't as if I can make you, but know that you wont find any peace until you do."

"That's a consequence I'll have to accept."

He nodded. "Are you coming to the house for dinner tonight? Your mother is going to want to talk about this poker tournament."

"I plan to be there."

"Good." He looked across the room at where the three women were standing, and then back to me. "I can see why you're drawn to her."

"Who?" I asked, and my father chuckled.

"Nice try, son. But Asha is quite a striking woman… and not at all the type I was expecting."

"Which was?"

"A social climber, like Robyn was. Overly refined and overly made-up. Overly polished. A socialite-slash-model-slash-actress, or… simply a liar, pretending to be one. Essentially, after looking at what we found on her, I was expecting a road we've been down before. But the woman is a pleasant surprise. Are you still seeing her?"

I scoffed. "No. Not at all."

"Why not?"

"What is with everybody?" I asked, with a weak chuckle. "First y'all were on my back about dealing with her, now you're on my back about *not* dealing with her. Decide which side you want to be on."

Laughing, my father clapped my shoulder again. "That's a fair point, but meeting someone will change your mind. And I've seen a marked decline in your demeanor since our conversation, whereas before that, you seemed content. In a way you hadn't in a while. Knowing what I know now… I'm thinking it was because you had a certain young woman on your mind."

"Give it a rest, man. Door is closed."

He cringed. “Not even cracked?”

I shook my head. “I’m not a fan of loose ends.”

Which was why the Sebastian Gray thing still bothered me so badly.

My father had other business to handle, so he left, and I wasn’t far behind him. Instead of lingering in the poker room when I had no cause to be there, I made my way to my office. I stayed there for hours, going over budgets, projections, and marketing plans for the casino and club.

By the time I left, it was hours later, and the poker room we’d used earlier was empty when we peeked in. Ace called down for the car, and instead of taking the back exit, I decided to go out through the front so that I could have a word with one of my pit bosses before I left.

When we came off the elevator, I stopped at the stairs that led down to the casino floor to look across the vast space. As usual, it was Asha’s red locs that grabbed my attention, even all the way across the dim room, but it was the person she was talking to that made my jaw clench.

Dorian had a hand around her wrist, leaning in close as he said something that made a pained expression cross her face. She shook her head, then tried to back away, but his hold on her kept her from doing so. Immediate rage flared in my chest as I headed in her direction, but when she pulled away again, he let her go, and she quickly disappeared in the crowd.

I glanced to my side to see that Ace had been watching the whole exchange too. She looked at me, undoubtedly knowing that I was bothered.

“What do you want me do?” she asked, and I scrubbed a hand over my face, trying to brush away the anger I’d felt at seeing him with his hands on her. If I’d been close enough to get to them, nothing would have made me happier than a good reason to put my fist through his face. For the distress he’d caused – and seemed to *still* be causing Asha, sure. But my disdain for him started before I even knew who Asha was.

"Did you or your boys sell to this woman?" I asked, shoving the phone in his face, forcing him to look at the picture. I was angry, drained, and still inundated with grief. He was the third mid-tier drug dealer I'd had the displeasure of talking to that day, and I was beyond ready for an answer that I knew one of them had.

It wasn't the right night to play games with me.

"I sell to a lot of junkie bitches," he said, pushing the phone out of his face without a glance. "You think I remember them? Unless she sucked somebody off for a hit, she's just another number around here."

He chuckled, and started to walk off, but I snatched him up by the collar. "You're going to look at the goddamnn picture, and tell me if you've seen her before."

"Yo, nigga do you know who the fuck I am?" he asked, trying to shove away. Around us, his boys approached, drawing weapons, but I didn't relinquish my hold. Ace was at my back, with two weapons of her own pointed at anybody who wanted to jump.

"Yeah, I know who you are. Dorian Haywood. One of Kimball's lieutenants, and I don't give a fuck about either one of you, because do you *know who* I *am?"*

"A dead man walking, nigga."

I grinned. "No. Kingston Whitfield. Nice to meet your acquaintance."

There was a noticeable shift in the atmosphere as it dawned on them who I was. We didn't have our hands in gangs, or drugs, but the Whitfield family had money that was long enough to dabble in plenty of legal places, giving us the ability to create the type of problems neither Dorian or Kimball wanted to have.

"Show me the fucking picture, man."

I put the phone in his face again, and he barely gave it a glance. But his eyes came back to it, lighting with recognition before he pulled himself out of my grasp.

"I never sold to her," he said, brushing off his clothes. "She bad as fuck though. Never struck me as a junkie."

"Because she wasn't," I snarled. No matter what the report said, I knew her. Knew she wouldn't do that to herself. "Where did you see her? Her art gallery?"

Dorian sucked his teeth. "Man, Nah. Fuck I look like in an art gallery? She was always with that shady French motherfucka that bought all those restaurants on the strip. I never sold to her, but she was in his office a few times when I did business with him."

"Sebastian Gray?"

He nodded. "Yeah, him. That's him."

"King?"

I blinked, then looked down to see Ace still beside me, waiting on instructions. I glanced in the direction where Asha and Dorian had both blended into the crowd.

"Find out how they're still involved."

FOURTEEN

ASHA

If it wasn't one thing, it was another.

Could I put in a request now, to have that engraved on my headstone when I inevitably died from the stress of taking on more responsibility than a woman in her twenties should have to bear?

After a night of fantasizing about what I'd do with my winnings in the tournament, – if I got that far – a fresh burden was an agonizingly hard pill to swallow. And as usual, I had no choice except to force it down as I stared at the bill in my hands.

"I… I don't understand this…" I looked up at Tim, my mother's husband, noting the defeat in his eyes. He was a good man, truly, one of the few consistent ones in my life. He carried his weight, but my mother's medical bills – the insurance was a joke – were more than he could handle. I didn't think less of him for that either, because he took on a lot. Things that would fall to me if it wasn't for him, like general living expenses.

But that didn't make the medical costs – especially unexpected ones, like this – any less of a headache.

Tim shook his head, scrubbing a hand over his steadily graying, buzzed hair. "I don't either. I took your mother to the treatment center this morning, and they turned us away. Said there was an outstanding balance, and they couldn't take her until it was paid."

"But I've been paying," I said, more to myself than him as my eyes settled on the low five-figure number at the bottom of the page, under a heading that said "Past Due". "How can they just suddenly pop up with something like this, refusing treatment over a bill we just got *today*?"

"I asked the same question. Your mother had a hard time over the weekend, so we were looking forward to today. I talked to the office manager – no payment plan is being offered. It's all or none."

I closed my eyes, leaning back into the soft plush of the armchair I'd settled into. "This is bullshit," I whispered. "They won't even make a *little* exception, since it's you?"

Tim was a security guard, working nights at the same treatment center my mother went to. Surely, because of the relationship there, they could…

"No. I already asked, but… one of the nurses told me the center is in trouble. Something about a lawsuit, and now they're strapped. I'm not even sure how secure my job is, and I've been there twenty years," Tim droned, bitterness evident in his voice. "But we have to do something. The emergency room is no help, every other clinic I've called either isn't accepting new patients or can't see her for weeks, and—"

"*Whaddup, family?*"

Ahmad came bounding into the room, with a pep in his step I hadn't seen from him in a long while. Most of the bruising was gone from his face, and he was back to the carefree kid – I couldn't help seeing him as that – kid I knew.

"Hey Ahmad," Tim said, standing to greet him with a half-handshake, half-hug. After that, Ahmad turned to me with a huge smile on his face.

"Ash, can we talk?"

I raised an eyebrow, leery of buying into his exuberance this morning. "What about? Why are you so happy?"

He glanced at Tim, then back to me, before shoving his hands deep into his pockets. "Well… come look outside."

Suspicion narrowed my eyes. "For what?"

"Just come look, damn," he insisted, grabbing my hand and pulling me up. Reluctantly, I let him lead me to the front door, which he opened, then pointed outside. I peeked out, then frowned at the shiny black car in the driveway beside mine.

"Whose car is that?"

When I looked back at my brother, he was grinning so hard his face had to be hurting. "Mine."

"Yours? *Yours?!*" Something in me snapped, and I shoved him back into the door. "You bought a fucking *car*, Ahmad? Are you crazy? What about your *debt*, huh? I swear to God, when I thought you couldn't get *any* stupider, you—"

"Man, kill that," he snapped back, pushing my hands away from him. "You're going off, without even letting me explain!"

My eyes were watering as I shook my head. "What is there to explain, huh? What year is that car? What are the payments? Can you afford them, or are you gonna run some more dope to pay it off, like you did with the truck?"

"I don't *have* any payments," he said dryly, absent of all his enthusiasm from before. "I sold the truck, since I owned it outright after… everything. I found the car used, had my homeboy who works as a mechanic check it out for me, make sure it was good. I got a good price, with enough left to handle a good chunk of our debt. The only reason I can't cover it all outright is because I paid to get Ebony out of that little hood apartment she was in. She's pregnant… I wanted her somewhere safer. Kita isn't really happy about any of it, but that's my seed, and I want to make sure I do right by them. I had to have a decent car to keep doing the Uber thing, and between that and my job, I can stack up the rest. It's off your head, Asha, which is what I was trying to do. But…" he pushed out a sigh, and shook his head before dropping his eyes to the ground. "It's whatever. I know after everything, that's probably not much to you."

My shoulders deflated. Partially in relief that he hadn't done something stupid, partly out of guilt for automatically assuming that he had.

"I'm sorry," I said, tipping my head down to catch his gaze. "Actually… it's a lot to me. I know how much you loved that truck, and after what you did to get it, I'm sure it was hard for you to let go."

He chuckled a little. "Yeah, it was. But… I don't want to always be looked at as a fuckup, man. Gotta be a man at some point."

"You're right," I nodded. "You do. And this was a great start… especially what you're doing to take care of your child on the way."

"I don't want to be the kind of father we had," he said in a low voice, dropping his eyes again. "I was thinking about it last night… I may not have had the example of doing it right, but I damn sure saw what doing it wrong looked like. I don't want to be on that path."

A different kind of tears welled in my eyes, and I reached up, hooking my arms around my brother's neck to pull him into a hug – something that felt like it hadn't happened in way too long. Ahmad confirmed that by squeezing me tight, holding on well past when we would have normally let go. When I pulled back, the gloss in his eyes matched mine, and I cupped his chin in my free hand.

"I'm proud of you, okay?" I said, and he nodded before he pulled away from my touch.

"We ain't gotta do the sentimental shit, Ash. Chill."

"Oh, I've got your sentimental," I teased, grabbing his face again to kiss his cheek. He squirmed away from me, laughing as he took my wrists to hold me back.

"What's this?" he asked, referring to the paper in my hand – a reminder that immediately punctured my freshly inflated mood.

I shook my head, then handed it to him. "A bill, from the treatment center. I want to fight it, but fighting it takes time that we don't have when they're saying they wont treat her until it's paid. She's back in her room suffering as we speak. Not that we can afford to pay it anyway."

"How much is it?" He asked, then turned his gaze to the paper. His eyes swelled when he got to the number on the bottom of the paper.

"Yeah." I wrapped my arms around myself, and leaned back against the wall. "My feelings exactly."

"And they aren't accepting any payment arrangements, begging, nothing?"

"Tim already tried. They sent her home without treatment," I said, pointing down the hall where Tim had disappeared to go check on her. "And I have no idea what we're going to do."

Ahmad shrugged. "We'll pay it."

My face twisted into disbelief. "Pay it with *what*? I have maybe a grand left in the tips from before the casino took me out of the club to work the poker tables. And the money I play with there? They're fronting me, Ahmad. That money isn't *mine,* not until the tournament starts next week."

It was a calculated risk that I'd selfishly taken toward my dream. I hadn't expected Ahmad to sell his truck – it hadn't even crossed my mind to suggest it – but between his regular paycheck and the money he was making from giving tourists rides around Vegas through that app, I was confident he'd make what he needed to pay Dorian on his own.

I'd thought I was in the clear to do something for myself, even though the timing was precarious. Apparently, I was wrong.

"We'll use the money I was going to give D. The payment to him isn't due for a few more days, so I'll… I don't know, give rides overnight for the next few nights. Maybe I can get a credit card, and take out a –"

"No!" I snapped, holding up a hand. "No, no more debt." I pushed out a sigh. My mind swung to the watch in my bedside table, then back again. I was kidding myself if I entertained the thought of selling it. "Call the medical center, and pay the bill so they can see Mama today. That's top priority."

He nodded, already pulling out his cell phone. "And maybe… I don't know, I'll talk to Kita and Ebony. Maybe I can get the security deposit and rent back, and Ebony can move into—"

"Kita will kill you, fool," I said, rolling my eyes. "She may not have broken up with you about the baby, but the suggestion of your pregnant side-chick moving in… no. Don't do that. Don't do anything except call and pay that bill. I'll handle Dorian."

Concern spread over Ahmad's face. "Handle him how?"

"Call and pay," I repeated, ignoring his question. And make them get her in as soon as possible."

I grabbed my purse and keys from the table beside the door and headed out, climbing into my own care. My stress level had already been through the roof, but just thinking about talking to Dorian, asking him for a favor… sent it even higher.

Just a few nights ago we'd been face to face, as I was leaving Reverie high on the happiness of being an official participant in the poker tournament. The smile I'd been wearing had melted from my face as soon as he appeared in front of me, wearing a grin of his own.

"You know what this reminds me of, you being dressed like this?" he asked, with a slow perusal that made discomfort prickle over my skin. He was referring to my slacks and blouse – the kind of clothes I only wore for "business". "Back when you had that little corporate gig, you wore stuff like this, and I clowned you about it. Little red worker ant," he said, grabbing my hand. "With a mean ass sting."

"Dorian," I started, but was quickly interrupted when he leaned in, closing a hand around my wrist.

"I want to have a conversation with you. One on one. Have dinner with me." I couldn't keep the disdain off my face as I shook my head and tried to pull away, but he wouldn't let me go. "You got a nigga out here fucking begging you for your time, Asha," he said into my ear. "Tell me what I have to do."

When I tried to pull away again, he let me go, and I got the hell away from him as fast as I could.

And now here I was, sweat building in my palms as I drove back to my apartment to get ready for the day. In the parking lot of my building, I closed my eyes, silently praying over what I was about to do. I fished my phone out of my purse, then dialed a number that wasn't saved, but was – and would probably always be – embedded in my mind.

It rang several times before it was answered, and I swallowed down yet another bitter pill of my stressful reality.

My mouth needed to be empty to articulate a deal with a devil.

I finished off the contents of my glass of Mauve and then sat back, looking at the documents spread over the desk in front of me. Drinking while I worked wasn't my thing – usually – but this was a special case.

Whitfield Inc. had never dabbled in the medical field before.

But here we were – *Sunrise Hospital and Medical Center* was in desperate need of an investment before they had to either close down, or eliminate some of the services they offered. They were floundering – between malpractice suits because of negligence from some of the doctors, changes to the ways they were reimbursed through insurance, and unpaid bills… I had a good feeling their CFO had been frantic when they made the decision to seek help. I *also* had a good feeling there was some shady shit happening, including taking advantage of some of the patients in an attempt to alieve the hemorrhaging of their coffers.

It would just take time to figure it out, and I wasn't about to be rushed to action about it. No matter how many times a day I got those hopeful emails, I would dig into this until it was figured out – I had to know it was a good investment before I made a move. This one was my call, not my father's.

I planned to get it right.

The sound of the door opening pulled my attention away from what was on my desk, and Ace walked in with a fresh cup of coffee that she silently placed in front of me. The look on her face said "*drink*" even though her mouth didn't. I picked up the cup, taking a deep swallow as she shot a glare in my direction before picking up the tumbler the liquor had been in.

I knew what she was thinking, but the two beverages were serving different purposes. The intention of the liquor was to ease the tension that had been building while I labored over this decision. The coffee was to wake up my fatigued body, giving my eyelids the fuel they needed to open again when I blinked, instead of giving in to exhaustion.

My sleep pattern had been fucked for the last few days – since I hadn't been able to shake my mental preoccupation with Asha.

Withdrawal symptoms, I mused as I took another big swallow from the robust coffee. Still, I felt like cold turkey was the way to do it.

I hadn't tagged along to another meeting, watched her on the poker floor, or even followed up with Ace about Dorian.

That didn't mean I could keep the damn girl off my mind though.

Shaking my head, I returned my gaze to the bookkeeping records for the hospital. Obviously, I would have them reviewed professionally, but I wanted to know as much as I could before that, in case I had questions. Around me, Ace moved through the office, cleaning it up before she settled at her own desk and started running down her tasks for the day.

Hours passed with us just like that, working in silence. The quiet was interrupted by the main phone line to the office, which was a rare occurrence. Most of the time, calls were routed to our cells.

"Kingston Whitfield's office," Ace answered, putting on her "professional" voice. She listened to the other line for a moment, then told whoever was there that she needed them to hold on. She pressed a button to mute the line, then looked over at me. "It's Asha's poker coach. He can't get in touch with Angela or Zora, and he says he needs to talk to someone."

"They're at their monthly spa date," I said, leaning back in my chair. "Their mother-daughter ritual. They'll be available in a few hours."

"So what do you want me to tell him? Because he sounds anxious."

"About Asha?"

Ace shrugged. "I would assume so."

I pushed out a sigh, then closed the folder on my desk. The coffee was wearing off and so was the liquor. It was late enough in the evening to call it a day. "Get him up here. Let's find out what's going on."

Ten minutes later, I had a poker legend in front of my desk, sipping a glass of liquor from my personal stash. Carl had seemed agitated when he came in, but once his grizzled hands had wrapped around the glass, his mood improved drastically.

"I don't know what the hell was wrong with that girl today, but her head was all over the place," he started, in a tone that was distinctly disappointed. "Usually, she's focused. One of the most gifted players I've seen in a *long* time. No flash, just… *talent.*"

I offered a slow nod. "But today was different?"

"Sure was," he said, then whistled. "Yessir, something heavy on her mind. Damn shame, young pretty thing like that, walked up to the tables like she had the weight of the world on her shoulders – and played like it too."

"How so?"

"Betting when she shouldn't, forgetting the cards, forgetting what went in certain hands. She was in bad shape. Usually a ripe player, but I was reminded of the fact that she's still a baby seeing her today."

It struck me as odd to hear him refer to her as a baby, but… it wasn't entirely untrue. Despite her demeanor, and the weight of her responsibilities forcing her to carry herself as older… Asha was *barely* twenty-seven years old. She'd just lived a lot of life in those years.

"Thank you for the heads up," I said, rising to shake the man's hand. He downed the rest of his glass and then accepted the gesture, nodding at Ace before he left.

She stood too, leading him to the door before she turned back to me.

"Before you ask," she began, but I shook my head.

"I wasn't going to."

Her head snapped back in surprise at my words, and she propped a hand on her hip. "You weren't going to… what?"

"Ask," I responded, taking a seat. "About Asha. I wasn't going to ask you to find out what's going on with her, because it's not my business. I'm trying to leave her alone, which is what you advised that day in the poker room, remember?"

Ace groaned. "Yes, and I've noticed your efforts. And I was willing to support you in those efforts, until what Carl just told us."

"Why does that change anything? My mother and sister have made it clear to Asha that they – and their abundant resources – are available to her if she needs help with anything."

"And you *really* think she's going to go to them? With what you know of her, you really believe that's going to happen?"

"Fuck, I don't know!" I said, pressing my fingertips to my forehead as I balanced my elbows on the desk. "Probably not. She's going to try to handle it herself."

"Which is exactly what I'm afraid of," Ace said, and I glanced up to see her going back to her desk, where she grabbed her tablet. She spent a moment pulling something up before she handed the device to me to look at – it was full of pictures, of Dorian and another, younger man.

With familiar light brown skin, red hair, and those heavily lashed eyes.

Asha's brother.

"What she told you that day at the spa, about giving up her money to save her brother? Mostly true." That was one of very few things I'd disclosed about the intensely personal – albeit one-sided - conversation Asha and I had shared that day, and only because it involved Dorian. "I did some digging though, which wasn't easy, because his guys… they're loyal. I had a hard time getting ahold of anybody with loose lips, but once I did… I found out that the fifty-thousand wasn't all baby bro owed. It was closer to seventy-five."

I felt the air leave my lungs. Asha hadn't mentioned a word of *that*.

"So what… this dude is shaking her down for more money?"

Ace's nodding response seemed to make the familiar feeling of betrayal sink in deeper. After everything else she'd divulged… why keep *that* aside? It was Robyn all over again – ample opportunity to tell me about some shit a man was holding over her head, but instead she'd chosen not to. *Why*?

"Apparently," Ace explained, "There were payment arrangements made, to pay for the rest. I'm assuming that he's pushing the issue because he had to pay Kimball back for what was stolen. Dorian doesn't want his boss on his ass, so he's putting the pressure on Ahmad, and in turn… Asha."

I shook my head. "It was always about Asha. I'd bet money on that. Look at this boy," I said, pointing to a picture of Ahmad looking goofy as hell. "That's not the nigga you put on the block for you, he's a disaster waiting to happen. Shit was probably a dream come true for Dorian."

"You could be right." Ace propped her hands on the back of the chair that stood in front of my desk, then blew out a breath that made the loose tendrils of hair around her face float up. "Every heterosexual man has that one woman… that soft spot. Knowing what I know… it's absolutely possible that Asha has the misfortune of being that spot – for more than one man."

I scoffed at the implication of her words. "Don't start, Ace. I know Robyn was my soft – no, fuck that – *weak* spot. But she's not here anymore—"

"So you got a new one," Ace cut in, with a teasing grin. "Come on, King. You know damn well you aren't about to sit here with what I just told you, after hearing what Carl said, and not do anything."

"I promise you, she doesn't want my interference," I argued, trying not to let it show on my face *just* how bothered I was. Men like Dorian lived by the same "no half-assing" doctrine as I did. If he was pushing the issue about the money, he was trying to prove a point, and he wasn't going to let up until he did. For whatever reason, Asha was stressed today in a way she hadn't been before, and connecting it to the money her brother owed Dorian was a logical conclusion.

I'd seen the fear and discomfort in her eyes when she talked to me about him that day at the spa, and I'd seen that same emotion mirrored the other night. It reminded me, more than I was comfortable admitting, of something I'd seen in Robyn's eyes… the final day I saw her alive.

The *last* time I'd let a woman in my life deal with a man she was afraid of without my interference… had to be the last time.

I looked up to find Ace's eyes on me, waiting, and expectant. I was sick of getting that look about Asha, but not enough to change my mind.

I leaned back in my chair again, blowing out a harsh sigh.

"Find out where she is. *Now.*"

ASHA

"You want some more wine?"

I ran my tongue over my dry lips, and then nodded. Anything to dull my senses enough to get me through the rest of the night.

Dorian raised his hand, motioning for the server to pour me another glass, and I snatched it up as soon as he was done, swallowing half of it down.

I was looking for a buzz.

Honestly speaking, dinner with Dorian hadn't been awful. Instead of going out to a restaurant, I was at his house, which wasn't ideal, but it wasn't like I was in much position to argue. I'd promised him dinner… it was my bad for not stipulating where.

He'd been a gentleman. Just as charming as I'd always known him to be. Putting aside my discomfort, the setting was beautiful. Outside, on the patio of his home, we could see the colorful lights of the strip in the distance. Before us, the firepit was lit, and lighted torches helped provide adequate visibility. At the table, Dorian sat right next to me.

He'd insisted on it, and then spent an absurd amount of time turned my way, watching me. His eyes stayed on me as I took another long sip from my wine, then placed the glass down on the table.

"What?" I asked, squirming underneath the heat of his gaze.

He shrugged, then leaned toward me, brushing my locs back from my face. "Nothing… just enjoying the opportunity to stare at you. It's been a long ass time. Too long," he said, his eyes boring into mine until I looked away. I sucked in a breath when he put his hand under my chin, turning me back to face him. "Come on, babe… you can't even look at a nigga now? It's like that?"

"Dorian, you already know what's up," I said, scraping my lip with my teeth.

He dropped his hand, and I looked away, searching out my wine glass.

Damn waiter should have left the bottle.

Just a few more hours of my time. That's all it would take to get him off our backs for this week, he'd promised me. He'd asked me to wear my hair down, because that's what he liked. Asked me to wear white, because that's what he liked. I'd honored both of those requests, hoping it would satisfy him enough that the night could end up being something that resembled pleasant.

So far… so good.

"So… I heard something about you playing in that tournament, at the Drake."

I nodded. "Yeah. The Reverie is sponsoring me."

Since you took the money from me.

"No shit? How'd you end up with a gig like that?"

I had his full attention. Something I'd craved as a teenager, before I understood that with a man like Dorian, his full attention meant his full… fixation. To an unhealthy degree.

Inside, I was a bubbling mess of anxiety, but I disciplined my features into an impassive expression, like I did at the poker table. And in some ways, that's all this was. I sat up a little straighter as I let that thought settle in my head. I just had to bluff my way through this hand.

I shrugged. "Just… luck, I guess. Angela Whitfield sees something in me, so she wants to support my dream."

"That's the boss man's wife, right? That's who you're working with?"

I pulled my eyes up from my picked over prawns. "Yes, her and her daughter. Why?"

"You were with their son that day I stopped you on the floor. Before that, you went upstairs with Kingston. Didn't come back down for a long ass time."

Was he… watching me? Following me?

My face remained aloof. "What? He came to retrieve me from the poker tables, and took me up to *Dream* for a meeting with his parents, and some pictures and stuff for the tournament. He didn't even stay."

"Really?" he asked, with an edge to his tone that was barely there, but enough to put me on higher alert than I already was. "So… you aren't really around him like that?"

I frowned. "No. Why, what's up?" I injected my voice will a carefully measured level of concern. "Is he… dangerous or something?"

Dorian shrugged. "Depends who you ask."

"I'm asking you."

A little smirk tugged at the corners of his mouth before he picked up the glass of whatever dark liquor he'd gotten three refills of since I arrived. "If you ask me, the motherfucker takes his name too seriously. Running around here like he's untouchable. Fuck around and get—" He raised a hand and mimicked holding a gun, drawing his finger back with the imaginary recoil of a pulled trigger.

"You don't like him or something?"

When Dorian met my eyes, his were just the tiniest bit bloodshot – he was starting to feel the effects of his drinking – and his smile came a little easier than before. "Nah, I'm just shooting the shit. I got no beef with old boy, but he ain't really feeling me. I know some personal shit he probably wishes I didn't. Shit about his dead wife."

Those words flowed out of Dorian's mouth so casually – so callously – that they stung. I blinked before I nodded. "So that's a sensitive topic for him. Not so untouchable after all."

"Nah, he is. He inherited that with his family name. They're straight now, but that wasn't always the case. Granddaddy was on the type of gangster shit niggas like me heard as bedtime stories coming up. Man got a family, cleaned his shit up, passed it down."

I raised my eyebrows. "That easy?"

"Not at all. Plenty of pushback, but he made it out on top, with his money and his respect. King's daddy used to have to bust heads to remind people wasn't shit sweet. Hell, King would too. But like I said… they cleaned all that shit up. They just still have the respect and the connections."

Looking away, I nodded. "Mmm. Interesting."

"What's so interesting about it?" Dorian asked, fixing his gaze on me. I could feel his eyes roving over the side of my face. "Why are we talking so much about that nigga? You got a crush or something?

I wrinkled my nose like I was disgusted, to hide the panic that shot through me. "Dorian… you're the one who brought him up. You tell me."

A chuckle broke free from his throat, and despite my complete aversion to him… the sound sent a ripple up my spine. My mind was made up about him – that was a road I had no intention of ever going down again. But my body, and my heart… they still remembered.

In fact, an uncomfortable flutter started in my stomach as his laughter died down, but his eyes remained on me, full of emotions that were frighteningly familiar. Three years, since that ugly, *ugly* night that was a dark stain on my heart and soul, and yet… *still.*

He reached out to touch me again, and for some inscrutable reason, I didn't give in to the compulsion to pull away. I remained still as he cupped my face, running his thumb over my cheek. "You're so damn beautiful. These eyes… it's like they hold more than just *you*. Like you've got a whole line of other lifetimes behind them or something."

It's called trauma, I thought, but didn't say out loud. He was being nice… there was no reason to turn things around.

Or so I thought.

When I didn't say anything, his hand drifted down, tracing my collarbone with his fingers. I shivered at his touch – a simultaneous blend of repulsion and arousal – and my reaction seemed to spur him on, until he was cupping my breast.

"Dorian!" I scolded, shoving his hand away. "I already told you, before I agreed to this—"

"*I'm not fucking you, D,*" he said, in a mocking voice. "Yeah, I heard that bullshit you were talking, but be real Asha. Don't act like I didn't have your little ass climbing the walls, screaming your brains out."

My nostrils flared, face heated in embarrassment as I glanced around, looking for the members of his staff that had been outside before, but were now painfully absent. "That was a long time ago. Things have changed."

"Yeah, and *people* change too."

I scoffed. "That's the argument you really want to make, while I'm only sitting here because I'm hoping it'll keep you from kicking Ahmad's ass?"

"How the fuck else was I supposed to get through to you, huh?" He asked, his eyes wide and wild as he got in my face.

Just like a million times before, I didn't back down, my face set into a snarl as I shot back, "You weren't! I told you to leave me the fuck alone!"

"And I did! For three goddamned years Asha, because I knew you were hurting, but you like to act like the shit didn't hurt me too. How long are you going to hold a mistake against me?"

"It wasn't *one* mistake, Dorian!" I said, but he kept talking like I hadn't even opened my mouth.

"How much time do you need? How many times I gotta apologize to you for that shit, huh? *I'm sorry*, okay?! I'm sorry for how the shit worked out, I'm sorry for what we lost, I'm sorry for… everything, okay? Aiight? Does that make you happy now?"

He'd growled those words right into my face, his voice breaking at the end with a crack of emotion that made my chest feel like it was caving in. I didn't say anything because I didn't have anything to say. I didn't bother trying to wipe away the tears that started dripping down my cheeks as we stared at each other. For the third time, he reached to touch my face, wiping away my tears, and I closed my eyes.

A few seconds later, his lips were on mine.

I didn't pull away, not at first. There was no force behind the kiss… he was barely there, until he was, and even then I didn't feel inclined. His lips got firmer, more insistent, and then the wetness of his tongue probed the seam of my mouth. I whimpered a little, trying to pull back, but he simply moved his mouth down to my neck, sucking and kissing me there instead of letting me pull away.

"Dorian, stop," I said, putting my hands on his shoulders in a vain attempt to get him off me. His fingers dug into my waist, and then down to my ass, pulling me against him. "Dorian!" This time I was louder, digging my nails into his arms. "I do not want you touching me like this, *stop*."

His eyes came up to mine, piercing me with yet another emotion that was achingly familiar – anger. "And what if I told you I didn't really give a fuck what you wanted, Asha? I'm sick of playing games with you."

"I'm not playing games," I told him, trying my best to keep the fear out of my voice. My eyes were trained on him, but in my peripheral, I was scoping out the table for a potential weapon. If I had to break a wine glass on the edge of the table and put the stem through his neck… so be it. I was done with being touched when I didn't want to be. "Just let me go, Dorian. I'll get you your money, all of it, and then we'll be done. Just let me go. I'll get a ride, you don't even have to take me home."

A slow, terrifying smile spread across his beautiful mahogany face. "Why the fuck would I do that?" he asked, his voice so low it was almost a whisper as he roughly tried to push a hand between my legs. "I've got exactly what I want right here."

I stretched my arm, trying to reach the table, knowing that even if I screamed, the only person here that could save me was myself.

As usual.

Dorian's hand went around my neck, squeezing as I fought to get away from him.

"D!"

A voice boomed through the night, seemingly right beside us, and I scrambled to get out of Dorian's grasp while he was distracted. I wasn't far before he grabbed my wrists, pinning me against his body in a way that put me at a painfully awkward angle.

"What?!" Dorian growled in response to the voice calling for him again. Now that I was upright, I could tell that it was coming from the other side of the patio's privacy wall, so whoever it was couldn't actually see us.

"You've got a visitor."

Dorian sucked his teeth. "Tell their ass I'm busy, and they better not come by my shit again without calling first."

For several seconds, there was no response, and then, "Nah," the voice drawled. "You might want to come talk to this one."

"The fuck?" Dorian asked, more to himself than the other person. "Bring your ass on," he said, yanking me along as he started walking back to the house. "You stay here," he directed once we were inside, leaving me in the hall that led back to the bedrooms. I nodded before he disappeared around the corner, but as soon as he was out of sight, I started looking around for an exit I could actually make it through.

I just needed my purse.

If I remembered correctly, I'd put it down in the kitchen at Dorian's insistence, one of many mistakes I'd made tonight. But to get into the kitchen meant going out into the open area of his house, something I wasn't very keen on doing… until my ears caught the soothing tenor of a familiar voice.

I eased close to where the voices were coming from, stopping when one of Dorian's security guard stepped into the hall at the other end of the open stretch that led to the kitchen. Somebody looking straight into the kitchen couldn't see either of us, but he could definitely see me, and he shook his head, raising his shirt to show me the gun at his waistband.

So I stayed still.

"We really don't have to drag this out all night, Mr. Haywood."

As angry as I'd been with him before, I'd never imagined the sound of King's voice being a relief to me again, but tonight… it definitely was.

"You're right. I'm not really a fan of unexpected, uninvited guests, you feel me? So…you and your people get the fuck off my property, and we'll call it good, aiight?"

King chuckled. "No. I know she's here, so you can cut the bullshit. Get her in front of me, and *then* we'll be "aiight". If you *don't* get her in front of me, really fuckin' quick, it's going to be the furthest thing from "aiight" in this motherfucker, if *you* feel *me.*"

She…

Is he here for… me???

"Oh, shit… you're gonna set it off in *my* shit, huh?"

"If that's what the fuck I have to do, so be it. We both know I don't mind. We both know I'm not about to argue about the shit for very long either, so what's it going to be?"

I glanced at the security guard to find him leering at me, which made me look down. A quick adjustment covered my exposed bra, which was what had gotten his attention. Quelling the urge to shudder, I smoothed a hand over my dress, flipped my locs over my shoulder… then darted out into the open before the "security" knew what was happening.

"I'm right here," I called out, and several sets of eyes turned to me. My attention went straight to the foyer, where Kingston was standing with Ace just behind me, facing off with Dorian. Or, that's what they *had* been doing. The verbal sparring had stopped, and now the attention was on me.

"Ah, the woman of the hour," King said, his tone disrespectfully casual. Dorian was fuming – tense jaw, tense shoulders, tense posture – while King was, visibly at least, completely relaxed.

He wasn't wearing a jacket. Just the slacks from what was undoubtedly a nice suit, and the sleeves of his button-up were rolled up to the elbows. He looked good… like he'd just left work.

He'd left work to come and get me.

"Asha," Dorian barked, nostrils flared. "I thought I told you to stay in the back?"

King didn't even flinch, as if Dorian hadn't spoke. "Asha… are you okay?"

"She's fine," Dorian answered for me, but King's eyes didn't leave me. They weren't cold like that day in his car – they were alive with concern.

"Is that true?" King asked, with his hands hooked casually in his pockets. "Do you want to be here?"

I forced myself not to look at Dorian, even though his eyes were boring into me. "No."

That word was barely out of my mouth before his hands were out, one stretched toward me. "Then come on. Let's get you home."

I took a step forward without thinking, and then hesitated. The tension around me was smotheringly thick, and as far as I could tell, any wrong move could set off a war.

"Nobody is going to touch you," King assured. His words were directed at me, but his gaze had shifted to Dorian, who was wearing an expression I recognized as a precursor to combustive rage. King's eyes came back to me, igniting a feeling I could only describe as… *safe.*

But then again, thinking about what he'd interrupted, anything was probably safer than where I was right now… so I moved my feet.

As soon as I made it to King's outstretched hand, he handed me over to Ace. "Take her to the car," he demanded, already dropping the soothing tone he'd used to get me to come to him. Ace's arm wrapped around my waist, steering me as she moved to follow his instructions.

"You keep coming to me like this about bitches, I'm gonna start thinking you're one yourself," Dorian growled behind me.

King chuckled – without any of the warmth it usually held. This was sinister, and dangerous… enough to send a chill up my spine as Ace hustled me out.

"Think whatever you want, nigga. *Know* that you'll be leaving that one alone," was the last thing I heard before I was pulled back into the pleasantly cool, fresh air of outside.

My eyes went wide when I saw not one, but four identical Escalades parked outside, with a trio of armed men in front of each one. Ace appeared unfazed by it, quickly ushering me past them, toward the third car in line.

"I-I forgot my purse," I stammered, turning around. Ace gave me a deadpan look, then lifted her wrist, speaking into the flat silver bracelet she always had on.

"She forgot her purse," she said dryly, then rolled her eyes. She opened the door to the SUV, motioning for me to get inside before she turned back to the guys. "If he's not out of there in the next five minutes, light this shit up."

The next few minutes were tense.

Ace climbed in with me and buckled her seatbelt, directing me to do the same. My hands were shaking as I did it, so it took me longer than normal. When I finally clipped it, I looked up to find her gaze on me.

"I didn't say this to you – and I won't bother making your death look like an accident if you claim I did – but… I've known him a good length of time. Enough to know that once he's yours… he's *yours*, and you've got a good thing. Don't fuck it up."

Before I could ask her what she meant, the door opened again. I automatically tensed before the faint hint of King's familiar cologne filled the space. He exchanged a few words with someone outside, and then he climbed in, his large body making the roomy interior feel much smaller. He took the seat beside Ace, then reached across, dropping my purse into my lap before he secured himself in his seat.

And then we were off. I wasn't sure where, but I was relieved.

I looked up, trying to catch King's eyes in the dark space, but they were closed.

After the night – hell, the *day*- I'd just had… I wasn't sure if I should feel slighted, or relieved.

FIFTEEN

ASHA

The whole ride was silent.

Not even Ace spoke up, to deliver a jab, a snarky comment, nothing, so I kept myself quiet as well, not knowing what else to do. This was unfamiliar territory to me.

The rest of the night, the parts with just me and Dorian… not so much.

Desperation had driven me to doing something I *knew* better than to do. Just because Dorian had never *struck* me, I'd somehow convinced myself that was the same thing as never *hurting* me, which wasn't the case, and tonight had brought those repressed memories back in vivid detail.

And maybe… that was for the best. Maybe I needed the reminder of why, in my head, I'd nicknamed the man the devil.

When the car stopped, I didn't move, because I didn't know if I was supposed to. I hadn't asked where we were going – wasn't sure if it mattered, as long as it was far away from Dorian.

Ace and King unbuckled their seatbelts, so I followed suit, then followed them out of the car. When my eyes adjusted to the sudden glare of bright white sidewalks reflecting the streetlights, I quickly realized we were in the parking lot of my building.

"Keys," Ace said, making a "gimme" motion with her hand.

I didn't argue – was too tired to, and too preoccupied wondering why King still hadn't said a word to me. I fished them from the purse and handed them to her, then followed her up the stairs that led to the unit I shared with Cam. King was right behind me, smelling so good it should have been criminal.

In the car, with his eyes closed, I'd gotten to study his face in the thin bands of light that shone through the window as we moved. His features, though still handsome as ever, had been etched with fatigue, and I couldn't help wondering why. Was he sick? Was he eating enough? Getting enough sleep.

I'd shaken my head at myself about the direction of my thoughts.

Guess nothing makes you forget you're mad at a man quicker than him saving you from bodily harm.

At the top of the stairs, I looked out into the parking lot. Only two of the Escalades had made the journey back to my house.

"Is your roommate home?" Ace asked as she pushed my key into the lock. "Or are you expecting anybody else to be here?"

I shook my head. "No, I'm not expecting anyone. But Camille is probably here, and sometimes her friends come over."

Ace nodded, then pulled a gun before she opened the door with one hand, quietly creeping inside. King and I followed, and out of habit, I turned to lock it behind us, coming face to face with his broad chest.

I skirted around him, not daring to let my gaze travel up further.

Awkward silence occupied the space as Ace checked the apartment. It wasn't until she disappeared into the back that I dared another glance at King, only to find him surveying my living space with curious eyes. At some point, he'd put his suit jacket back on, and even in a suit he'd probably been wearing all day, he looked… too expensive to be *here*.

"Why did you come tonight?" I blurted, then immediately dropped my eyes. The question had flashed in my mind, sure, but I'd intended to leave it there – not speak it out loud.

"Because Carl reported that you weren't in a good headspace. After looking into things… I didn't feel like you were in a safe situation, so I rectified it."

I nodded, still looking at the tall, strappy nude heels I'd worn tonight. "So… it goes back to poker then. Like, protection of your investment or something, right? Nothing… personal."

"No," he said, paired with a chuckle that didn't give me the slightest inclination he found something funny. "It was personal as hell, and I'm gonna have to hear about it tomorrow. Maybe even tonight, but… you're protected."

I raised my gaze to his, and was immediately swallowed by an intensity that made me take a step back. There was so much there… raw sincerity, anger, lust… *consideration.* Heat rushed to my face as I considered the implication of his words. At the poker table, and often in real life, I could read people – it was impossible for me with him. When he told me there was nothing intimate between us, I hadn't doubted him. But now…

"Why?"

That one-word question tore his gaze from mine as he swiped a hand over his face. A heavy sigh blew from his mouth, and he angled himself away from me, shaking his head. "I don't know."

"So your roommate isn't here," Ace said, not bothering to keep her voice low since we were alone. "We'll have security out there overnight, and I'll show them her picture. As long as she's alone if she comes in, she won't be stopped or anything, so we can avoid drama there. If she has company… they have to be vetted."

My mouth parted. "Do you think he would come, or send somebody here tonight, after that?"

"I think Dorian is fucking psycho, and we can't be too careful." She patted me on the shoulder as she passed, heading for the door. "Goodnight."

They're leaving me alone?

But I quickly discovered that *they* weren't leaving. Only *she* was. When the apartment door closed behind her, King was the one who locked it, then turned to me with yet another indecipherable something in his eyes.

"Go to sleep," he told me, making me wonder what he saw in *my* face. "It's been a long night. I'm sure you're tired."

My feet started moving before my brain caught up. I was halfway to the hall that led to my room when I stopped, and turned around.

"Are you angry with me?" I asked, and his jaw tightened before he nodded.

"Yes."

"Why?"

"Because you shouldn't have gone to his house. You should have known better."

My nostrils flared. "You don't know my situation," I said, lifting my chin as the defensive words spilled out. "I was doing what I always do – what I had to, to survive, and take care of my family."

"You didn't *have* to."

"I owed him money."

King shrugged. "And now you don't. I could have solved that problem for you weeks ago, Red. All you had to do was ask."

I shook my head. Was it really that simple to him? "I don't like owing people anything."

"Again – now you don't. You're Welcome."

"Yeah, right. I'm really supposed to believe you just… did all this for me? It wasn't because of anything I did, and you don't expect anything in return?"

He shrugged, raising his hands as he did so, like he was baffled by my confusion. "You don't owe me shit," he said, a way that was probably supposed to be soothing, but only served to further frustrate me. Instead of saying anything else, I shook my head, and went to my room.

There, I couldn't get out of my clothes fast enough, leaving the dress in a ball on the floor. I'd never wear it again. Once I was stripped down, I went into the bathroom, stopping when I caught a glimpse of myself in the mirror.

My eyes were glossy, and rimmed in crimson like I'd been crying. I stepped closer to the mirror, sweeping my locs over my shoulder to expose my neck, where I caught a glimpse of redness – irritation from where Dorian's hand had been. There were similar marking on my thighs.

I looked away as a sob caught in my throat, and turned the shower on as hot as it would go. While it warmed, I went back into my room to grab panties and an oversized tee shirt. I left those on the counter, pulled my hair into a high ponytail, adjusted the temperature, and the immersed myself in the spray of hot water.

Who the fuck does he think he's kidding?

Men's kindness never came without a price. I'd learned that lesson from an early age, watching the gendered interactions of the people around me. Women gave. Men took. Sometimes, they afforded you a lifestyle that made it worth the sacrifice.

But, invariably, there was a price. Women paid with their bodies, their health, their time, their sanity, their money, for the privilege of having a man to take these things, and sometimes it was good enough to seem like an investment. Dorian's price had been the little youthful innocence I had left, my sexual agency, and almost… my humanity. I got lavish clothes, gifts, the status of being his girl as the return on my investment. But leaving that life was like leaving a cult – you left *everything* behind.

Kingston Whitfield wasn't fooling anybody. He *had* a price. Either he knew it, and recognized that it was more than any smart woman would accept, which was scary. Or… he hadn't discovered it yet, which meant he'd used me to figure out just how much abuse and stress he could dole out. Which was even more terrifying.

I shook my head, carefully angling myself to not get my hair wet while I let the water stream over my face. Maybe I was wrong. Maybe… I was just jaded. But even if that were true, it didn't change the fact that his no-strings generosity was both foreign and frightening to me.

I couldn't comprehend how I earned it, which made it difficult to fathom how to accept it.

I scrubbed until my skin was sensitive to the touch, then turned the shower off. I dried off, brushed my teeth, lotioned, then dressed, all the things I usually did before bed… and then I went to see what King was doing.

When I stepped out of my room, the apartment was quiet. No low murmur of him talking on a cell phone, no TV. I'd left him in the living room, with the lights on, but it was dark now, and empty. The kitchen was in a similar state.

Despite the limbo I was in over how I felt about him… I had to admit that him leaving while I was in the shower packed a little bit of a sting. My shoulders drooped as I went back to my room, but as soon as I stepped through the doorway, I stopped.

He was there.

In my room.

The chair in the corner, where I draped things I intended to put back in the closet, was occupied, even though I'd emptied it the day before. King's large frame swallowed it up, but I could see a peek of his jacket draped over the back, and his shoes were tucked neatly underneath.

The room was dark, but the subtle glow of the streetlight bloomed through the window. He was staring at me just as hard as I was staring at him, with a slight glint of amusement in his eyes. Probably about the disappointment he'd seen in mine.

"I thought you'd left," I said, stepping into the room, and leaving it dark. I didn't need him to see it in the full light, which would only serve to illustrate how… magnificent… he was, compared to the Walmart – occasionally Target, or IKEA – furnishings of my modest room.

"Nope. Babysitting tonight."

I didn't look at him as I slid under my covers, but the smirk I could hear in his voice irritated me. "I'm not a baby."

"In many ways… you are."

"Am not."

He snickered. "Are too."

I sat up, glaring at him in the dark. "Whatever. Are you sleeping here, or were you just waiting on me?"

"I intended to sleep."

My glare softened. "In the chair?"

"Where else?"

I started to offer the couch, but it occurred to me that he could have started there in the first place. I looked down, at my perfect-for-just-me full sized bed, and licked my lips. "I'd tell you we could share the bed, but… if you're babysitting, that's not exactly appropriate, is it?"

His eyes shot in my direction. There was silence for a moment, and then, "Asha… are you inviting me into your bed?"

It sounded ridiculous out loud. After what he'd just rescued me from, and my musings in the shower… was I *really*?

"Yes. You look like you need a good night's sleep, and it's not happening in that tiny chair."

Not to mention you saved me a few hours ago, and this is the least I could do.

He stood up, and I watched, enthralled, as he stripped down to black boxer briefs. I hated that I enjoyed the show so much, relishing every inch of his rich, smooth brown skin, tinted blue by the darkness as it came into my view. He came to stand at the foot of the bed, staring without speaking for a moment.

"Scoot over."

I glanced down at the bed again, then back at him. "Over where? There's nowhere to scoot."

King shook his head, and then… his knees were on the bed. Then his hands, planted on either side of me as his long limbs made short work of climbing onto the bed. He positioned himself on his side, facing in my direction, and I tried not to inhale too deeply. If I did… I might get more wrapped up than I already was.

If such a thing were possible.

"How the hell are you going to invite somebody into this little ass bed," he grumbled, after I'd laid back down. I was on my back, staring up at the ceiling, and he was so close to me that his words were a pleasing rumble in my chest.

A rumble that turned to a ripple of awareness, working it's way down between my legs. "You didn't have to accept the offer," I whispered.

Why was I whispering?

Maybe it just… felt inappropriate to be loud in the dark.

Or… to talk at all.

So we didn't.

We laid there, until I recognize the telltale signs of his shift in breathing. His eyes were closed when I turned in his direction, and I took the opportunity to stare, as questions ran through my head. *Why is he here? What is happening right now? What the hell am I doing?*

"It's creepy as fuck to stare, Red."

For a second, I didn't breathe. Instead of responding to his words, I turned over to the other side, and my eyes fell on the glowing numbers from the clock. It was barely ten at night, but it felt much, much later.

My breath caught in my throat as his arm snaked around my waist, pulling me closer to him. Even if I'd wanted to resist, my body didn't get the memo. My hips moved immediately, bouncing back to be in line with his. I tried to ignore the groan he let out by closing my eyes, pretending his baritone *hadn't* had my nipples pebble underneath my thin tee-shirt.

I *couldn't* ignore the steady hardening of his dick against my butt check. It intensified the flood of arousal between my legs, and before I could help it, I was squirming.

"Stop that shit," he growled, right against the back of my neck. He was so close that his lips brushed my skin as he spoke. "I'm trying not to fuck you right now."

A smile came to my face, over those crudely spoken words.

He was handsome, rich, and influential. Physically stronger than me. *His* people waiting outside. I'd invited him into my bed. All of the power dynamics played in *his* favor, and yet… he'd chosen to put the control in *my* hands.

If I wasn't wet before…

Instead of "stopping that shit", as he'd asked, I did it harder, grinding into his dick until he grabbed me, pushing me on my back before positioning himself over me, bearing his weight on his knees. He'd pinned my wrists over my head with one hand. With the other, his thumb and pointer finger hooked under my chin while his other fingers rested against my neck with a vague hint of pressure.

"What are you doing?" he asked, boring into me with that same intense gaze from before.

I swallowed as hard as I could with his hand at my neck. I wasn't nervous, or tense, or worried. My body was under his control, but fear never crossed my mind. I was… *hot.* Very, very hot.

I met his eyes, spreading my legs open and hooking them around his thighs. No ambiguity. No chance for him to misunderstand, or second-guess me when I told him, "I'm calling your bluff."

So… he laid down his hand.

We met in a bruising, heated mash of his lips against mine, and a second later, he introduced me to his tongue, swiping it into my eagerly parted mouth. He didn't move his hand, he used it to maneuver me into his will as he devoured me in deep, fervent kisses that forced shortened, desperate breaths. His hold on my wrists dissipated, and his hand made a welcomed reappearance between my legs.

I bucked into him as soon as he touched me, barely feeling the clumsy click of our teeth as he pushed his fingers inside of me. I was so wet I'd already soaked the seat of my panties, and he groaned his appreciation into my mouth as he buried them deep, probing. That thought had barely made it from one side of my mind to the other when his exploration ended with his fingertips toying with the spot that made me want to crawl out of my skin in pleasure, and his thumb circling my soaked clit.

"*Ahhhh*," I whimpered, pulling away from the kiss to throw my head back. The hand that had been around my neck pushed the covers to the floor, out of the way. The cool air tingled against my heated skin, creating another level of stimulation that only intensified when King pulled my shirt up, exposing my breasts. Then he occupied his mouth again.

The tautness mounting in the depths of my stomach snapped as soon as his teeth grazed my nipple, followed quickly by the hot rasp of his tongue. My mouth fell open, but nothing came out – I didn't have enough air in my lungs to come and make noise at the same time. I clenched around his fingers, involuntarily pulling and releasing as he pumped me harder, stretching the orgasm out. I sucked in a breath, letting it out as a strangled moan as pleasure overloaded me, engulfing me to the point that everything seemed to freeze for a moment, coming back in warp speed as I released, then collapsed into my sheets.

But only for a second.

Because after that, he was tugging my panties down my thighs, past my knees, off my feet. The shirt was next, leaving me completely bare, and my eager hands found the waistband of his boxers, tugging them down. They weren't even off before I wrapped my legs around his waist again, and he sank inside of me.

The sound that rumbled up from his throat when our hips met sent a tremble down my spine. He dropped onto me with his face in my neck, sucking and biting as he stroked into me. My fingernails dug into his arms, holding tight as he filled me up. Out of nowhere, a flash of déjà vu hit me, and the memory of Dorian's mouth on me, my nails in him, fighting to get free, flashed in my mind.

"What's wrong?" King's voice brought me back into the moment, and I opened my eyes. He was still inside of me, but not moving as his eyes roved over my face, waiting for an answer. "You tensed up on me," he explained. "And you're shredding my arms."

I released the breath I'd been holding, running my tongue over my lips, which were suddenly dry.

"Do you need to stop?"

"*No*," I said immediately, finding my voice. My hands moved to cup his face, bringing his mouth to mine. "*No*," I repeated as I kissed him, over and over again. I pushed my tongue into his mouth, tasting him the way he'd tasted me, feeling empowered by the way his dick twitched in me until he started moving again.

We were back in rhythm. Deep, slow kisses synced with deep, slow strokes that stoked the flames of another climax in the pit of my belly, then got steadily faster. Harder. Deeper, as he pushed my legs up further. From his waist to his back, then spread wide, hanging from the bend in his elbows as he drove into me. Then, up on his shoulders while he slowed down. Deep kisses and deep strokes again, so slow and intense that I started thinking I wouldn't mind at all if he wanted to take permanent residence inside of me.

With my feet still up on his shoulders, he rose up on his knees. My weight was on my shoulders until he hooked his arms around me, holding me as he plunged into me.

It felt so good I couldn't hold back a scream.

Length, thickness, and *gravity* were apparently the perfect combination to drive me out of my mind. He let my legs drop from his shoulders to the bends of his arms again, using it to keep me spread wide open for him as he… ruled me.

By time we dropped to the bed, dripping with sweat, my legs were like jelly. They couldn't do anything but hang open uselessly as he kissed, sucked, bit my neck, branding me with memories for this night that overthrew anything else.

He moved up, catching my lip between his teeth before he sucked it, then gave me another kiss that would've made me weak in the knees, if I could feel my knees. And then he drew back, just enough to look me right in eyes as he stroked me.

I didn't look away – couldn't even if I wanted to. I was in that narrow, hazy space right between having and not having an orgasm, and the sweet, slippery, delicious friction created by the in-and-out of his dick had me paralyzed. My eyes wanted to roll back in bliss, but couldn't. I was stuck. *We* were stuck, magnetized to each other as our bodies held this conversation.

We were in tune.

Somehow.

I fell into the abyss of an orgasm, and King fell with me, gripping me hard and pumping harder, expending the last of his strength to release.

I was drained.

Like someone had picked me and wrenched out every last bit of my energy. Inexplicably, I was also… giddy. High.

Insanely happy.

Which was just… confusing.

Beside me, King groaned, then pressed a kiss to my bare shoulder. I found the energy from somewhere to blush, over that of all things, after what we'd done. "You hungry?" he asked, his words muffled against my skin. "I'm fucking starving."

I turned my head, casting my gaze to where he was. Slightly below me on the bed, and it took him a second to look up, but when he did, there it was…

Butterflies.

I didn't say anything, just looked. And after a moment, he maneuvered his large body up a little so that we were… back in sync. His arm came around my waist again, pulling me close, in a move that was so intimate… I didn't know what to do with it.

So I did nothing. I just sat with the feeling, letting myself enjoy it, and I didn't even feel the usual sense of dread attached with most times I gave in to that particular emotion.

Interesting.

I woke up in a panic.

While last night had ended on that sticky-sweet note, this was a new day, and reality came rushing to me as soon as I opened my eyes and recognized that I wasn't alone in my own bed.

King was like a rock covered in thick moss – the pliant presence of muscle and skin covered the hard angles, making him a comfortable resting place, but he was heavy, and immovable. It took me several minutes to maneuver my way out of his grip, and once I was free, he rolled onto his back and spread out his arms, drifting right back into a deep sleep.

Jesus.

In the bright, revealing light of day, his large frame seemed even bigger, taking up most of the bed. A blush heated my face as it occurred to me *just how close* we had to have been last night for that sleeping arrangement to work out.

Kingston Whitfield slept in – is currently sleeping in – my bed.

Naked, under my covers.

Well, somewhat. In the confusion of me climbing out, they'd gotten twisted and disheveled, leaving his chest and midsection bare, all the way down to where fine sprinkles of hair started their trail to his groin. There were no tattoos marring the smooth expanse of his skin, no piercings in his ears, none of that. Just him, unadorned, with one powerful thigh peeking from underneath the covers, as gloriously naked as we'd both been when we passed out.

Now that I was upright, gravity began to take course. The sudden feeling of moisture between my legs – not cause by my arousal – pulled me out of my reverence of King, and I snatched up my phone from the bedside table, hurriedly unlocking it before I tiptoed into the bathroom.

"Come on, come on," I urged, as I waited on the app to open. Before my eyes, a calendar popped up on my phone. I found the day's date, and relief sunk my shoulders when I saw that the little box was empty. This same day, exactly a week ago, had a bright teal starburst inside, indicating the most fertile day of my cycle.

I blew out a cleansing breath, silently thanking God for *that* miracle. We'd been… I didn't want to call it reckless, but certainly not thinking it through when we'd gone at it multiple times without protection. But at least – *at least* – I wouldn't be worried about not getting my period because of an unplanned pregnancy.

As I moved into the shower to clean myself up, I thought about the things I *did* have to worry about.

Like Dorian.

No matter how rich, powerful, whatever, King was, I knew Dorian very well. There was virtually no way he was going to let last night go without some type of answer, some type of payback. And while stepping out had felt right in the moment, I couldn't help wondering how he would collect – and he *would* collect.

I'd lied.

I'd looked him right in the face and told him I had little interest in King, acted like I barely knew him. But King's actions to retrieve me from Dorian had been too bold, too discourteous, too dominant for it to not be clear that there was *something.* They were the kind of actions a man did for someone he either cared about, or badly wanted, or both. And the comment Dorian made to him last night, "*If you keep coming at me like this about bitches"*... had King done something like this before? Was this just his M.O.?

What the hell was I getting myself into, by getting into this with him?

When I exited the bathroom, he was still sleeping. I retrieved a fresh shirt and shorts and pulled them on, intending to go to the kitchen for a glass of water. But when I got there and saw Camille sitting at the counter eating a yogurt and a banana while she tapped away at something on her phone, that went out the window.

"Camille!" I hissed, and she looked up, startled at first, but then she grinned.

"*You* look well-fucked," she teased, and nodded her head in approval. "Good, cause you've been stressed the hell out ever since you started getting ready for that tournament. Did you meet another big-dicked gentleman to sweep you off your feet for the night?"

I blew out a sigh, then motioned for her to follow me. She climbed down from her barstool and followed me down the hall to my room, where I peeked in first to make sure King was still sleeping, and at least partially covered.

Cam's eyes went wide when I motioned for her to look in. She grabbed the doorknob, pulling it almost closed as she turned to whisper, "Girl, is that Kingston Whitfield? As in… *the* Whitfields? As in, Black Vegas royalty?"

I gave her a sheepish nod, and her mouth fell open before she peeked in again, slowly shaking her head. "*Damn he's fine*," she muttered, then turned back to me, fully closing the door. She propped her hands on her hips, and frowned. "So… wait… your little hotel tryst, weeks ago… K.W…" I nodded again, and she twisted her lips. "You, my dear roomie, have some explaining to do."

And… she was right.

I did.

So I explained.

Back in the kitchen, I told her everything I'd been keeping to myself, from finding out about who K.W was, to the strip poker, to Dorian showing up, to the spa, to the surprise hospital bill… everything. She listened without interruption, letting me tell it all at my own pace, and when I was done, she shook her head, lifting her hands to her face.

"How the hell did I miss all of this?" she asked, looking distressed. "What kind of friend am I that all of this was happening and I didn't know?"

I shook my head. "A *busy* one, Cam. You're the *star* of the show you're working right now, and that's stressful enough. I couldn't burden you with any of this."

"Says *who*?" Cam lifted her hands in disbelief, then pushed out a sigh. "Asha, I know you think that because I'm bubbly or whatever that I'm… soft, I guess. That I can't handle things. And I'll admit, the way I handled things with Jared probably contributed to that. I was naïve, and silly, and couldn't figure out for myself that I needed to leave, until you forced the issue for me. You have no idea how grateful I am to you for that, for you and Cree getting him to leave me alone. But you have to understand… I don't play about the people I care about, girl. You can come to me anytime, with *anything*. I'm not too pretty to ride out, okay?"

I laughed at the serious expression she was giving me, and kept grinning when she stood to give me a hug. "Whatever, Cam. This isn't the type of stuff I should be putting on you. I'm *supposed* to be able to depend on my family."

"So I'm not family?" she asked, drawing back. "And as protective as Jackson is about you, he ain't family?"

I sighed. "You know what I mean."

"Nope," she shook her head. "I most certainly do not. Blood is not the only thing that makes people family, and hell… sometimes blood does the worst things to you. You want family, Asha? You've got it. You just have to expand your definition."

I dropped my gaze for a moment, considering her words. My eyes started watering when I realized she was right. In the time we'd known each other, Camille had *always* felt like a bestie. When I moved into the extra bedroom in what was just *her* apartment at the time, all I'd had was a security deposit and a month of rent, a small suitcase, and the clothes on my back. Over the years, she'd been nothing but generous to me. Never tripping if I needed a little help covering the rent because of an unexpected expense, making sure I ate, checking on me after I'd worked a long shift… things I'd probably taken for granted a little because my eyes were so wide open with the lack of consideration from my… family.

Maybe she was right.

I needed to rethink my definition.

"Anyway, I'm kinda mad at you," Camille said, stepping away to go back to her breakfast. "We haven't talked about it yet, but you're bogus for *all* that talk about "Jax" while never bothering to mention he was that *fine*. I was already in love from the things you'd told me from the club, but now…" A sly grin took over her mouth as she squirmed in her seat.

I laughed. "I wasn't looking at Jackson like that – on purpose. I had to compartmentalize the fine-ness and lock that shit up. He's my boss!"

"You still have eyes though," she accused. "But that's okay… I see he wasn't really trying to give me any attention."

A knock sounded at the door before I could respond to that, and Cam seemed ready to change the subject from the way she practically dived at the door.

She unlocked and opened it without looking through the peephole first, a habit of hers that I hated. I didn't even have a chance to scold her about it before Ace walked through the door, uninvited, holding up a duffel bag.

"King requested this from the car," she said, looking back and forth expectantly between Camille and me.

My eyes went wide. "Wait…he's awake?"

"For at least the past few minutes," Ace shrugged. "Are you taking this, or am I?"

"I'll take it," I said quickly, hurrying to retrieve the bag. I wasn't sure why – I knew she'd seen King in his boxers at least once, the day of our strip poker game, and… probably in less than that, at one point or another. Hell, I'd just set out his semi-nude body for my roommate. But still… it didn't feel right for anyone to take that bag in, except me. "Cam, this is Ace. Kingston's…"

"Assistant," Ace supplied. I left the two of them looking at each other awkwardly to take the bag to my bedroom.

The bed was empty.

A quick glance in my bathroom showed King's naked ass in front of my toilet, as a steady stream of liquid broke the surface of the water. Aside from the fact he was relieving himself, even *this* view was delicious. Those strong thighs, firm ass, the corded muscles of his back and shoulders…*geez.*

"I have your bag," I said when he was finished, stepping into view as he washed his hands. He caught my gaze in the mirror, motioning for me to come to him, and I did, more out of compulsion than anything. He took the bag from me and put it on the counter, not saying anything as he dug in, then came up with a bag of toiletries.

"So how'd you sleep?"

His eyes came to me, seemingly surprised by the question. "Like a baby on his mother's titty," he said, smirking as his gaze dropped to my breasts, which immediately responded with hard nipples. I rolled my eyes, crossing an arm over them as I leaned into the doorframe. He took out a toothbrush and rinsed it, then picked up the toothpaste. My eyes went to his back, examining him as he moved. This time, the scar across his back caught my attention.

"What is that from?" I asked, reaching to touch it. He didn't pull away, but he didn't look at me either, keeping his focus on loading his toothbrush with paste.

"Ace," he said, casually. "And a fucking antique sword. She swears she only hit me with the flat of the blade."

He put his toothbrush in his mouth after that, as if he'd told me a completely normal, every day thing. I didn't get the impression he was interested in offering more, so I picked up my own toothbrush, set it up, and started brushing.

He finished first, and then said nothing before he climbed in the shower. I took the opportunity to complete my morning skin routine, then returned to my room where I eyed the bed.

I had to change the sheets.

In the time I'd lived here, I'd *never* had to change the sheets because of a man. I'd slept with them, yes, but kept them out of my space, out of my psyche. Now that King had been here, I didn't know if I'd be able to look at it the same again.

I stripped the sheets off, then picked up one of the pillows to get the case off. The scent that hit my nose – familiar, but still alien enough in the context of my bedroom to catch my attention – made my stomach clench. I closed my eyes and lifted the pillow, bringing it to my nose.

What an overdone cliché to become, Asha.

My eyes popped open.

Was I *really* about to stand here and inhale his scent from my pillows like a love-struck teenager? I let that question play in my mind for a few seconds, and then closed my eyes again, because… yes.

Yes, I was.

It was so, so good. Clean and leathery and woody with a little touch of spice. I groaned a little – *so gooooood* – and then quickly snatched it down when I heard the water in the bathroom shut off. All of the linens were shoved into a pile, and I was coming out of my closet with a fresh set when King emerged from the bathroom, pulling a black tee shirt over his head. I stopped in my tracks, a little mesmerized by the sight of him dressed down, after only ever seeing two versions – Naked King, or Suited King. This new one, Casual King, was just as delicious.

"Just so there's no ambiguity," he started then moved to start picking up his clothes from the floor, "I told Dorian not to bother you again. He doesn't have shit to bother you about. You don't owe him anything. I took care of it. If he's a smart man… he'll let it go."

I looked up from my work of attaching the new fitted sheet. "We both know how often the heart overrules the head."

"That's true." King caught one of the corners for me, tucking it underneath the mattress. When he straightened, he had my panties from last night in his hand. He smirked, then slipped them into his pocket. "But in his business, he should know better. So like I said… you don't owe him."

"And what about you?" I asked, unfolding the flat sheet. "What do I owe you?"

"I told you last night that you didn't owe me anything."

I scoffed. "Yeah. And you still seem to think that's comforting."

"Why wouldn't it be?"

"Because nobody gets something for nothing, and nobody gives it either. So… name your *something*. At least give me the courtesy of letting me know what you expect from me."

"*Nothing*," he said, shaking his head. "I don't expect shit from you, Red. You don't have anything I need."

Those words suck the air from my lungs, and my hands stilled from smoothing out the sheets. "Not… anything?"

That question came out as a whisper, and King cursed under his breath. "Shit, you know what I mean."

"No, I don't," I snapped, standing up straight. "You're so fucking reticent with me, I don't *know* anything."

"Materially." He stepped into the bathroom and grabbed his bag, then came back out. "I have everything I need, *materially*. I'm not Dorian's bitch ass. I don't need to take anything from you to make myself feel like the man – I just *am*. I came for you last night because I'm haunted by enough shit already. I didn't need another thing."

"So it was about easing conscience. Not about me?"

He gave another of his humorless chuckles. "Here you fucking go."

"Yes, here I fucking go!" I jeered, coming around the bed. "You're saying *all* these words, Kingston, and still, somehow, not saying *anything*."

"Not sayi—" he stopped himself, shaking his head before he mumbled under his breath, "*I'm* not saying anything?"

I moved to stand in front of him, blocking his access to his bag. His chin went up, eyes pointed at the ceiling. "No," I declared. "You really, *really* aren't. Unless you're speaking some language I don't understand, you're not saying *shit* to me."

"Well maybe your headstrong ass needs a translator," he barked, glaring down at me. "Letting you keep your job – saying something. Getting you in that tournament – saying something. Running up in another nigga's house like goddamned Batman – saying something. Not walking away from this irksome conversation – fucking *saying something.* It's not my fault if you aren't listening."

I scowled right back, swallowing the lump of emotion trying to build in my throat. "How *dare you* act as if you didn't stand in my face and rip my heart out of my damn chest with that "*it's not personal*" shit? I was *so* grateful, *so* happy, thought it was your way of telling me that we'd made some sort of connection and then you kicked me right back into my place. So you and your mixed signals don't get to—"

The rest never came out.

King's arm went around my waist, snatching me into him as his mouth covered mine. It pissed me off… but I didn't pull away. I let him kiss me, and with every nibble on my lips, every swipe of his tongue, I wondered if *this* was saying something too.

"I made myself clear to you last night… and I don't like repeating myself, Red." He was hard again, pushing into my stomach. I tried to ignore it, focusing on his words. "It was always personal. And don't ask me *why*. I don't know *why*, it just is. Are you still confused?"

I swallowed again. His eyes pleaded with me to say *no*, but I nodded instead. The truth. "Yes."

His nostrils flared as he pushed at frustrated puff of air. "Join the fucking club."

He let me go after that, then gently pushed me aside to get to his bag. He pulled out socks, and immaculate black and white Jordan's, then sat down in the chair to put them on. I went back to making my bed in the silence that followed, and was almost done when another knock sounded at the door.

Thinking that maybe it was Ace again, I moved to leave the bedroom, but King stopped me at the door. "Where are you going?"

I raised an eyebrow. "To answer my front door."

"Isn't your roommate here?"

"Yeah, but—"

"So she can handle it."

The retort I wanted to give died on my lips when the distinct sound of Ace saying *"What the fuck are you doing here?"* reached my ears. King obviously heard it too, because he led the charge down the hall, where the first thing I saw was Cree standing at the door.

Ace was in his face.

"I should be asking you the same thing," he said back, scowling at her. "I'm here to see my damned sister."

In a flash, Ace had pulled a gun, aiming right for Cree's chest. A loud "*Whoaaa!*" came from me, Camille, and King at the same time. Camille and I were shocked, and afraid. King was trying to calm her down.

"She doesn't have any siblings," Ace said in a cold voice. "I know that because I looked into her when I looked into Asha. And *you* don't have any siblings either, so tell another fucking lie! Why. Are. You. Here?!"

"He's not lying," Camille said, approaching with her hands up. To both of our surprise, King stepped forward, snatching her behind him. "We were in a foster home together," she called from around his back. "We aren't blood, so we don't have the same last name, but he's my brother."

"Asha, is that true?" Ace asked, and I stumbled over my answer.

"I… I… um, I guess?"

Ace jabbed Cree in the chest with the gun, and he didn't flinch. He was stone-still, waiting for a chance to act without ending up in the hospital.

"I've always known him as her brother," I said, trying to keep my voice steady. "I didn't know they weren't blood. I assumed their parents had divorced or something."

King's voice rang out, as soon as I was quiet. "We're good here. We *know* Detective Bradley isn't about any of Dorian's shit. Chill."

Ace's eyes went to King, and in that moment of distraction, Cree had the gun out of her hand. Before she could fight it, he'd turned around, pinning her arms behind her. "The very next time you pull a gun on me, you'd better pull the trigger," he hissed in her ear, then shoved her away.

Immediately, Ace caught her balance and turned around with murder in her eyes, but a sharply delivered "*Ace*!" stopped her in her tracks. "Fuck!" she growled, then turned away, speaking into the bracelet at her wrist. "How the hell was he allowed up here and nobody said shit to me?"

Cree adjusted his collar, then turned to look at me and Camille, who'd emerged from behind King's back. "Somebody wanna tell me what the hell is happening?"

"Alicia and Kingston are Asha's guests," Camille said, looking over to where Ace had moved into the kitchen, and was cursing out whoever was on the other end of her earpiece. "And it would seem that the beautiful armed woman in the kitchen has beef with you, Cree. Something you want to tell me?"

"Not at all," he said, dryly. While I hadn't gotten quite the same impression, I could certainly see why Ace might be interested in Cree. He was ruggedly handsome – dark brown sugar skin, baldhead, bearded, well built, and pretty hazel eyes that had made me blush more than a few times.

"She's on edge," King offered. "We may have had a little incident with Dorian Haywood."

Cree whistled. "An incident, huh? A different one?" His eyes came to me, lighted with amusement before he shook his head and looked back to King. "You sure know how to pick 'em."

"Wow, shade!" I said, crossing my arms. "And right here in my face?"

He grinned. "You know that's the only kind I throw." He turned to Camille. "I need to talk to you baby girl."

"About what? Is everything okay?" Camille asked, stepping closer.

Cree glanced over his shoulder, noticing Ace standing close by, with a scowl on her face. "Why don't you ask Alicia? She might know, since… she looked into me."

"Oh, kiss my ass," she muttered, rolling her eyes.

He chuckled, in a flirtatious sort of way that made me and Cam both cringe a little. "Finally, an invitation?"

Ace didn't respond. Instead, she stomped out, slamming the door behind her.

"We'll let you two talk," King said, then grabbed my hand, pulling me back down the hall. In the room, he picked up his bag, then turned to me. "I'm going to head out to handle some business, but we're leaving security. If you leave, they're going to follow. Okay?"

I nodded, and my eyes went wide when he turned like he was really leaving. "Wait!" I called, then went to the nightstand, where I pulled out his watch. "Um… I'm sure you want this back," I said, holding it out to him.

He looked at it for a moment before he took it from my hands. "I thought you'd sold this. To pay for the tournament, or… the debt to Dorian."

"I thought about it. But… it wasn't really mine to sell. Or at least, it never felt like it."

"My father gave me this watch. When I first started at Whitfield Inc."

"I know," I told him, then removed it from his hands to slide it on his wrist, and clasp it. "It's special to you. I don't know why in the hell you gave it to me."

He chuckled. "Because I'm a man of my word. I set the terms of the game, had to follow through."

"And… you didn't think I'd win. You underestimated me."

He lifted his shoulder in a shrug. "Maybe."

"Big mistake," I teased, running a finger across his chest. He caught my hand, pulling me into him while he stared into my eyes with that now-familiar, heart-pounding intensity.

“Or not,” he said, then pressed a kiss to my lips that wasn’t nearly long enough. “I’ll see you later.”

I nodded, hating it when he let me go, and disappeared through the doorway.

I bit down on my lip, trying to keep myself from smiling, but it broke free anyway.

SIXTEEN

KING

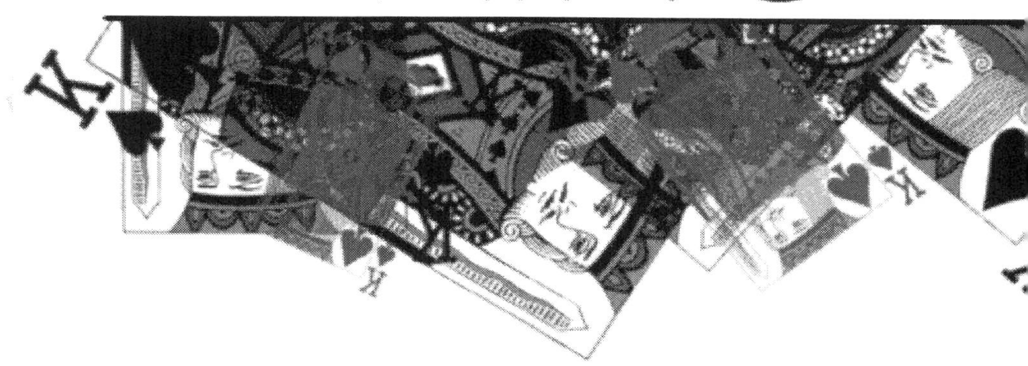

"Have you lost your goddamned mind!?"

My jaw clenched as I looked straight ahead. You didn't survive thirty-plus years with parents like mine without taking your fair share of verbal lashings. I was a grown man, sure, but there was a certain boundary of respect that I would be very, *very* hard pressed to cross.

I wouldn't call my father a harsh man – especially not in dealings with family – but he wasn't exactly easygoing either. When he got in his head that you'd made an egregious mistake – or even just a stupid decision – he wasn't shy about making it known. Never hesitated to let you know exactly what he thought, even if it was ugly.

But I could shoot back.

We were men, and it was understood that while I would stay on the side of respectfulness, there was a high likelihood of me saying some slick shit back. This kept things balanced – two grown men having a conversation.

But in *this* conversation, there was no balance.

My mother didn't play that shit.

At first, it had been just me and my father, discussing the events of the night before. But then, the door to his office flew open and my mother stormed in with the force of a tornado, hands on her hips, brow pinched in a scowl.

"Well?" she snapped, repositioning her arms to cross her chest as her nostrils flared. "Are you going to answer my question?! Let me repeat it for you, just in case – *Have you lost your goddamned mind*? And here's a bonus question – *Do you need some help finding it*?"

She didn't want me to answer that.

While it could be an actual conversation between my father and I, with my mother, you shut your ass up. She had the questions and the responses, saw past, present, and future, and wouldn't think twice about hurting your grown ass feelings.

Best practice was to shut the fuck up.

"Maybe I'm stupid," she said, hip propped against my father's desk. I was seated in front of it, with him seated behind. He had his elbow on the desktop, chin clasped in his hand, eyes full of amusement at the scene going down in front of him. *Of course* he thought this shit was funny. My mother, by default, had a calm, soothing sort of demeanor. Nurturing. But on the other side of that… was what I was seeing now.

"Is that what it is?" she asked, with a quizzical look etched into her elegant features. "You think your mama *just* fell off the turnip truck, don't you?" she stared at me like she was waiting for an answer, but as soon as I opened my mouth she waved a hand, dismissing anything I was about to say. "You *have* to. Because that's the only, *only* scenario where this makes any sense. You think your mama is *stupid*," she accused, jabbing a finger in my direction. "But I promise you, I am *not*."

Nobody thinks you're stupid, woman.

"Then why the hell did you run your ass out of here with a small army?" she snapped, like she'd heard my private thoughts. "Who the *hell* do you think you are, Liam Neeson?"

No.

"Oh, that's definitely it. You think you're in a movie, or on TV. You're an action hero now, huh son? That's what you think?"

"Mama—"

"Don't you mama me, boy! Your father, and *his* father, and *his* father before him did not build this wealth, this name, so you could leverage it to run behind every hussy that convinces you her legs have the secret to happiness between them. You *barely* escaped jail time over the first one, and here you go again!"

"Mama—"

"*Be quiet!*" she bellowed, voice breaking with emotion. "What if… what if… you'd gotten… *hurt*?"

There it was.

The *real* reason she was so upset.

Not because I thought she was stupid – wherever the fuck that came from – or because I was messing up the family name, or because I might go to jail.

No.

She was mad that I'd put myself in danger.

"We do not fool around with drug dealers and criminals," she said, clearing her throat. "Legitimate business is cutthroat enough, and we worked too hard to leave the other stuff behind, with our legacy intact, to be drug back into it. Especially not by the likes of a Dorian Haywood."

"And no one is trying to," I replied, attempting a soothing tone that earned me a scowl. "I promise you, the last thing I intended to do was end my day on a note like that, but I couldn't just sit back and let something happen to her."

My mother rolled her eyes. "Who is implying that you should have? *No one.* But the fact of the matter is that if you had come to one of us, we could have helped in a way that was a helluva lot more discreet than the SWAT team mess you pulled. Was all of that really necessary?"

"With the likes of Dorian Haywood, as you put it yourself… yes. It was. Disrespect, and strong shows of force – those are the only things he understands. If I'd gone in there without any insurance, it would've tripled the chances of a bullet in my head."

She propped her hands on her hips. "No. He would have done no such thing, knowing who you are. He *knows* the hierarchy in this city."

"Regardless of the hierarchy… love and obsession can make you act against the proper order of things, and against your own self-interests."

My mother just blinked at me for several seconds before she shook her head. "You'd know, wouldn't you?"

"Yes. I would."

She looked to my father, who was still trying to appear as though he wasn't paying attention, but I know he was tuned in to every word. "Are you going to say something to him?"

He shrugged. "Say what exactly, Angela? The boy is grown. And it's not as if I would have reacted much differently."

Hmm. A big difference from what he said about me trying to rescue Robyn.

"But the context is different Daniel," my mother argued. "You and I are *in love,* of course you would risk things for me, but your son isn't…" she stopped, with a quizzical look on her face as she turned to me. "I mean… *are you*?"

"No! *Hell no*," I said, standing from my chair. "Listen, I don't mean to be rude, but… is my trip to the principal's office over now?"

"It's over when I say it is." My mother gave me a stern, piercing look that had my knees bending to deliver me back to my chair. "Just because you're Mr. Fightclub around here, doesn't mean *I* am scared of you. You're not too old for me to make your Daddy take off his belt."

"And neither are you," My father teased, making her giggle, and I groaned. He was deflecting her anger and calming her down, which I should have been grateful for, but these were still my parents.

Ugh.

"Call whatever it is you're feeling for Ms. Davis whatever you want, son. Explore it, it's good for you. Not to mention, I actually like this one. But – and I plan on delivering this message *personally* to her as well – what I *will not* do, not this time, and not ever again, is sit back and watch another woman run my baby into the ground."

I scoffed. "Nobody ran me into the ground, and I'm not a—"

"*Call it what you want*," she said, not even acknowledging that I'd spoken. "I am not blind or stupid, and I know what I saw. I should have burned that girl's entire life down, but I let it ride because you loved her, and you needed to make your own mistakes. Everyone knows that I am a woman who finds strength and dignity in restraint, but the very next time someone hurts one of my children… I will be downright hedonistic in my indulgence in, and execution of, their very worst nightmares and sorrows."

When she finished speaking, her eyes were dark and cold, face set in the harsh lines of anger. But then she blinked, and it was gone. She smiled at me.

"With that in mind, *now* you may go."

I didn't have to be told twice.

I stood and shook my father's hand, then turned to my mother, wrapping her in my arms. "Stop trying to be a gangster, woman. You're not tough," I teased before I kissed her cheek.

She caught my face in her hands and returned the gesture before looking me in the eyes. "If anything else happens, you *call your father.*"

"Aye, captain."

"I'm serious, King. You… you don't understand how it hurt me to see you hurting, and then to find out what she'd gotten herself into. For us to have to send you halfway across the world to keep you out of trouble…"

"I know, Mama. Stop worrying. I'm going to be okay."

"You'd better be."

"I will."

Finally, she nodded, then dropped her hands to wave me out of the room. I tossed a last word to my father, and then I was out into the lobby that preceded my father's office, where Ace was waiting.

When she saw me, she didn't even hesitate. She got up, got on the phone, and we headed for the car to get to *Reverie.* Everything else aside… there was still work to be done.

"So it looks like that's the only time that will work for both of us?"

I slid the folder that held the medical center paperwork aside to pull my tablet from underneath the pile on top of my desk. I tapped a few buttons to wake up the screen, then navigated to my mobile calendar.

"Uhhh." My eyes scanned the boxes filled with meetings and important dates. "Yes. Some stuff will have to get moved around on my end, but that should work. I'll have Ace call Penny, and we'll get it set up."

"Bet," Trei said. "I'll see you in a few days, man."

We hung up the call, and I sat back in my chair. All morning, and into the afternoon I'd been swamped with work, but still preoccupied. It was a wonder I'd gotten anything done, but I'd somehow managed to be productive.

I'd made a decision about the hospital – we would invest, which was a decision I'd made before I found out Asha's mother was one of their patients. I wasn't saying anything about it to *her* yet – I wasn't looking forward to a conversation where I had to convince Asha my investment wasn't about her – but in a few weeks, her family, among others, would be getting reimbursement checks about those bullshit charges they'd put out. That was the *first* demand I would make after the paperwork was signed, but I hadn't said anything to the hospital yet either.

I would definitely give them an answer before I left for the trip I'd just arranged with Trei, for the two of us to represent Whitfield Inc when we went back overseas for a second look at a few potential casino properties. I'd finished up a few other things here and there, but no matter how much I tried to busy myself…

Asha stayed in the peripherals of my mind.

And, in what seemed to be a growing trend, because she was on my mind, not even five minutes later Ace strolled in with Asha at her heels, wearing an expression that was the exact opposite of the serenity I'd hoped she would find after I left her at her apartment this morning.

"She's trying to dodge her security," Ace explained. Annoyance dripped from her tone.

Beside her, Asha crossed her arms. "I do *not* need to be followed into the bathroom. It's too damn much!"

"That's not for you to decide."

Ace's response obviously set Asha even more on edge, because she drew her head back and scowled. "Excuse me? How the hell is it *not for me to decide*?"

"That's not obvious to you?"

Asha sucked her teeth. *"Obviously* not. Whose decision is it then, if it's not *mine*?"

Ace let out a contented sigh, and a smirk spread over her lips as she looked pointedly in my direction. As if she was just now realizing I was there, Asha turned to me and crossed her arms too, in the same stance as Ace. Only difference?

Asha wasn't smiling.

"You said there would be people outside of my apartment. Fine. You said they would follow if I went somewhere, just to make sure I was okay. *Fine.* You *didn't* say that they would come in the casino, standing over me like damn sentries while I tried to play poker, get a drink, while I peed! That isn't fine! I need you to tell them to give me some space."

I shook my head. "No can do. I need to make sure you're good."

"There's enough security inside the casino that–"

"The security *stays*, Asha. There's really no point in you arguing."

That… may have been the wrong thing to say.

Somehow, Asha's demeanor turned even more frosty, and she narrowed her eyes. "Are you telling me that you are going to blatantly disregard what I want?"

"To keep you safe? Yes."

"Bullshit," she snapped. "This isn't about me. This is your Jamie St. Patrick wannabe ass wanting to control me, and I am *not* on board!"

Ace busted out laughing as I squinted, confused.

"Wait, back up… who the fuck is Jamie St. Patrick? Do I know a Jamie? Is that one of the owners from the Rainbow Resort? " I asked Ace, who seemed to laugh even harder at the question.

"No," she sniffed, wiping tears from her eyes. "She's talking about this soft ass "crimelord" from a TV show, and you should be offended. She's roasting the fuck outta you."

I frowned, looking at Asha. "So I'm… soft, now? *Me*?"

"What?!" she asked, eyes wide. "No! I don't think that! Ghost isn't soft," she insisted, looking at Ace, who pursed her lips in incredulity.

"You think I'm soft?" I asked Ace, and her eyebrows pulled together dramatically.

"You know, I think I hear somebody calling my name," she said, then turned on her heels to head out.

"What the *fuck*," I growled. "Ace you better turn your ass back around and explain this shit to me. Who the fuck do I need to set straight?"

She was rolling her eyes when she turned around. "*Nobody*, geez! You're… hard when you need to be." She shuddered, and shook her head as soon as those words came out. "Ugh," she gagged, like she was dry heaving. "That was the double-entendre from hell, and on that note… I'm going to let you two talk. Bye."

Ace was gone before I could wrap my head around a response, leaving me with Asha, who, from the look on her face, was ready to go toe to toe.

"I'm busy right now," I told her, which earned a deep scowl that in the moment, I didn't really give a fuck about. "Security is not something I'm going to negotiate with you. Not now, or ever." I dropped my gaze to my desk, reopening the folder I'd been reviewing before.

"Are you serious right now?" Asha asked. When I didn't give her the attention she wanted, she moved closer to the desk. "You *seriously* don't even give a damn what I want? I don't have a say in the matter?"

Finally I looked up, leaning back in my chair as I met her eyes to make myself perfectly clear. "No. On *this* matter, I *don't* give a damn, and you *don't* have a say. After I had to sit and take it while I got my ass handed to me about *your* shit this morning, you're just going to have to learn to live with it, Red."

"I don't *have* to do shit."

I grinned at her, then turned back to what I was doing. "Yeah, we'll see."

She let out a frustrated growl as she turned for the door. "*Fuck you!*" she said as she stomped away. "I don't know why the hell you think I'll sacrifice everything to get away from Dorian only to end up with someone just like him, but you thought *wrong.*"

Just like…

I was on her so fast I damn near shocked myself. Her hand was reaching for the door handle when I snatched her back, turning her to face me with alarmed eyes. I pressed her back to the wall.

"I give you a million miles of leeway with this mouth of yours," I started, putting my hands flat on the wall on either side of her. "I'm surrounded by women who aren't afraid to say what they're thinking; My mother, my sister, Ace – sometimes it's rude, crass, disrespectful, whatever. I accept and welcome you speaking your mind because that's the type of man I was raised to be. The shit doesn't bother or threaten me. *But.*" I moved in closer, bending so that my eyes were level with hers. "What you won't *ever fucking do again* is compare me to a motherfucker like Dorian Haywood unless you're getting ready to compliment me."

I didn't bother to ask her if she understood – she did.

I turned away, intending to leave her there until she felt the compulsion to get the hell out of my office. But – and this didn't surprise me at all – she still had shit to say.

"Then don't act like him," she said, in a low voice. "You may not like it, or want to hear it, but when you're trying to control—"

"*Protect,*" I growled, turning back to her. "If you're going to critique me, get the shit straight. Maybe you're too jaded to see the difference right now – I can accept that – but nobody is trying to control you. I'm trying to keep your obstinate ass alive, well, and free, so you can beast this damn tournament, get the fuck outta Vegas, and do the shit *you said you wanted to do.*"

"So you couldn't just say *that*?" She tossed her hands up, emphasizing her confusion. "I was supposed to get that from the boorish, domineering shit that *actually* came out of your mouth?"

"You're not a stupid woman, Asha, read between the goddamn lines!"

"I wouldn't have to read between lines if you would *make yourself clear*."

I shook my head, paired it with a dry chuckle. "Are we really doing *this* again?"

"We'll do it as many times as it takes to be on the same page, or we can leave whatever this is right here. I did the guessing game shit for too many years – I won't spend the next… for however long… doing it again."

"I don't have time for this shit right now," I said, heading to my desk. "We'll discuss it later… or not."

When I made it to my desk, I looked up to find her standing in the same spot, lips parted, eyes cold. She closed her mouth, swallowed, nodded. "I get it now. Understood."

"You get *what*?" I asked, crossing my arms.

"This. This," she gestured between us, "Is a game to you. Entertainment. And it always has been, hasn't it?"

"Will you calm down? Damn!"

She forced out a bark of laughter. "Calm down? Oh, you think this isn't calm? Okay." A grin that was anything but pleasant spread across her face as she nodded. "Don't send your security after me if you don't want them arrested for stalking, and you can tell your mother not to worry – if her son gets in some shit with the underbelly of Vegas, it *won't* be in my honor because I don't want anything to do with him. I'm going to go somewhere and *calm down.*"

Damn it.

She was heading for the door, and once again I caught her, turning her around. "I'm not going to run after you to make shit right every time you're upset. I'm not a fucking orator, Asha – I'm not going to go against my nature and articulate every single little thing I feel for you just because that's how you'd like things to be. Leave the shit that turned you cold in the past and learn how to read for context – you do the shit at the poker table, you can do it in real life."

"Whatever, Kingston." She shrugged off my hold. "You won't go against *your* nature, but here you are expecting me to do exactly that, at every turn, and it's not *fair.*"

I scoffed. "Life isn't fair. That's a fairy tale."

"You're right," she nodded. "It isn't. So when I gave in, and let my imagination run free with the visual of me in a relationship that was healthy, and full of balance, and… *love…* I shouldn't have been naïve enough to hope that might eventually happen between you and me."

Air filled my jaws and I blew it out in an exasperated sigh. "Will you *relax,* damn!"

Asha crossed her arms, looking up at me with defiant eyes. "Give me a reason to, and maybe I will."

Fuck.

What the hell was I supposed to do with this? I'd never been good at this type of shit, and didn't anticipate becoming that way any time soon. She was looking for some spilled emotions, bleeding heart type of shit that just wasn't in my temperament, no matter how much I – inexplicably – wanted her to be happy. The longer I stared at her, what I'd initially read as insolence in her eyes became transparent, exposing the reality she was trying her best to hide.

She was scared.

Of what, I couldn't be sure, but knowing some of what she'd been through, I had an idea. I could understand her demand for clarity, her desire to know exactly where we stood, her reluctance to go with the flow. She was trying to avoid another situation like the one she'd ended up trapped in for years with Dorian.

I *got* that.

I just couldn't give her the words she needed to soothe the fear.

So instead of saying anything… I kissed her.

I poured my frustration into her and she gave it right back, pushing up on her toes and wrapping her arms around my neck as I invaded her mouth with my tongue. My hands hooked under her thighs, pulling her against my body until her legs were around my waist.

I carried her to the desk, where I shoved a stack of folders out of the way to make room to put her down, not caring about the ones that fell to the floor in a jumble of documents. With each stroke of my tongue against hers, I wondered if it was enough, even though I knew better. You couldn't fuck someone into trusting you – I *knew* that, logically… but I damn sure intended to try.

My hands went to the soft fabric tie of the dress she wore, making quick work of getting it open, revealing half of the bra she wore underneath. I opened the other tie and then pulled the dress apart, baring her to me – creamy honey toned skin, accented with black lace. Her loose locs framed her face, spilling onto her shoulders and down her back as she looked up at me.

"I just don't want to have to wonder," she whispered, even though it was just me and her.

I pushed a handful of locs behind her shoulder so I could kiss her there, and then trailed up to her ear. "About?"

"How you feel." Her words came out in a gasp as I nipped her neck, then moved my hands under her ass to pull her closer. "If you won't verbalize… how am I supposed to know?"

"You let my actions speak for me." I closed my mouth over her skin, sucking until she squirmed in my arms. "They always, *always* will," I told her, punctuated the words with kisses to soothe the spot that would soon be a dark mark on her light brown skin.

"What if they don't?"

"They will."

"And what if they contradict?" I stopped my teasing to meet her eyes, glossy with tears. "What if you say you love me, but… a "no" never means no to you?"

That question sucked the air out of my lungs. I didn't even have to ask if that was what she'd lived through. It was right there in her eyes.

"That won't happen."

"How can I know for sure?"

I shook my head. "You have to trust me."

"Why?"

"Why not?" I shrugged. "Because of what the last nigga did to you?"

"Yes," she said, then swallowed hard, like she was trying to hold back her tears. "That's *exactly* why."

I chuckled. "But you want to talk about shit not being fair?"

"I never said it was. But… that's life."

"You're right," I nodded. "But… have you considered that by that same reasoning…" I leaned in, speaking into her ear. "Maybe I shouldn't gamble on *you*?" I pulled back, meeting her eyes again. "You aren't the only person in the world with trust issues, sweetheart."

Understanding softened her expression. "Your wife…" she murmured, almost under her breath. "She hurt you?"

I pulled my gaze away from hers and took a step back, shaking my head. "*This* is some shit I'm not about to do."

"It's a yes or no question." Asha reached out, hooking an arm around me before I could get any further away. With her free hand, she cupped my face. "Just… yes or no? You're just as fucked up as I am, because whatever happened between you and her before she died… it hurt you?"

It wasn't just before she died. It was the shit that I found out after, the depth of the secrets and lies from a woman I'd … poured *everything* into. For a long time, it consumed my thoughts when I was awake, haunted my dreams when I tried to sleep. I couldn't get away from it, no matter how I tried. Fucking, working, drinking, fighting, traveling… nothing seemed to clear the shit from my brain, not until very recently.

Not until…

"Yeah."

… Why did that feel like such a weight off my shoulders, to admit out loud that yeah… the shit with Robyn fucked with me? Maybe because I wasn't "supposed" to cop to that type of thing, but… my dick was still where I'd left it, and as far as I could tell, nobody had stamped "bitch" across my forehead, so… I accepted the feeling of relief.

Asha nodded about my answer – I was just confirming what she'd already construed. She moved her hand to the back of my neck, tugging me down so she could kiss me. "They say," she said against my lips, "That "hurt people hurt people", right? But maybe… if I'm already hurt… and you're already hurt… maybe it'll just cancel out."

I chuckled at that, and after about a second, she joined in, giggling as I kissed her. And then, we suddenly weren't laughing anymore – we were devouring each other.

Her hands went to my waist, undoing my belt, and my pants.

"I see you calmed that ass down," I teased as I pushed her dress away from her shoulders, leaving it to pool around her on the desk.

"Not because you said so."

I smirked. "Yeah, that's what you think."

Her fingertips went into the waistband of my boxers, cupping and squeezing before she pulled me free. "You really think you have the power to just *make me* calm down, huh?"

"Oh, I *know* I do."

She released her hold on my dick and leaned back on her elbows to look at me. "How?"

It took me less than two seconds to slide the seat of her panties to the side, line up, and then bury myself inside her in one fluid stroke. That's *just* how wet she was. She gasped as our hips connected, arching her back to pull herself up and grab onto my arms. She clenched around me as I ground into her, making a grin spread over my face as I dropped my head to speak into her ear.

"That's how."

There were too many people around for me to relax.

Not to mention, this wasn't my hotel, so while I had a wide berth of privileges because of my friendship with Lincoln, Braxton, and Nashira, I didn't run shit in here. Usually not a problem, but when it came to one particular person… it was.

There were too many moving parts in play here.

The Ace of Spades tournament had packed out the Drake Casino and Hotel, and Asha was a good part of what people wanted to see. Granted, people were going to come to see poker played regardless of who was in the tournament, but the gorgeous Black woman with distinctive red hair was definitely getting attention.

A lot of it.

It was day two of the tournament, and she'd done well. The whole thing was being televised live, so instead of being on the poker floor with the action, my family and I – along with a wide range of other VIP guests – were watching from a private room with a screen that took up the whole wall.

"It looks like newcomer Asha Davis is going to fold this hand – her third time in a row folding a hand since she arrived here at today's

last table. What do you think, is she getting nervous?" one announcer asked the other, words the players couldn't hear from their seats at table.

"Maybe so, Todd," the other announcer responded. *"She came out of nowhere this year, representing The Reverie, another casino resort here on the strip. I don't know that anyone was really expecting her to come this far, but surprisingly, she's been dominating."*

"I don't know that I would call it dominating, but she can certainly play, and she's not hard to look at either."

"We should be thanking Reverie for their contribution to the diversity of the competition."

I shook my head at that "diversity" comment and then tuned out their voices as they moved on to actually discussing the gameplay. When the cameras happened to catch her, my eyes were on Asha, who instead of looking bored and disinterested, paying no attention like the other players who'd folded, was keenly tuned in to the table.

This was something I'd noticed and admired before – she kept her focus where it needed to be, learning her opponents even when she wasn't actively playing. As always, she wore her poker face.

Some of the players wore sunglasses to cover their faces, hats low on their heads. Today, Asha wore her locs down, framing her face and falling in a way that called perfect attention to her collarbone, exposed in the off-shoulder style top she wore.

Tastefully distracting was how my mother described the look. Who knew – or cared – if it was working? She looked *good as hell* on my TV screen, she was doing well in the tournament, and there were at least seven security guards in the room ready to act if anybody decided to get stupid.

Those were the only things that mattered.

Leading up to this, she'd been nervous, but none of it showed in the perfectly poised woman at that poker table.

Another round started, and the tiny cameras at the table showed us that Asha had a queen of spades and a nine of spades – decent enough cards to play. But, the guy next to her had been dealt a pair of aces, and the other one had a jack and ten of hearts.

The little number on the screen, predicting her possibility of winning, only said 15%.

But she stayed in.

When the other guys raised the bet, she matched them, and dealer turned over the first three community cards – the flop. Those cards were a queen of diamonds, a jack of spades, and a 10 of clubs.

Her probability moved up to 31%.

That round of betting went fast. The guy with the jack and ten of hearts was confident, with good reason – his probability was at 41%. He was raising the bet with a clear purpose – to come out on top. Only two people from this table were going to the next round.

I hoped one of them would be Asha.

Her chips were getting lower fast as they kept betting, and the fourth community card wasn't turned yet. Her shoulders were high, and her face held her usual bland poker expression.

She wasn't bothered.

The "turn" card was finally flipped – a seven of spades that sank her chance of winning down to 21%, and raised his to 57%. The player with the pair of aces went all in – *why the fuck did he do that?* – and the other player matched his bet. When it came around to Asha, she seemed to hesitate, deliberating longer than usual about whether she was staying in or not.

She pushed in enough chips to match the bet, leaving her with just a few more.

And then… it was the moment of truth.

Right now, Asha was in the "bubble". If she was eliminated now, she would walk away with nothing. If she at least made it through this round, to play tomorrow, even if she was eliminated in the very first round she played, she would walk away with seventy-seven thousand dollars, which wasn't bad.

There was only a 21% chance of her winning. An eight would give her a flush. A nine or a queen would give her two pairs.

A hush drifted over the room as the dealer pulled a card from the deck and discarded it, then picked up the "river" card – the fifth community card, which would benefit or hurt all players. Her hand seemed to move in slow motion to put it down, and the room collectively gasped when she finally did.

"A fucking nine of hearts," Zora shouted, the first person to speak. "She *won!* How the fuck did she—do y'all see this? How the hell did she pull that off?"

Asha could barely believe it herself.

Or at least, that's how it seemed, when the guy who'd bet it all on a pair of aces was currently on the poker room floor crying, and the other player was simply shaking his head as the huge pile of chips was scooped into Asha's pile.

She hadn't moved.

She was still sitting there, frozen, like nothing was happening around her. But then someone touched her shoulder, getting her attention to shake her hand, and suddenly she was smiling and full of charm.

"*An unbelievable upset by newcomer Asha Davis, who has eliminated poker veteran Paul Williamson from this tournament with a nine and a queen. Certainly none of us saw that one com—*"

The announcers were still expressing their disbelief over Asha's win when I excused myself from the room, followed closely by Ace. We took the private elevator down to the poker floor, and she stood in the corner wearing an amused smirk the whole ride.

"What's with the face?" I asked, knowing she was dying to say something.

She shook her head. "Nothing."

"Oka—"

"I mean, since you insist," she interrupted, flipping her long French braid back over her shoulder. "You rushing down to meet her, after her win… it's cute. I like seeing you like this."

"You're going to make me stop this elevator and go back upstairs."

"No," she laughed. "Don't do that. It will probably mean a lot to her that you want to celebrate her moment. Everything doesn't have to be about… ripping phone books in half, and pillaging. You want to be with your woman, go be with her! If somebody says some slick shit… kick their ass. Or I'll do it for you—wait, no, that would be counterproductive. Yeah, you kick their ass."

I shook my head. "I'm so confused right now. When the hell did you get all… pink and romantic?"

She shrugged. "I don't know. I've been reading… watching movies I guess."

"You guess? Either you have or you haven't."

"Well, I *have*."

"Reading and watching what? Romantic comedies and shit?"

She shifted away, staring at the number panel on this slow-ass elevator as it climbed down.

"Reading and watching *what*?" I repeated, and she shot a scowl in my direction.

"It's not *shit*," she mumbled. "And it's *research* more than… pleasure."

I raised an eyebrow. "What are you researching?"

She shook her head, just as the elevator stopped. "I've told you enough of my business."

I chuckled as we stepped off the elevator, then made our way through the mass of people. Security wasn't letting family or friends in to see the players yet, as they were talking to press first, but name recognition got me through.

Ace and I held back for a second, waiting as Asha finished up an interview. She walked away from the reporter only to get stopped by another group wanting to stop and offer congratulations. Even now that the shock had to have worn off, she still seemed reserved, as she shook hands and smiled, offering all the pleasantries that were expected of her.

And then she looked up.

I grinned at her, and she smiled back before she could catch herself. Immediately, she excused herself from the conversation, and made her way over to where Ace and I stood.

"So," I said, pushing my hands into my pockets. "No matter what happens tomorrow, you're walking away from this a winner. How does it feel?"

She shook her head, and when her eyes came back to mine, she was blinking away tears. "Amazing. Not even because of the money, just the fact that I'm… *here*," she said, gesturing at the room around her. "I can't even explain how grateful I am. If I hug you, you aren't going to play me this time, right?"

"Bring your ass here," I said, and she walked into my arms. Behind us, the increased volume of the crowd told me they were finally letting family and friends come in to talk to players. I leaned in, speaking into her here. "I'm going to leave so you can talk to your people, but… how about letting me treat you to dinner, champ?"

She looked up at me with a grin as she stepped back, and nodded. "I'd love that."

"You are *such* a cheater," she said, accepting the glass of wine I offered before walking away to continue her slow perusal of my home.

We'd passed that giant white canvas on our way inside. She stopped then, and came back to it now, staring for a few seconds before she tilted her head, then shifted her position to stare again.

"What *is* this?" she asked, turning to where I was standing a few feet back, studying her as closely as she was studying the piece, trying to get it to make sense in her head. She'd changed from earlier – her hair was pulled up now, in an intricate-looking knot, and she was wearing a gauzy, pale coral dress that skimmed her body in an understated, sexy way that made it hard not to imagine what was underneath. But… I didn't *have* to imagine.

I knew.

So… maybe it was just hard not to strip it off of her. But I managed.

"You have to figure it out for yourself."

She frowned in my direction. "You're not being a very good host. First, you offer to "treat" me to dinner, then bring me to your house. Then, you won't even tell me about your art. What's next? Are you kicking me out after dinner?"

"I hardly think that a meal prepared by a private chef is anything to complain about," I grinned. "As far as the art… it's a custom commission from a young artist in California. The medium is wax. And no… "kicking you out" does *not* appear on the list of things I plan to do to you after dinner."

I groaned at the sight of her lip pulled between her teeth as she considered my words, then took a sip from her glass. "And what *does* appear on that list?"

"You'll find out after dinner."

"See? Bad host. You're telling me I don't even get dessert?"

I smirked. "Have you tasted yourself? You *are* dessert."

She blushed over that, then shook her head as she moved from the entryway to look out of the window in the open living area. Not that far away, Chef Miri was in the kitchen – cooking something with scallops, obviously – and the aroma of butter and sautéed herbs drifted to where we were standing side by side, looking out at the cliffs. From this side of the house, there was no view of the strip, just purple and orange bands of color moving across the sky as the sun sank behind the horizon.

"This is weird," she said, finally breaking what I'd considered a comfortable silence.

I sipped from my own wine, then glanced in her direction. "What is?"

"This…" She used her glass to gesture between us before she lifted her gaze to mine. "*Not* being at odds with you, the chef, the fireplace, the wine, the view… it's downright romantic, and it's… idyllic. Disarmingly so."

I nodded. "Give it time. I'm sure we'll be at each other's throats again soon enough."

"So am I," she laughed. "So I should probably just enjoy the moment, huh?"

"I sure as hell I am," I said, then turned so that I was facing her direction and put my back to the window. "Why are you so surprised though? What, you think I'm some sort of brute?"

She shrugged. "I mean…"

"Oh come on, Red," I chuckled. "The very first night we met, I was nothing but a gentleman to you. If I recall correctly – you picked *me* up at the bar."

She laughed. "Yes, but if *I* recall correctly… you almost put me out of your room."

"Because you were acting like you'd changed your mind." I shook my head. "I don't play that shit – if you changed your mind, I'm not convincing you of *shit*."

"I was nervous!"

I scoffed. "You? Nervous? Please."

"I *was*," she insisted, shaking her head. "Talking shit at a bar to a stranger is one thing, but backing it up once the stranger takes you up to a very expensive hotel room… that's something else."

"Duly noted. So… you really had no idea who I was?"

She shook her head. "Not a damn *clue*. I'd heard your name mentioned, heard rumors about you, but… as you know, my personal life is a bit of a mess. I had my own shit going on, and I just wanted to go to work, make my tips, and go home. It never occurred to me to look up the owners – just like I never looked up the owners when I had my corporate job."

"But you've looked me up now?"

"Of course. You looked into *me*, didn't you?"

I nodded. "Yeah… I checked you out. Found some interesting things."

"I could say the same about you – though, my little google searches probably didn't yield *nearly* the type of answers *your* investigation did. It's really not fair, to be honest."

"Is that right?"

She took a long sip, then nodded. "Yep. It is. Bad hosting again."

"Wait," I chuckled. "How the hell does that figure into my hosting skills?"

She shrugged. "I'm just saying… a *good* host would… answer some questions."

I tipped my head to the side, thinking about it for a moment. "Alright. I don't have shit to hide. Go for it."

"What happened to your wife?"

I damn near choked on the gulp of wine I'd just taken. I quickly cleared my throat, then shook my head as I turned back to the window. "Damn… straight to the good stuff, huh?"

"No point in wasting my questions asking what your favorite football team is, or who's your favorite rapper."

I gave a deep nod. "I guess I can understood that. Connecticut Kings, and Young Lord, by the way. But you're not interested in that."

"I'm not."

"This is an answer you could easily find on the internet."

"But I want to hear it from you," she said, quietly. She'd stepped closer to me, and I glanced in her direction when I felt her hand on my arm. "You… you know a lot of uncomfortable truths about me. I don't think it's out of line to want to know some about you."

"You're not wrong." I pulled in a deep breath, casting my gaze out of the window before I spoke again. "Robyn… was a beautiful woman. Devastatingly so. Very poised, well-educated, cultured, whole package. I was young – we both were. It didn't take very long to fall, and once I did… I was a goner."

A fucking *goner*.

I would've done anything, given her anything, just to keep her happy. As far as I knew at the time, that feeling was reciprocated, and neither of us was really bothered that she didn't easily mesh with my family. They were good to her, but they kept their distance, and if I asked, I could never get a clear answer on why. They didn't have anything solid, no evidence, but… they must've felt something I was blind to.

"It was all built on a lie. I didn't know until after she died, but she was born and raised in France. Worked hard as hell to create a whole new persona, new identity, everything, because of some shit she was running from back there. It was… *airtight.* At the time though, I just knew she was suddenly acting strange. Lying, being out all hours of the night. I couldn't figure the shit out, but I knew something wasn't right. So I had her followed. Found out she was spending a lot of time with a gallery "client". I didn't know anything for sure, but… I confronted her. Made it seem like I knew something I didn't. The day I confronted her… was the last time I saw her alive."

When I finished speaking, I finally turned back to Asha, who was looking at me with her eyes wide.

"So… you think she committed suicide because of that confrontation?"

I nodded. "Yeah, I did. For a long time. But then… I found out that the "client" knew about her life before me, back in France. Was holding it over her head… blackmailing her. Using her to manipulate *me* into making deals that were favorable to him. Fucking her."

Asha's lips parted. "He made her do that?"

I shrugged. "Maybe? Maybe she felt like she had to, or maybe she was willing. I only have his word, and what I found on my own, cause she never told me any of this shit."

"Why wouldn't she just tell you, if you guys were married?"

"That's another question in a long ass line of questions I never got a real answer to." I shrugged. "You just… learn to live with it. But… it wasn't like it was some shit I couldn't have gotten past. She came from a fucked up family, and she was… just trying to get away from all of that, didn't want to be associated with them."

Asha let out a dry laugh. "She'd made herself into something… maybe she didn't want the world to know about the particular type of nothing she came from. Look at you, King. Look at who your family is.

You met and fell in love with a certain woman, of a certain stature and presumed pedigree. Maybe she was afraid you'd see her differently, and… she couldn't bear the thought of losing that."

"Maybe so. That's why I like figuring out exactly who a person is before I let them into my life now. I won't go through that shit again."

She scoffed. "A dossier doesn't tell you who a person is, or even what they've done, really. It only shows you what *other* people know about them. Only the stuff that's on paper."

"That's true," I nodded. "So… what about you? What's not on your file, Red? You have any secrets some fool is going to come out of nowhere to hold over you?"

She went very, very still at that question, and I silently willed her not to tell a lie. I could accept, and handle, a long list of bullshit – lies weren't anywhere on that list.

"Yes," she said finally, then gulped down the rest of her glass of wine. "But I'm not about to talk about it right now."

"Will you ever?"

She nodded. "Maybe."

"Fair enough," I said, then stared at her until she looked up, meeting my eyes. "Who knows?"

She frowned. "Excuse me?"

"The fuckboy who'll show up with his hand open to keep his mouth closed. Who?"

From the shudder that washed over her, I knew who she was going to say before she even spoke. "Dorian."

I nodded. "Okay. Okay."

She narrowed her eyes. "That's just… it? Okay? That's all?"

"What else do you want me to say, Red? You were honest about there being… something. I appreciate that. You were forthcoming with a name – I appreciate that too. When the food is ready, we're going to sit down for our meal, and enjoy it, because we're going to talk about something else, and not let the past linger in our minds. And then… I'm going to fuck every bit of energy out of both of us, so we won't dream about the shit either. And tomorrow, we'll consider this a successful night."

She stared at me for a long moment, and then the ghost of smile came back into her eyes, then onto her lips. "That sounds like a wonderful plan."

Just as soon as those words left her mouth, Chef Miri's voice rang out from the kitchen, letting us know it was time to eat. I extended my hand, and Asha took it, letting me lead her out to the balcony where our dining area was set up.

Already, our plan was the only thing on my mind.

SEVENTEEN

ASHA

This is so, so weird.

But I didn't care.

I buried myself a little deeper in the sheets of King's massive bed with a deep inhale, enjoying the remnants of his scent. Just the memory would have to suffice for now.

The man himself had left late the night before, on a private international flight, and he'd offered – no, *insisted* – that I stayed where I was instead of going home. Instead of balking, or arguing, I tried a different route – I accepted his offer.

Mainly because it was late as hell anyway, and I didn't feel like moving.

Still, it was weird – just as I'd mentioned to him two nights ago. This was such a change from our former dynamic that I could barely believe it was happening.

And yet… here I was.

I sat up, glancing at the clock before I flipped the covers away from my aching body. King was supposed to be gone for a week, and he'd made sure to implant his conscience on me. I was sore, and my limbs were stiff as I made my want to the bathroom for a shower, but… I felt good.

I wasn't operating under any delusions about being in love – wasn't even sure I was capable of letting myself be that person again – but whatever this feeling was, it felt more like the way things were supposed to be than anything else I'd experienced before. I didn't feel like property. I could come and go as I pleased. I felt *safe.*

Yeah… this could work for me.

The bed was already made when I left the shower, so I knew King's house manager had been through. I dressed simply, in jeans and a tee shirt, then found my purse, keys, phone, and headed out, sending up a mental *Thank You* to King for making sure my car had been made available to me, even though I'd been chauffeured to his home.

Even *that* – simple gratefulness, without wondering about his angle – was new. Spanking, brand new, and was the result of a long conversation with Angela and Zora that had started off as awkward, and morphed into something I didn't know I needed.

After last night – the third night of the tournament – Angela and Zora had descended on me before King could, whisking me off to a private dinner. Once they were done gushing over me, and offering congratulations on making it to a point where my *definite* winnings were over one-hundred and sixty thousand dollars, they moved on to what I had a sneaking suspicion was the *real* point of this dinner.

"I want to talk to you about my brother," Zora had said, looking me right in the eyes like she dared me to deny something was going on. Even without that look, I wouldn't have bothered with that lie. The whole intervention with Dorian had pretty much spread that little tidbit among the family, and the day after that, Angela had made it clear that I'd better not get her son in any more trouble.

The thing was, while I was a teensy bit terrified of Angela, she hadn't come across as if she *minded* the thought of me being with her son. She'd even seemed sort of pleased by the idea, unless I was remembering through a rose-colored lens.

She just *also* wanted to make sure I knew she didn't play about her babies.

Anyway, Zora had gone on to give me something of a rundown on King, of things I already knew. He had a tendency to be an asshole, he could be bossy, he was cagey, and slick at the mouth. "But… he's also dependable. Generous. Kind. *Faithful.* And God help anyone – and I mean *anyone* – who would try to do any type of harm." She took a sip from her wine, then raised her hands. "I know, I know, I'm his sister, of course I have good things to say about him, right?" She shook her head. "Nope. I'm the *last* bitch to give a man a pass just because he's halfway decent and has more than a couple of inches of dick."

"Zora…" Angela warned, and her daughter shrugged it right off.

"What? It's not like I'm just making shit up Mama! Women are expected to endure, and ignore a lot, but that's not my ministry, Sister Whitfield, okay?"

Angela sucked her teeth. "And what *is* your ministry, little girl? Men in dick slings?"

Zora snickered. "Well, I mean, I prefer the oiled abs, but that works too. By the way, Asha, *Waterfalls* night at *Dream* in two weeks, you should come, bring your homegirls. But anyway… back to my point… I don't know what you endured with Dorian, but I have my experience with men like him. Been there, done that, got the antibiotics and the stiches," she said, pointing to a faint, razor-thin scar under her eye. "But what you shouldn't do is treat every man after him like he's the same. I know you're probably cautious, and you *should* be. That's *smart*. But King is a good man, point blank. Far from perfect, but a good one."

"Why are you telling me this?" I asked, intrigued. This little conversation didn't strike me as something King would have agreed to, and would probably flip about if he knew it was happening.

"Because of what I've seen over the last couple of months. He was up, then down, and now he's up again, and I know it's because of you. I saw the change in how you two were interacting when we first started working on the tournament – he'd done something to piss you off, and you were probably paying him dust – to now. I know my brother very well, and as much as the man will talk, he doesn't… *talk.* So this is me doing my sisterly duty for his majesty, trying to throw him a little rope. He's feeling you. You're feeling him. It's still really early... just let it flow."

So… I was going to try to do just that. I was going to check my neuroses at the door, and instead of waiting on King to adhere to my dysfunctional preconceived notions about men… I was going to let *his* actions speak for him.

But what if he's just a really good actor? What if Zora is too? They're family… of course she's on his side, duh! Rich people are always fucked up… this is entertainment for them.

I shook my head.

Not obsessing over what could go wrong was easier said than done, and the last thing I wanted was to be naïve, and stupid. But the *first* thing I wanted was… peace. And even with everything else swirling around me, the sense of dread lingering in the balance, there was no denying that when I was with King, on some level, I felt it. There was no judgement, or maltreatment, no need to put up a façade, not really.

He *got* me. In a way that no one, not even Dorian, ever had.

How could something like that *not* put a smile on my face?

As soon as I was in my car, the phone rang. I answered Camille's call before I pulled away from the house, putting it on speaker and propping it in the cup holder.

"So, you didn't come home *last* night either," Camille sang from the other end of the line, and I smiled. "Should I start boxing your things for you? Are you moving into Whitfield Manor?"

"Hell no," I shook my head. "Pump those brakes Cammy!"

She snickered. "Oh please, you know you want the keys to your new boyfriend's kingdom!"

"He is *not* my boyfriend," I corrected, immediately. "We've only been getting along for like a week – I'm not even sure if what we're doing qualifies as dating."

"You like him?"

I shrugged as I pulled to a stop at a light. "I mean… I guess so, if that's what to call it. Yeah."

"And he likes you?"

My face twisted into a scowl. "How the hell should I know? I… hope so? If not, all of this shit is pretty damned weird."

Camille laughed. "Whatever, Asha. You like him, he likes you, you're spending time together…you're dating."

"If you say so, Cam. Why does it matter?"

"Ugh, attitude," she teased, and I shook my head as I pulled onto the highway to get back to the main part of the city. "And I guess it doesn't, not really. The title doesn't have to be a thing."

"There's nothing to put a title on yet anyway."

"Asha."

"Camille."

On the other end of the line, she snickered. "Fine, *fine*. What I *really* called about was to ask if you wanted to go hit the buffet with me this afternoon. I know you have today off, since the last day of the tournament is tomorrow, and *I* am off for the next two weeks, so what better time for both of us to stuff our faces?"

"How the hell did you get two weeks off?" I asked as I pulled onto my mother's street.

"Major beef between the producers and the director. Show is on hiatus while they work it out – as long as my check clears, they can beef all they want."

I chuckled. "I know that's right. But, yeah. We can meet later. I'm about to check in with my mother, and see what she needs. I'll call you back after I know what my free time looks like."

"Works for me! Talk to you later."

We ended the call just as I pulled up to my mother's house. At first, the black Escalade that pulled up behind me put me on edge, but then the window rolled down, and a man I recognized as the security King had hired for me waved.

Shit.

I hadn't even thought about them.

I went inside to find my mother bustling around the kitchen. Tim was seated at the table, sorting out jar lids and labels that would soon hold the contents of the sticky-sweet smelling pots bubbling on the stove.

"Oh my *God*," I groaned, mouthwatering at the aroma of cinnamon and nutmeg in the air. I took a deep inhale, basking in the off put of fresh apple butter and peach marmalade. Canning was a hobby she'd picked up – and mastered – in just the last two years.

Both Tim and my mother greeted me warmly, and I was glad to see her condition was much improved. I was still pissed about that surprise bill – and the consequences involved with getting it resolved – but at least the hospital actually did its job, and had her feeling better.

"You look good today Mama. Have you talked to Ahmad?" I asked, as she put a pair of tongs in my hand, for me to take over the job of sterilizing the jars while she did something else.

"He came by here yesterday with his little girlfriend," she said, stirring the pot of marmalade with a long-handled spoon. Despite her use of "little girlfriend", she actually really liked Kita – we all did.

Hell, sometimes I like *her* better than I liked Ahmad. She'd talked him out of plenty of stupidity over the years.

"He told me he's thinking about proposing to her," Tim added, with a deep nod.

I grinned. "About time. They've been dating for what… six years? She stayed with him through losing an NBA contract and knocking up another woman, a ring is the *least* of the ways he could repay her," I laughed, and they joined in.

I spent the rest of the morning there with my mother and Tim, and then headed out. The security guys were leaning against the car when I stepped out, and I tossed up a wave to let them know I was leaving. Not sooner than I'd lowered my hand, my phone rang, and I pulled it from the back pocket of my jeans to see a number that was Vegas local, but still not one I recognized.

"Hello?" I said once I'd hit the button to answer, then tucked the phone between my ear and shoulder as I dug in my purse for my keys.

"So you're fuckin' him?" Came the cold voice from the other end. My fingers froze, and my throat seemed to close up immediately. "You sat your ass in my face, asking questions about the mothafucker like you were just curious, but that wasn't it, was it? What did you call yourself doing, baby? You're what, a fucking spy now or some shit? Is that it?"

I swallowed hard, desperately trying to bring moisture back to my mouth. I must have looked spooked, because the security guards hadn't gotten into the car, instead they were eyeing me with concern. I raised a hand to stop them as they headed my way. "He told you to leave me alone, Dorian," was all I could manage to get out, in a low enough voice to not cause any more alarm.

"I don't give a *fuck* what his bitch ass said. *You owe me,* lil mama, and I intend to collect what's mine one way or another."

I turned away, facing the house as I hissed, "I don't owe you *shit*!" into the phone. "If you'd left me alone when I asked the first time—"

"Shut the fuck up with all that," he growled. "I'm sick of you blaming the shit on me. If your ass had been more grateful for the life I gave you, you wouldn't have had it in your head that you needed to leave in the fucking place!"

"More grateful?!" I screeched, louder than I intended, before I laughed. "Dorian, you are a *monster*, and you were turning me into one too. There wasn't anything about my life to be grateful about, other than the material bullshit you thought would keep me on my knees."

"But you let *this* motherfucker get you on your knees for free? Funny how that worked out."

"*Fuck. You.*" I spat into the phone, holding up a hand again to the security guards. "You will not lay any guilt over the way we ended at *my* feet. The day my body failed because of *you,* because of *your* actions, was the best damned day of my life. That was the day I was *finally* free. So thank you, asshole. But I don't owe you a damned thing."

He was quiet for a long moment. "Best day of your life? *That* was the best day of your life?"

"That's what I said."

He chuckled. "Wow. *Fucking wow.* You always did know how to go for the jugular, didn't you Asha?"

"Just how you taught me, Dorian."

"Bet."

In my hand, my phone started buzzing, silently notifying me of a new incoming call. I pulled it from my ear long enough to glance at another unfamiliar Vegas number.

"Asha…" Dorian said, but I didn't respond. "You're going to give me what you owe me, or I'm going to take it. Bottom line. When that number that you just ignored calls you again, you may want to answer it… it's the only warning I'm giving you."

A second later, my phone chimed to let me know he'd ended the call. Immediately, it rang again, with the number I'd ignored before. This time, I answered.

"H-hello?"

"Is this Asha Davis?" a female voice asked, in a brisk tone.

“Yes.”

“You’re listed as the emergency contact for an… Ahmad Davis?”

I drew in a breath. “Emergency conta… yes, that’s my brother. What the hell is going on?”

“Well, your brother needs some treatments, and we’ll need your consent, since he’s unable to give it right now.”

Around me, everything seemed to fade into a haze. I only stayed on my feet because of one of the security guards grabbing me under the elbow, steadying me. “Wh-why can’t he—”

“I *can’t* say any more over the phone, ma’am, we would need you to come in.”

I swallowed hard, then nodded as if she could see me. “What hospital? I’m on my way.”

I should have been afraid.

After seeing the state Ahmad was in when I arrived at the hospital, beaten and bruised and swollen to the point that I could barely recognize his face, I probably should have been *terrified.*

But I wasn’t.

"Will he have me attacked while I'm working?" should have been the question on my mind. After all, that's what he'd done to Ahmad. Gone through the car service and requested a ride, then had him jumped, and beaten nearly to death. This was Dorian's "thing", and he was very good at it. He'd experimented enough to exactly how much abuse the human body could take, which points were weak, where it hurt the most, all of that. And he wielded that knowledge as the primary weapon of intimidation.

But *this*? This attack on my innocent – this time – brother, and that little phone call intimating that after the hell he'd put me through, I actually owed *him* something?

Sitting in the semi-darkness of the private waiting room, I smiled.

Finally, Dorian had broken his very last straw with me.

I was going to put a bullet in another psychopath's head.

My plan was already developing.

No sketchy man in a dark alley this time. I had another resource – Ace. I knew that if I went to her, asked her to get me what I needed, she would oblige. Sure, I'd probably have to spill a secret or two to make her understand that not only was I serious, I was *capable*, but that was okay. I would do anything – *anything*. No matter what I had to sacrifice, Dorian's ass was mine.

"Asha?"

I looked up to see King's prominent frame taking most of the width of the doorway, and my mouth fell open. I recovered quickly, clamping it shut before I stood, shoving my hands in the back pockets of my jeans.

"What are you doing here? You're supposed to be on the other side of the world right now, aren't you?" I asked, taking a step forward.

He took more than one, crossing the room to get to me. "Not quite. We had to stop in New York first to handle a few things before we headed to Sun City. When I heard about what happened…"

"… you came back."

He nodded. “Sent Trei ahead without me, which will be a good experience for him anyway. All the groundwork was laid… this trip was a follow-up.”

“Yeah, you explained a little to me before you left. You didn’t have to modify your plans for me though.”

“I don’t do shit I don’t want to do, Red,” he shrugged. “Why didn’t you call me?”

“Why *would* I have?” I asked, mirroring his shrug. “This isn’t your problem.”

His eyebrows lifted, and he nodded. “If you think that, obviously I’ve dropped the ball again on making myself clear.”

“I don’t even know how to respond to that.”

“Then don’t. How is he?” King gestured toward the door where Ahmad lay sleeping on the other side. Kita and my mother were in there with him. The room – hell this entire hospital and its’ facilities, were just over the line of lavish, as far as medical treatment could go. When Ahmad had been moved from the first hospital to this one, and placed in the most private quarters I’d ever seen outside of television, I didn’t have to question why he was getting such treatment. I already knew.

“The doctors say he’ll be okay. Some broken ribs, broken nose, concussion, lots of bruising. Probably a painful healing process, but he’ll get through it.”

King nodded. “Good.” He moved in closer to me, putting his arms around my waist. I welcomed the contact, molding myself into the hard contours of his body as he pressed his lips to my forehead. “And… how are you?”

“Managing.”

He took my hand, leading me to the chairs that lined the wall, and sat me down, leaving a seat between us when he took a seat. “Explain.”

“Nothing to explain,” I shrugged. “I just… hospitals aren’t my favorite places. Last time I was in one for myself… wasn’t a very good time.”

King let out a sound that was half groan, half sigh. "Yet another thing we have in common." Silence settled between us for a few moments, and then, "Tell me what happened."

"I'm sure you already know."

"But I want to hear it from you."

I knew, from experience, that the chances of him letting it go were incredibly slim. Nonexistent. I remembered that day at the spa, when he'd offered me the choice of telling him what he wanted to know, or having him call Dorian for information.

Maybe I should have let him.

If I had… maybe things wouldn't have gone this way.

"Dorian did this. He thinks that I owe him something, still."

King frowned. "This shit can't be over a few thousand dollars."

"It's not. It's not about money at all."

"Then what?"

I dropped my gaze to the floor, and pushed out a sigh. "… a baby. He feels like I owe him a child."

King's frown melted into confusion as I looked up, searching his face to gauge his reaction. "What the hell do you mean he thinks you owe him a goddamned child, Asha? Why would he think some crazy shit like that?"

"Because I lost the first one."

Another thick layer of silence fell over us before King sat back in his seat, studying me. "When?"

"Three years ago," I whispered. "I was four months pregnant. I told him I was leaving. He didn't like it, said I couldn't, so he grabbed me. I lost my balance when I snatched away from him, and fell. I'm sure you can figure out the rest."

I looked at anything except him. I hadn't said those words out loud, to anyone, before now. That was before I knew Camille, before I'd ever even heard of *Dream*. Back when the world I lived in with Dorian was the only one that existed.

"I'm sorry you had to go through that," King said beside me. When I didn't respond, he continued. "Since we're divulging… you should know that particular grief, of losing a child… we have *that* in common too."

That got my attention. I turned to him, eyebrows pulled together. None of the many articles I'd read about him had mentioned a child, no pictures of a pregnant Robyn.

"What are you talking about?" I asked the side of his face, since he was no longer looking at me. I watched his Adam's apple bob as he swallowed, then shifted in his chair.

"I don't know if I'm really feeling you right now."

I frowned, baffled by what seemed like an out-of-nowhere statement. "Excuse me?"

"You heard me," he said, turning to me, glaring. "What the fuck is it about you that has me spilling shit nobody needs to hear?"

I shrugged. "I could ask you the same thing."

"I'm attractive, charming, and a great listener," he said easily, crossing his arms.

I sucked my teeth. "Oh really? And what the fuck am I, a blank wall?"

He shook his head. "Don't put words in my mouth. You're… hell, attractive, charming… the great listener part is still to be determined."

"Oh kiss my ass," I said, and rolled my eyes. "You're saying stuff. Me? Charming?"

King chuckled. "Just the fact that you don't think so… is endearing."

"Okay, so then… why are you confused about the urge to talk to me?"

"Because it's shit that I *don't want* to talk about."

"And I'm not forcing you. But… you can't really drop a bomb like that and just leave it there."

He pushed out a heavy sigh, and tucked his hands behind his head. "Fine. But I'm telling you now… I'm not talking about this shit again."

"Good. Me either."

"Robyn…was pregnant when she died."

Something clenched in my chest at the careful way he said that, like it was hard to get the words out. As a woman, I felt awful for her, and the horrible position she must have felt she was in to be carrying this man's child and decide to end her own life. On the other side of that though… I felt for him too, for his whole family to be lost.

A little twinge of guilt pricked me then – I didn't feel badly for Dorian anymore. He'd lost his family too, but by his own doing. This wasn't the same situation, at all. Ours was full of… dysfunction.

But then again… so was theirs.

I remembered what he'd told me just a few nights ago, about how his wife had a sketchy past of her own. Because of that, she'd gotten tangled in blackmail, with a man who hadn't been afraid to claim her body as payment somewhere along the road. And if *that* was the case… wasn't there a possibility, even if it was vague…

I looked up at King to find him already looking at me, like he knew the question that was on my mind. I would never, *never* have asked – as far as I was concerned, it was a past that was his, the same as I considered my own. I was curious, of course, but I didn't *need* that. But… I was discovering more and more that he saw right through me. He already knew what was on my mind, and shook his head.

"It's something I live with every fucking day, but no… I'm not sure. Like I said the other night… a lot of things I don't know, even though she was a huge part of my life. The one thing I *do* know… she didn't do that to herself. She wanted that child. *I* wanted that child. So… yeah… I get it."

A different guilt stabbed in my chest that time, and I looked down again, unable to meet his eyes. I shook my head. "No."

"What?"

"No," I said, louder. "It's not the same. You… you grieved… you're *grieving* a child you wanted to love, and cherish, and give a good life. That's not the same thing as what I felt after I lost that baby."

I felt his gaze on me, but didn't look up. "Which was…?"

"*Relief*," I whispered, then reached up to roughly scrub tears from my eyes. "Dorian is… a monster. As much as I loved the baby that was growing inside of me, I hated that I was bringing her into that environment. Hated that she would tie me to him forever. So many times I asked myself, *Asha, what have you done*? Why on earth would you willingly give this man another potential victim? I saw the things he did to other people, and I couldn't say for sure what he was, or wasn't capable of. That's what was in my mind that day. I was leaving him, so that I could be okay, and so that she could too. And then… she was gone. And I think it fucked *him* up so much that he didn't even want to look at me after that. Losing her set both of us free… and he's not going to drag me back. Ever. And I can't sit here beside you, hearing the anguish in your voice over your loss, and pretend like I can relate. It's not fair to you."

When he didn't say anything, I looked up to find him studying me, yet again. "It's always about fairness with you, isn't it?"

"What do you mean?"

"I mean what I said. You're always wanting things to be fair – for you, for me, for everybody."

I shook my head. "I… I hadn't realized."

"Trademark of someone who's used to being taken advantage of. You refuse to go back, and refuse to do it to anyone else. Probably why you have a hard time handling someone not expecting anything in return when they do something nice for you – you can't help wondering about the balance."

I chewed at the inside of my bottom lip as I considered his words, then raised my chin. "I don't think there's anything wrong with calculating my odds before I place a bet."

“There isn’t,” he said, and gave me a little grin. “But you have to be willing to play when you’re dealt a good hand. Can’t refuse to bet just cause the others ones were shit cards. Right?”

I tried my best to suppress a grin. “Don’t hijack my metaphor. I’m not agreeing with that.”

“You just did.”

A shift in energy pulled both of our attention to the doorway, where Ace suddenly stood, missing the usual hint of impishness in her eyes. She held up a cell phone, and King immediately stood, towering over me as he moved in front of my chair.

“I have to go,” he said, then used two fingers under my chin to angle my mouth for his access. He didn’t linger, but the feeling of his lips against mine did as he pulled away. “I’m sorry for not considering the threat to your family, or friends. That’s been rectified. Are you playing tomorrow?”

Shit.

I hadn’t even thought about the tournament since I got that phone call.

“I don’t know, honestly.” I shook my head. “Maybe if Ahmad is awake, and doing better.”

He nodded. “Okay. You’ll be protected, whether or not you decide to go. And it won’t be held against you if you decided not to.”

“Okay.”

He leaned in to kiss me again, and this time, he stayed longer. I whimpered a little as his teeth nipped me, just before his lips closed over mine.

And then he was gone.

KING

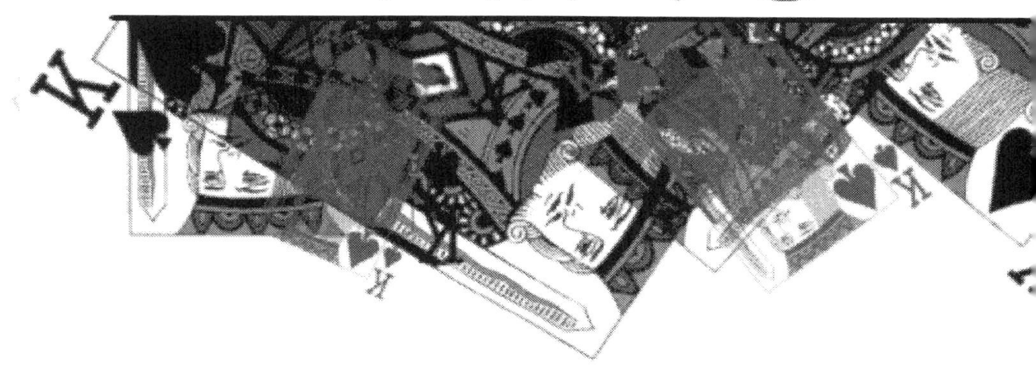

I told him to leave her alone.

I understood why it might be hard, or why it might even *seem* impossible, but really… it was simple fucking task. Don't call her. Don't talk to her. Don't follow her. Don't go anywhere she might be. Don't even think her fucking name. Don't dream about her.

Simple. Fucking. Instructions.

And yet… apparently I should have added "Don't fuck with her family either, you pussy ass motherfucker" – a caveat I thought was implied.

Obviously not.

"Get him on the phone," I growled to Ace, who simply did as I asked, without getting in her feelings about it. She knew that the barely controlled state of rage I was in right now had nothing to do with her, and everything to do with *him.*

There was a good chance I might kill him.

When Ace handed me the phone, it was still ringing. My strides were quick as I headed out of the hospital for the vehicle waiting down in the garage.

"Who is this?" was the rude ass greeting that came from the other end of the line, and my anger turned up a notch.

"The wrong one to fuck with," I answered, and there was silence for a few seconds before Dorian snickered.

"You know… you're a funny ass dude, King. You walk around like you really are royalty, bitches falling all over themselves to get to you, and instead of just luxuriating in that shit… you choose the most broken ones to really fuck with. What's up with that?"

"I'm not your goddamn friend, nigga. We're not about to shoot the shit and bond. I told you to leave Asha the fuck alone, and you're acting like you're deaf, or dealing with a mental deficit, something. For your sake, I'm hoping that's what you tell me, that you just don't have the brain capacity to do the right thing. Is that what's happening here?"

He grunted. "Yo, you can kill that shit, acting like somebody's stupid. I know exactly what the fuck I'm doing."

"Do you?"

"Better than your pussy-whipped ass. Yeah, I know it's sweet. Tight. Wet. Deep. That was *my* pussy. I had it first. Wrote my name *all over it*. Did that bitch tell you she killed my seed?"

My jaw clenched – at the question, and over the way he was speaking about Asha – as I climbed into the vehicle and we pulled off. "Not the way I heard it happened."

"Of course not. If her stupid ass had just appreciated the position I'd put her in, wouldn't have been any argument, she wouldn't have thought she was leaving, and she wouldn't have ended up facedown in the driveway. As far as I'm concerned, the shit is her fault, and I'm not fucking leaving her alone until my seed is replaced. How about that?"

"Why don't we have a sit down, face to face. Talk about it, you can tell me your side."

"Nigga I ain't stupid. You and that trigger happy bitch aren't about to set me up."

I chuckled. "A gun is the least of your worries if you're in the same room with Ace."

"That ain't the bitch I'm referring to. She walks around high and mighty, but don't let the face fool you. Ask her about her Pops. Or better yet… maybe that's a conversation she needs to have with LVPD."

My eyes narrowed. "Don't do any shit you're going to regret, Dorian," I warned, clenching my free hand in a fist. As soon as I got ahold of this dude… God help him.

"Too late for that, chief. This shit with me and her goes deeper than fucking street politics, and I've waited long enough to settle up. I'll face my consequences after she faces hers. Like I told her earlier – Ahmad was just a fucking warning."

"You're a dead man."

He scoffed. "Ain't the first time I heard that. You do what you gotta do… I'll do the same."

The line went cold, and I tossed it over to Ace's waiting hands. "*Find him.* Bring him to me. I don't give a fuck who you have to call, whatever. I want that nigga's head on my desk."

Ace smiled – full, genuine joy – and my concern that her little crush on Detective Bradley was making her too soft flew right out the window. Shit like this – violence, intimidation, duress – was her bread and butter. "It'll be my pleasure."

While she went to work making that happen, I pulled out my personal cell.

Fuck.

I didn't want to have to make a call like this, but that shit Dorian had said, *"Ask her about her Pops*"… that didn't sit well with me.

I dialed a number that was embedded in fucked up memories, and lifted the phone to my ear. Disgust turned my stomach when I heard the sluggish voice on the other end of the line.

"Sebastian. Wake your bitch ass up. I need a favor."

EIGHTEEN

ASHA

"It's your dream, Ash... you can't just not show up..."

Ahmad's voice played in my head over and over, offering the words that should have made me feel okay about leaving the hospital to participate in the last day of the tournament. But it didn't feel like a dream, not anymore. It felt like a nightmare, and I was just waiting to see how it was going to play out.

There were too many variables. Too many places for Dorian to be, even if he wasn't physically there. Was someone waiting in the dark to snatch me? Right now, was there a gun aimed at my chest? Even though King had promised protection – and I believed he could make it happen – there was still that lingering question in the back of my mind... *What the hell is about to happen*?

My hands shook as I sat down at the final table, waiting to begin. I closed my eyes, searching for a happy thought to hold on to, to get me through this. I had to suppress a smile when my mind settled on a memory from less than thirty minutes ago, when King had pulled me aside for a private, quiet moment, only to have it interrupted by Zora bursting into the room looking for me. She'd spoken to Kiely, the woman from the spa desk, and was coming to ask when I needed to come to *Waterfalls* for my "vassage".

King… didn't like that.

I pushed out a cleansing breath as the dealer started shuffling the cards.

If I couldn't do a single other thing well under pressure, at *least*, I could play poker.

In theory.

In reality, I was too frazzled. Too preoccupied with the thought of my brother in a hospital bed because of an enemy I'd made – an enemy who was apparently *still* looking for some sort of payback.

An enemy I hadn't even realized I had to consider as such.

That was silly of me, honestly. I'd thought, for these three years, that it was just… done. I'd moved on, to some degree, and I figured he had too. It never occurred to me that he was still harboring that sense of ownership, or resentment, or animosity, or whatever it was that made Dorian want to torment me.

As if I'd *forced* him into the lover-oppressor dynamic we lived with for nearly a decade.

The poker rounds went fast. I managed to not be the first, or even the second person to have to leave the table, but just barely. My usual "gut" was missing today, so I was relying purely on the logic of a game that was almost entirely based on chance. Sure, there were skills involved, but when it came down to it, none of us knew what the next card was going to be. All we could do was guess.

It wasn't going super well for me.

My chips were low, because of a bad decision early in the game, but I'd been managing to hang on. When the next hand was dealt, I peeked at my cards to see I had both the ace and ten of hearts, which was a good starting place. I stayed in long enough to see the first round of community cards – ace of spades, ten of diamonds, and queen of spades.

I was working with two pairs.

Not the best hand in the world, but those aces were high, which was an advantage. I kept my face neutral, and stayed in the game. The betting went a little higher than I wanted, but I needed to see that fourth card.

When it came, it was the ten of spades, turning my hand into a full house.

I blew out a rush of air through my nose.

I *hated* full houses.

But, despite the negative connotation my past had created, there was no denying the power of such a hand. It was the third best hand possible, and the two that were higher were hard to make – even *harder* when the community cards had created a perfect full house.

"All in," I said, when the betting came around to me. The pile of chips I pushed in was flimsy, but the one I would pull back would fuel me through the rest of the day. A hush went around the gallery of watchers, as it always did when someone put it all on the line.

The final community card was turned – a jack of hearts – but it meant nothing to me. My hand was already made. I kept my face neutral as I waited for the time to turn my cards. I'd never been one to taunt and cajole my opponents unless provoked, and I wasn't about to start now.

I simply flipped my cards over when it was my turn, no flourish, and waited to be declared the victor so I could collect my winnings. Only… that moment never came.

I was frozen to the spot as the dealer scooped the pile of chips into someone else's pile. My opponents were clapping – clapping for *me*, I quickly realized. In the moment before they left their places to step in my direction for the customary pats on the back as I left, I glanced at the cards on the table. The player who'd won – *not me… what the fuck just happened?*- had a king and jack of spades.

Ace.

King.

Queen.

Jack.

Ten.

All spades, all on the table.

"*...A goddamn royal flush.*"

My spine felt infused with a steel rod as I plastered a smile on my face and played the role of a good sport. I'd calculated, and lost – I could hear the gallery audience rumbling about my loss, how I'd played a good hand and just caught a bad break.

Story of my life.

I was ushered into a section full of reporters for an exit interview, but all I could think about was getting back to Ahmad. If it was over, it was over – I could process that later. I wanted to get back to where I should have been in the first place.

"Ms. Davis, how does it feel to be the first black woman to make it *this* far in a professional tournament with stakes this high?" Someone asked, sticking a microphone in my face.

I blinked, hard. "Umm… amazing, I guess? I hadn't really considered that, until now. It doesn't feel like the type of thing we should still be having "firsts" about, but I'm grateful for the opportunity, and really proud to have made it this far. Maybe further next time. Black women can do anything."

"What's the first thing you're going to do with your winnings?"

I frowned. "Winnings?"

"Your tournament winnings – fourth place finisher takes home almost four-hundred thirty-five thousand dollars. What are you buying first?"

I shook my head, trying to clear away the sudden feeling of dizziness. "I… I can't even fathom that at the moment. Ask me again tomorrow. Right now, a *drink* would be wonderful."

Someone else started to shout a question in my direction, but it was overshadowed by a commotion nearby. A moment later, a small group of uniformed police parted the crowd, and my eyes narrowed when I saw who was at the front, leading.

I rolled my eyes at Jared's coward ass and turned back to the reporters to finish my duty. As far as I was concerned, Jared wasn't worth my – or anyone's – time, or attention.

But then I realized he was coming for *me.*

"Asha Davis," he said with a smirk, roughly pulling my arm behind my back. "You're under arrest for the murder of James Davis. You have the right to remain silent—"

Any other words were drowned at the in the blur of noise and activity around me. The security King had assigned couldn't really interfere with the police, and there were cameras going wild, people screaming questions, and pushing, and just a general mash of… crazy.

I glanced around wildly as I was dragged from the poker room with what seemed like a million people watching. For what? I didn't know. There was no one I could lock eyes with to make this better, or get me out of it. Deep down, I'd always expected this moment, to the point of anticipation. As horrible as my father was, my guilty conscience wouldn't let this one go. I'd committed a crime, and *this* was the balancing moment.

As badly as I wanted it to disappear, this wasn't going away.

It was cold.

The flirty, sleeveless black dress I'd worn for the tournament had been perfect for that setting, but in the stark, disarmingly gray inside of an interrogation room, I may as well have worn nothing. The cold bit right through the thin fabric.

I'd been waiting for what had to have been an hour or two, with no phone, no company, no nothing. By the time the door swung open and Jared strolled inside, wearing his usual stupid smirk, I was *almost* glad to see him. Just to see *someone.*

"You made the wrong enemy, Red." He put a large cardboard box down, and then sat across from me at the table. He should have been considering himself lucky I was handcuffed to the back of my steel chair. "We got the tip about your father from a concerned citizen with a very, *very* detailed story. I never would have taken you for a pillow talk kind of girl."

He wanted me to respond. Everything from his tone, to his expression, to his body language screamed it. He wanted a fight where I couldn't *really* fight back, unlike the one where I'd walked in on him screaming at Camille and given his weak ass a run for his money.

I wasn't going to give it to him.

I simply stared at him – just as I would if he were sitting across from me at a poker table. No – *through* him. And that *really* made him mad.

"Why so quiet now, bitch? You're usually at level ten with your mouth, what's wrong? Afraid to say something and incriminate yourself?"

I said nothing.

He sneered at me, then reached for the box, pulling out a plastic bag. I swallowed once, and then swallowed again, forcing myself not to respond to the very, very familiar gun in the bag that he put down on the table between us. Surely it wasn't loaded, but if I hadn't been handcuffed, it would be hard not to give in to the urge to beat him with it.

"Just tell the truth. Maybe the prosecutor will be easy on you, since you were a kid. But if you keep sitting here looking stupi—"

"You don't have any evidence, do you, Officer Price?" I asked, catching him off guard. He frowned, and then tapped on the gun.

"I beg to differ."

"Beg all you want. I haven't been fingerprinted, processed, given a phone call, offered a lawyer in any sort of meaningful way, and since *when* did beat cops do interrogations? *Nothing* about this is legit, so before you go advising me to tell the truth… you go first," I spat, nostrils flaring as I spoke. The more I thought about it, the more pissed I got.

"I told you, you made the wrong fucking enemy." He leaned across the table, and it took everything in me to reign in the urge to spit in his face. "I would've helped him for free, just because it was you… but getting paid to make sure you lose your freedom? This just might be one of my happiest memories."

"Fuck you. You don't have any evidence."

His smirk grew wider. "But by the time we're done… we'll have plenty."

A sharp knock on the glass startled both of us. Jared hopped up, dropping the bagged gun back into the box before he went to the door.

I heard voices arguing on the other side before the heavy door shifted closed. Several long minutes passed, and relief sank my shoulders when it swung open again, and a pissed-looking Cree stepped into the room.

"Are you good?" he asked, immediately coming to the back of the chair to release the handcuffs.

I nodded. "Yes, but I don't understand what's happening?"

"Fucking *Jared*," Cree growled as he pulled the cuffs off my wrists. He hated the man, and with good reason, after the way he'd treated Camille. "Overstepping every possible boundary, stomping all over proper protocol for a bogus fucking arrest. His ass is grass," he told me, as I stood. "Don't you worry about this shit."

I swallowed. "But, I…" I took a deep breath. "So am I free to go?"

"In a minute. We have to figure out what all this fool did, but like I said… this isn't something you'll have to worry about."

Something in his voice made a heavy feeling settle on my chest. "Wait…" I said, meeting his eyes. "What do you mean?"

"I mean what I said. This won't happen again. It's closed."

I blinked, as the implication of his words sank in. "Forever?"

He gave me a little smile. "Yeah… forever. You've got some valuable people on your side, Red." He patted my shoulder. "Sit tight. I'll be back in a minute."

I nodded, absently, and he left, but the door stayed open this time, probably for my benefit even though he'd told me to stay put. My mind was racing, trying to figure out what the hell had just happened.

It didn't take much to assume that one way or another, if I looked hard enough… that path would lead to King.

KING

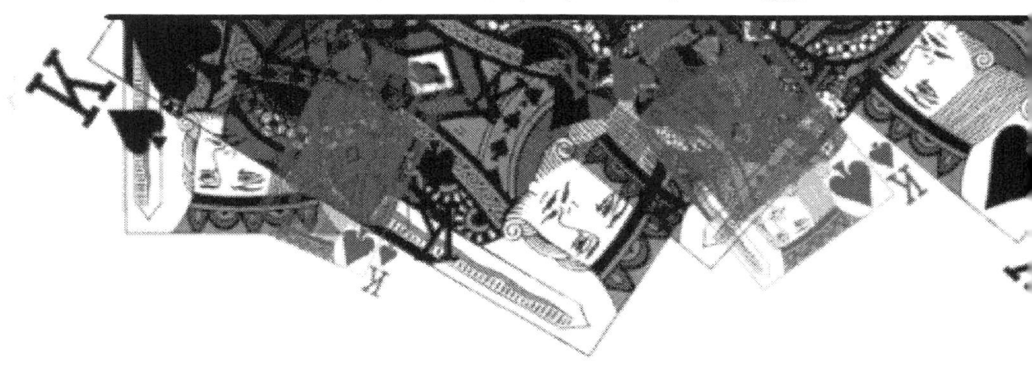

"She's perfectly fine," Cree said when he walked into the room, stopping my pacing.

"When can we leave with her?" I spat, stopping in front of him. "I need to get the fuck out of here before my foot ends up in your officer's ass."

Cree chuckled, and shook his head. "Don't worry. Jared Price will be handled."

"Not my way."

"No, not your way. But handled, nonetheless," he said, pushing his hands into his pockets. "Speaking of your way… who'd you get on board to make this happen? Evidence tampering is a pretty big favor to call in… especially when you know I could've been of assistance here. She's my sister's friend."

I nodded. "I get that. But, I didn't want to dirty your hands. I had another route, so I took it. Someone with less to lose."

"I get that. And, I appreciate it. But… who did you think they would call?"

My eyes widened, just a little, as I realized what he was saying, and he nodded.

"Yeah. Imagine my surprise when I get a message that Sebastian Gray, of all fucking people, needs a few suspicious footprints and witness statements of a small figure running away from the scene to disappear. I knew what this shit was as soon as I saw the name on the case."

I shrugged. "Not sure what you want me to say, Detective."

"I don't want you to say anything, man. I'm guessing that with this favor… there won't be any more slaughtered pigs on Sebastian's doorstep?"

I chuckled. "I didn't do that shit, man. If we're being honest… I was waiting on his ass to think I'd forgotten. But…" I let out a deep sigh, and shook my head. "He and I are as even as we'll ever get now. Assuming the discretion of everybody involved."

Cree raised his hands. "You won't have a problem out of me. There's no copies, nothing lingering. She's good. Jared tried to scare her by showing her a gun, but the actual one was never found. Probably never will be."

"Good. May I?" I asked, gesturing toward the door, and Cree nodded.

"Of course. She's probably anxious to get out of here."

I didn't say another word as I pulled open the door and stepped out, but I paused when Detective Bradley called out for my attention.

"What's up?" I asked, turning to see him leaning in the doorframe.

"I know you're trying to get to Asha, just one more thing – *Seriously…* what's up with that fine ass bodyguard?"

I laughed, and shook my head. "You're on your own with that one Detective. I'm not touching it."

She was exhausted.

Even though it was early in the evening, by the time we walked through the front door of my home, her usual feisty energy was gone. She wore the look of a woman who was emotionally depleted.

After leaving the police station, I'd taken her to the hospital to see her brother. Her mother and stepfather were there, waiting, after having seen everything that happened from the live cameras at the tournament.

She had explaining to do, and I'd stepped out of the room, leaving her to have that moment with her family. I peeked in at one point, concerned about the reception of her news, to find Asha, Ahmad, and their mother, crowded together on the hospital bed, in a tearful embrace.

Immediately, I stepped back out.

When my phone rang, I quickly picked it up, listening intently to the voice on the other end. At first, a spike of anger filled my chest, and from the tone of Ace's voice, she wasn't pleased either. But… maybe the fact that we'd gotten to keep our hands clean was for the best.

After the call from Ace was one from Cree, wanting to know if I was responsible for the fact that Dorian and several other members of his crew had been found with bullets in their heads. Truthfully – but grudgingly – I told him no, and hung up.

A few moments later, Asha had stepped out of the hospital room.

Her face was swollen, eyes glossy and rimmed in crimson from crying. We exchanged very few words – just enough for her to communicate that she was ready to go, and okay with coming to my place instead of going home.

In the car, she was quiet for a long while before she looked up, and cleared her throat. "Um… I feel like I should probably explain why—"

"Nah," I said, with a wave of my hand. "You don't. Teenage girls don't shoot their fathers just for the fucking fun of it, Red. And I know what he was doing to your mother. You don't have to say another goddamn thing today if you don't want to."

She nodded, and didn't say anything else until we made it home. When she walked in, she initially passed that big white canvas in my entryway. But then, she took a half-step back, staring at it like she was seeing it for the first time, and then turned to look at me.

"I think I'm going to take it down," I told her, approaching where she stood to put an arm around her waist.

Her eyes came up to my face. "Why? It's beautiful."

"I agree. But… it's also a constant… probably unhealthy, reminder. Considering all the circumstances."

"Yeah," she whispered, and then turned fully toward me and cupped my face. Her lips were salty from tears, but I devoured her mouth anyway. When she pulled, after several long moments, she cast one last glance at the canvas – a replication of an ultrasound picture from Robyn's pregnancy – and then walked away, telling me she was going to take a shower.

I studied the canvas myself for a minute, then joined her.

After the shower, I left her alone. She hadn't had that all day – the police department didn't count – and even though she didn't say it… I had a feeling she needed it.

I went to my home office and got in touch with Trei, and because of the time difference of him being overseas, was able to sit in on a meeting, which was sure to make my father happy. He hadn't been thrilled about me backing out of the trip, but after hearing what had happened with Asha – and seeing what went down the next day too – he understood.

As a matter of fact… if I knew my father like I thought I did, he'd probably had his hands in this shit. I sat back at my desk after the meeting was over, thinking through what Ace had told me when she called. The more I thought about it, my thoughts about if my father were involved went from maybe to definitely.

Nobody *smart* wanted Whitfield family problems.

When I went in search of Asha, I found her in my personal poker room, with cards spread across the table. I'd had clothes brought over for her, but she was wearing a shirt from my closet, and had the watch she'd won – and then subsequently returned – around her wrist.

I pushed my hands into my sweats as I ambled in, surveying the scene in front of me. She was sitting in front of an ace and ten of hearts, and the other cards were set up exactly like the game she'd gambled on and lost, getting her put out of the tournament. Her gaze left the table and came up to me, and she shook her head.

"A fucking royal flush," she muttered, then looked down at the cards again. "The odds of a royal flush in Texas Hold'em is like… thirty-thousand to *one*. That's not even… a quarter of a percent. You've got a better chance of slipping and killing yourself in the bathtub, or cutting your foot off with a lawn mower."

I laughed. "Seriously?"

"Yep. Seriously. I've never lost with a full house."

"Wow."

She nodded. "Yeah. Wow. You know… I considered it like a curse though. My daddy bet me in a game, when I was fifteen. Won with a full house. Every time I get a full house, I think about it. It reminds me of the day I decided he had to go."

"I told you… you don't have to explain that to me."

"I know. I just wanted you to know. My curse is broken. So if you never see me pick up another deck of cards, you'll know why."

My eyebrows went up. "Damn. You're saying… you don't want to play anymore?"

Asha stared at the table a long time without answering, then shook her head. "Just the thought of not playing makes me a little sick to my stomach. And now I feel like I *need* to play, to get rid of that feeling," she laughed.

"So lets play," I said, moving to where she was sitting down. I brushed her locs behind her shoulder, then bent to kiss her. "Maybe I'll even win this time."

She giggled. "Yeah, sure. We *have* to play now."

"Shuffle the cards then, Red." I smacked what I could reach of her ass with her sitting down. "I know you can lose now, I'm feeling confident."

She faked an offended laugh. "Oh, now that's just mean. I *did* win four-hundred thousand dollars, *Mr. Whitfield*."

"You did, didn't you?" I asked. I'd actually not even thought about it again. "So… that's enough for you to do what you wanted, right? Start over somewhere?"

It took her a moment, but she nodded. "Yeah. A lot to get away from."

"Not really," I offered – probably overstepping, but fuck it – then took the seat beside her. "That shit with your dad… it's taken care of, in a way that can't be reversed. And if you're talking about Dorian still… his boss didn't really like the kind of enemies he was making out of the Whitfields. You know how people talk, and he didn't want it to create a problem for him. So… he eliminated the issue."

Asha's eyes went wide. "So… Dorian is…?"

"Yeah. Ace saw the body herself."

Instead of the happiness or relief I expected, she rolled her eyes. "Shit."

I raised an eyebrow. “Shit?”

“Yeah,” she nodded. “I… kinda wanted to handle him myself.”

I couldn’t help the grin that spread over my mouth as I looked at this angelic-faced woman, mad at not being able to plan… whatever the hell she’d had in mind for the man who’d abused her, and tried to bulldoze her life when she didn’t shut up and fall in line. I pulled her into me, and kissed her again before I murmured against her mouth, “Join the club.”

She giggled as she pulled away, and gathered the cards in her hands. She was quiet again, thoughtful, as she shuffled, then turned to me. “Okay,” she said. “So what are we playing for this time? Money? Clothes? What?”

I propped my chin on my elbow, and my elbow on the table. “How about, if I win… you stay in Vegas. And if *you* win… you stay in Vegas. You good with those terms?”

Her eyes smiled as she rubbed her chin, considering it. After a few moments, she took two cards from the top of the deck and put them in front of me, then took two for herself.

“Okay. Ante up.”

- the end –

If you enjoyed this book (or even if you didn't!) please consider leaving a review/rating on Amazon and/or Goodreads. Not only does it help others decide if they'd like to meet these characters, it's how I know you're out there, and I would love to know what you thought about the book!

You can also visit me at my website (you can email me there from the contact page), like my Facebook page, or connect with me on Twitter, at @BeingMrsJones.
Team CCJ – Love in Warm Hues
Want updates on new releases and giveaways? Join my mailing list!

Christina C. Jones is a modern romance novelist who has penned more than 25 books. She has earned a reputation as a storyteller who seamlessly weaves the complexities of modern life into captivating tales of black romance.
Prior to her work as a full-time writer, Christina successfully ran Visual Luxe, a digital creative design studio. Coupling a burning passion for writing and the drive to hone her craft, Christina made the transition to writing full-time in 2014.

Christina has attracted a community of enthusiastic readers across the globe who continue to read and share her sweet, sexy, and sometimes scandalous stories.
Most recently, two of Christina's book series have been optioned for film and television projects and are currently in development.

Other titles by Christina Jones

Love and Other Things

Haunted (paranormal)

Mine Tonight (erotica)

Hints of Spice (Highlight Reel spinoff)

The Truth – His Side, Her Side, And the Truth About Falling In Love

Friends & Lovers:

Finding Forever

Chasing Commitment

Strictly Professional:

Strictly Professional

Unfinished Business

Serendipitous Love:

A Crazy Little Thing Called Love

Didn't Mean To Love You

Fall In Love Again

The Way Love Goes

Love You Forever

Trouble:

The Trouble With Love

The Trouble With Us

The Right Kind Of Trouble

If You Can (Romantic Suspense):

Catch Me If You Can

Release Me If You Can

Save Me If You Can

Inevitable Love:

Inevitable Conclusions

Inevitable Seductions

The Wright Brothers:

Getting Schooled – Jason & Reese

Pulling Doubles – Joseph & Devyn

Bending The Rules – Justin & Toni

Connecticut Kings:

CK #1 Love in the Red Zone – Love Belvin

CK #2 Love on the Highlight Reel

49002247R00184

Made in the USA
Lexington, KY
19 August 2019